They'd been comrades-in-arms. Comrades in art. And comrades in the passionate political idealism that had brought them together. And now they were torn apart by a cold war that pitted fame against loyalty—a war without bullets, where names were the weapons . . . and love and friendship were the casualties. . . .

COMRADES

"Panoramic in scope . . . an impressive achievement"
—Frank D. Gilroy, Pulitzer Prize-winning author of *The Subject Was Roses*

"The complex struggle between these two friends makes the era come alive in all its contradictions."
—*Booklist*

COMRADES

A NOVEL
PAUL LEAF

A SIGNET BOOK

NEW AMERICAN LIBRARY

Copyright © 1985 by Seagate Company, Inc.

All rights reserved. For information address New American Library. This book previously appeared in an NAL Books edition, published by New American Library and simultaneously in Canada by The New American Library of Canada Limited.

 SIGNET TRADEMARK REG. U.S. PAT. OFF. AND FOREIGN COUNTRIES
REGISTERED TRADEMARK—MARCA REGISTRADA
HECHO EN CHICAGO, U.S.A.

SIGNET, SIGNET CLASSIC, MENTOR, PLUME, MERIDIAN and NAL BOOKS are published by New American Library, 1633 Broadway, New York, New York 10019

First Signet Printing, March, 1986

1 2 3 4 5 6 7 8 9

PRINTED IN THE UNITED STATES OF AMERICA

You never reach maturity until
you've faced the moral choices
and have either survived or succumbed.
—Harold Clurman
  The Fervent Years

PROLOGUE

1951

Three men stopped in front of the panel of photographs in front of the Shubert Theater in New Haven. Director Mike Rossano, in black turtleneck, looked at them through intense black eyes. Robert Thompson, in tweed jacket and work shirt, held a pipe in a large, strong hand, portrait of the playwright. Over them, seeming to look benevolently down on his protégés, was the producer-critic Alex Tarasov, in his broad-brimmed black fedora.

They passed under the marquee, which read 84 AVENUE FOCH in large white letters, and through the iron gates into the dark backstage alley that no glint of sunlight ever reached. The stage door scraped noisily as they entered.

"Afternoon," the doorman said. He wore a heavy sweater under his rumpled suit, held a steaming coffee mug with both hands.

"Everyone in, Harry?" Mike asked, looking at the actors' sign-in sheet on the call board, its stubby pencil hanging from a dirty string.

"Yes, sir." He sipped. "Oh, and by the way, that gentleman there is waiting for you."

As Alex brushed snow from his black coat with his pearl-gray gloves, they looked at the nondescript man trying to warm himself by the feeble heat of the radiator. His skin had the texture of paper, his eyes were a faded blue. Robert and Alex looked at him with the indifferent curiosity reserved for the autograph hunters who frequent backstage alleys. But Mike was jolted by the shock of alarm that shot up his spine. He'd never seen the man but knew who he was.

"Mr. Thompson . . . Mr. Rossano?" the man asked in a light voice. He approached tentatively.

Mike nodded. Robert merely stared at him as Alex puffed on his cigar, which had gone dead.

"Yes," Robert responded. The man put his hand into a frayed pocket of the too large coat. Mike tensed, knowing what was coming. The man withdrew two envelopes.

"Please accept these," he said, handing them each one. The envelopes had the seal of the United States in the left-hand corner, and under it the legend "United States Congress." Robert and Mike looked at each other. As they did, the man gazed at the envelopes.

"Oh, excuse me," he said, and reached for them. "I gave you the wrong ones." He exchanged them and handed them back. "Good day," he said softly and left, the door scraping in the silence.

Robert, his throat constricting in the old reaction to fear, tore open the envelope and withdrew its pink contents. The subpoena read, in bold black letters, "House Committee on Un-American Activities."

Mike took a deep breath. "When is it for?" he asked.

"Nine-thirty A.M., December 16th, 1951."

Mike opened his envelope with difficulty, as if his fingers were uncoordinated.

"Same time," he said quietly.

"What can we do?" Alex asked in the cold hush, throwing his dead cigar into a can of water.

Mike shook his head. "Appear," he said, almost inaudibly.

They walked down the aisle of the darkened theater toward the stage, where the actors were already assembled on the set under the glare of the single thousand-watt worklight. A large Nazi flag, its black swastika in a brilliant red field, hung over the audience from the proscenium arch as if from the window of Gestapo headquarters in Paris. Robert and Alex took seats as Mike climbed the steps to the stage. The actors broke from their clusters and turned to him.

"We'll start with the rewrite of two-one. And Jimmy," Mike said to the stage manager, "would you call Boris and ask him to meet us at five to go over light cues?"

Jimmy made a note and nodded to his assistant, who left for the phone. Mike gave copies of the new scene to Jimmy, who handed them out to the actors involved. They started to rehearse.

So damned normal, Robert thought, as if nothing's happened.

Onstage, Mike tried to listen to the words and fit them to new moves, but his concentration was fuzzy and his direction lacked its usual pointed clarity. Have to call Odets, he thought.

Robert, imprisoned in a web of his own thoughts, leaned to Alex and whispered, "I'm going to call Katherine."

Alex nodded slightly. "Give her my love." Robert rose and went up the aisle, his six-foot frame bent at the shoulders as if carrying a heavy pack. Alex returned his attention to the stage. He frowned at Mike's distracted work. The actors glanced at each other over their new pages, antennae alive to the change in Mike, wondering what had happened.

———

Dr. Katherine Thompson listened to her patient's distress. The woman was sitting tensely on the couch, legs tightly pulled together, hands twisting a wet handkerchief. Katherine replaced some stray hairs that had gone awry from her tightly pulled bun of reddish gold. The phone rang. Startled, the woman looked at Katherine angrily.

Katherine looked back apologetically, thinking it had to be a wrong number—unless something had happened to Bobby. The nursery school had this number for emergencies. She picked up.

"Katherine," Robert said from the backstage phone.

Katherine drew a sharp breath. "Yes, Robert? What is it?" He'd never called her on that phone.

"They subpoenaed us today."

"For when?" She tried to sound calm.

"December 16th." His voice rang hollow.

"Not much time. Mike too?"

"Same date."

"I don't like that. Sounds like a setup."

"What do you mean?" he asked.

"You should be able to see that," she said almost sharply. "Maximum drama."

"What do you mean?" he insisted.

The patient cracked her knuckles, and Katherine was aware of her growing anger at the interruption.

"Robert, I'm with a patient and I've got appointments all day. We'll have to talk tonight."

"I'll call you after the show," he said.

"I'm sorry, Robert," she said softly as he hung up.

———————

The light cues had been smoothed, but the new scene was rough. Robert spent the performance pacing in the back of the theater. Alex took notes and Mike watched from backstage.

Afterward, they had a postmortem at Kaysey's Restaurant across the street from the theater.

"I think the new scene will work," Alex said, trying to raise their spirits. They nodded silently. Mike lit a cigarette and stared out into the restaurant crowded with actors and theatergoers.

Robert rose. "I'm going back to the hotel," he said.

It had stopped snowing, and the air was hard and cold. He breathed deeply, looked up at the stars, and listened to the crunch beneath his feet, thinking of Iowa snow, French snow, German snow—all the snow his feet had traversed and left his mark on was now gone. He took another deep breath and made his way through the New Haven streets back to the hotel. As he sat on his bed deep in thought there was a knock at the door.

"Robert?"

Robert went to the door and opened it. Mike stood there, his coat open, radiating cold, as if he'd also been walking.

"C'mon in," Robert said.

Mike crossed to a striped satin chair and sat without taking his coat off, hands jammed deeply into his pockets as if they were still cold. He looked at Robert sitting on the edge of the bed.

"Well . . ." he said.

"How do you feel?" Robert asked.

"Like *The Seven Who Were Hanged*," Mike laughed, referring to a Russian play. "What'd Katherine say?"

"She thought it was suspicious having us appear together."

"She may be right."

"Why?" Robert looked at him sharply.

"More press," Mike said, taking his hands out of his pockets and leaning forward. "What are you going to do?"

"I haven't talked to my lawyer yet. And you?"

Mike looked at his hands, then rubbed his eyes. "I've known it was coming, but just like shells or mortars, as many as you've heard, you never get used to them. Remember how death shook us that first day at Jarama when that farm kid got it in the throat? And the morning after when the English officer took a slug through the head? But the second day of battle we were less shocked than the first, and pretty soon we passed the bodies without looking. It was easier not to know how a buddy got it, because we had to go on. That's how it is in Hollywood! It's a war zone, with as much fear. More!"

Robert took his arms, stared into the dark face, and spoke with pleading intensity.

"Mike! Mike! I've always looked up to you because you're strong. I survived because of you . . . because nothing frightened you!"

"Death never frightened me," Mike said quietly. "But I'm scared now. That committee can destroy me."

———

The New Haven tryout ended on Saturday, and Alex took the company to Boston. Robert and Mike went to New York to prepare for Monday's appearance in Washington. Katherine canceled all her appointments to go with them.

The train was almost empty as they rattled through the Sunday-afternoon countryside. As they looked out of the train window they talked of the trip from Paris to Perpignan.

"It's almost fifteen years," Mike said.

Each nodded. A sadness had descended on them.

"Hey!" Mike suddenly said. "What're we so sad about? We've faced worse than this. They can't kill us, for Christ's sake. Let's go and get a drink."

By the time they'd finished their second round, as they rolled into D.C., they felt more confident. But no one slept that night.

As they walked along the corridors of the old Federal Building on Monday, flashbulbs popped, reporters surrounded them, and TV crews shot them. They said nothing as they walked arm in arm toward the committee chamber, where they met their lawyers.

Every seat in the room was taken. The committee had a sellout for this performance and wore smiles for the cameras, especially the Representative from California, Richard Nixon. The current chairman, Thomas Wood, rapped his gavel. His predecessor, J. Parnell Thomas, hadn't been able to make it to Washington this morning, since he was in the Danbury State Prison for payroll padding and income tax evasion.

"This session of the House Committee on Un-American Activities will come to order," Wood intoned. "We have two witnesses this morning, and I can see by the crowd the public thinks them important. I'd like to remind you of Congressional decorum. Demonstrations will not be tolerated by anyone. Mr. Jenner, would you begin, please."

The committee's chief counsel, Jenner, rose from his chair, straightened his tie, and cleared his throat. "The committee calls Mr. Robert Thompson."

Katherine squeezed her husband's hand. Mike smiled at him and his attorney patted his shoulder as he rose to cross to the witness chair. Robert walked slowly and with dignity. His shoes hurt a bit. He swore to tell the truth.

"Mr. Thompson, I'll get right to the point," the committee counsel said. "Are you now or have you ever been a member of the Communist Party?"

The committee members sat forward, as did the audience. Mike bit his lip. Katherine put her hand to her face. Robert looked at Jenner and considered his answer.

"Are you going to answer the question?" the chairman asked.

Robert looked at him. "No," he said finally. The audience breathed again.

"Is that an answer to my question or the counsel's?" the chair asked in exasperation. Silence. "Mr. Thompson, are you pleading the Fifth Amendment?"

"No."

"Are you pleading the First Amendment?"

"Perhaps."

"There is no perhaps in law, Mr. Thompson. Have you been advised by counsel?"

"Yes."

"Then what is your position?"

The crowd waited.

Robert looked straight at the chair until the man grew uncomfortable.

"My position is that you have no right to ask these questions."

Robert's lawyer's breakfast curdled in his stomach. There was a wave of whispering in the room.

"Mr. Thompson, this is a legally constituted committee of the United States Congress and you have accepted a subpoena to appear before it, which means we have the right and duty to ask you questions. You have the right to refuse to answer on the grounds that you might incriminate yourself. That is, taking the Fifth Amendment, a refuge of—"

"I know what it means," Robert cut him off.

"Then declare a position," the chair said angrily.

"I have," Robert said.

"Will Mr. Thompson's counsel advise his client of the proper behavior before this committee?"

Robert's lawyer sighed and went to him. They had a whispered conversation, at the end of which Robert's lawyer shrugged.

"I've advised my client, sir," he said, and took his chair.

The counsel asked his question again. "Are you now, or have you ever been—"

"I am not now nor have I ever been a member of the Communist Party of the United States," Robert said slowly and deliberately.

The chairman seemed satisfied. "You realize that by answering you have waived your rights not to answer any more questions," he said.

Robert was silent for a moment.

"But that doesn't mean that I will," he said.

The chairman frowned. Nixon whispered to him.

"If you follow that course, you may be found in contempt."

Robert nodded.

"You fought in Spain with the American Abraham Lincoln Battalion in 1937 and 1938?" counsel asked.

"I did."

"Was Michael Rossano in that unit?"

"Mr. Rossano will answer for himself."

Counsel looked to the chair for his cue. The committee conferred quietly, then the chair nodded for counsel to continue.

"Were you aware that there were Communists in the Abraham Lincoln Battalion?"

"I was aware that there were Communists and lumberjacks, seamen and soldiers, schoolteachers and—"

"Mr. Thompson," counsel interrupted.

"—and writers and—"

The gavel banged. "Mr. Thompson, just answer the question."

"I was."

"You were in the OSS during the war?" counsel asked.

"I was."

"Did you know any Communists there?"

"It's possible. We had all kinds of guys in that outfit. Just like any other. There were also a lot of Ivy Leaguers."

"But the OSS was a special unit organized for clandestine work—something the Communists are very good at—was it not?"

"I'm not aware that Communists are any better at it than anyone else, including the FBI," Robert answered evenly. "They didn't have a monopoly on fighting the war."

Laughter. The chairman was aware that Robert was getting the better of his counsel, whose discomfort was revealed in his reddening neck and cheeks. "The FBI informed General Donovan that a Mr. Irving Goff was a Communist. On their honor roll, as a matter of fact. Did you know Mr. Goff?"

"I'll tell you General Donovan's response to the FBI. He said, 'I don't know if he's on the Communist honor roll but he sure as hell is on ours,' or words to that effect."

More laughter and gavel banging were followed by a conference among the committee members. Robert's young attorney had a puzzled look on his face. The chair nodded for counsel to continue.

"Do you know a Mr. Milt Felsen?"

"I do."

"He also fought in Spain?"

"He did. And very well."

"Was he in the OSS with you?"

"You can check his service record or OSS files."

"You are not answering the question, Mr. Thompson."

"I thought I was."

Robert's attorney leaned to Katherine and whispered, "I don't know why they're letting him get away with this."

"You were asked if you knew Mr. Goff," the counsel went on.

"I know Mr. Goff," Robert answered.

"Do you know him to be a Communist?" Counsel insisted.

"You'll have to ask him that," Robert replied.

"Mr. Thompson," the chair said, "will you answer the question?"

A long silence.

"No," Robert finally said.

"Mr. Thompson," the chair said wearily, "we are trying to establish evidence of Communist infiltration into even the most secret of our organizations so that we may protect ourselves from outside threat. Do you want to help us?"

"I'll stand on my combat record, sir. I fought the Fascists in Spain, North Africa, France—"

The chair rapped sharply. "You were not asked for your service record! You were asked about Goff!"

"Goff didn't infiltrate the OSS. He was recruited by General Donovan on the basis of his experience in Spain as a guerrilla fighter and won several high medals for his combat service in the OSS."

The chairman took a deep breath and looked at his counsel.

"Are you aware, Mr. Thompson," counsel continued, "that the Joint Anti-Fascist Committee is on the Attorney General's list of subversive organizations?"

"There was no such list in 1939."

"But there is now."

"Unfortunately," Robert volleyed back.

"Were you a member of that organization?"

Robert took a deep breath. "I refuse to answer that on the grounds that you have no right to inquire into my political beliefs."

The room tensed. Katherine and Mike sat forward.

"You refuse to answer?"

"I do. You have no right to—"

"You are in contempt of this committee and the United States Congress!" the chair shouted and rapped his gavel for emphasis.

"And you are in contempt of America and everything it stands for!" Robert shouted back.

Katherine breathed again. Mike bit his lip. Robert's lawyer held his head in his hands. The chair rapped as the press wrote furiously and the gallery chattered, while one group applauded.

"Sergeants at arms, remove the witness!"

"You are in contempt of the Constitution and the Bill of Rights!" Robert continued shouting as he was removed from the witness chair by two men in black suits and flung back to his place.

Katherine and Mike embraced him. His lawyer shook his head in disbelief.

"Order! Order!" the chair demanded. The room eventually quieted. "The next witness will be Mr. Michael Angelo Rossano."

Robert and Mike looked at each other and smiled. Robert gave his friend a thumbs-up gesture. Mike crossed himself, something he hadn't done since he was a child. He walked to the witness chair and swore to tell the truth.

"Are you now or were you ever a member of the Communist Party?" counsel asked.

"I was."

Murmurs.

"When was that?"

"For about a year and a half in 1934 to 1936."

"Why did you leave?"

"I didn't . . . leave."

"You didn't leave?" counsel asked, surprised. The committee now sat forward. Richard Nixon licked his lips.

"No. I was kicked out."

Robert now sat forward. Katherine's hand went to her face. They hadn't known this.

"Why were you kicked out?"

"Individualism."

"What does that mean?"

"That I was too much of an 'individual,' a lousy member of the group, which was funny because we were in the Group Theater."

The committee laughed, as did the audience. The chair did not rap for order. Robert and Katherine tensed, expecting the worst now.

"They called me an anarchist or a Trotskyite deviationist because I wouldn't follow the 'line.' I was unreliable."

"What was the line?"

"It changed." Mike shrugged. "Sometimes a hundred and eighty degrees. They called it 'tactics.' One day you could be for accommodation with capitalism, the next day against it. It depended on the leadership. We fought Hitler in Spain, but when Stalin signed the nonaggression pact with him, you were supposed to rationalize it. That was pretty tough even though you knew Stalin was buying time and Hitler was a threat through Finland. But that was the beginning of the end for many Communists. It was too cynical."

"Why did you go to Spain, sir?" counsel asked.

It wasn't lost on Robert and Katherine that counsel called Mike "sir."

"I went to Spain to fight Fascism. Like the others I was a 'premature anti-Fascist' and proud of it. We recognized earlier than the rest of the country that Spain was Hitler's and Mussolini's rehearsal for World War Two."

"Were there Communists in Spain? In the Abraham Lincoln Battalion?"

"There were. They were anti-Fascist."

"Please answer the questions without comment," counsel said, his voice getting edgy. "Were there Russians there?"

"There were."

"If American foreign policy was against intervention in Spain and you had to be smuggled in, why did you go?"

"I told you. I'm an individualist. I follow my own line," Mike said.

"Did you know Mr. Goff in Spain?"

"I did."

"And in the OSS?"

"We were on the same team."

"Was he a Communist?"

There was a pause. "You'll have to ask him that."

Counsel looked to the chair, whose eyebrows were raised. Whispered conferences among the Congressmen. Robert took Katherine's hand and squeezed.

"Mr. Rossano, you have not sought protection of either Amendment, so please answer," the chair said.

"I have, sir."

"You have not," the chair shot back.

"Then my answer is that I don't know."

The chairman rubbed his eyes and nodded for counsel to continue.

"Mr. Rossano, who was in your party cell in the Group Theater?"

There was a long pause. Robert held his breath as he and Mike looked at each other.

"I won't answer that."

Robert breathed again and smiled broadly.

"You refuse?" the chairman said sharply.

"Yes, sir."

"Who were some of your fellow members in the Joint Anti-Fascist Committee, now on the Attorney General's list?" the counsel pressed on.

"I won't answer that either."

"Then you are in contempt, Mr. Rossano," the chair said, his voice rising.

"I will answer any questions about myself, sir."

"We are asking you questions about yourself. The other persons relate to you."

"That is sophistry, sir," Mike said.

"What is sophistry?" the chairman asked.

"Are you asking me to define the word?" Mike asked.

"I don't happen to have a dictionary here," the chair said.

"Faulty logic, sir. I will not give you any names."

The chairman was obviously taken by surprise, and there was a hurried meeting among Congressmen as the gallery buzzed. The committee caucus was marked by knitted brows and intense whispers. Finally they took their seats again and the chair rapped authoritatively.

"I'll ask you once more, Mr. Rossano," he said, staring hard at Mike. "I'll give you one more chance to answer. Who were your fellow members in—"

Mike didn't give him a chance to finish. "I won't give you any names," he said, staring back.

A great weight fell from Robert's shoulders.

"Then this committee finds you in contempt of Congress. You may step down, Mr. Rossano. Meeting is adjourned."

The Congressmen rose, clearly unsatisfied with the morning's show. The gallery buzzed as Robert, Mike, and Katherine embraced. Photographers and press surrounded them, shouting questions.

Mike looked at Katherine as if to say, "I fooled you, didn't I?"

"Yes, you did," her eyes said.

Robert was on the verge of tears as they walked down the long hallway in triumph, feeling again the thrill of the last farewell in Barcelona in 1938.

"I'm so happy for you," Katherine said at the airport as Robert and Mike boarded the plane for Boston.

Robert smiled back at her. It was a smile that said, "I told you so."

From the doorway of the plane, Mike waved for Robert to hurry.

"I've got to go," Robert told his wife. "Hug Bobby for me."

Katherine watched the taxiing plane with mixed feelings.

———————

Alex met them at Logan Airport. In the taxi they told him about Washington and he briefed them on the setup in the Boston theater.

"The Colonial's good for us," he said. "It's not too large and I like the stage."

"I remember it well." Mike laughed. "Froze our asses off there before the war in the Odets play."

"We seem to have a hit, so they're giving us heat." Alex lit a cigar, its Havana aroma filling the cab.

Robert was glad the laughter was back in their lives, the ugliness behind them for the moment. They still had to face the contempt charges, but they had survived without castration. It was one of Alex's favorite phrases—survival without castration.

Alex had checked them into the Ritz Hotel. They crossed the small but elegant lobby to the desk for their keys. Mike was handed several messages, which he glanced at quickly, biting his lip.

Upstairs, Mike sat on the silk spread of his large bed and looked at the slips of paper again. Ziggy, his agent in Hollywood; Gene Milford, his film editor in New York; his wife; and Stavros Miarcos, in France.

He placed the transatlantic call first.

———————

Stavros Miarcos, the powerful-chested, thick-necked head of 20th Century–Fox, sat at a table in Le Pyramide in the small town of Vienne, near Lyon, breathing in the fumes of the 1934 Lafite as it swirled in his glass. He lifted the large but delicate bowl to his lips and closed his eyes, as if concentrating on the levels of taste in his mouth. When he opened his eyes to the beautifully appointed dining room and returned to a *cassoulet de cailles aux morilles*, he saw the headwaiter approach. He had the opportunity for one more mouthful of quail and wine before the man bent to him and spoke quietly.

"Telephone, Monsieur Miarcos."

Stavros nodded, and the man withdrew. He looked regretfully at his food and meaningfully at John Farrell, a producer at Fox. Farrell returned the gaze, understanding it. Stavros rose and went to the phone in a small alcove with fleur-de-lys wallpaper and fresh flowers.

The hisses of the transatlantic cable were loud. "Hello," he said.

"It's Mike."

"You double-crossed me, kid," the studio head growled. "I'll kill you for that."

In the bedroom in Boston, even through the rising and falling hisses, the disembodied voice carried threat.

"I couldn't do it, Stavros. I couldn't go through with it."

"You put me on the spot with the committee. You embarrassed me. You damaged my credibility with them, and I'll destroy you for it. Do you know what it means for them to call me in France to tell me you blew it and they're pissed?" Stavros shouted. "You're finished, Rossano. Dead. I'll bury you and dance on your grave."

He slammed the receiver back on its hook, adjusted his beautifully tailored suit that nevertheless did not hide his bulk, and strode purposefully back to his table to finish his meal.

Mike slumped back against the pillows, staring at the ornate ceiling.

PART ONE

Shame is worse than death.
—Mike Rossano, Spain, 1937

CHAPTER ONE

1936

Music filtered into the storeroom of the Café Montparnasse on the Boulevard Saint Michel in Paris, accordions and a female voice warm with promises. Piaf's song of love permeated the room filled with wine cases, candlelight, the smoke and pungent aroma of strong Gitanes cigarettes.

Mike Rossano mounted a reckless attack to the center of the chessboard. Robert Thompson cautiously parried with a classic defense.

The two men had met earlier that evening in this room, where they were to wait for their International Brigades contact. When they shook hands, Mike looked up at the tall young man in the blue chambray work shirt and tweed jacket, took in the broad planes of his face, the gentle, intelligent eyes and warm smile, and thought this could be a friend.

Robert Thompson had looked down at Mike in his leather jacket and immediately felt the tension that radiated from the compact body, the intensity of the black eyes, the quivering awareness of a forest animal on the alert. Robert had been delighted when Mike responded to the offer of a game on the small portable chess set Robert carried in his pack.

Twenty-two-year-old Katherine Loesser had arrived with Dr. Leonard Barkin, the oldest member of the group, already a successful New York surgeon. When introduced to her, Robert had held her hand and stared at her face as though in a trance.

"Can I have it back?" she'd laughed.

"Oh . . . sorry." Reluctantly he'd let go as Barkin watched, amused.

Now, as the two men played, Katherine and Barkin watched, weighing their own moves. Barkin's Phi Beta Kappa key, hanging from his vest, glinted in the soft light. Katherine's blue-lavender eyes moved from Robert's serious face back to the board as he moved a pawn into a blocking position and lifted his head. Their eyes met. She smiled, flushed, and returned her attention to the game, thinking, This is crazy. We just met.

Mike caught the exchange.

Katherine was disturbed by the thrill of attraction. She hadn't come to Europe for romance. She and Dr. Barkin had come to serve in a medical unit of the Abraham Lincoln Battalion as part of the International Brigades fighting the Fascists in Spain. She folded her hands into her plaid woolen skirt and looked down at them. She was ashamed of the long, tapering fingers and well-manicured nails that had never known any physical work.

Mike wondered at the attraction Robert seemed to feel for this refined-looking girl. She'd be lousy in bed, he thought. Probably still a virgin.

The door opened and closed quietly. A short, stocky man in a rumpled suit entered, a cigarette dangling from his heavy lips, a worker's cap tilted rakishly over one eye. "Good evening. I am Paul Fresnay of the International Brigades. Who is Dr. Barkin?"

"I am," Barkin said, raising his large body from the chair and putting out his hand. Fresnay took it heartily.

Barkin winced at the strength of Fresnay's grip.

"I am sorry," Fresnay laughed. "I always forget. Too many years on the docks. I am glad to meet you. We need you. We need all of you." He noted their youth. Except for the thirtyish Barkin, they were all in their early twenties, he judged. As they introduced themselves, he looked at each as if judging who would survive.

Barkin was large and handsome, but unathletic. Everything about him was soft and round, his face, his gold glasses, his fingers, his voice. Everything but his eyes. There was resolution there.

Fresnay found Katherine Loesser fascinating. She had reddish-blond hair pulled back against the pale skin of her face. Her eyes were striking, radiating warmth, and there was a warm, accepting air about her. She could be very strong, though, Fresnay thought.

He looked at Robert, who was tall, like Katherine, but where she was assured he was all awkwardness, shyness. His feelings are too close to his skin, Fresnay guessed. And he's unfortunately tall for battle.

Pete Pappas and George Carver were remarkably alike, although Carver was black. They were of medium height and heavily muscled, unhesitant in their movements, frank in their physicality. Pete, a former boxer, moved on the balls of his feet as if he were still in the ring. Carver, a steelworker, moved more slowly, but with sureness. They have a chance, Fresnay thought.

He noted Mike Rossano's tension, that of a cat ready to leap. Mike's eyes were restless and probing, his mind ceaselessly working. Sizing me up, Fresnay thought. This one was a survivor.

"We leave tomorrow morning at six," Fresnay said.

They all looked at one another.

"Any news from Madrid?" Robert asked.

Fresnay took a newspaper from his pocket. "I have here an English paper." He unfolded it and read. "From November 16th until November 19th, Hitler's Condor Legion bombed Madrid, killing one thousand people. For the first time in the history of warfare, mass bombing of a civilian city is being used as an act of terror. The flames caused the capital to appear like a place of torture. Over the crackle of flames could be heard, like the beat of a distant drum, '*No Pasaran! No Pasaran!*'—'They Shall Not Pass!'"

There was silence.

"Checkmate," Mike declared.

Everyone was startled. Fresnay rubbed out his cigarette and stared at Mike.

"You're kidding," Robert chided.

"No, I'm not," Mike said, illustrating his trap.

Wow, Robert thought. He won't allow himself to lose.

"Drinks on me!" Mike announced happily.

They entered the café and put several tables together. Fresnay patiently answered questions. Were the Loyalists holding? Was there any chance France would lift its embargo on arms for Spain? What about medical supplies? No, the French government was adamant, even though Hitler and Mussolini were pouring fully equipped divisions and air squadrons into Spain. Like England, France had even tightened restrictions and was deporting volunteers they caught trying to cross the French border into Spain. Especially Americans, whose passports were stamped "Not valid for travel in Spain."

"You must be very careful," Fresnay said. "You are a tour-study group. Nothing more."

Robert, sitting next to Katherine, was thinking about her incredible lavender eyes.

"Whaddaya think?" Mike asked him.

Robert turned out of his reverie. "What?"

"Hey, we're in Paris and the night is young," Mike said, punching Robert playfully on the arm and smiling.

Katherine smiled too. She'd been watching Robert. "Where were you?" she whispered.

"With you," he whispered back.

"You're funny," she said, blushing. The byplay was not lost on anyone at the table. Rag ends of conversation floated about them, but they barely listened. Carver asked Barkin if he'd ever been to Harlem.

"I worked the emergency room at Harlem Hospital. Lively place," Barkin said.

"I want to go to New York after this war," Carver declared, his skin mahogany in the candlelight. Totally self-educated, he'd worked as a steel-union organizer in the mills of Detroit and had traveled a greater emotional and intellectual distance than anyone else in the room.

Peter Pappas had had enough of New York. In his last fight in the Coney Island Velodrome, Pappas had hit his opponent so hard the Guinea Kid had never regained consciousness and had died two days later in the hospital. As a result, Pete looked like a contender and his manager got him a bout in Madison Square Garden. Sick with guilt, he had decided to go to Spain instead.

The group walked through the dark streets in a light snow illuminated by Napoleonic lamps. Mike, almost a head shorter, fell into step with Robert and Katherine as Katherine talked about her life in Princeton as the daughter of a history professor.

"Loving and secure. Chamber music on Sunday nights, Maine in the summer. A well-orchestrated life, few discordant notes. I started medical school, then decided to come to Spain as a nurse."

"Why?" Robert asked.

"Photographs, newsreels of men, women, and children fighting for their country, some with rakes and hoes against machine guns and tanks. The torn bodies, the lost eyes. Dr. Barkin was one of my professors, and I really admire him. When he told me he was going to set up a medical unit, I decided to go with him. My parents fought it, even denounced Dr. Barkin as irresponsible. But they knew I'd go without their blessing. In the end, they cried, smiled, and wished me well."

Robert took her hand in a gesture of understanding.

"And you?" she asked.

"The death of a poet."

Katherine glanced questioningly at him.

"The execution of García Lorca by Franco," he explained. "And other writers. Anyone who executes poets has to be fought. Besides, fighting seems to run in my family. My great-grandfather, who was German, fought on the Union side in the Civil War, then went west as a cavalry scout. My grandfather was with Teddy Roosevelt's Rough Riders and got his legs shot off in Cuba. There's a picture of him with Teddy in our parlor." Katherine noted the word "parlor."

"My father fought on the Allied side in World War I, but never talked about it," Robert continued. "Maybe because we were German. I grew up speaking German. There was a group of us in the town, a vaguely Populist-Socialist group that gathered to discuss politics and literature and carry on

German culture. Then I went to the writer's workshop at Iowa University, studied French and German literature, got major letters in track and baseball. I turned down a Rhodes Scholarship to come here because I thought it was more important to stop Fascism now. I figured the scholarship could wait."

Katherine looked at Robert's serious face in the lamplight and felt a great warmth for his youthful gravity. She also noted Mike's intent listening.

"My father's in the feed business," Robert continued. "Chicken feed." He laughed. "But my mother'd been a dancer in New York. You've seen those modern dance recitals, Greek tragedies in long, black skirts. . . ." Robert paused. "I always wondered what she saw in him. He's so unimaginative. And how she could live in Iowa after New York. But she seemed happy, taught kids, read a lot, wrote poetry."

Katherine sensed his need to talk about his parents. Were his parents part of the answer to why he came, just as hers were?

"I could never see them together, and yet they seemed to have a good marriage," he said, then stopped and looked at her, smiling almost in embarrassment. "God! I haven't talked so much about myself in my whole life!"

"I'm a good listener," she said, smiling back, then turned to Mike. "What about you, Mike?"

He looked at her, at the snowflakes in her reddish hair, the pale skin made paler in the lamplight, the lavender eyes that looked questioningly at him, and he decided he liked her even if she wasn't his type.

"My uncle wasn't a poet, but he was executed by Mussolini's Black Shirts." They stopped to listen as the others in the group drew near. "He was my father's older brother. He'd stayed in Sicily, and I grew up on stories about him. My father loved him and always talked about him. They both were *Garibaldistas*, followers of Garibaldi, who believed in democracy and fought the monarchy and the 'oppression of the workers.' My father used phrases like that. Now you have Franco trying to destroy democracy and restore the monarchy and the oppression of the workers. Uncle Roberto worked for Mussolini when Mussolini was a Socialist, but fought against him when Benito became a Fascist. The Black Shirts beat him up and drowned him in Palermo harbor. His letters are still in my father's drawer. Maybe I've come for revenge because Mussolini is fighting in Spain."

Katherine and Robert were silent in the wake of Mike's emotion.

The three of them started to walk again.

"Where did you go to school?" Katherine finally asked.

"CCNY," Mike said.

"What did you major in?"

"Opera and girls."

Robert and Katherine laughed. As they did, the group arrived at their hotel

"*Bonsoir*," Fresnay said. "Have a good sleep."

"*Bonsoir*," they called back, standing under the streetlight of the Hotel Monsieur le Prince.

They entered the faded lobby, observed by the sharp-eyed concierge.

Katherine had her own room. Barkin was rooming with Carver; Robert, Mike, and Pete were together.

As the three men lay in the dark, the streetlight slicing across the worn carpet, Robert spoke quietly.

"Mike?"

"Yeah."

"Did you really major in opera?"

"Sure. Not that it was part of the curriculum. I got a job at the Metropolitan. In the claque."

"The what?"

"Claque. I was a potcher."

"Potcher?"

"Yeah. Must be a Jewish word. You get paid to 'potch'— applaud—besides getting in for nothing. I was there all the time, sometimes in the chorus. I knew everyone. Even the stars."

"Wow! How did you get that?"

"My poppa was a potcher. He was a real opera nut. Used to take me when I was a little kid. Sneak me in under his coat. But it was a game he played with the guy at the door, who was Italian. You know how the Italians are about opera."

"No, I don't. I never met one before."

Mike laughed and went to sleep.

———————————

In the semidarkness of the huge Gare d'Austerlitz, locomotives snorted steam in the cold; passengers, vendors, trainmen, rushed about carrying luggage, swinging lanterns. Fresnay led them past engine 77, its black, oily, muscular wheels and pistons shrouded in steamy puffs.

Aboard the train they moved through the beautifully varnished wooden compartments of the first-class carriages and the worn velours of second class to the bare Spartanness of third class, with its hard wooden-slatted seats. Some of the cars had compartments; others were open like trolleys, already crowded with men in working-class clothing and berets, who looked at the clean Americans, especially at George Carver, the only black, and Katherine, the only woman.

A tall man with eaglelike features and a fresh, livid scar across his cheek greeted Fresnay. Fresnay introduced him as Jean. They compared names on the list. Jean pointed out a compartment.

As they were putting their luggage on the overhead racks, the train lurched backward, coupling new cars. Katherine fell against Robert, and they toppled to the seat. A vendor came through, and as they sipped hot coffee and hungrily bit into brioches and flaky croissants, the train began to roll through the white Paris winterscape.

The compartment door opened. A red-haired young man appeared. His accent was deep Cockney. "Yanks, are you?"

They nodded.

"Tourists?"

They smiled.

"Good show. So are we." He winked. "Imagine . . . the 'ole bloody lot o' us goin' fer a 'oliday in the South. What a coincidence." He laughed. "Well . . . join us for lunch. Cheerio." He smiled and closed the compartment doors.

"By the way," Barkin asked Fresnay, "where are we going?"

"For tonight, Perpignan."

"That's near the Spanish border, isn't it?"

"Yes. We'll make the crossing somewhere nearby."

"How long will we be in Perpignan?"

"A couple of days. It depends on how many men are to be crossed and the number of guides."

They looked out at the French countryside, farms with wheat stubble sticking through the snow, small railroad stations, a horse and wagon, a convoy of trucks, a small boy waving.

Fresnay had a newspaper; Carver, Dos Passos's *Three Soldiers*; Pete, a copy of *New Masses*; Barkin, Hemingway's *The Sun Also Rises*; Katherine, a book on surgical techniques for medical officers; Robert, Ibsen's collected plays; and Mike, *Stanislavsky Directs*.

Mike looked at Robert's book. "You interested in the theater?" he asked.

"Uh . . . yeah. I've been writing short stories, one novel. But I'm leaning toward the stage. Maybe as an excuse to leave Iowa."

Katherine glanced up at him. Mike laughed. "Looks like you found it," he said, indicating the countryside. Then, after a short pause, he continued, "I've worked in the theater."

"Really?" Robert asked, interested.

Mike tried for modesty. "I was an apprentice in the Group Theater. I studied with Alex Tarasov, and I was in *Waiting for Lefty*."

Mike got his expected looks of admiration, then they all went back to their books.

The train rolled on as they read. Later, the doors slid open again and a dark face proclaimed, *"Mangiare . . . mangiare!"*

"Me voglio," Mike said, stretching. The man left.

"I'm hungry too," Pete agreed.

Robert looked at Katherine. "Ready?" he asked.

"I'm not a big eater." She smoothed her plaid woolen skirt. "But I like the company." She smiled.

They entered the car. Its long wooden benches were filled with men from many countries, who cheered the Americans and crowded around Katherine, impressed with her French and her flushed beauty.

Mike spoke to the Italian group as they passed bread, cheese, sausages, and wine. Soon they started to sing. Mike knew the obscure arias of Puccini, Rossini, and Bellini and twenty-six ways to cook linguini. They were soon calling him *maestro*.

"I was the Toscanini of the Group Theater," he laughed.

"Hey! Anyone here know any Greek?" Pete shouted.

"No Greeks, only Turks," someone yelled back.

"I know few words," a young Italian said. "I work in Greek restaurant."

"Probably my cousin's," Pete shouted.

Robert spoke with some Germans who were joining the Thaelman Battalion, the anti-Nazi unit of the International Brigades.

Wine flowed, guitars appeared. They sang songs of freedom and struggle in every European language. As the lights of the towns came on in the dusk, they entered Perpignan.

Katherine turned to Robert. "This is why I came. For this feeling of being together in something important."

The train stopped. The men moved to the platform, embraced, formed into groups, and quickly disappeared into the night.

"Where are they going?" she asked Fresnay.

"To houses, farms. You are going to a hotel."

"Why?"

"Because Americans can pass for tourists."

A block from the hotel they were stopped by a gendarme and a civilian. Fresnay took them by the elbows and walked a few paces. The group exchanged nervous glances. Could they be detained for "suspicion," deported after they'd come so far?

After a brief conversation Fresnay walked back, their passports in hand.

"Everything all right?" Barkin asked.

"I don't think so. They reminded me your passports are stamped 'Not valid for travel in Spain.' But I got a recommendation for a restaurant."

Jean was waiting for them at the small hotel. He had a whispered conversation with Fresnay, then they went to Fresnay's room, where Jean addressed them.

"I am sorry. I know you have had a long journey, but you must leave tonight. We have brought too many and the authorities are on the alert. You will be taken to the crossing point in two cars tonight and met by Spanish guides. Go to dinner, act normally."

The man's rasping authority irritated Mike.

"Why us?" he asked. "Why not another group?"

"You will learn to do as you are told," the man said coldly.

Mike's temper flared. "That's not why I volunteered," he shot back.

Fresnay leaped in. "They are tired, Jean."

"Anarchist! Trotskyite!" Jean spat at Mike. Robert could see Mike's fists clench.

"Can't you make other arrangements?" Fresnay asked.

"Have them ready at eleven o'clock," Jean said, turning and leaving.

Fresnay looked embarrassed. "I am sorry," he said in answer to their stunned silence.

Silence extended to the restaurant. Surrounded by photos of bicycle racers, they ate soberly. The plainclothesman watched them over his own dinner.

———————

The lobby was lit with one small bulb. Dressed in army surplus and backpacks, the group waited. The concierge whispered anxiously to Fresnay, "They'll take my license."

Fresnay handed him some bills. A gendarme rode by on his bicycle, flashing his light in the lobby. They pushed back into the shadows until he passed. A car pulled up to the door. Fresnay sent Mike, Barkin, Carver, and Katherine into the street. Before Katherine got into the car, she waved to Robert. The door closed and she was gone. Robert felt a pang.

What if he never saw her again? Suppose this was a trap? Another car stopped outside. Fresnay shook hands with the concierge and hurriedly left with the rest of his group. The small bulb went out and the lobby was in darkness.

———————

They drove without headlights on a road to nowhere. Katherine turned to see if there was a car following. There was none. Mike took her hand reassuringly. "It'll be all right."

Robert's body ached from the strain of looking ahead. After fifteen minutes there was a flash on the side of the road. They flashed back. Fresnay said something Robert couldn't hear to the driver. Was this betrayal?

He leaped out almost before they'd stopped, ran to Katherine. They took each other's hand. The rest of the group were on the side of the road with an old man and a young boy in ragged sheepskins.

Fresnay listened to the sound of swiftly approaching tires. "You must go quickly. *Bonne chance!*" He embraced them hurriedly and entered his waiting car. Both cars ground gravel and loose snow as they sped off.

The old guide turned up the trail, and they followed. The approaching car passed, and there was no sound now but the sweeping wind. They looked at the huge, dark mountains they had to cross.

The stony trail was bitterly cold and tortuous. Mike led them, behind the old man, Pete and George on his heels. Robert put out his hand to help Katherine over a slippery stretch, but she refused: "I want to do this alone." Barkin, last, slipped and fell, pulled himself up and continued.

The young boy, who'd been farther up the trail, returned and spoke excitedly to his grandfather, who silently motioned them backward, then started climbing in another direction. They scrambled after him. Soon a three-man French army patrol passed beneath them. The Frenchmen laughed as they went by, but suddenly fell silent and returned as if looking for something. The group tensed. The old man drew a knife. Then they heard the sound of peeing.

Climbing higher, they paused for rest, breathing hard, stamping feet, and clapping hands for warmth.

"If I see the sun again, I'll die happy," Katherine said.

"Hey, you know what night this is?" Mike asked. They all looked at him. "It's New Year's Eve."

"And we've come for a party," Robert said, taking up his mood.

"Happy New Year!" Pete bellowed, his voice ricocheting off the Pyrenees. "Happy 1937!" he yelled.

"Sssshhh!" The old man looked at them with alarm as they all hugged. *"Andiamos."* He motioned them forward again.

Barkin looked gratefully at the guide, who had stopped and motioned toward a pile of rocks that formed the entrance to a cave. They entered, glad to be out of the wind. The shepherd took a candle from his pocket, lit it, and started a fire with wood that had been prepared. They surrounded it, rubbed their hands, and then stretched their tired bodies on the ground.

"Can you believe we were in Paris this morning and now we're in the middle of the Pyrenees?" Katherine asked, just before she fell into a deep sleep.

They woke with daylight filling the cave, looking at each other for orientation. Robert's and Katherine's bodies had been close, and they woke with their hands touching.

"Good morning," Robert said, smiling at her.

"Good morning," she said, returning the smile and wondering how many more mornings they would share.

"Don't I get a good morning?" Mike joked.

"Good morning, Mike," everyone chorused. The old man turned from the mouth of the cave, where he'd been looking at the weather. His young grandson was boiling water and slowly feeding the pot strips of dried meat.

Robert, Katherine, and Mike went to the entrance and looked at the crest of the mountains, the rising sun coloring the valley below.

"España." The old man pointed.

The strips of boiled dried meat reminded Robert of Chaplin eating his shoelaces in *The Gold Rush*.

Mike went to his pack and withdrew two chocolate bars.

"My mother gave them to me," he said, offering them. "Nuts or no nuts?"

"We're all nuts," Pete laughed, breaking off a piece.

Katherine was struck by Mike's generosity. "Thank you, Mike," she said with that dazzlingly warm smile.

Despite himself, Mike was touched by it. Later, Mike looked up from the chess game he was playing with Barkin and saw Robert and Katherine at the mouth of the cave, Robert holding her hand. He wondered at the piercing feeling that possessed him.

"It's crazy," Robert said, "but I've never felt such a crush on anyone so quickly." His face was open and vulnerable.

"I know," Katherine said, rubbing her thumb over his large hand. "I feel the same. Maybe it's love on the edge of death."

———

They descended that night in a snowstorm.

Holding one another's hand in a chain, slipping on small stones down the canyon passes, unable to breathe in the tearing wind, they never thought to see the dawn. As the sun began its orange ascent, the snow stopped and they found themselves finally on the valley floor of Spain. They looked back at the towering snow-covered Pyrenees and then joyously, breathlessly, ran through a field of winter flowers.

The shepherd led them to the fairy-tale fortress at Figueras, where he and his young grandson were to leave them. Katherine gave them a bunch of wildflowers she'd picked, and Mike gave the boy his last bar of chocolate.

They spent the rest of the day and night in the heavy stone-and-timber fastness of the ancient fort, talking with others they recognized from the train. The next day they were on a train rolling south, filled with hundreds of volunteers from all over Europe. A guitarist struck the opening chords of "Ay Manuela" and their voices shook the old cars. The machine gunners on the roofs listened and scanned the skies for enemy planes.

Katherine, her eyes shining, seemed to sing even louder than Mike. Carver quickly learned the Spanish words, and everyone complimented him on his accent, for he'd never studied any foreign language. He beamed in delight at his accomplishment. The ancient wooden cars creaked and swayed over the roadbed, and at every station, no matter how small, the crowds gathered, throwing them food and shouting the Loyalist slogan, *"No pasaran! No pasaran!"*— They shall not pass!

"As long as we live, we'll never forget this," Robert said.

At day's end, in the small town square of Albacete, in the dust created by military trucks and marching feet, as orders were shouted and engines revved, Robert stood with Katherine as if they were alone. She put her hands to his face.

"Please be careful. For my sake," she begged. "I know it's crazy when we've just . . ."

"I want you to take care. I feel the same!"

Impulsively they kissed. It was their first, and they held it as if it were to be their last.

Mike watched from the back of a truck, and as it started to move slowly from the square, he shouted, "Hey, Robert! We're movin' out!"

They kissed once more, then Robert broke from her, running to the truck.

"Write me at the brigade hospital," she shouted.

"I will," he shouted back as Mike pulled him aboard.

The truck turned a corner and they could no longer see each other.

Barkin crossed to Katherine and gently took her arm. "Come," he said.

In the crowded truck, Robert put his pack between his long legs and sat next to Mike with a look of joyous confusion.

"You're lucky," Mike said. "To find someone like that."

"It's nuts, though, isn't it?"

"Don't question it," Mike said. "It doesn't matter that you just met, or how. What matters is what you feel."

CHAPTER TWO

They arrived at their training camp at Villanueva de la Jara and entered the barracks as the sun fell, creating slanted rays through the dusty air of the parade ground. They hadn't eaten all day and were brought to the mess hall immediately. It was a high, vaulted room with long tables and flickering lamps, and it was filled with lively sounds of men eating, talking, joking.

"Pete! Pete! Hey, you fuckin' Greek!" a short, muscular blond man who was standing on a chair shouted at them.

"Irv! You Coney Island beachrat bastard!" Pete shouted back and ran to him. They embraced and punched each other affectionately. The others joined them, and Pete made introductions. "This is the jerk who talked me into coming here," he said. "Irv Goff. Said if we didn't stop the Fascists in Spain they'd be invading Coney Island and taking over the pool room. You son of a bitch, you still owe me two bits from the last game." He playfully punched Irv again. "How long you been here?"

"About a week. Came in through Bordeaux, then a leaking rowboat. Ruined my new Tom McAn's. But it was easy for me. Other guys had to swim in under fire. Italian gunboats and German subs. Murder!"

"How's the training going?" Robert asked.

"Yeah, what kinda rifles you got?" Mike asked, already eating from the mounds of food on the tables.

"So far, we got one rifle per squad and not many cartridges that fit. The machine guns are always jamming, the bayonets are rusty, the hand grenades are wood. But the officers are good."

"So . . . whattaya do?" Pete asked.

"Run a lot," Irv said. "We run a lot."

A cold wind swept the barren plains of La Mancha. The bare olive trees trembled against the winter sky. A whistle blew.

"Let's go," ordered Mike, the squad leader. Field stubble and stones became hundreds of charging figures.

"Cover your flanks! Cover your flanks!" shouted Captain John Scott over the wind. "I don't want to lose a single man to a mistake. We're outnumbered and outgunned, but goddammit, we're not going to be outsoldiered!" Grasping their dummy rifles, they turned down the hill once more and disappeared among the rocks.

Mike field-stripped the rifle blindfolded as he and Robert talked in their room. Guitar music and singing rose from below. Carver sprawled in a corner, book in hand. When Mike had reassembled the rifle, he pulled the red kerchief from his eyes. The faded red square had been his father's.

"How about a chess game when you finish the letter, Robert?"

"Uh-uh," Robert replied. "If I beat you, you'll be sore at me."

"You won't beat me."

"If I can't beat you, what's the point of playing?" Robert went back to his letter.

Mike shrugged, turned to George Carver. "How about a game, George?"

"I don't know how to play," George said, surprised.

"I'll teach you."

Carver put down his book. "My daddy always said, 'Never turn down a chance to learn anything new.'" He moved to the board.

Mike picked up each piece, explaining its moves. The others watched. Carver played surprisingly well, and Robert noted that Mike played without his usual killer's instinct.

"My daddy and I used to play checkers with this set he'd whittled," George said, moving a piece. "He was a good man." Mike moved as George continued. "When the man owned our farm tried to cheat my daddy on the cotton count like he did the other 'croppers who were afraid to complain, my daddy wouldn' back down. He wouldn' take less than he was owed."

"What happened?" Pete asked.

"They busted through the door with shotguns, wearing white sheets like they was the Klan, but I recognized the owner's voice. We found my daddy the next morning. He was hangin' from a tree over the county road. They'd tarred and feathered him and hung a sign on his chest. 'Here hangs a uppity nigger.'"

George told the story without emotion, as if it no longer had the power to hurt him.

"How old were you?" Mike asked quietly.

"'Bout ten."

"So was I." Everyone looked at him. "When my poppa was killed." He paused again, then continued. "He was a bricklayer, working on a project over on the East Side. The builder was putting too much sand in the mortar. The men knew it. The foreman knew it. The city inspector who was paid off knew it. When Poppa said he'd quit, my mother screamed, 'You crazy, Angelo? How we gonna feed the kids? You worry too much. Come to bed.'"

Mike looked at them, and sure of their attention, continued. "Poppa was always telling me about 'the job,' about workers and bosses and the girls who passed. Sometimes I'd hitch a ride on the back of the trolley car to where he was working. One day, ambulances and police cars passed me, sirens screaming. I knew before I saw the dust and smoke, and the cops and workers trying to pull guys from out of the collapsed building. I found him under a pile of timbers and bricks, his face covered by dust, blood coming out of his mouth. I tried to pull a big timber off his chest, but I was too small. Some men helped me, and I threw myself on him. His eyes were closed and he couldn't hear me screaming, 'Poppa! I need you!' The ambulance took him away. Later, a man came to the house and told us he was dead." Mike paused in the silence of the barracks room. "I swore I'd never be crushed like he was. By anything."

He let the words sink in. "We had a dozen funerals on the block. A dozen fathers killed for a few bucks' worth of mortar. That's capitalism."

Mike's words hung in the small room. The silence was broken by a commotion down the hall. Scott put his head in the door. "The Fascists have taken Málaga! A whole division of Italians, with two battleships in the harbor. They're shooting all prisoners!" Scott disappeared. The men in the room looked at each other. Would Madrid be next?

———

With the fall of Málaga, the battalion trained harder in the disciplines that required no weapons: scouting, map reading, infiltration, communications. They were becoming a high-spirited, coordinated battalion of almost five hundred.

Without weapons.

One chill night Mike and Robert lay on the ground in a pine woods, waiting for the signal to "attack."

"Why wouldn't you play me the other night?" Mike asked.

"I told you."

"Are you afraid of losing?"

"I may be more afraid of winning," Robert answered as if the words had wanted to escape forever. "Winning means responsibility. You have to win again. It's expected of you. If you lose, no one expects anything."

Mike nodded thoughtfully. There was a low whistle, like a bird call.

"That's us," Mike said. "Go ahead. I'll cover you."

———

In the surgery of the base hospital at Albacete, Katherine and Barkin received their baptism. The casualties from Jarama poured in. Jarama was a valley that straddled the road to Madrid from the south. The Fascists were again trying to take the capital, and the Franco forces were attacking fiercely there. As in the late fall of 1936, the International Brigades stood in their way.

Katherine had never seen blasted bodies, nor could she have imagined them as they were placed before her and Barkin in the surgery. Neither had Barkin with all his experience in the emergency rooms of New York City hospitals. They spent days on end without sleep at the operating table.

On Valentine's Day, 1937, the town of Villanueva de la Jara gave the Lincoln Brigade a going-away party. Rumor had it they were going to another base for advanced training.

"Bullshit," Irv said. "We're gonna get on-the-job training."

The party was held in an old building that passed for a town hall. It was festooned with spirals of crepe paper, and a band played.

Mike danced with Florita Mendez, a beautiful young Spanish girl with amazingly long lashes over her dark eyes. Her olive cheeks were flushed with color, and her black hair was loose over her slightly perspiring neck. Mike held her firm body and smiled at her. Her returning smile was one of complete adoration. Mike basked in it, but what attracted him most was her eighteen-year-old innocence and vulnerability, her total trust of him.

Earlier, he and Robert had been invited to her family's small house for dinner. They'd sat in the tiny candlelit dining room trying to converse with Florita and her father, who was the town shoemaker. Mr. Mendez was dressed in his funeral and wedding suit, his white shirt without collar or tie. He felt greatly important for having the two Americans in his home. His own son was at the front fighting on the Franco side, which tormented him. Mrs. Mendez, in her one black dress, brought food to the table, and Mike immediately started to eat. Robert, who'd been served first, waited, but Mrs. Mendez served no one else. Robert looked first to the mother, then at the others with a questioning look.

"*Come, come,*" Florita said, motioning them to eat.

Robert pointed to the empty plates. Mendez shrugged and pantomimed, "Eat, eat." Robert kicked Mike under the table.

"What's the matter?" he asked.

"They don't have any," Robert whispered. Mike looked at their empty plates, then got up and took his plate to Florita, sharing the food. Mendez's neck flamed in embarrassment. Robert did the same with Mrs. Mendez. She was mortified. Mendez put the food back on their plates, shouting he'd been shamed and would kill himself.

"What do we do?" Mike asked Robert.

"He's not giving us a choice."

They ate under the family's approving scrutiny.

Mike remembered the dinner as he danced with Florita. Robert remembered it as he danced with Mrs. Mendez in her black dress. Mendez remembered it with satisfaction as he played the trumpet in the band and watched his daughter dancing with Mike.

The music stopped as the mayor stepped onto the little stage and motioned for silence, then spread his arms.

"*Amigos!* Friends of the Spanish peoples! We will never forget that you came to fight for our liberty and ask nothing for it but our friendship. You will have it forever!"

The Lincolns applauded, and the music started again. They danced, drank, sang until three o'clock in the morning, when Mike disappeared with Florita.

He didn't show up until six as the battalion was lining up on the drill field.

"God, she's sweet," Mike said to Robert as he fell in next to him.

The trucks rumbled into the early quiet of the Villanueva town square. The battalion marched in company formation, their mood still party-gay, waving to their friends. Florita was among the admirers, throwing a bouquet to Mike. He caught it, rushed to the sidewalk, and kissed her. Then he embraced Florita's mother and father.

Mr. Mendez, tears in his eyes, felt he'd replaced his own son. *"Buenos suerte, mi hijo. . . . Vaya con dios."*

Mike felt an unexpected swell of emotion as he returned the embrace and kissed Mendez's unshaved cheeks. Then he ran back to his squad.

They arrived in Albacete late in the afternoon and stopped outside the Guardia Nacional barracks, hungry and thirsty, their muscles cramped from hours in the trucks. A staff car with the star of the 15th Brigade pulled up, and Katherine emerged. The men whistled.

"Katherine!" Robert yelled.

They ran to each other and embraced.

"I had to see you," she said as they kissed.

"I've missed you," he said. "Your letters have been so short."

Mike watched them as he smoked.

"No time to write. I've just worked forty hours straight. I can hardly keep my eyes open. I feel as if I'm going to drop in the middle of an operation."

"How'd you know we'd be here?"

"Barkin heard you were moving up to the line."

"Then it's true," he said incredulously. "But we don't even have any weapons."

"The 15th is in terrible shape. They've been getting the worst of the Madrid offensive. The wounded keep pouring in. I never imagined anything like it."

A motorcycle screamed into the plaza. The driver jumped off and handed the officers who were standing in a group a packet of orders.

"Hey, Thompson!" Captain Scott yelled. "Let's go. We're movin' out."

Katherine and Robert embraced.

"I will see you again, Katherine."

He kissed her and pulled away. She watched as he joined Mike. When the troops started to march toward the local bullring, she got into the staff car and fell asleep almost instantly.

In the bullring all was confusion, troops milling about waiting for orders.

"Some fucking army," Mike said.

Night fell without food. It got cold. A convoy grunted into the bullring, forming a circle. The drivers jumped from the cabs and unloaded crates of rifles, machine guns, ammunition. Hearts pounding, the troops grasped the weapons and were loaded onto trucks once more.

Robert, Mike and the others passed the gates, where a single swinging light bulb fleetingly illuminated their faces.

They were on their way to war.

CHAPTER THREE

The trucks stopped once during the night.

"Piss call!"

They lined the sides of the road and when finished were ordered to fire five rounds into the side of a dark mountain from their 1903 Springfields. It was the extent of their rifle training.

Robert and Mike huddled next to each other in the cold night. The canvas covers of the truck gave little protection, and eddies of freezing air coming through the openings blew sparks from Mike's cigarettes. Robert drowsed, Mike stared.

Just before dawn they stopped at a British field kitchen for coffee. It was weak but warm, and the metal cups brought life back to their numb fingers. Nobody said much. They huddled together in groups, shoulders touching.

When the sun had reached its zenith, they paused for lunch. The long convoy was strung along the length of country road when a cry went up.

"*Avion!*"

The men looked up to see the German dive bombers sweeping down on them, engines screaming. The troops scattered, their mess kits clattering on the road. Robert started to seek the shelter of a truck. As he crawled beneath it, he could feel Mike's hand on his arm. Mike was shouting, but it was hard for Robert to understand.

"In the ditch!" Mike pointed. "They'll bomb the trucks." Mike pulled insistently until Robert understood. As the planes tore at them, machine guns spitting, Mike, on his back, fired in futile anger. Everyone else seemed paralyzed. The planes arced away after the first pass, and Mike yelled, "Come back, you bastards!" As they prepared to return, Republican planes appeared, Russian Chatas, small and fast. They broke up the German formation with their skittering tactics and then engaged them, downing one. Everyone cheered as a German Stuka fell in a trail of smoke and exploded on impact. The rest fled.

"Thanks," Robert said as they climbed out of the icy ditch. Mike shrugged as if it were nothing and adjusted his father's red kerchief around his neck.

"Hey, I lost my hat," Pete said.

"It's probably in the ditch," Irv said. Irv knew how Pete felt about his Spanish Republican hat. Pete even slept in it. The men were reloaded in the trucks as Pete searched the culvert. Their truck started to move without him.

"He'll get in another truck," Mike assured Irv.

"He'd lose his head if it wasn't attached," Irv said with affectionate concern. "And I'd be the one who'd have to tell his mother."

Pete found his woolen hat. It was muddy, but he put it on his head, smiled, and climbed to the side of the road as the trucks rumbled by. The last one in line stopped for him.

They were closer to the fighting now, and artillery alternated with the clanks, grindings, and whirrings of war vehicles, punctuated by the rat-tat-tat of machine guns. They felt the first stirrings of nervousness. It increased as the convoy arrived below the Jarama trenches during an intense artillery barrage from the enemy. There was confusion as orders were shouted and men ran about on the road looking for their squads, forming into their companies.

"Into a skirmish line!" Captain Scott shouted. "Company One ready to go!" He shepherded them up the hill. "Spread out. I don't want one shell getting you all."

Robert, his heart pounding, stayed next to Mike as they ran.

In the trench the noise was devastating.

"Welcome to Suicide Hill," a grimy, gaunt-eyed soldier said, fixing his bayonet to his rifle.

"What's goin' on?" Mike asked.

"Counterattack," the soldier said, forcing a clip into the breach of his ancient Remington.

Mike's squad grouped together, crouching, waiting for the whistle.

"Wonder where Pete is," Irv said.

"He'll find us," George said reassuringly.

Mike looked over at Robert, who was trying hard to swallow. His throat was constricting in fear, and he could only nod in response to Mike's glance.

"Good luck," Mike said, patting his shoulder. Robert nodded gratefully, and as he did, the whistle blew. They looked at each other, then started to go over the parapet as Scott led them.

"Cover your flanks!" he shouted.

The machine-gun fire from the opposite ridge was murderous. Mike motioned George and Irv to his left, Robert to his right, where he felt he could watch him better, then made a short dash forward, throwing himself behind a shattered olive tree. Robert followed, running a fast zigzag pattern, and as he threw himself next to Mike, Mike smiled at him. Irv and George were farther up the hill. Next to Robert was a young Minnesota farmboy with cornsilk hair who was a champion hog caller. He'd demonstrated his skill for them at Villanueva. As he rose to go forward, he fell suddenly, between them, clutching his throat, blood oozing between his fingers. Robert removed his hand. He had been almost decapitated by machine-gun bullets.

Robert and Mike looked at each other in shocked recognition of sudden death. Mike emptied his clip furiously at the opposite ridge, jammed another clip into the breech, and dashed below, falling behind a rock. Robert followed, but his legs felt as if they were rubber and he was bound in a nightmare.

George and Irv were already climbing the enemy hill. Mortars began to drop in on them, and an enemy plane strafed. Cries of the wounded mingled with the mortar whomps and the hammering of small arms. George dragged a groaning man, half his thigh gone, to a clump of trees at the bottom of the hill, where a medic worked. It seemed as if all the enemy fire had been directed at them.

"That was fantastic," Robert said to George as he joined him and Mike behind the rock. George shrugged.

Mike nodded and patted George's shoulder, then looked around them. "No one is advancing," he said.

"Too much fire," George said.

"Pull back at sundown! Retreat in the dark!" called a messenger as he crawled from group to group.

Mike snuggled down and calmly lit a cigarette. "Nuthin' to do but wait," he said as the bullets whined above.

My first battle and I haven't even fired a shot, Robert thought.

———————

Pete's truck had stalled. The fuel pump was clogged with dirt, and it was two hours before they had taken it apart, cleaned it, and got the truck going. The convoy was long gone with no one in sight. The men were angry. They might miss their first day of battle.

The empty road seemed peculiar to the driver and he wondered if he'd made a wrong turn. He thought he was driving toward the sounds of battle, but they could be deceptive as they echoed off the surrounding hills. His thoughts and concerns were interrupted suddenly when from the deep culverts at the sides of the road enemy troops in long capes appeared in front of them. His blood turned cold as he jammed on the brakes.

"Fucking Moors!" he exclaimed.

The assistant driver grabbed for his rifle, but they were surrounded by Franco's Moroccan mercenaries, who waved submachine guns at them. Resistance was useless.

In the back of the truck the men didn't know why they'd stopped again, and they began to bitch. But they fell silent when they saw the swarthy North Africans pointing their weapons and motioning for them to unload. On the road, the Moors took their captives' watches and rifles, then pushed them into the culvert. The men huddled together and looked up at their captors, wondering what they were going to do.

The answer came when the Moors put their hands under their capes and withdrew hand grenades. The grenades exploded in their midst. As the Lincolns screamed and tried to run, the Moors gunned them down with automatic fire, then went among the twenty-seven men and shot them individually.

The last rays of the sun fell beneath the horizon. Almost immediately it was dark and cold.

"Let's go," Mike said, shivering and turning up the hill. Hot coffee and food were waiting for them. Some, like Mike, devoured it; others sat in stupefied exhaustion.

Robert was elated. "We did it," he said. "We went against all that and didn't panic."

"Who didn't panic?" Irv asked. "I shit in my pants."

Mike dipped his bread into the stew and swallowed almost without chewing. "For greenhorns, we did okay," he said.

"I wonder where Pete is," Irv said.

Captain Scott appeared. "I'm proud of you boys," he said. "That was quite a baptism, and you did really well." They smiled and nodded. "We attack again at midnight," he added dryly and left.

Robert's heart fell. The rest looked at the moon shining on the shattered battlefield.

"Look at that fuckin' moon!" Mike exclaimed. "We're gonna be perfect targets."

The same moon shone on the murdered men in the culvert, their bodies stiffening in the cold, creating grotesque shapes. A breeze rustled over them, caressing the mangled bodies. There was silence until a body shifted heavily, then was pushed upward as if by some force beneath it. A head emerged, covered in blood. The rest of the body followed, elbowing its way forward. The man stopped and listened, looked about, and then climbed over the rest of the bodies and out of the culvert. Pete Pappas straightened his hat and walked down the road in the moonlight.

———————————

Robert and Mike looked out at the battlefield in the cool, pale light. Wounded were still being brought in.

"Looks like a stage set for a war play, doesn't it?" Mike said. "Could be Irwin Shaw's *Bury the Dead*."

Robert nodded, thinking he could be one of those sacks being carried up the hill, arms dangling, head rolling from side to side. He tried to still the panic he felt rising at the thought of the midnight attack.

Mike was calm now. His heart beat regularly. He had come down from the exhilaration he'd felt on his first entrance to the stage of war. He'd made the right moves, followed the script Captain Scott had outlined for them, and if his performance hadn't been outstanding, there would still be other scenes to play, performances to come. He lit a cigarette and hid its glow in the palm of his cupped hand.

The footsteps came from behind them, creating a stiffening alert. Mike shoved a round into the chamber of his rifle and focused on the sound, turning toward it, finger on trigger.

The steps were slow and deliberate, climbing the hill from the road behind. Then the figure appeared, macabre in the moonlight above them.

"Who's that?" Mike asked sharply.

Silence.

"Pete?" Irv asked in disbelief.

"Yeah. It's me."

"Pete!" Irv shouted, moving toward him, embracing him in relief.

"They killed us all," Pete said in a dead voice. "The Moors killed us all." Pete felt as though he'd left his life behind him with the others. He had no right to be alive.

Irv hugged him again, feeling the spasm that shook Pete.

Pete told them the story.

It could have been me, Robert thought. But I wouldn't have survived.

At ten minutes to twelve a tank rumbled and clanked into

position to lead the attack. Captain Scott came through the trench patting a back, giving an encouraging word or a piece of advice.

"Remember to cover your flanks. I don't want anyone cut off in a counterattack."

Then, down the line at battalion HQ, the whistle blew. They moved forward behind the tank. Pete had insisted on going with them.

Their machine-gun company had already opened up, and the tracers made long arcs toward the enemy. They responded with flares which threw the attackers into silhouette in the bluish-white light; then their own concentrations of machine guns started a constant hammering.

Bullets pinged off the armor plating. Robert's throat was tight. He tripped on a tree root and fell. Mike took his arm and pulled him up. They made it to the bottom of their own hill and had started to climb toward the enemy when the tank took a direct hit from an antitank shell. It blew up in a ball of fire. They scattered and hit the ground, seeking cover among olive trees and grapevines. They watched the tank burn. Only one flaming figure emerged from the hatch.

Mike motioned his squad toward the yellow-blue matchlike fire of the machine guns above them. His heart raced, and the blood drummed in his ears, but he was lucid, calm in his center, aware of everything around him as if he were above the events looking down on them.

Pete went blindly ahead, leaving them, throwing grenades and firing. Irv went after him, then George.

"Let's go," Mike said to Robert. "We got to cover them." They rose to a crouch, but the intensity of the fire forced them down. They went forward, digging with their elbows, knees, and feet into the rutted, stony hillside. They could no longer see the other men of their squad, but found Scott ten yards from the enemy wire. Robert fired as Mike and Scott lobbed grenades. The sputtering flame of the machine guns seemed close enough to touch.

As Scott rose to throw his last grenade, a mortar that was falling short whistled and exploded nearby, sending hot metal fragments cutting the air with a high whine. Scott fell heavily, groaning.

"Where you hit?" Mike asked quickly.

"Seems like everywhere. Stomach . . . chest . . ."

Scott was on his face. Robert and Mike slowly rolled him over, and as they did so, Scott's guts spilled out of him. They looked at each other and, despite their rising bile, placed the intestines back in the open cavity.

"I'll get a stretcher," Robert said.

"Don't bother, friend," Scott said slowly. "It's too late."

The call came to retreat.

———

The warm sun and sounds of mess kits being scraped woke Robert and Mike. They filled their tin plates from the huge pot and joined Irv and George, scrunching down beside them.

"Where's Pete?" Robert asked.

"Coffee . . ." Irv replied.

"How is he?" Mike asked.

Irv shrugged. George merely stared ahead over his mess kit, shrouded in thought.

Pete returned. He still hadn't washed the blood from his face, but no one said anything about his bizarre appearance. An occasional bullet whined above them.

"Fuckin' snipers," Irv said. "Don't they eat breakfast?"

Two men approached them. One was an English officer with a swagger stick. "You laddies did well yesterday," he said. "We were on your left flank."

"*Ja*," the second said. He was wearing a long leather coat and had a thick German accent. "For green troops you do okay."

Robert was about to start a conversation in German with the man when they heard the whine of a bullet and the small cry of surprise from the Englishman. He'd been hit in the forehead; his brains spilled out the back of his head, spattering into their coffee.

"*Gries Gott!*" Robert said involuntarily.

February 27 was cold, and the sky threatened rain. Occasionally the sun revealed its position, breaking through the heavy clouds, but it gave no warmth. The men huddled in the trench, checking their equipment over and over, and tried to still their rising apprehension over the coming attack. The promised artillery preparation never materialized, and Major Merriman, the battalion commander, was furious. No artillery, no air cover. How could they be expected to succeed? He'd objected to the coming attack without support at the regimental staff meeting that planned it, and it was only Colonel Copic's threat of court-martial and replacement that kept Merriman from disobeying. He took off his horn-rimmed glasses and rubbed his eyes, then looked at his watch. Ten minutes to twelve. He signaled for the messengers to go down the line.

"Ten minutes," they said as they ran.

"Sounds like a stage manager's call," Mike quipped. No one laughed.

They affixed their bayonets. Robert's throat tightened. Pete wet his lips. George closed his eyes as if praying. Mike chewed his lip.

The field phone rang in Merriman's dugout.

"It's Copic," his operator said. Merriman eyed him. "He says, 'Go.'" Merriman nodded. He went out to the trench, put his whistle to his lips, and reluctantly blew it.

With Confederate yells, the Lincolns sprang over the parapet as their machine guns started their chatter. The rows of enemy guns yammered back, and their mortars started falling. The English on their left flank also streamed down the hillside. The Spanish 24th on their right stayed in their trenches.

Merriman went down almost immediately, a slug through his shoulder. Captain Scott's replacement was cut down. His adjutant, Father McGrotty, a priest from Dublin, rose to command the company and was killed. More than half those who had reached the olive trees below were already dead.

The rain was now a downpour, rivulets of water carrying

blood. Mike's squad lay in the muddy puddles all afternoon. Somehow, Mike felt cheated. He knew there would be no climax to this scene, only exit. As he lay there, smoking a damp cigarette, he felt slightly bored at withdrawal.

The intensity of Robert's fear had diminished. He breathed easier, although the attack had been a disaster. His throat didn't hurt as much.

At dusk, soaked and freezing, they returned to their trenches, covered in mud, too exhausted to care, grateful to be alive. The seriously wounded were still lying on the cold, bloody hillsides of no-man's-land, the bullets whizzing over them.

The rain turned to sleet. There was no food and no dry clothing, and there were very few men left. Of five hundred, sixty were in the trenches, forty down below in search parties for the wounded. That's what was left of the Abraham Lincoln Battalion after Jarama. But they had stopped the enemy's advance with their attacks, and Madrid had been saved once more by the International Brigades.

———————

Katherine worked in a trance of exhaustion, a sleepwalker's state that ignored even the bombings of the hospital. The operating room was bloody. There was no time to clean it as the casualties from Jarama poured in, men patched at the front needing surgery to stay alive. Many died waiting. As men were put on the table, Katherine looked at their faces, terrified one would be Robert's.

Barkin no longer worried about her survival. He feared for his own. He was processing human bodies like a butcher in a Chicago slaughterhouse, struggling to keep his feelings intact, struggling to remember these were men as he sought to put them back together.

———————

Lying like muddy rag dolls in their trenches, the survivors waited for spring. The Jarama front was in stalemate, and the enemy put its efforts elsewhere.

Over and over they recounted the battle, the sounds and

textures of war, the anecdotes of machismo and death. Mike's dark eyes lit with luminescence as he described his feelings. His heart had never pumped so hard, but it was not fear. He felt the same lucidity that came to him on stage. It was a height that did not drop off into emptiness.

Robert wasn't sure that Mike's exhilaration was something to be admired. But he knew he felt safer with his friend when he feared he'd drop his rifle for the trembling in his hands.

Irv was matter-of-fact, almost enthusiastic.

Pete was silent.

George said, "We were the pawns."

Mail call. They all dashed into the gray, drizzly morning from their dugout and sloshed to the mail truck. It had been raining almost steadily for two months. Mike received a package from Alex Tarasov, containing some plays, cigarettes, and a letter from Clifford Odets. Robert received a letter from Katherine, and one from his parents.

Pete wrapped a colorful scarf around his neck. "From my mom," he said. "And some baclava."

"What's baclava?" George asked. He had received no mail.

"Food of the gods," Pete replied. "They used to make it on Mount Olympus, now they bake it at Coney Island."

Irv got a letter from the former dance partner with whom he'd toured the Loews circuit. "We had the best adagio act in Brooklyn," he said.

Katherine wrote about the surgery and their total exhaustion. There were no endearments. Robert sensed an emotional detachment. His mother wrote about a poetry class she was taking, and his father sent news of the grain store.

Alex wrote about the Group Theater's season in New York, and Odets said the new play he was working on would have a big part for Mike. It all seemed very distant here in their muddy dugouts, and Mike sometimes wondered why he'd come when he could have been advancing his career. Someone has to do it, he told himself. Someone has to take a stand. But why me? Why did I volunteer? Was it really because of my uncle, my father?

Reinforcements arrived daily as both sides waited for spring. When it came, mud turned to dust under the hot sun. It got into their food, their clothes, their red eyes. But at least it was warm, and the warmth healed them emotionally. Out in the sun once more, they stretched, smiled, touched one another, and trained with the almost six hundred new men. They played baseball, shared their thoughts, letters, food, and hopes for the future.

As they spent days together in conversation, Robert and Mike knew that they complemented each other. Mike admired Robert's intellect, his powers of analysis. Robert was moved by Mike's gut intuition and volatile emotion. It had never been easy for Robert to express emotion, perhaps because of his father's remoteness.

The warmth between them released a flood of writing for Robert. One day, as they discussed a scene Robert had written, Irv sneaked up on them.

"Smile," he said. As they looked up at him he snapped their picture. They went on discussing the scene.

On July 2, Mike left for Albacete in a convoy of three trucks to load supplies. The front was still quiet and the trip was uneventful. They were to lay over, return the next day. Mike traded cigarettes for chocolate bars to give to Florita and hitched a ride to Villanueva.

The car arrived at six, and Mike went straight to the Mendez house. All that was left of it was the shoemaker's sign hanging from the doorframe. He knocked frantically at the next house, which was untouched. An old woman in a black shawl appeared, staring at him.

"Que pasó con la familia Mendez?" he asked breathlessly, knowing the answer.

The black eyes in the walnut face held his own.

"Muertos. Una bomba."

"Todos?" He felt a terrible chill.

"Sí. Todos."

Numbly, he turned from her and looked at the family's remains. A doorway and a chimney.

Overcome with bitter guilt, he got drunk at the wine

shop he used to go to with Robert. He had easily manipulated Florita's feelings, overcome her protests, and taken her in an open field, vowing to return after the war to marry her. Love was the condition of her first surrender, and he'd shamelessly sworn it. He didn't expect belief, but Florita had. How could she suspect his motives? He'd come to save her country.

Dazed, Mike returned to camp and sought out Robert. Outraged by the bombings of Guernica and Barcelona, by Hitler's Condor Legion, Robert was moved even more by Mike's news.

"I wrote about them when you were gone, Mike," he exclaimed. "I wrote the story of the dinner!"

Mike closed his eyes and turned away. Robert crossed to him and put his arm around his shoulders. He didn't tell Mike that he'd gotten a letter from Katherine while Mike was gone, saying she was arriving with Ernest Hemingway for their Fourth of July celebration.

———

The troops raised the American and Spanish Republican flags, made a bonfire for the hot dogs Hemingway had promised, and cleaned the baseball field, while Robert nervously waited for Katherine to arrive.

"Hey, you guys," Irv called. "Smile." Robert put his arm around Mike, and Irv snapped the shutter.

"Battalion formation! Battalion formation!" the runner from HQ cried, surprising everyone.

"What the fuck for?" Mike asked.

"We're moving out."

"To where?" Milt Felsen, one of the new guys, asked.

"Brunete. Big attack."

When Katherine arrived, they were gone.

———

Their marching created clouds of dust. Their faces were caked, their lips dry, their canteens empty. The road stretched endlessly between hills under an unmerciful sun. It seemed they'd been marching their whole lives in this blistering hell.

And George had been killed.

After the air attack from the huge German Heinkel bombers in which Robert expected to be blown to pieces, they found George near a tree, his body perfectly intact. But blood was trickling from his ears, nose, mouth, and eyes. His skin was sun-warm, his heart still. He'd been killed by blast concussion.

Robert's hand shook as he touched George's face.

Mike bit the inside of his lips. "Pawns," he said. "We're the pawns."

They looked at each other and then at the shimmering heat waves of the road as they stood to march again.

———————

Brunete was a costly disaster.

Three weeks earlier, on July 4, there had been nine hundred Americans. Now there were 280.

They were pulled back to recover.

CHAPTER FOUR

Robert closed his eyes as they bounced in the truck. Mike smoked a dung-smelling Spanish cigarette. Pete played gin rummy with Irv as they drove toward Madrid.

"Remember the year I took the AAU state diving and tumbling championships?" Irv asked. Pete nodded and threw out a card. "Boy, that was some year." Irv picked up a card and discarded one. "I was in really good shape." He nodded and stretched.

"Yeah, I remember how you used to show off for the dames on the beach."

Irv laughed. "It was the back flips that really got 'em."

"Gin," Pete said, putting down his cards.

Robert opened his eyes and cracked his knuckles.

"Nervous?" Mike asked him.

Robert nodded.

"Don't worry." Mike patted Robert's shoulder. "It'll be okay."

But Robert wasn't sure as the truck entered Madrid. Katherine's letters had been cool and factual since she moved to the base hospital in Madrid. "Maybe she found someone else," he worried.

"Not Katherine," Mike observed. "If she did, you'd know it. I'm telling you, Robert, it's gonna be good."

Robert smiled in appreciation. But still, he worried that Katherine would find him shallow and reject him. When they met in the lobby of the Hotel Florida, where she was living, he was sure he had lost her. Her face fell on seeing him.

Katherine was shocked at Mike's and Robert's haggard faces. Their shaved cheeks accented the hollows, their eyes were shot with red, rimmed with blue rings no amount of sleep erased. Their bodies were like stick figures from loss of weight.

Robert choked when she hugged him warmly, but thought he detected disappointment as she hugged the others.

"Where's George?" she asked. The men looked at each other without answering. "I'm sorry," she said quietly. "Where did it happen?"

"On the road to Brunete," Robert answered, remembering George's still-warm skin.

They stood awkwardly in the bustle of the lobby. Mike finally broke the silence. "Enough," he said. "We've done our mourning. Life goes on." They all nodded and turned toward the street.

Katherine wore a light cotton dress in a small floral print, and her hair was atop her head in a tightly pulled bun, accenting the length of her neck.

Mike looked speculatively at her as she went through the doors ahead of him.

Robert and Katherine joined hands as they walked behind the others down the Gran Via toward the Café Chicote. Robert felt as though his palms were sweating and was vaguely embarrassed. He pretended to be preoccupied with the antics of his buddies as they horsed around on the street ahead of them.

"Why are you so quiet?" Katherine finally asked.

"Because you're disappointed."

"What do you mean?" She stopped and turned to him.

"I saw your face when we met in the lobby."

She impulsively put her arms around him. "That wasn't disappointment. I was shocked at how you all look. I couldn't believe the change. You don't look twenty-three anymore."

"I never will again."

"Oh, Robert . . ." She held him tightly there in the street. Passersby looked at them curiously.

Mike had turned and looked back for them. He felt a pang of emptiness as he saw their embrace. "Come on," he shouted gaily. "There won't be any tables left."

The café was filled to overflowing with leather-coated tank drivers, jacketed fliers, journalists, secret servicemen, Spanish cavalrymen, Germans, French, English, Scandinavians, nurses, hookers, newspaperwomen, all those who accompany a war.

"Two days ago we were getting shot up—tonight we're in a bar."

Robert laughed at Mike's observation.

"It's a trolley-car war," Katherine said, returning the laugh.

"I like that," Robert said.

"I can't claim it as mine. It's Hemingway's. He says it's the only war he's ever heard of where you can commute from the hotel to the front by trolley car. It starts at the Casa del Campo at the end of the Gran Via. You see those tankers over there?" She pointed at the burly men in the long leather coats. "They live in the Florida and go to work every morning by trolley as if they had normal jobs."

"So you know Hemingway pretty well." Robert was impressed, and afraid of the writer's reputation as a womanizer.

"He lives in the hotel," Katherine said simply.

They had one drink at the crowded table and left the roar, leaving Pete and Irv behind with two British nurses.

At the Gran Via restaurant the crowd was different. The clothes were expensive and stylish, the clientele drank champagne and dined on little lobsters, hair was coiffed and bosoms were in evidence in an atmosphere of gaiety.

"This goes on every night?" Mike asked.

"Don't ask me," Katherine said. "It's the first time I've been here. Hemingway suggested it. I thought we'd have a celebration."

"I thought I was fighting for the Mendez family," Mike said bitterly.

Katherine was sorry they'd come. Mike's hostility to the

upper classes was apparent, and the waiters treated them badly, even telling them there was no more food in the kitchen.

Finally the mention of Hemingway's name to the maître d' brought them a decent bottle of wine and the Mediterranean lobsters the other diners were eating.

In the hotel lobby Katherine asked them if they wanted to go up to Hemingway's room. "It's always open even if he isn't there, which is often."

Robert looked at his watch, wondering how Katherine knew Hemingway's habits so well and also if she was stalling about going to her own room with him, since it was late.

"I'd like that," Mike said, wanting to continue the evening.

Hemingway wasn't there, but his room was jammed with men and women, filled with smoke and the sounds of the latest American phonograph records. The bed was covered with bodies; beneath it, discarded wine and champagne bottles; on a desk, Hemingway's typewriter, which Robert looked at in awe, and on the other side of the bed, a hot crap game. The room was headquarters for writers, journalists, aviators, and their entourages.

A dark young woman gave Mike a glass and filled it. "Who're you?" she asked. "Anyone important?"

"Yeah, I'm a star visiting the front," he replied.

"Seriously?" she asked in a French accent.

"Why? You a celebrity fucker?"

"Ah, how wicked you are." She smiled. "What's your name?"

"Errol Flynn."

Robert and Katherine nearly choked on their drinks.

Mike looked at the crap game.

"How much money do you have?" he asked Robert.

"Three hundred pesetas."

"Lend 'em to me."

"Why?"

"I feel hot tonight."

Robert emptied his wallet. "Don't lose it. That's six months' pay."

"Errol Flynn never loses," Mike said. The girl laughed

and followed Mike to the game. "New player! New player!" Mike shouted.

"Hey, fresh money," someone called. Most of the players were aviators, who had more money than anyone else in the war, and it was a high-stakes game. Mike took the dice and examined them carefully.

Robert and Katherine watched from a corner with the correspondent from the London *Times*.

"Betting three hundred." Mike threw down the bills.

"Three hundred!" someone said derisively. "This ain't no kid's game."

"Gotta warm up." Mike threw a seven on his first roll. "Betting six hundred."

"Fade you."

Mike rolled an eight and made his point in three rolls. He quickly ran the stake up to five thousand.

"Betting five thousand," he called, and started singing an aria from *The Barber of Seville*. Robert shook his head at Mike's audacity and looked to Katherine, who shrugged. Everyone in the room crowded them as the bet was covered. He rolled.

"Nine! Nine's the point." Side bets started as Mike held the dice. He rolled again. The dice hit a shoe and came up nine. Mike started to pick up the bills.

"No dice," said a huge tanker. "They hit a shoe."

Mike sized him up and knew he couldn't take him. "Okay. You're gonna lose anyway."

Mike made his point in three passes. The tanker stalked away. "Ten thousand! Betting ten thousand!" There were gasps, and Mike loved it. "Any takers, or are you all just a bunch of chicken shits?" There was a conference. Nobody bet ten thousand.

Robert stared at Mike as if seeing an aspect of him he hadn't revealed before. Finally the others got up the money and Mike smiled, took a deep breath, let out a blast of Puccini, and rolled.

"Seven!"

That broke up the game.

The French girl took Mike's arm. Mike handed Robert a thousand-peseta note.

"You only owe me three hundred."

"Interest. And tomorrow, dinner's on me."

Michelle lived on the fourth floor with a correspondent who was away covering Franco. Katherine lived on the fifth. They took the elevator together.

Mike held a bottle of champagne. "*Mañana*," he called as they left the elevator.

Outside Katherine's door she fumbled for the key. "I've never done this before," she said in explanation of her nervousness.

"Neither have I. I'm just a hick."

Katherine's room was small and plain, but she'd tried to make it homey.

Robert examined the photographs on her dresser. "Who's this?" he asked, looking at a picture of a young man in tennis whites.

"My brother."

"You didn't tell me you had a brother."

"I'm full of secrets," she said playfully, trying to conceal her nervousness. "It's painful," she added, more seriously. "I'll tell you another time." She was sitting on the bed. Robert sat down next to her. She put her arms around his neck. "Well . . ." she said, smiling.

They kissed gently, quietly, then sank together, kissing more hungrily. They undressed each other slowly. Robert's hands stroked her body, and her nipples rose as he sucked them; warm liquid flowed between her legs.

"Now, please," she said, and guided him, alive to the shock of entry. Yet as soon as she began to relax she felt the heat of his release. Is that all there is to it? she wondered, as he relaxed on top of her.

"*Mon Dieu*, you are a focking machine," Michelle cried out in delight, coming for the fifth time. Her correspondent always fell asleep immediately.

"You're not bad yourself, baby," Mike said, lighting cigarettes and handing her one. He was playing Bogart, Cagney.

"Where you learn to fock like that?"

"It's like talent, kid. You got it or you don't."

"You have a *big* talent!"

Mike laughed in delight. "You want to go for the double whammy?"

"What is the 'double whammy'?"

"I'll show you," he said, stubbing out the cigarette.

Michelle dropped hers in the tray as Mike's tongue slid down her belly.

"Was it good, Katherine?" She was silent. "I have so little experience."

"Disappointing," she finally said.

"Do you always tell the truth?" he asked, hurt.

"It's the only kind of relationship I can have."

"Good," he said, and started stroking her again. She marveled at the lightness of his hands.

"How gentle you are," she said, trying to give herself over to sensation, while a corner of her mind held on as if to a ledge, afraid of falling into the abyss. Finally, the resistance ended and all of her became alive to sensation. Her neck arched backward as she held Robert's shoulders, and now her entire back was a span as she held the thrust and they came together, falling onto the bed in breathless tremors.

Michelle was coming as a result of Mike's tonguing, and he entered her as she did. She gasped, and he thrust at her with long, slow strokes. She grasped his shoulders and dug her nails into them, holding on as she threw her pelvis at him. Their breaths came faster and faster, and her moans became one prolonged cry as she disintegrated.

The man in the next room banged on the wall.

They collapsed in laughter.

Michelle sprawled across the bed in sweetly exhausted sleep. Mike smoked and stared at the ceiling. He was unsatisfied and lonely.

Below them, Robert and Katherine slept in each other's arms with the innocence of children.

When Mike left Michelle the following morning, she smiled sweetly and said, "I have never been focked so good in my life. Will I see you tonight?"

"I don't go in for relationships," he answered.

Robert and Katherine woke, still in each other's arms. Robert smiled at her. "How are you?" he asked.

"Lovely. I feel . . . lovely," she answered, hugging him.

The flickering black-and-white images were familiar. They were of war, but they were different. They were the enhanced images of film, somehow larger than life. Mike sat entranced as they watched their attack on Mosquito Crest in the Brunete campaign. All they heard was the whirr of the projector, but they could remember the rattles, whines, and thumps as plumes of smoke and geysers of earth fountained in the air. They felt both removed and part of it, as though watching someone else's dream. The screen went white as the film ran out.

"Well, what do you think?" Hemingway asked as the lights in the hotel room came on and he adjusted his horn-rimmed spectacles. Hemingway was making a documentary on the war in Spain. He hoped to use it to change the U.S. policy of nonintervention and embargo of supplies to the Loyalists. The men looked at each other.

"That's the way it was," Robert said.

"Only more so," Mike said thoughtfully. "It seems to have a super reality on film."

"That's what pictures are all about," Robert Capa said, his cigarette dangling at the edge of his lips, smoke curling into his eyes. "Let me show you some stills." He went to a battered leather briefcase and withdrew a sheaf of 8 × 10s, placing them on the bed as they gathered over them. One particularly stood out. It was the moment of death for a

Republican soldier. He was on a hillside outlined against the sky.

Katherine squeezed Robert's hand and whispered, "I'm glad I saw this."

Robert, Mike, and Katherine walked the sunny Madrid streets, avoiding shell holes from the night before. The German artillery on a hill nearby always opened up as the movie theaters let out. They passed the marquee of the Capitol Theater, and the Marx Brothers grinned from posters on a wall. *A Night at the Opera* was playing.

"We've got to see this," Robert said.

"Tomorrow," Mike replied. "Today, we walk."

They approached a hunting shop with beautiful leather goods in the window. "Hey, let's go in here," Mike said impulsively, taking their arms. He bought new boots for himself and Robert and a handbag for Katherine, and a Castilian steel hunting knife, which he strapped to his leg under his trousers.

"You're too generous, Mike," Katherine said.

"Bullshit." He shrugged.

"You spent a fortune on us," Robert said.

"What else are friends for?" He shrugged again. "Besides, it wasn't my money, and there's plenty left."

"How did you know you were going to win last night?" Robert asked.

"I knew I was hot. Like you're in a basketball game and everything you throw goes into the hoop, or a pool game and you sink every shot."

"I know what you mean," Robert said, smiling.

Katherine wondered what women had among themselves that was similar. She couldn't think of anything. Perhaps only intuition.

Despite Robert's protests, Mike took them back to the Gran Via for dinner. Katherine wondered why. Mike had said he hated the place. He'd also given Irv and Pete a thousand-peseta note to take out the two British nurses.

Afterward they returned to Hemingway's room. It was as if the party had never stopped. The crap game was in full swing, champagne flowed, the music blared.

"You gonna give us a chance to get our money back?" one of the aviators called out.

"It's gone," he called back. "Easy come, easy go."

Michelle was on the bed talking to another aviator. Mike nodded to her, and she immediately crossed to him, her cotton dress clinging to her body in the heat. Mike found himself getting hard.

"Hallo, Mike."

"Hallo, babee," he said, mimicking her French accent.

"You had a good dinner?" she asked.

"We had an expensive dinner."

"Why didn't you ask me?"

"I forgot about you," Mike answered simply.

"I didn't forget about you," she said.

Later, they left together.

As the perspiration cooled on their bodies, Katherine snuggled comfortably against Robert and closed her eyes. They listened to an occasional artillery shell, the sound of someone's radio, a car backfiring. Robert held her and wondered at their relationship. He never thought of himself as a romantic, as a lover, and yet here he was in the middle of what would certainly be a romance if he read about it in a novel. He marveled at his luck and wondered if it would last.

Katherine wondered at his preoccupation. "What are you thinking about?" she asked.

"How lucky I am and whether it'll hold."

"It will."

Robert closed his eyes for a moment. "Tell me about your brother," he finally said.

Katherine sat up, her mouth tightening slightly, a fleeting shard of pain crossing her eyes.

"I loved him very much. He was my big brother, handsome, brilliant, gallant. Everything you'd want in a brother. He played the piano beautifully and football just as well. I think he must have been the most popular boy in Princeton." She stopped.

"What happened to him?"

"He died."

"How?" Robert asked, shocked.

"We don't know."

"What do you mean, you don't know?"

"We never found out. He grew depressed for no apparent reason. One day he was in the full swing of his life, and then he began to grow dim, like a bulb without power. There didn't seem to be any cause. He stayed home, stopped going to class or seeing friends. He didn't eat and lost weight. Then he got into bed and stayed there until he died. He wasted away. It wasn't anorexia or cancer. We had every doctor with a theory. Nothing worked. It was as if he decided life wasn't worth living. We went from a happy, doing family to a mystified depression. Even the chamber music stopped. But at his funeral, my father's group played a piece Mozart wrote on the death of his father. . . . It seemed a needless, useless death, and I decided to become a doctor."

"How old were you?"

"I was in high school."

"Did your parents blame themselves?"

"Not outwardly. But they must have felt they'd failed somehow." Tears began. "It's terrible for a parent to outlive a child." The tears continued.

Robert took her gently in his arms and kissed her softly, thinking of his own parents, how unlike each other they were.

Katherine's tears stopped, and as she wiped them she could see his absorption. "What are you thinking?"

"About my own parents . . . and a trip I took with my father." He stopped.

"Please tell me about it," she said softly.

He started slowly. "It was the summer of 1933. My father wanted to visit Germany. I grew up speaking French with my mother, German with him. It was one of the few things we had in common. Although he read all the German classics and listened to German composers, we never spoke about his origins. He was a silent man. My mother either didn't want to go or felt it would be good for our relationship if we went together, just the two of us. We went on the *Bremen*, visited Berlin, Goethe's house in Frankfurt, listened to Mozart in Salzburg, then went to Oberhausen, a small Bavarian town where my father's folks had come from. It's a mountain town, looks like a postcard, where the men all wore lederhosen and spoke about Hitler, how he was going to save Germany from the Jews who owned everything. I was angry with my father because he said nothing. His wife, my mother, is Jewish," Robert said emotionally. "He has lunch with the Jewish owner of the dry-goods store down the block from his place almost every day!"

Robert's voice was rising. "He was silent when they talked about the 'dirty Jews.' On the train, I asked him why he'd said nothing to his relatives. He stared out the window without answering me. I was furious, and he knew it.

"The next day, we were in a bookstore in Wiesbaden when storm troopers smashed the window and dragged the Jewish owner out into the street, kicking and punching him. My father looked at me and ran out to help the man. As I also came out, one of them clubbed my father to the ground. I went to him. His head was bleeding. The bookstore owner was lying on the sidewalk nearby, and the SA men walked away laughing. And people just walked by as if nothing had happened. No one even stopped.

"My father started crying. It wasn't the pain. It was the shame. This was his Germany, the Germany he was showing off to his son!" Robert fell silent.

"But he fought the Germans in the War, didn't he?" Katherine asked.

"Yes, he did. And never spoke about it. He never talked about his war experiences as Grandpa did."

"I can understand that. The Germany of Beethoven was his."

"He used to sing me a funny German song when he put me to sleep." Robert started to sing. "*Ich bin der Doktor Eisenbard, Willi, Willi, vip voom vooom. Ken machen das di blinden gehen und de lamen vedersehn . . . Willi, Willi, vip, voom, voom . . .*" He smiled.

Katherine hugged him. "Oh, Robert, I'm so happy when I'm with you."

———————

The following day, Robert, Katherine, and Mike went to the Prado. In the cool rooms and corridors they stared at the Goyas and Velázquezes. Then they went to the Capitol Theater to see *A Night at the Opera*. The Marx Brothers in wartime Madrid were surreally funny. As they walked out into the late-afternoon sunshine they met Pete and Irv, who also were recounting the movie's antics. Then the shelling began. The group waited under the marquee, still laughing, as if waiting for the afternoon rain to stop.

Their mood changed when they saw the military trucks in front of the hotel.

"Roundup time," the drivers called. "Back to the ranch."

The abruptness shook Robert and Katherine. Walking in the street hand in hand had given them a false sense of normalcy.

Mike stood aside as they embraced.

"Do you think we'll ever have more time?" Katherine asked.

"We'll have our whole lives," Robert replied.

When Katherine opened her eyes, she saw Mike watching them.

"I'll take care of him," Mike said.

CHAPTER FIVE

"Six months of winter, six months of hell." That was the peasant description of Aragon, a string of towns called Quinto, Belchite, Zaragoza—names never heard in Brooklyn and Iowa.

Quinto was the first victory for the "Internationals" after so much defeat, and in high spirits they went on to Belchite, a small hilltop town well fortified by the best of Germany's military engineers.

The fighting was cruel and merciless. Every house had to be taken from the stubborn defenders. Even the church tower, which commanded a clear field of fire, was infested with the machine guns.

Robert, Mike, Irv, and Pete worked with the precision of a practiced backfield. Mike's energy was boundless and his instinct for danger flawless. But he couldn't have foreseen the booby trap that exploded in Pete's face.

"Fuckin' grenade attached to the door," Pete shouted through the blood that covered his face. His clothing was in tatters and he was bleeding all over his body from fragments.

"Aidman!" Irv shouted as he leaned over Pete.

Mike threw a grenade and charged as soon as it exploded, heading for the cellar. Robert followed. A Moor stood up, hands in the air. As Mike approached him in the heavily beamed room, another Moor stepped from under the stairwell behind Mike, bayonet raised at his back. Robert shot him.

"Thanks," Mike said as he rushed past him after calmly shooting the other Moor.

Irv wiped the blood from Pete's face, cradling him, cooing, "You'll be all right, Pete. You'll be all right."

They took the town after the sixth day of sleepless fighting.

"Hey," Mike shouted, "today's my birthday!"

"If I'da known I'da baked you a cake," Big Abe said.

"How old are you?" Robert asked.

"Twenty-three."

"Me too." Robert smiled.

"Pete's twenty-two," Irv said.

They sang Happy Birthday around a large fire as the *sanidades* carried the dead past them. They hardly noticed the stench of corpses in the air. They had forced their bodies beyond the borders of endurance, and now sleep was even sweeter than victory.

They rested briefly before the next attack, and during the respite, Irv volunteered as a guerrilla behind enemy lines. Robert thought it was suicidal.

Mike laughed.

"You think what we're doing is healthy?" he said.

They hoped for another victory, but the attack on Fuentes was a disaster. The artillery was nonexistent; the tanks were late and so were the Canadians. When the tanks did arrive, some of the units hadn't been informed about them and, thinking they were the enemy, fired at them. One tank crushed two friendly Spaniards.

The terrain in front of Fuentes was flat, an ideal field of fire for the enemy. Men started falling.

The hot shell fragments tore into Robert's leg. They felt like a branding iron as the points of steel made their way through the soft flesh. He went down with a cry that was lost in the sounds of the battlefield.

Mike was ahead and to Robert's right. When he turned, Robert was gone. What he saw made his blood run cold.

Robert was lying among the charging tanks. As Mike ran back, a clanking monster rumbled toward Robert's prostrate body. Mike frantically waved his arms, running directly at the tank. At the last moment the driver saw him and swerved but came so close Robert could feel the treads brush past him.

Mike knelt. "Where you hit?"

"Leg."

"Bad?"

"I don't know. I can't feel anything."

Mike slung his rifle and managed to get Robert across his shoulders, carrying him through the crossfire to a clump of trees where an aidman was working on another wounded man.

"Leave him," Mike commanded.

"What?"

"Leave him!" Mike pointed his rifle.

"You're fuckin' crazy!"

"I know. Just take care of my buddy."

The aidman tore Robert's trousers and looked at the bloody leg. "Bad," he said.

"Give me the bandages and go back to the other guy."

He finished bandaging Robert himself, touched his cheek.

"Thanks, Mike. I'll be okay."

Mike went back to the attack trying to feel nothing but fury. But he was cold and empty.

Robert passed out as the stretcher bearers shoved him into the ambulance. It was already full. A medic tried to close the doors. A foot was in the way. He had to move it. The man screamed.

The road was crowded with the traffic of war. The driver crashed the gears in the stop-and-start dash to the rear. The lurching of the ambulance brought cries of pain. The driver cursed the stalled truck in front of him. He started to go around it and nearly collided with an oncoming tank. He slammed the brakes, bringing more cries and curses. He pressed on the horn and stepped on the gas as the tank passed him. It was hot. Robert was in and out of consciousness.

The ambulance was unloaded at the mobile surgery. Two of the men were set aside. They were dead. The young man with the peach-fuzz face looked for identification.

"Robert Thompson," Robert whispered, and passed out.

Dr. Pike poked expertly in the thigh. Robert groaned.

"Heavy lacerations, shell fragments, bone intact," the doctor said crisply to the nurses and the aidman. "It has to be cleaned out or amputated. I don't have time for either. Evacuation. Next."

Robert was lifted from the operating table and put outside. He came to and looked at the blue sky and hot sun. For an instant, he thought he was in Iowa, lying in the fields, looking at the sky, wondering about the universe. Was his mother calling him? No, it was the young clerk telling him he'd be all right. He went out again.

Every lurch of the ambulance was an agony. His leg began to throb and the skin to tighten, a drum in the football field orchestra. Boom! Boom! Boom! Iowa! Iowa! I love the fall, he thought. He was alternately hot and cold in the sweltering heat. The road was bumpy and endless, a vacuum into which he fell.

He regained consciousness briefly as they put him on the hospital train to Madrid. A nurse was rebandaging his leg. He smiled weakly at her. She smiled back, and when she'd finished, she gave him some water. He swallowed and went out again.

It was summer. They were playing baseball in the noonday heat. The bases were loaded, and Robert was at the plate. He was tall for twelve and a good hitter. He smacked one all the way out into the tall corn. As the outfielder looked for the ball, Robert trotted home. Then they all ran to the well and poured water from the bucket over themselves. Oh, the water was cold and sweet dripping over their faces, cooling their skin.

He was feverish, his skin hot, his throat parched.

"Water," he whispered weakly to the nurse's back. She didn't hear him. "Water," he croaked as she turned. She nodded and put the canteen to his lips. As the water trickled down his dry throat, he heard his mother calling him from the house.

"Robert! Robert! Lunch! Bring in the boys."

The car was loaded with groaning men stacked along its sides and floor, leaving a narrow aisle for the nurses. It was hot with a suffocating airlessness. He was kissing Katherine.

"Now, try not to get into trouble today," his mother said, kissing him on the lips. He loved his mother. His mother became Katherine again as he kissed her.

Robert was dimly aware of crashing sounds as the train rocketed and lurched. Were they explosions? The lights went out. Or did he? Hitler's Condors were bombing the clearly marked hospital train.

The men lined the corridors of the hotel leading to the surgery. Katherine had long ago stopped searching the faces of the wounded. It hurt too much. She didn't look at the tall man with the festering leg as he was lifted to the operating table. She looked at wounds. Wounds were her focus.

"It'll have to go at the knee," Barkin said.

Katherine reached for the bone saw. The man moaned. She got the large scalpel from the sterilizer, handed it to Barkin, and sponged again. The man opened his eyes and whispered. Did he call her name? Imagination. Barkin cut away the infected flesh, called for the saw. She handed it to him. The man whispered again. Yes! He'd said "Katherine."

She looked at his face.

"*No!*"

"What is it?" Barkin asked, alarmed.

"It's Robert," she said, finding her voice.

"Oh, no."

"He can't lose the leg."

"I hope no one dies out there while we do this," Barkin said, sighing.

They spent what seemed like hours picking shrapnel, stitching skin.

Robert woke in the morning. The sun streamed through the windows. He looked about the room. A man sat in a chair, outlined against the light. His head and face were covered with bandages. Only his mouth and nostrils were visible.

"Hiya," he said.

"Hi."

"Where you hit?"

"Leg," Robert answered, looking at the heavy bandages.

"Must be bad, they brought you here."

"I guess so."

"You feelin' okay?"

"I don't know yet," Robert said, feeling nothing.

"Your voice sounds familiar."

"So does yours. What's your name?"

"Pete Pappas. What's yours?"

"Pete!" Robert exclaimed, moving forward and falling back in pain. "It's me, Robert. Robert Thompson."

"Robert Thompson!" Pete got up and felt his way to the bed. The two men embraced. "You know who's here?" Pete asked. "Katherine."

"I thought I was hallucinating last night in the operating room," he cried. "I thought she was there! Jeez, how lucky can a guy get? But what about you?"

"I lost 'em both."

"Oh, no!" Robert put his arms around Pete's shoulder once more as tears came to his eyes.

Katherine entered the room.

"I thought you two would find each other," she said.

Robert gathered her into his arms as if his survival depended on her.

———

It was three in the morning when Katherine woke to Pete's whimperings. She disengaged her hand from Robert's and went to him, cradling him in his nightmare.

———

Just when Katherine had thought she'd seen every cruelty that could be inflicted on human bodies, she'd learned she'd seen nothing. The building she entered with Barkin after a bombing by the Condor Legion was a clinic for pregnant women and young mothers. She gulped her fear and disbelief, forced herself into rooms that would haunt her for the rest of her life.

Hopelessly, she and Barkin looked at the beseeching

eyes of young women Katherine's age who were dying, ripped apart by men in airplanes who'd dropped high explosives on nonmilitary targets for purposes of terror. Holding a dying woman in her arms whose hand still reached for the baby that looked like a smashed doll, she thought of how she sometimes held Robert. Would he also die like this?

Days melted into nights and then months. It was fall when Mike showed up at the hospital during a lull in the Aragon fighting. He was like an electric wire, eyes burning, cheeks gaunt, body alive with tension.

As Robert embraced him he could feel his ribs through the shirt. He was like a starved cat.

"I brought you some plays," Mike said, going to his pack. "The Group's in London, and Alex sent some stage magazines too. How's your leg?"

"Healing," Robert said, looking at him fondly.

Pete asked Mike if he'd heard from Irv.

"Only rumors that he's in the mountains with the peasants." He turned to Katherine. "How's the den mother?" Katherine looked at Mike's pinched face and felt a surge of sympathy for him that took her forward to hug him. Mike was slightly flustered.

"Well, I hope there's a restaurant that still has some food. I haven't had a decent meal in months," he said.

Barkin watched Mike as he spoke at the table. Mike's eyes glittered as he told of the recent fighting, and Barkin's look was caught by Katherine. She understood what it meant. Mike was lyrical in his descriptions of war.

In Katherine's small room, she and Robert listened to the nightly shelling. It mingled with a flamenco guitar playing on a radio somewhere.

"You love him, don't you?" Katherine asked.

"Yes . . . he saved my life. I'll never forget how he stood in front of that tank as if he were offering his own life."

Katherine sighed. Robert looked at her questioningly.

"It's almost as though he's found himself in war," she said. "The way he lights up when he talks about it. He's a war lover."

"I saw that tonight," Robert admitted. "And I'm not."

"But it won't stop you."

"No," he said quietly. "I'll go back as soon as I can."

But Katherine was to go before him.

———————

Teruel was Spain's Valley Forge.

It was twenty below at the front, and blood stained the snow. The Republicans, on the offensive, threw Franco's forces back. Barkin and Katherine went with the mobile surgery units working in the rubbled stone of destroyed buildings, in ambulances torn by shrapnel and bullets; stitching, patching, cutting around the clock.

"I feel like the wife being left behind," Robert had said to her as Katherine packed a small bag.

She had put her arms around him. "You don't have to feel like Mr. Macho. Leave that to Mike."

His body had stiffened. "Leave Mike alone," he had said quietly. It was the first discordant note between them.

Katherine thought about the conversation now as another patient was put on the table. The noise outside was deafening. Her hands were cold despite the rubber gloves. She and Robert had apologized to each other, but the rough edges remained as they said goodbye.

"Katherine . . ." Barkin's voice reached her, and she turned her mind to the wounds of the man in front of her.

———————

It was snowing in the mountains.

The small group in peasant sheepskins came through the ravine and saw the railroad bridge ahead. Irv pointed to the guard shack at the other end. A grizzled old face nodded at Irv. They crouched in the falling snow, quiet as the rocks, waiting for darkness.

When it came, they made their way to the tracks of the bridge. Irv gave a final twist to the dynamite caps that were wired to the pressure detonators. The large explosive charge was neatly bundled under the track. He was nervous, although he knew the guards wouldn't leave their brandy and the potbellied stove whose smoke curled whitely into the cold air. Still, one might have to piss and check the track.

He nodded when he was satisfied with his work, and they ran back across the bridge and up the trail of the mountainside, then stopped breathlessly in the heavily falling snow. Just in time. They could hear the chugging of the train, see its bright eye as it snaked through the passes. Finally, it was on the flat stretch before the bridge that spanned the rushing river below.

The headlight blazed as the train slowed, waiting for the guard's signal to cross. They could see him outlined against the bright light waving the engineer ahead. The locomotive picked up speed.

In the center of the span there was a flash and a roar as the dynamite exploded. Then the munitions the train carried ignited. Bombs and artillery shells lit the sky, tracers flew in crazy arcs, and the span collapsed with the train into the river. The screams of men could not be heard.

If the earth shook, it was from explosions.

———————

Robert rewrote the story he'd written about the Mendez family and started a one-act play. But he worried about Katherine and Mike. The news from the Aragon front was bleak. Having captured northern Spain, Franco had put the full weight of his armies into a counterattack at Teruel. Never before had such numbers of planes, tanks, artillery, been put together. The Republican defense crumbled under the weight of the massive assault.

The ambulances and several field hospitals were ordered back to Madrid. They had almost no medical supplies left. The wheels churned in the snow, stalled on the icy roads, came under air attack. Katherine no longer trembled. She was too numb.

———————

At Caspe there were less than a hundred Americans left. They were the last defenders. When they ran out of ammunition they retreated toward the Ebro.

The terrain was rocky, filled with gullies and arroyos. Mike looked to the stars for direction but couldn't figure out where he was. He was a city kid. He'd always depended on Robert for that. Now he was lost, and it was too late for him to hide when he heard the gun bolts click.

"*Manos arriba!*" a voice commanded. Mike put his hands in the air and found himself surrounded by Moors in long capes, their submachine guns pointed at him.

Robert was asleep when Katherine entered the room. He'd awakened only slightly when he heard the engines outside in the street and thought nothing further of it, shifting his weight to his good leg for comfort. He didn't hear the door open but vaguely felt a presence in the room. He was a child in Iowa again and his mother had come in to check him as she did every night, sometimes sitting on his bed and stroking his head.

As Katherine bent over him, he was confused, but reached up for her, feeling an erotic impulse. As she kissed him he opened his eyes and smelled the salty perspiration of her neck and the antiseptic odor of her hands.

Katherine's hair fell as she buried her head in his chest and cried, "I love you, Robert."

He held her in his arms as she shook.

The patrol of Moors marched Mike to a nearby village and herded him into a bombed-out church where there were other captured Loyalists. Mike wondered why they hadn't shot him in the field and soon learned that the captives were being executed outside against the churchyard wall. He decided he had nothing to lose in an attempt to escape.

He still had the knife he'd bought in Madrid strapped to his leg, since the Moors hadn't searched him carefully. They'd stopped when they found his watch. As the next group of prisoners was marched out to the courtyard, only one guard was left to watch them.

"Ask him for a cigarette," he said to the Englishman next to him. "I'll work my way around him."

"You're crazy," the man said.

"What have you got to lose?"

The man frowned and rose, crossing to the guard, who pointed his submachine gun at him. *"Tiene un cigarillo, señor?"* the Englishman asked. *"Un cigarillo antes de mi muerta."*

"Por usted? Está loco? Usted no vale un cigarillo."

"Ahora no," the man agreed as Mike sprang from the shadows, grasped the guard in a headlock, and cut his throat. They dragged the Moor behind a column, and Mike put on his cape, then went to the door. As the two other guards returned, Mike put the submachine gun in their backs and disarmed them. The other prisoners bound and gagged the guards with belts, then left for the courtyard. Mike and two other prisoners, wearing the capes, pretended to be the guards marching the prisoners outside to their execution. The prisoners nervously stood against the wall as Mike and the two others got behind the firing squad. As the Moors raised their weapons, Mike and the others fired into their backs.

"For Pete," Mike said.

They left the silent village and headed toward the Ebro.

Company One had forty Americans left. The rest were in hospitals or prison camps, wandering the countryside, or fighting with other units until they could rejoin their own. Franco announced the annihilation of the Abraham Lincoln Battalion, but its surviving members made their way singly, and in pairs, half naked, starved, and exhausted from hiding, running, fearing they'd never see a friendly face again.

Slowly, the International Brigades started to rebuild. Robert got a letter from Mike saying, "We need you, kid."

CHAPTER SIX

Katherine held Robert's hand.

They were in the day room of the hospital listening to Paul Robeson sing. She knew Robert would be gone soon. Robert no longer needed crutches, and the tissue had healed well. Pete had gone back to the States. Others were getting ready to leave for the encampment on the Ebro where the Republicans were preparing for the final offensive.

Madrid was warm in May 1938, and a light spring breeze ruffled the curtains of Katherine's open window. Robert sat on the bed tying the laces of his boots, the boots Mike had bought him with his crap-game winnings.

"Do you think there will ever be a time when we won't be saying goodbye?" she asked.

He sat up and went to her, taking her in his arms, looking at her beautiful eyes. "Someday."

———

With the coming of spring, Mike felt better. The sun warmed his skin and he tried to forget about the freezing defeats of Aragon. And he was reunited with Robert. They talked for days as they trained new recruits, felt restored as they worked together again.

On a warm night in July 1938, small campfires dotted the landscape. There was a bright moon and many stars. Hundreds of voices sang softly, mutedly, a wave of whispered sound. Night was also movement. In the dark, convoys of trucks, tanks, pontoon bridges, boats, were moved and hidden along the banks of the Ebro.

Katherine walked from fire to fire looking for one face. In the middle of a refrain she found it and stopped in the firelight. Mike watched Robert go to her, take her in his arms, and kiss her.

"It's you," Robert said, finally finding his voice.

"Yes. We've come for the offensive."

Robert led her to Mike, and the three embraced. Katherine kissed Mike, seeing the needy child in his face.

"I love you too," Mike said.

———————————

Night. Tanks and trucks rumbled into position. Katherine sat between Robert and Mike as they sang. Twenty-four-year-old Milt Wolff, commander of the battalion, gave them their last briefing: "We're not coming back."

At one in the morning, the first crossings started while the moon was obscured by clouds. The Poles were in the middle of the river when the moon came out, and the Germans raked them with gunfire. The anti-Nazi Germans streamed across the footbridge while the Canadians and Spaniards rowed.

They were next. Robert's fear rose from the pit of his stomach to his narrowing throat as they got into the boats. As Mike was about to shove off they heard a voice shouting, "Hey! Wait for me!" It was Irv.

Katherine was on the riverbank in an ambulance waiting to cross as enemy artillery started. "Don't stall now, Jimmy," she cooed to the ambulance donated by James Cagney.

They took the town of Faterella from the surprised enemy and then marched to Hill 666 by nightfall. It was a difficult climb over crumbling rock. As they reached the top, a breeze brought the odor of rotting flesh. It also brought Moorish music, with its strange wailing melodies. In the morning, the Lincolns looked down the sharply descending slope to a moonscape of blackened shrubs and bodies. There was no earth, only twisted shrapnel, splintered stone, shellholes. Its only value was strategic. For the moment.

The next morning they attacked.

They made it as far as the enemy barbed wire, where they exchanged hand grenades, covered on their flanks by the Canadians and the Spanish 59th. There was no chance of taking the position. As they withdrew, Mike got a slug through his arm, but refused to be evacuated.

"It's just a flesh wound. Help me bandage it, Robert." As Robert wound the gauze he wondered to himself, How far does he have to go to prove himself?

————————

Hill 666 stood in the way of a Fascist counterattack, and they held the position for weeks despite continual bombings and artillery and infantry attacks. Then one afternoon Irv rushed into the trench waving a newspaper.

"We're being withdrawn," he shouted. "'The Spanish government has decided to withdraw immediately and completely all non-Spanish combatants who are participating in the fight in Spain on the side of the government,'" Irv read excitedly. "'The Spanish government asks the League of Nations to supervise withdrawal.'"

"If they think the Germans and Italians will withdraw too, they're crazy," Mike said angrily. Robert thought Mike sounded disappointed.

As if in response to the news, enemy artillery started, signaling another attack.

"Here they come," Robert said, sighting a target.

Waving red-and-gold flags the enemy started up the hill, shouting, "Surrender! Surrender!" Robert was so busy firing he didn't notice the Spanish sergeant in their midst leap up with a white rag yelling, "I surrender! *Yo soy un amigo.*"

Robert was too late to stop Mike from shooting him.

"Good shot," Irv said.

A grenade dropped into the trench next to Robert. He quickly picked it up and threw it back. "That was close," he said.

"Ah . . . you had three seconds," Mike laughed, throwing one of his own at the charging Moors.

The enemy retreated, leaving a field full of flags and bodies. That night, as they listened to the cries of the wounded below and the keening Moorish death songs, Robert thought about the callousness of Mike's action that afternoon, picked at it in his mind like a scab. Yet no one else thought Mike was wrong. He thought back to an incident that had occurred months earlier. Six Lincolns had deserted in an ambulance but were caught. The battalion was asked to vote whether to court-martial them, which meant death, or return them to their units. Robert and Milt had voted they be spared. Mike and Irv had voted for the death penalty.

"We'd be doing them a favor," Mike had argued. "Shame is worse than death."

On what was to be their last day on Hill 666, Mike volunteered to take over a machine-gun position in the British lines. They were being attacked and had no more gunners. He looked at Robert, who looked back at him with questioning eyes. Why? Hadn't they done enough? Was this his last opportunity to be a hero? Even Irv said, "Don't be a shmuck, Mike."

"See you later, kid," Mike said to Robert as he still held his eyes.

"I'll go with you," Robert finally said.

In the British lines, the officer led them along the trench, swagger stick under his arm, as if conducting them on a tour, while the gunfire rattled about them.

"Here you are, lads," he said, taking them into the timbered bunker. "Fine Maxim, plenty of ammo." Again he pointed at the weapon, then turned. "Good luck . . . and thanks." He left.

"Nice gun," Mike said as they settled into the bunker.

"Yeah, but look at that," Robert said, pointing through the slits. Below them, the Moors were assembling for another attack, this time behind masses of tanks. The attack formed on the British position.

Two of the tanks burst into flame as they were hit by antitank shells. It didn't dissuade the rest. The Moors made more noise than the machines. The bullets from their machine gun bounced off the armored hulls.

"These aren't armor-piercing," Robert said as he fed while Mike fired.

"So I've noticed."

A tank exploded, sending the Moors behind it scattering. Mike cut them down. Another tank came right at their position, and they realized it was the end.

"I always knew I'd go this way . . . that I'd be crushed. Goodbye, Robert."

"Goodbye, Mike."

They kept firing until the tank rolled over them.

————————

Night. The clink of shovels on stone, faint voices that were unintelligible.

"Mike?"

"Yeah. . . ."

"You okay?"

"I think so. You?"

"Just ache a lot. Can you move?"

"If you grab my hand."

Gradually, Mike's hand appeared above the rubble. Robert took it. They pulled together until they had worked free. Robert felt Mike's shoulders shake in spasm as the sobs left him. Robert held his own emotion, kept it from forming, immersed in Mike's.

"It wasn't our time," Mike said. "Not yet."

They became conscious of the voices down the line.

"I think they're ours," Robert said as they cautiously set off down the trench until they could hear the words.

"Blimey, it's the Americans. It's a bloody miracle. We were sure you lads had had it."

"You guys held," Mike said in admiration.

"Takes more'n a few bloody tanks to push us off."

————————

In the morning they marched and sang in the September sun, their voices strong, their spirits high.

> *"There are rats, rats*
> *in bowler hats and spats*

> *in the store, in the store*
> *There are rats, rats*
> *with bowler hats and spats*
> *in the quartermaster store.*
>
> *There is cheese, cheese*
> *that will bring you to your knees . . ."*

As the remnants of the battalion came over the rise and down the dusty road, Katherine ran toward them. Tears streaming, the three comrades embraced.

The International Brigades marched together for the last time through the streets of Barcelona, where hundreds of thousands cheered from balconies and rooftops, throwing flowers, shouting, singing, while Republican aircraft flew overhead to protect them.

It was October 29, 1938. One month earlier, Chamberlain of England and Daladier of France had met with Hitler and Mussolini and had given Hitler Czechoslovakia.

"Today, you are going away. Many of you, thousands of you, are staying here with the Spanish earth for a shroud." La Pasionaria's voice rang out. La Pasionaria, tall, dark, black eyes burning, threw out her arms as if to embrace them. "Come back! Come back to us! You will find the love and gratitude of the whole Spanish people, who now and in the future will cry out with all their hearts, 'Long live the heroes of the International Brigades!'"

Robert smiled down at Mike, who returned the smile and raised his clenched right fist in salute, knowing what Robert's smile meant. They might not have won but they'd given everything they had. Half the young Americans who'd come to fight for democracy were dead, but they were alive, Mike thought with a thrill. They had survived.

Down the line, standing with Barkin in the medical detachment, Katherine looked across the square at the ranks of Frenchmen, Poles, Germans, Slavs, English, Italians, Mexicans, Canadians, who had come to offer their lives for a cause they believed in. Who could do more? She bent her head slightly forward so that she could see Robert and

Mike. Robert was also looking toward her, and their eyes met as La Pasionaria's voice soared through the roar of the planes overhead.

"Come back to us when the olive branch of peace . . ." her voice drifted off, then rose. "Long live the heroes of the International Brigades!" Her words reverberated through the square, and every man and woman there knew they would remember this moment forever.

CHAPTER SEVEN

Mozart's *Don Giovanni* filled the New York living room as the late-afternoon sun faded softly. Mike sang as he held the bookcase Robert was hammering. Katherine hung the photos of Robert and Mike that Irv had taken at Jarama.

She stepped back. "How do you like them?" she asked.

"Pretty ugly guys," Robert laughed.

"Looks good there, next to Orozco," Mike commented, putting down the bookcase. "I've got to check my sauce. Hold this, Katherine." As she took his place at the bookcase, Mike went to the kitchen of their Greenwich Village railroad flat.

Robert finished hammering the nail and kissed Katherine.

"Our third New Year," he said.

"And it's going to be lovely," she said, kissing him as Mike returned.

"Eeeetsa beeeooootiful. Pasta Rossano eesa famous all over Leetle Eetaly," he said, kissing his fingers.

"I'm glad you like to cook, Mike," Katherine said. "Otherwise we'd starve to death."

"We're lucky you found this place," Robert said. "You think we can swing it?"

"Robert, we can do anything," Mike assured him.

"I'll contribute my living allowance," Katherine said. "My parents can't take that away from me, as long as I'm in med school." Katherine's parents did not appreciate her moving into an apartment with two men.

"I'm pretty sure I got the job in the carpenter's shop, so I can write at night," Robert said.

"And I'll get a job at night so I can make rounds during the day."

"As long as it doesn't interfere with your cooking." Katherine laughed. She laughed a lot lately. She was very happy. Their apartment was filled with Spanish Civil War posters, lithos by Kollwitz, Gropper, Goya, and Orozco, and photos of Spain.

"Well, I'd better make myself beautiful," Katherine said, leaving for their bedroom.

Robert put the rest of the books away. He was especially careful with the autographed copy of *The Sun Also Rises*. He turned to Mike. "You talk to Alex today?"

"Yeah. He's gonna drop by tonight, so you're finally gonna meet him."

"I can't wait."

Mike went to the kitchen to stir his sauce. Robert carried his typewriter into the bedroom he shared with Katherine. She was drying her hair with a towel, her skin pink from the hot water. He felt a stirring that was both affectionate and erotic.

"My God, you're beautiful."

She laughed. "You always say that when I come out of the shower."

"You're always beautiful." He kissed her breasts. The nipples rose. She took his head in her hands and gently moved it upward, kissing him.

"Later. We've still got a lot to do."

He subsided. "You think your parents will ever get over it?"

"I don't think so," she answered.

When they'd arrived at the dock on the French ship, Katherine's parents had brusquely said hello to Robert and Mike and whisked her off to Princeton in their new Packard. Katherine was embarrassed and angry at their treatment of her friends.

"Aren't you glad to see us?" her father asked stiffly from behind the wheel.

"Not like this," she replied.

Katherine stayed in the beautiful white-and-green house in Princeton for only two days. Two days of argument. Her parents could not accept the woman she had become, the woman who had seen so much. She wanted to tell them about Spain, but they wanted to talk about Princeton, about the past. They wanted their little girl back.

"Who were those men?" her father finally asked.

"Robert is my lover," she replied simply. Her father paled and left the room. Her mother sat in her sewing chair, eyes blank, picking at her nails.

Perhaps it was a needless cruelty, Katherine later reflected. But she needed her father's rejection so she could leave without guilt. She had stayed with the Barkins until Mike found the apartment, then she and Robert had moved in with him.

They heard Mike's footsteps in the hall, then the sound of plumbing. Railroad flats were not built for privacy. Katherine continued drying her hair as Robert put a piece of paper in the typewriter he'd bought in a pawnshop.

The first thing he'd written on the typewriter was a letter to his parents telling them why he wasn't coming home. He told them about Katherine and Mike and that he wanted to get to work without any more loss of time. He told them about Mike's mother, with whom they'd stayed, about the brown apartment in Little Italy with its crucifix over the living-room couch, its constant scream of neighbors anxious to see "little Mikey." Mrs. Rossano had wanted them to stay longer so that she could fatten them up. "You boys so skinny," she said. Mike had promised they would return for her pasta.

Robert's father had been hurt, and, as usual, silent. His mother was disappointed but understood, as did his grandfather. "But I hope to see you soon," he'd written, trying to soften the blow of his not returning.

"The summer soldier and the sunshine patriot . . ." he continued.

Irv and Pete were the first to arrive. Then the apartment began to fill up as Milt, Abe, and others of the battalion followed. Later, Alex Tarasov came with Clifford Odets and John Garfield, who was starring in Odets's *Golden Boy.* Alex was wearing the black overcoat and broad-brimmed black hat that had become his trademark. He'd bought the ensemble in Paris, where he'd lived after graduation from Columbia. He talked with an energy and passion that made him the center of any group.

Garfield was well built, with a handsome rugged face, dark hair, and an infectious smile, very much a street kid as Mike was. Odets was tall, bushy-haired, intense, with startling blue eyes behind his glasses. Robert could sense his strong ego.

"I'm sure glad to meet you, Mr. Tarasov," Robert said.

"Please. It's Alex. Mike tells me you want to be a playwright and you've got some talent." Robert shrugged. "Don't be modest. It's not an asset in the theater, and Mike's a good judge. Have you met Odets?"

"Not yet."

"Cliff?" Alex called. "Come over here." Odets turned and crossed to them, his intense gaze on Robert. Alex made introductions.

"You were in Spain with Mike," Odets said.

"Yes."

"I admire the hell out of you guys."

"I admire your plays."

"It takes a different kind of courage. You can get killed by the critics, but it's not permanent. Have you seen my play yet?"

"No. We just got back, and—"

"Come as my guest. Julie's wonderful in it." He nodded toward Garfield, who was talking with Katherine. "We'll have a bite afterward."

"Thanks," was all Robert could say.

Another wave of guests arrived. More actors and the folksong contingent, Will Geer, Woody Guthrie, Pete Seeger, and a black man named Leadbelly.

"Irv used to talk about you," Robert said to Guthrie. "About the house you used to live in in Sea Gate."

"He say anything nice?" Guthrie asked in his Okie twang.

"How could he?" Will Geer said, laughing. He towered over the small singer, who wore overalls, a leather jacket, and work shoes. Geer looked like a lumberjack and dressed like one. Seeger was tall and thin and wore a seaman's turtleneck. Leadbelly was small and of indeterminate age.

"Nice folks," he said, looking around. "Look like actors."

"Leadbelly thinks all city folks look like actors," Geer said.

"Well, they are," Leadbelly laughed.

They got out their guitars and started playing. Seeger launched into "Los Quatros Generales" and the vets joined him. The actors picked up the choruses.

Horns blew outside, and Mike entered with his huge pot of steaming spaghetti. "Happy New Year!" he shouted.

Everyone kissed. Pete put his hands to his mouth and shouted as he did in the Pyrenees, *Happy New Year!*

More actors arrived: Cobb, Bromberg, Carnovsky, Farmer. Robert's head swirled with the names of actors he'd read about. All over the apartment people were in animated conversation about politics, books, music, theater. Robert and Katherine held hands and smiled at each other as they looked at the new people in their lives. At five in the morning they sang "Goodnight, Irene."

It was quiet except for the radio playing "I've Got My Love to Keep Me Warm." Robert and Katherine were dancing in the living room. Mike was in the bedroom with an actress. The music changed to "A Foggy Day in London Town."

"I'd love to go to London with you someday," Katherine whispered in his ear.

"I'd love to go anyplace with you. Especially to bed." They stopped dancing and kissed. The embrace increased in intensity until it became hungry. Robert leaned to the radio, turned it off.

"London will have to wait."

Twenty-six days later, Barcelona fell to the Fascists.

On Valentine's Day 1939, the guys got together at Pete's

cousin's Greek cafeteria on 41st Street. It was two years since they'd danced at the party before going off to Jarama.

Even as they sang, Mike got depressed and then drunk. He'd been thinking of the Mendez family.

"Florita was the only girl I ever loved," he said to Katherine and Robert, then went for another drink.

"It's perfectly safe for him to love her," Katherine said. "She's dead."

Robert looked at her in surprise.

Mike came back with a fresh drink. "What'samatta, Robert, you look mad," he said, sitting.

"It's nothing. Let's go home."

"I'm not going home. I got a date."

"You can't go like this."

"Who says so?" he asked belligerently, as he fell off the chair. Robert and Irv sat him up.

"Gotta sober up for my date. Gemme some coffee, Irv."

"Who do you have a date with?" Robert asked.

"Girl."

"What girl?"

Mike thought about it. "Don' remember her name."

Robert looked at Katherine. "How do you know where to go?"

"Got her address in my pocket. Beekman Place."

Irv came back with the coffee.

"Thanks, Irv buddy." Mike drank the thick, sweet Turkish brew and shuddered. "Gotta go." He stood uncertainly.

"Mike, it's after midnight. You sure she expects you?"

"She doesn' come home till after twelve. Curtain comes down 'leven-twenny."

"You ought to call."

"I ought to go, that's what I ought. Night, everybody," he shouted and walked unsteadily out the door.

"I've never seen him like that," Irv said, concerned.

"Neither have I," said Robert, watching through the glass window as Mike wove down the street.

———————

The night was crisp, the stars cold, as Robert and Katherine walked home.

"What'd you mean, Katherine?"

"I never thought you'd ask."

"Don't be cute."

"I wasn't being cute. I was preparing an answer."

"Well . . ." He took her arm. It was a gesture of hostility.

"I don't like the way he treats women," Katherine said, removing her arm from his grasp.

"I thought it would be more profound than that."

"I'm not finished. I don't think he really cares for women."

"How can you say that? He's always got one."

"So does Alex. But Alex is a man who loves women. Mike is a man who uses them."

Robert was silent. "Is that it?"

"Not quite. I don't think Mike can commit himself to another person."

"There was no one more committed in Spain!"

"That was a different kind of commitment. It was a commitment to action, not emotion."

Robert looked at her sharply and stopped, taking her arm again. "You mean he's not committed to me?"

Katherine looked at his face in the streetlight. "I don't know how far," she said slowly.

"He's risked his life for me."

"I know that."

The rest of the walk was in silence.

They heard it on the radio as they drank their morning coffee.

Hitler had marched on Czechoslovakia.

Franco had murdered hundreds of thousands.

They were gloomy days. Mike drove a cab at night and made rounds of producers' offices during the day. One Sunday he decided to cook a huge dinner for his actor friends. The kitchen was crowded with members of the Group.

"Reminds me of Sundays at Franchot Tone's and Joan Crawford's," Alex said, laughing.

"Does this look like Hollywood?" Mike roared. "Besides, Franchot was a fink for leaving the Group."

"If it makes you feel better, Mike, he suffers from guilt," Alex said.

"Hah!" Mike exclaimed.

"Does Odets feel guilty?" Robert asked.

"Clifford loves it. The first time I went out there and stayed with him in Beverly Hills, I was struck by its over-powering pleasantness. We took a walk. The sun was warm, the gardens beautiful, the air divine. We ran into Edward G. Robinson, who told us about his new Renoir. We continued walking and Cliff pointed to his new world and said, 'Not bad, huh?' He was very impressed."

"Do you think he'll come back?" Katherine asked.

"Yes. When he succeeds there. He wants them to love him or he wants power over them. Maybe both."

"That's pretty deep, Alex," Katherine said.

"Did you expect less of me?" he chided, then continued, "I had an argument with him. I said, 'Hollywood is the symbol of money-making unrelated to any other ideal.' He said that was nonsense, that Hollywood had raised more money for Spain than any other place in the world and had made *Blockade*, which was pro-Spain. You were over there when they made it . . . with Hank Fonda and Madeleine Carroll. It opened at Radio City Music Hall, but the American Legion picketed and the studio withdrew it."

"That's what I call the courage of one's convictions," Mike said sarcastically.

"Which is my point!" Alex now shouted. "You never reach maturity until you've faced the moral choices and have either survived or succumbed. Virtue is only lack of opportunity."

———————

Katherine had gone back to the Columbia College of Physicians and Surgeons, where Barkin taught. In terms of experience, she was way ahead of her class, and the students seemed very young to her, but she had two years to make up academically.

Robert worked in a small kitchen-cabinet factory nearby. He liked working with his hands and he liked the other workers, Italians for the most part. Mike visited often for the old-world camaraderie and to speak Italian. Katherine said he was still trying to replace his father. Robert wrote in their bedroom at night, while Katherine studied in the kitchen.

Mike drove a cab on the four-to-twelve shift. His schedule allowed him to take advantage of the more lucrative theater trade while leaving his days free for acting class and "making rounds." Alex bought him lunch and encouraged him. Robert and Mike each made twenty-five dollars a week, enough for their expenses and a concert, play, or movie. A contribution to some cause meant giving up something, and they still believed in causes.

———

Across the stage of Mecca Temple, a large meeting hall in Manhattan, was a banner reading JOINT ANTI-FASCIST COMMITTEE. Under it were smaller signs. Local 65—CIO, Teachers Against Fascism. Furriers and Leather Workers. Artists and Writers for Freedom. Merchant Seamen Against . . . No More Munichs! Stop Hitler Now!

Paul Robeson was singing. His huge voice boomed out across the packed hall. Katherine squeezed Robert's hand. Robeson's voice brought her back to his Christmas concert in the Madrid hospital. Robert and Mike also remembered. Robert put his arm around Mike's shoulder.

When Robeson sat down, a small, fiery man went to the lectern. "Friends of the Spanish peoples! The battle goes on. Tens of thousands of former Loyalist soldiers, proud fighters for liberty, are being shot by Franco. Four hundred and fifty thousand refugees are behind barbed wire in France. In these internment camps, they have no shelter, no clothing, little food. They are concentration camps for our comrades." The speech went on, finally culminating as it usually did in a collection. He asked the vets of the Abraham Lincoln Battalion to stand. The request came as a surprise to Mike and Robert. As they rose, the crowd cheered. They could see Irv, Pete, Abe, Milt, and a lot of others.

"Our heroes of the International Brigades who were willing to give their lives will now go among you to collect your dollars."

"Did you know anything about this?" Mike asked afterward. The others shook their heads. "The usual lack of organization on the left," he said disgustedly. Although they didn't mind, they would like to have been asked. They had gone to a number of meetings of the Joint Anti-Fascist Committee with the other vets. For them, the war wasn't over. The committee was trying to raise the consciousness of the country to the dangers of Hitler and Mussolini. Mostly it was distributing leaflets, talking to people.

Nobody listened.

———————————

In April, Mike got a job in *Golden Boy*. One of the actors was leaving the cast to go to Hollywood for a film, since the play would close at the end of June.

Robert and Katherine went to Mike's first performance. He was playing a gangster, and the dark, dangerous side of him came through in the part. His inner turbulence drove his performance, and he was electric.

Alex had been pacing nervously at the back of the theater, and he greeted them with a huge smile as they went up the aisle.

"Some performance, huh? That kid'll never let you down. Let's go backstage."

Mike's dressing room was on the second floor. His door was open, and actors were congratulating him. Mike's eyes were shining.

"Ah . . . here they are," Mike said, his arms outstretched to Katherine.

She kissed him. "You were wonderful," she said.

Robert embraced him. "All I can say is, *wow!*"

"You see?" Alex laughed. "Writers are always at a loss for words."

"I am," Robert said, returning the laugh.

"Hey, look at this," Mike said excitedly, showing them a bottle of champagne. "From Odets." He popped the cork and poured into water glasses. "To us," he toasted. "Forever."

Alex took them to Sardi's. The walls were lined with sketches of Broadway stars, playwrights, directors. The room was crowded and festive. Robert and Katherine joined hands out of excitement and a need for security. Alex was greeted and waved at many others.

"Don't get the idea I'm here every night," he said. "I can't afford it. We're running an art theater, and unfortunately, that means wearing a hair shirt."

"I like your hair shirt," Katherine said, looking at Alex's impeccable attire.

"Don't let it fool you. This suit is five years old."

Several actors wandered over to say hello to Alex and ask Mike about his performance.

"It felt good," he said. "But I've got a way to go."

"I can't imagine that," Katherine said.

Mike exchanged glances with a blond actress having dinner with a producer. When she left her table, Mike got up.

"Excuse me a minute," he said. He stopped her outside the door to the ladies' room.

"Will I see you later?" he asked.

"See you! I don't even know you."

"Mike Rossano. Now you know me."

"Ruth Gilbert," she said, nonplussed.

"Can you dump the guy you're with?"

"Dump him? He's a producer."

"There's plenty of producers."

"And plenty of unemployed actors. Which I don't intend to be."

"I'm an actor and employed."

"What play are you in?" she asked doubtfully.

"*Golden Boy*. I opened tonight."

"Oh, you're *that* Mike Rossano," she said with interest. "I've heard about you. Damn, I can't tonight."

"Your loss."

"How about—"

He didn't let her finish. "Another night? Sorry. I'm leaving for the Coast soon and I'm really busy. I just happened to be free after dinner with Alex Tarasov." He turned and left her standing there.

"I'll have the cannelloni," Mike said to the waiter as he returned to the table.

"How's the writing going?" Alex asked Robert.

"Pretty good," Robert said modestly. "I'm doing character sketches of the men I work with. Maybe there's a play there."

"I'll be glad to read what you've got."

"Oh, it's really not ready."

As Ruth Gilbert and the producer were leaving, she stopped next to Mike and bent at his chair.

"You dropped this," she said, giving him a piece of paper.

"Thanks," Mike said, smiling.

She left with the producer, neck arched on shapely shoulders with the right amount of wiggle. Mike watched her retreating back appreciatively, then smiled at the phone number.

———————

On a warm Sunday night in June they went to see *Ninotchka* with Garbo, but the evening was spoiled by a "March of Time" newsreel showing Hitler decorating the Condor Legion as it returned to Berlin. The music sent chills through them.

Two weeks later, *Golden Boy* closed. Mike wasn't looking forward to a New York City summer in a taxicab.

Katherine enrolled in summer school and Alex looked for a place the Group could spend the summer together. It was valuable and necessary for their growth, he maintained. They would train new actors and develop new plays. He invited Robert to join them. Katherine and Mike were pleased. It showed Alex's interest in Robert's talent.

"I don't have the money," Robert told them.

"Nobody does," countered Mike, surprised.

"Are you afraid?" Katherine asked.

"Of what?" Robert stiffened.

"Of the challenge. Of exposing your work to criticism."

Mike knew she was right. "Plays are for the stage, Robert," he said gently. "Not the page." Robert felt pinned like a butterfly they were examining. "You know, there are actors who never audition," Mike continued. "They go to class and study for years and say they aren't ready. They call themselves actors, but they aren't because they're never on a stage. If you're a playwright, actors have to say your words and an audience has to listen and react to their truth."

Robert looked away and then to Katherine. "You might find someone else while I'm gone," he joked nervously.

"So might you," she shot back. "All those ravishing actresses waiting to pounce on a brilliant new playwright who will write great parts for them. And a handsome one, at that. But that's the risk of growth. And you've got to grow, Robert."

Mike put his arms around Katherine and kissed her. "Why can't I find a girl like you?" he said.

"You're not ready for a girl like me."

"What do you mean?" He held her at arm's length.

"I'm too serious for you."

"You mean I'm not serious?"

"Not with women."

"I don't know anyone who's more serious about them."

"Chasing them. Not relating to them."

"I relate to women."

"In bed. Not on a serious level."

"I'm serious about sex."

"That's not a relationship."

"That's because I never found anyone like you."

"That's sophistry," she said. "I'll ask you a question which you certainly don't have to answer."

"I will if I can."

Robert was immediately apprehensive. He knew Katherine's sometimes stinging directness.

"Why do you have to screw so many women?"

"Because I keep trying to feel something."

Her eyebrows rose.

"Even boredom," he went on. "But all I feel is nothing. I stare at the ceiling wondering why I can't feel something. Anything. Only with that sweet girl in Spain. With her it was joyous, full. . . . With her, I felt like a man."

Katherine had not expected the truth and was unprepared for it. What she felt was overwhelming compassion. She put her arms around him. "Oh, Mike," she said sadly.

Robert wondered at his answer. Florita? Only with Florita? Mike had been with her only that one night! What fantasy was he carrying around with him? What did Florita mean?

———————

"Surprised you, didn't he?" Robert asked as they prepared for bed.

"Yes," she said, preoccupied.

"What are you thinking?"

She looked at him and paused. "There was something theatrical about the admission."

"You were moved."

"I was. Until I decided I'd been manipulated. I felt as though I'd witnessed a performance and been taken in by it."

"You don't believe him?"

Katherine paused again in concern for Robert's feelings. "I believe it's the truth," she said carefully, "but I also feel he was using it."

"How?" Robert felt an edge of anger. "How was he using it?"

"This is very difficult, Robert." They looked at each other, Robert with some hostility. She felt conflicted about whether to go on. "I can't help feeling he was saying, 'See how naked I can be, how honest?' But I think that 'honesty' is a disguise, a mask of his true feelings."

"Which are . . . ?"

"Hostility. I think it's the motor that drives Mike."

"I don't know anyone more generous," he flared.

She felt her own heat rising and tried to control it. "I didn't say he wasn't. But I think it's a cover."

"You don't trust him?" It was both a question and a statement.

"I can't," she said quietly.

"You're jealous," Robert said. "You're jealous of our relationship because there are things you can't share. Things that only men can share."

"I don't think that's true, and I'm not jealous." Her own

anger began to rise again. "What I don't like is your dependence on Mike."

"It's not dependence. It's admiration."

"Call it what you like. I wish he'd move." There it was. She'd finally said it, although she hadn't meant to.

Robert stared at her for what seemed like moments.

"What do you mean by dependence?" he asked softly.

"You rely on him for a great deal, and that's why you don't want him to move. You don't want to grow up."

Robert continued to stare at her. "I think what you mean is that you want me to be dependent on you."

"No, Robert," she said. "What's important between you and me is that you can't be independent without him."

Robert took a deep breath. Katherine recognized it as the pause before dangerous decisions. "Robert, I'm not asking you to choose between us. I might lose."

———

In July, Robert went off with Mike and Alex.

A wealthy woman who fancied herself a patroness of the arts, and who also fancied Alex, had lent him her summer mansion on Long Island. It was quite a change for the Group. Formerly, they'd been in cabins in the Catskills. The mansion's twenty bedrooms could house a whole theatrical company. Its gardens were beautiful and enormous, its living room large enough for lectures and workshop performances.

Alex's only problem was running faster than Gertrude, whose husband had made a fortune selling scrap iron to Japan. Gertrude had also proved her investment savvy by making a good profit on her stake in *Golden Boy*. Now Gertrude was trying to get her husband to fund the whole of the Group's next season. A hundred thousand dollars.

"I didn't know my body was worth so much," Alex laughed.

"It's your mind I adore," Gertrude cooed, then continued business. "Albert is in London now cornering the sterling market. He'll make another killing when he's proved right about there not being another war in Europe. Sterling's going to zoom."

"And if there is a war?" Alex asked.

"Wipeout. Albert will be broke."

"What a deductive mind you have."

"What about my seductive body?"

"It's your mind I adore. Let us pray for peace."

The weekdays were full. Robert, engrossed, went to acting and directing classes in the mornings, while afternoons he spent on his play, *The Shop*. It was about a small Manhattan factory, the unfulfilling romance between a bookkeeper and her married boss, the conflicts between the younger and older Italian workers when put to the test of a strike.

In the evenings they listened to music, talked politics and literature, and gossiped. Sometimes they went to a nearby roadhouse for a midnight hamburger.

Katherine remained in the city. The argument over Mike had left its rough edges, but was smoothed when they were together on weekends. There was something fresh about their meetings now, and sex was all the sweeter for its reduced availability.

Mike went through the company of females like a mouse through cheese. He nibbled everywhere. What amazed Robert was that the other women knew and didn't seem to mind. They didn't expect permanence with Mike and weren't disappointed when it wasn't offered. They were like shipboard romances, butterfly love affairs. They were meant to die with summer.

But if Mike wasn't serious about women, he was deadly earnest about his work. He was full of ideas and talked endlessly. He wanted to be in and part of everything. He helped Robert with his play, especially the character of an old Italian drunk who was outsized, both buffoon and pathetic figure, having been glorious in youth and unable to fathom age. Mike did "exercises," playing a bear, practicing different walks, grew a large mustache, drew on all the old men in his Little Italy childhood. The character became his reality.

It was a long one-act play in two scenes, taking place in six months. It became Mike's project. He directed it, helped Robert with rewrites as they rehearsed, and then decided it was ready for a workshop performance.

Katherine came with Irv and Pete.

The rococo living room became the Greenwich Village factory. As Robert sat with Katherine, his anticipation was worse than on the eve of battle. Sensing it, Katherine squeezed his hand.

The lights came up and the shop was empty. Slowly, each character entered. It was winter, and they shed their overcoats, blew on their hands, unwrapped their scarves, took off their galoshes, spent a wordless eternity of silence on their "cold" exercises. They were, after all, the first "method" group.

Robert began to fidget. God, they're all wrapped up in their technique, he thought in dismay. What about my play?

The room came to life on Mike's entrance. The onlookers loved his walk, his presence. They moved forward on their chairs as the play developed, and they became involved in the characters.

There was applause at the end of the first scene. People smiled at Robert when the lights came up.

The next scene was summer. Now it was hot. And so were the actors. They sweated; they played every variation of heat before they spoke. Robert anguished again. But again they regained the balance of the play and the audience's attention. There was warm applause at the end when the actors yelled in chorus, "Strike! Strike! Strike!"

As the applause ended and they were still in darkness, someone shouted, "Odets, where is thy sting?" It brought the house down, and when the lights came on, the audience was still laughing at the barb.

Mike rushed over, still in costume, his face flushed. "I find the guy who said that about Odets, I'll take him apart!" he said angrily.

"I thought it was terrific, Robert," Irv said. "Showed a real working-class consciousness."

"I liked what I heard," Pete said.

"It was wonderful," Katherine said, embracing Robert.

"Good work," Alex called out to the cast, who were milling about with their friends. "Postmortems tomorrow. Let's go to the roadhouse for a drink."

It was a redneck kind of place, loud with "Beer Barrel Polka," which someone played continuously on the jukebox. The conversation swirled around Robert, who half listened, still absorbed in the hurt of the Odets remark.

"Hey, kid, it's your first production," Mike said cheerily. "You should be celebrating. You can't let some idiot get you down. Everybody liked it. You heard the applause."

"The applause was for you, Mike."

"Bullshit! They liked the play. Ask Alex."

Alex had been listening and watching from across the table. He smiled reassuringly. "We'll talk tomorrow," he said.

Later, in bed, Robert was still self-absorbed. Katherine wondered if that was what it meant to be an artist and tried to think of an analogy in medicine. She couldn't. Unless it was a doctor who had lost a patient.

The next day was bright and pleasant. At breakfast the actors gossiped as Alex moved among them. Mike entered with the play's ingenue, obviously having spent the night with her.

"Mea Culpa on the Lawn," Alex called out.

"Yes, Father Tarasov," they called back.

Mea Culpa on the Lawn was their description of the postmortem discussions of their strengths and weaknesses, their admissions of theatrical excess. Katherine sat on a lawn chair, a little to the side of the group, listening as the dissection took place in the sun. The critiques were neither mean nor carping. Everyone in the circle of friends and co-workers each stated his feelings.

"There's nothing wrong with an ode to Odets, especially in a first play," Carnovsky said. "We all want to be like the artists we admire. And if there are plot similarities, that's a minor fault. I think Robert succeeded very well with a number of characters, especially Lorenzo."

"A lot of it is my fault," Mike said. "I got too involved with my own character to see the whole. As a director I should have been able to guide Robert in the integration of idea and character. I ran across something by D. H. Lawrence I'd like to read. 'The essential function of art is moral. But, a passionate, implicit morality. Not didactic. A morality which changes blood rather than mind. Changes blood first. The mind follows later, in the wake.' In other words, Robert, write from the balls."

Everyone laughed and clapped. Katherine was impressed.

"That's good, Mike," Alex said. "Also, there's a certain amount of living that has to be done. The central character lacked the maturity you yourself lack." Katherine certainly agreed with that. "I think the play revealed genuine theatrical instinct. More instinct, though, than accomplishment. More rough substance than created form."

Someone ran from the house shouting excitedly. "The Russians just made a deal with Hitler! Stalin signed a non-aggression pact with him!"

"What!" everyone chorused, shocked.

"I just heard it on the radio. Von Ribbentrop is in Moscow and Stalin signed it!" There were murmurs of disbelief.

"Despite the importance of this news," Alex continued, "I would like to finish discussing Robert's play. We also have to read Clifford's new play by the end of the week and discuss it intelligently. He's waiting for an answer."

"Alex, you would fiddle while Rome burned," an actor said.

"I'm a fiddler, not a firefighter," Alex shot back.

———

That night there were violent arguments about the pact.

"Stalin's trying to buy time," said the apologists.

"He's also taking a part of Poland."

"As a buffer."

"That's what Hitler says."

"How can you compare the two?"

It was August 23.

On September 1, Hitler's Condor Legion marched on Poland.

On September 3, Britain and France declared war on Germany.

Gertrude's husband went broke.

CHAPTER EIGHT

On September 17, the Soviet Union invaded Poland and Robert got a telegram.

> GRANDPA DIED TODAY STOP PLEASE COME
> FOR FUNERAL STOP LOVE MOM STOP

Alex gave Robert an advance copy of Thomas Wolfe's *You Can't Go Home Again*. "Nothing like a long train trip to think about your life," Alex said.

Wolfe's speculation on change brought Robert's own. He put the book down and closed his eyes. In a vacuum of time his mind floated. The sounds of the train brought images of the trip from Paris to Perpignan, down the coast to Barcelona, Pete's bright eyes, George's death.

Increasingly, the images narrowed to Katherine and Mike. If a choice had to be made, who would it be? He shook his head, opened his eyes. What did each mean to him? He went back to the book. But the words blurred and the question persisted. Who was he now? How would he define himself? I'm a writer. I'm a playwright. Does that mean I'm closer to Mike? I don't know.

He thought about the war. Was he more or less of a man for having killed other men? The war in Europe was close. It was only a continuation of Spain. Was he going again? He sighed. "I want to be a writer, not a soldier."

His mother was as pretty as he remembered her, his father as bland. She had her long black hair tied in a bun, as she always did, and only a few strands were gray. He saw the same hairstyle worn by young dancers in Greenwich Village.

"It's so good to see you," she said tearfully, as she held him in her slender arms, looked at him again. "You're not a little boy anymore."

"I wasn't when I left, Mom."

She shook her head. "There's a difference. It's your eyes."

His father waited patiently, awkwardly, in his Sears suit and shoes, twisting his hat in his large hands. Robert had his father's hands. He waited, as if in line at church, waiting to say hello to the minister.

"Hello, son." Frederick Thompson put out his hand. Robert took it. "How are you?"

"I'm okay." Then, impulsively, feeling he had to break whatever held them apart, he took his father's shoulders and embraced him. "I'm sorry, Dad. I'm sorry about Grandpa."

At first, his father's back stiffened, the shoulders tensed, and he blinked. But Robert held him. He took a deep breath and the shoulders relaxed. "He loved you, son," his father said. "Grandpa Frank loved you and believed in you."

"I loved him too."

The train station was empty as Robert picked up his bag and they went to the Ford. The streets seemed smaller. Robert sat in the front seat next to his father, who pointed out the changes.

"They put a blinker up at Four Corners. Truck had an accident with a hayrick. And the drugstore got a new sign. The old one fell down in the last big wind."

His mother sat behind them. Were these events for her too? Could he ask her? They were passing Thompson Grain and Feed.

"Hey, Dad," Robert exclaimed, "you've expanded!" Despite himself, he was excited.

"Took over Grover's Hardware. The old man died, and Tom went to Chicago."

"Tom Grover went to Chicago! What's he doing?"

"Playing in one of those jazz bands."

Robert remembered fat Tom playing on the football field in the Ames High School Marching Band, slide trombone, cheeks puffed and red, in the fall cold. "What happened to Suzie?" he asked. Robert had had a crush on Suzie Grover. His father didn't answer. "What happened, Dad?"

"Ask your mother."

"What happened, Mom?" Robert asked, alarmed, fearing death.

"Suzie had to leave town. She got pregnant."

Robert almost laughed in relief. He realized his standard of bad news was death. The world was about to blow up, but in Ames, Iowa, a pregnant girl was still a scandal.

"Do you want to see Grandpa first or freshen up?" his mother asked.

"I'd like to see Grandpa."

———

He's so small, Robert thought. Without his legs, the old man took up barely half the casket. The funeral director had considered using a child's coffin, but the only one he had was painted with flowers and angels. Robert looked at the rouged cheeks and lips and thought how his grandfather would have hated it. The hair was closely cropped as it had been in life, but badly cut. There was a razor nick above the lip.

"I'd like to go out to the farm tomorrow after the funeral," Robert said after dinner. His father nodded and was silent. Is he thinking about chicken feed? Robert wondered. What does he think about? Robert didn't know.

"You think there's goin' to be another war?" his father asked, surprising him.

"Yes. It's a continuation of the war in Spain."

"Best thing could happen would be if the Bolsheviks and the Nazis would finish each other off," his father said quietly. "We're not going to get involved. That's for sure."

"The war may be forced on us."

"Not if we're smart."

"We may not have a choice."

"America first is what I say," his father said forcefully.

"There can't be a free America without a free world."

"Is that what they say in New York?"

Here it comes, thought Robert.

"Is that what the Jewish bankers and the Commies say? Get us in a war to save Russia?"

His mother was getting nervous.

"The war is to save democracy, Dad. Ours, England's . . ."

"I heard that one before, Robert. My head was filled with it and I went to fight the war to end all wars. What I saw I've spent the rest of my life trying to forget. You know what was left of my company? Me!" His father was agitated, his hands clenching and unclenching. "All those fellas I went over with died. Are you telling me they died for nothing?" Robert was silent. "Grandpa charged up San Juan Hill with Teddy and took a cannonball for his trouble. You know what it is growing up with a daddy with no legs?" his father burst out. "And you went. What good did it do?"

"Frederick, please," his mother said.

"Okay, okay, Rose, I'm sorry. I didn't meant to attack you, Robert. I'm tryin' to tell you, we've got to mind our own business. We lost enough boys over there. Let 'em fight their own battles. This family has done enough! I don't want to see you comin' home in a wheelchair . . . or a wooden box."

Robert went to his father as he stared in anger and pleading, and held him.

A sob escaped his father. "*Ich liebe dich, sohn*," he said, lapsing into German.

———————————

Robert was lying in bed reading *The Sorrows of Young Werther* in German. After his parents had gone to bed, Robert had scanned the rows of classics in German in their "parlor," books collected for years by the family. As he read the Goethe, his mother entered. The room was just as he'd left it, a college boy's room with books and banners, athletic equipment and trophies. She sat down next to him.

"Are you all right?" she asked.

"Sure, Mom."

"Your father never got over it."

"I finally know why he never talked about the war." He decided to ask her. "Mom, how come you married him? You're so unlike each other." He couldn't imagine them in sex. "How did you ever meet?"

She was silent for a moment. "I met him at the university. I was on tour with a dance company and he was at the party afterward. He was very shy and very nice. I was attracted to his silences, what I thought were his depths. At the end of the evening he startled me. He said he loved me."

Robert looked at his mother in amazement.

"Oh yes, it was crazy," she continued, "but I believed him. Perhaps I wanted to."

"Why?"

"I had no real confidence in myself as a dancer. I was afraid I'd never really be as good as I wanted to be, and that's all I ever wanted. When he followed me to Chicago and asked me to marry him, I said yes." His mother took his hand and held it firmly. "But I don't want you to be afraid. And Grandpa didn't want you to be afraid. He had faith in you, and wanted you to have a chance. He's left you all his money. Five thousand dollars. Now, go to sleep." She tucked him into his blankets, turned off the light, and left the room.

Robert stared into the dark.

———————————

The service was a simple one in the town cemetery. The remaining buddies who had gone to war with Frank Thompson laid a wreath on the coffin as it was lowered. Robert looked from the wreath to the sky. It was the same sky he'd looked at when he lay wounded in Spain. A sob shook him. His father put his arm around him, and they left.

Later, his father gave him a box and an envelope. The

cardboard box contained his grandfather's medals. The envelope contained a letter and a check.

> Dear Robert,
>   Every man has to face his end, and I do so calmly, knowing I've tried to make this world a little better than when I came into it. I don't know if I've succeeded, but I sure tried. I think you'll do a better job than me and I want you to have a chance. So, I'm leaving you the pension money I've saved up. I know you'll use it well.
>   You're a good boy and I loved watching you grow up. Goodbye, till we meet in that place where old soldiers go. Until then, I know you'll do your best.
>
>   Grandpa

Robert folded the letter and put it down with the box of medals. His eyes were wet.

Robert went to the farm alone. He wanted it that way. His mind seemed blank as he drove along the endless fields of harvested corn. The farm was just as he remembered it. He went to the well and drew some water. It was as sweet and cold as it had been when he was a boy. He looked at the field where they'd played baseball. He heard his mother call, "Come in for lunch, boys."

The old house stood empty in the sun, and a breeze touched him. "I'll try, Grandpa," he said aloud.

Some birds twittered in response.

"How was it?" Katherine asked, as she met him at Grand Central.

"Thomas Wolfe was right, but I'm glad I went."

Robert put the letter and the medals in his drawer and went to his typewriter. Mike and Katherine were in the kitchen cooking dinner. He could hear their voices as low murmurs, the scraping of a pot, a snatch of aria Mike sang.

"Well, how do you feel about being rich?" Mike asked, twirling his pasta.

"What's mine is yours, Mike," Robert replied seriously.

"You mean I can stop driving a cab?"

"Whatever you want to do, Mike, I'll help you."

"I'll remember that. But I don't want any money."

———————

It was a quiet afternoon in November, a Sunday. A Mozart symphony filled the living room. The remains of a chess game and the Sunday *New York Times* were on the floor. The paper was filled with news of the Russo-Finnish war and pictures of Finnish ski troopers in white devastating their Russian attackers. Robert put down the news section with a sigh. Katherine was reading the book review, Mike the theatrical pages.

Mike was working as assistant stage manager and understudy in the Group's first play of the season, for which he was being paid fifty dollars a week. He was waiting for Odets to finish his new play, in which Mike would have a good part. "Why don't you two get married?" he asked suddenly, lighting a cigarette.

Robert and Katherine looked at each other in surprise.

"It seems like the wrong time," Robert said. "The world is so unsettled."

"If you wait for the world to get settled, you'll never get married," Mike said, laughing.

"I can't see that it makes much difference," Katherine said.

"It's a different kind of commitment," Mike said.

"That's odd coming from you, Mike," Katherine said.

"I'm a terrible example," he said.

"I think Mike is right," Robert said with sudden conviction.

"It's all right with me," Katherine agreed.

"Great! I get to direct a wedding," Mike laughed, hugging them.

———————

The apartment was bursting with actors and veterans of the battalion. Mike was Robert's best man, Katherine's college roommate was her bridesmaid, and Barkin gave her away. Her parents had refused to come.

Robert's parents made the trip from Iowa. His mother was flushed with excitement as she made her way from group to group. His father stood shy and frightened in a corner, staring at the strange people who were his son's friends.

"I love walking these streets again," his mother told him. She was dressed in a long skirt and wore a ponytail like a Martha Graham dancer.

Alex made them a gift of a painting by an unknown Russian named Chagall. It was of a wedding in a small East European village in which the two lovers kissed high in the air above the spires of the church.

On Christmas Day, peace on earth seemed farther away than ever. Everyone talked of art and war. After the wedding party, they left for the theater. Mike had gotten them tickets to Lillian Hellman's new play, *Watch on the Rhine*.

"I wish I could write like that," Robert said as they left the theater. It was snowing. They walked downtown, the snow crunching underfoot. "The way she's able to synthesize character and idea without sentiment just knocks me out," he continued.

"And the economy," she added. "It's as if she writes with a scalpel. She just slices to the bone."

"Not a bad image for a surgeon," Robert laughed. It was snowing harder now. "Hey, do you want to walk, or do you want to splurge on a taxi?"

"Walk first, splurge later."

"Great idea. A fire and some brandy."

"And a Beethoven quartet."

"Aren't we lucky?" Robert said, as they kissed.

———————————

Katherine gathered kindling while Robert went to the kitchen for brandy. He found a note on the table from Mike.

"Don't worry—I won't be home tonight, so let yourselves go. Love, Mike."

Robert read it to Katherine as she lit the fire.

"That son of a bitch." She smiled. "He knows I'm inhibited with him in the next room."

"Oh . . . is that the reason?" Robert kidded.

"Is what the reason?" she challenged lightly.

"Why you're so quiet."

"I'm very genteel, in case you haven't noticed. I was brought up a respectable young lady, not a rowdy."

Robert took her in his arms. "Let's make love in front of the fire, like in the movies."

"It's cold in here."

"You're so romantic."

"I can't be romantic when I'm cold."

"I'll warm you up."

"Promise?"

"Promise," he said. "Instead of Beethoven, let's have something to dance to."

Robert turned on the radio. Walter Huston was singing "September Song." They came together, kissed, and danced to Huston's warm, raspy voice.

"Getting warmer?"

"Hmmmm," she said, putting her head on his shoulder, taking a sip of brandy. "That's good." They kissed, and Robert stroked her.

"Is this a seduction?" she asked. "I like seductions."

"You never told me that before."

"I don't tell you everything. If I don't have secrets, I'll be dull."

"You'll never be dull."

They kissed suddenly, as if moved by the same need, and started to undress each other. The song changed.

"I'll get the blanket," she said, going to the bedroom.

They lay on it now, the hard floor creaking beneath them as Robert moved within her. Slowly . . . slowly . . . then faster. Katherine started to moan. Robert was surprised, then her sounds ignited him and he moved deeper. She came in a long cry as he exploded.

When their breathing became normal, she asked, "Was that loud enough?"

He collapsed in laughter.

"We are lucky," she said, as they huddled in the blanket, watching the fire. "Often, just before I fall asleep," she continued, "I see you on the operating table."

"Sssshhhh," Robert said.

"No. I want to tell you. We were so busy, men became only wounds. You whispered my name and I thought I was hearing things. Then you called me again. It still haunts me."

"Sssshhhh." He took her in his arms.

"I'm so happy, Robert."

"So am I. Because I have you and work that I love."

She was silent for a moment. "Do you think Mike will ever be happy?" she asked.

Robert sighed. "Mike will only be happy when he no longer feels the world will come down on him and crush him like his father. And I don't know if that will ever happen."

CHAPTER NINE

Mike got the lead in Clifford Odets's new play. He was inwardly ecstatic and outwardly sober. He worked in total concentration. Even food meant nothing to him. He ate dinner with the script in front of him, ignoring conversation. When his plate was empty he went to his room. He never brought anyone home. He was like a monk in training. They celebrated New Year's Eve quietly.

It was cold and blizzardy in Boston that January of 1940. The notices were like the weather, and no one came to the theater. The management turned off the heat, and the company rehearsed rewrites as if in cold storage. The dressing rooms were freezing. Alex bought electric heaters. The house manager turned them off when the actors were onstage. The few people who came to the play because they were Odets fans sat bundled in their coats. They applauded to keep their hands warm.

The opening-night audience in New York was thrown. The play was not what they expected from Odets. This was no working-class drama of ideas. It was lyrical and fanciful. Some of his strongest past supporters were the most bitter in their comments at intermission.

"Bourgeois entertainment."

"Poetic bullshit!"

"Frivolity."

"More Saroyan than Odets."

"Whatever the hell that means," Alex said angrily to Robert and Katherine when he overheard the remark.

Robert confided to Katherine when they were back in their seats that he thought Mike was miscast. He had the energy but not the poetry. Katherine was inclined to agree.

The applause was warm if not enthusiastic on the curtain calls, out of respect for Alex and Odets. Mike managed a good hand on his own bows.

"I liked it," Alex said to Robert and Katherine as they met backstage. "But God knows what the critics will make of it."

Odets crossed to them from across the stage, where he was congratulating actors. His eyes were bright. "Alex, I think this is the finest production of the best play in New York," he said.

"That's what worries me," Alex said dryly. "Let's go downtown to the Café Royal. I don't feel like being in the water with the sharks tonight."

Odets was somewhat deflated by Alex's mood. "Good idea," he said. "I'd rather be insulted by a Jewish waiter than complimented by my friends who are writing my obituary."

"What about the notices?" Mike asked in his dressing room.

"The press agent will call me down there."

They all crowded into a taxi, and they rode in silence.

"You didn't like me tonight," Mike said as the cab made its way down Second Avenue. "Did you, Robert?"

Katherine tensed. The others were alert.

"It wasn't that I didn't like you. I thought you were miscast."

"What does that mean, 'miscast'?" Alex said. "He should play everything."

"I just meant—"

Alex didn't let him finish. "You just meant he should play it safe, get good notices, and further his career rather than stretch himself," Alex said heatedly.

Katherine shrank into her corner, knowing how Robert must feel being attacked by a man he admired so much.

"Yes, what did you mean?" Odets asked with an edge.

"I just meant this part's very far from Mike's reality."

"Playing his personality isn't acting," Alex said, but with less heat. There was some truth to Robert's perception.

The argument ended as they passed the Jewish theaters that lined Second Avenue and stopped in front of the Café Royal.

The Sardi's of Second Avenue, it was brightly colored and garishly lit. "I love it here," Alex said as they swept in. Alex wore his long black coat, broad-brimmed fedora, and gray doeskin gloves and carried his walking stick.

"So do I," echoed Odets, "and it's been ages since I've been here."

"My usual lousy table," Alex said to the maître d'.

"I see by your costooom you had a optown opening," the maître d' said with a thick, Russian-Jewish accent as he appraised Alex and led them to a table in the middle of the room.

The restaurant was crowded and the voices loud to match the clothing. Robert and Katherine had never seen anything like it. Odets smiled as hands flew in front of faces like gesticulating birds, fists pounded tables for emphasis, eyes and gold teeth flashed in anger or enthusiasm. Waiters ran about with food that still steamed with the heat of the kitchen and threw them on tables in front of their customers.

"Do you have a quieter table?" Alex asked.

"This is the best table in the place," the maître d' said, surprised. "Everyone can see you."

"It's very noisy," Alex insisted.

"For quiet, you don't come to the Royal. For quiet, you go to the cemetery," the maître d' answered, throwing stained menus on the table in front of bowls of pickles and baskets of bread. "For a good heartburn, have the mushroom-barley or the potato latkes." He left with a smile.

"It's part of the charm," Odets explained to a bewildered Katherine and Robert. "You're rated by the level of insult."

The waiter was dyspeptic and sallow-looking.

"So, *nu*?" he growled impatiently.

"We haven't looked at the menus yet," Odets said.

"So what? Order anything. It's all good."

"We'll start with some chopped liver," Alex said.

"Take my advice, don't." They looked at him. "The chopped liver is pure poison, believe me."

"I believe you," Alex said. "We'll have the matzo-ball soup."

"A wise choice. And for the main course?"

"Blintzes," Alex ordered.

The waiter shook his head negatively.

"No?"

"No."

"There's a reason?" Alex asked.

"Do I need a reason?" He shrugged. "Take the pot roast. It's well burned tonight. And I'll give you some latkes on the side."

"Jack said the latkes are sure heartburn," Odets said.

"First of all," the waiter intoned, "Jack is an idiot. Second, what's wrong with a little heartburn? It's a natural condition."

Alex and Odets laughed.

"My mother always called it 'the fire of life,'" Odets said. "It would be very cold in Philadelphia without it."

They ordered the pot roast and followed the waiter through the noisy bedlam.

"There's more energy and passion here than on the whole of Broadway," Alex said. "But my heart can't take it too often."

The waiter arrived balancing five large soup bowls in one hand. With the other, he threw them to the table, the liquid sloshing to the rim without spillage. It was all a skillful act.

"Jewish cannonballs," Alex said, slicing a matzo ball with his spoon.

"We should have had them in Spain," Mike said. He ate with concentration for a few moments, then looked up at Alex. "You worried about the notices?"

"I don't worry about notices anymore," Alex said. "Some critics will love us, some will hate us, and all for the wrong reasons. What's important is survival intact. Survival without castration."

Robert nodded, as did Odets.

As the waiter delivered the pot roast, the maître d'
crossed to them importantly. "Telephone, Tarasov."

Alex shrugged and went to the pay phone. They watched
him make notes and return sober-faced.

"If we don't get heartburn from the pot roast, we'll get it
from the notices," he said, sitting.

"Not so good, huh?" Odets said.

"Stupid," Alex shouted. "Listen to this. 'Now that Odets
writes like Saroyan, Doomsday is near.' Or, 'Mr. Odets has
been around long enough to improve instead of to subside
into mannerisms, the mannerisms of a new playwright who
has not yet learned to use the theater expertly.'" Alex
banged the table with his fists so that the plates jumped.
"Odets like Saroyan! Idiots! This isn't criticism. It's con-
sumer reports!"

Odets was silent.

"What did they say about the production?" Mike asked.

"Here, I have to agree with them. 'The best acting organization in this country is offering a superlative performance . . . a brilliant Group Theater production.'" Alex
smiled and turned to Mike. "'In Mike Rossano, they are
presenting one of the most exciting actors in America.'"

"They're not such idiots," Mike said, smiling.

Odets looked at him speculatively.

———————

The play limped along, and they settled into a routine.
Katherine went to school all day and studied all night. Robert woke early with her and they had breakfast together.
Then Robert went to his typewriter. With his grandfather's
money he was able to leave the cabinet factory. Mike took a
long time to unwind from his performance and always had a
date afterward; he usually got up at eleven. Mike ate breakfast while Robert ate lunch.

They usually talked about Robert's play.

"I'm really up a tree, Mike. I can't seem to hook into the
emotion."

"Maybe you don't have enough distance. It's the tough-
est kind of play to write."

Robert was trying to write about his own family.

"But I want to explore it. I seem to have a need to explain my mother."

"To yourself, or to an audience?"

Mike's questions always went to the heart of motive.

Twice a week, they went to Alex's midnight class for professionals. It was filled with actors and directors working on Broadway. Robert learned what actors needed to make a scene work. The class ended at two in the morning, and, stimulated, he and Mike usually went to an all-night cafeteria. When they got home, Katherine was often slumped over her books, asleep at the kitchen table. Robert would gently wake her and lead her to bed.

Katherine tried to sort out her feelings about the amount of time Robert spent with Mike and the relatively short periods she had with him. But what could she do? She had the same compulsion to excel that they did, and there was little she could share with him about medicine. Despite her jealousy of Robert's relationship with Mike, there was no question of asking Mike to move. He had found the apartment and they had moved in with him.

Spring 1940. They laughed at Chaplin in *The Great Dictator*, but the newsreel showed Hitler's Wehrmacht *Blitzkrieg* through Holland and Belgium, the same Stuka dive bombers, tanks, and artillery first tested in Spain. When they went to see *The Grapes of Wrath*, they also saw Dunkirk. On June 14, Hitler rolled down the Champs Élysées in his big black Mercedes convertible.

It promised to be a lousy summer.

Mike was out of work, but he'd saved enough not to have to return to a hot cab. He spent more time with a despairing Robert.

"I'm just not getting anywhere, Mike. I don't think I should be a writer."

"Why do you say that?"

"I can't make this play work."

"Then try another."

But Robert was obsessed with it.

Katherine tried to decide whether she should go to summer school. She and Robert needed more time together. A compromise was struck when he suggested they go away together for a couple of weeks between terms. She was delighted.

"Alex is going away to the Cape," Robert said, implying they might go too.

"I like the Cape," she countered, "but I love Maine even more. You haven't lived until you've seen a Penobscot Bay sunset."

"Maine it is," he said, hugging her.

"I know the greatest little island," she said, happy to have the time away with Robert and still be able to attend summer session.

When they left, Robert sensed that Mike was angry. But why should he be angry? Did he expect to be invited along? It *was* a kind of honeymoon trip.

"What are you thinking?" Katherine asked, turning from the window, the sunlight glancing off her reddish hair, striking sparks of gold, as the train rolled toward Boston.

"Nothing," he replied. Did he want Mike with them?

———————————

Bucksport was a small Maine seaside village with one turn-of-the-century hotel. The bedsprings in the Jed Prouty Tavern and Hotel squeaked with rust, age, and complaint. Katherine started to laugh.

"They must hear us all over the hotel," she said.

"Everyone here is deaf with age."

"Are you sure?" She laughed again.

"Now you've ruined it," he said, shrinking.

"I'm sorry," she said, continuing to laugh. "I grew up in a quiet house."

"You don't think your parents did 'it'?"

"I never heard them." She laughed again.

"What are you so giddy about?"

Katherine stopped laughing and leaned over him, her breasts and hair touching his shoulders. She kissed him.

"I'm happy. I'm very happy you suggested going away together. Now, try to be quiet."

The ferry to Deer Isle was a platform towed by a boat. It

reminded Katherine of the ferry across the Ebro. There were two cars, and they were the only passengers.

Mr. Eaton waited for them at the other end. He was a stark New Englander who said little more than "Eh," as his Model A Ford putt-putted toward Stonington, the largest village on the island. Eaton was a lobsterman who made ends meet by renting rooms to occasional visitors in summer. Deer Isle was not like its northerly neighbor, Bar Harbor. It was not chic. Only fishermen lived there and a few "summer folk." It was one of the reasons they loved it.

"I've never seen anything so clear," Robert said as he looked out over Penobscot Bay. The small white lobster boats made their way between the pine-grown islands, picking up their traps. The sun was warm, the air cool. They explored the island on foot and bicycle, made love among the pines at Burnt Cove as the sunlight sliced through the heavy green branches and made patterns of light on their skin. Looking upward through the trees at the sky, Robert thought of Spain, and with Katherine over him, studying his face, tears came.

"Why?" she asked.

"I'm so lucky to love you."

"Me too."

Eaton took them out in his boat as he made the rounds of his traps.

"If I were a painter, I'd be here every summer," Katherine said.

"We had a fella stayed with us was a painter," Eaton said, slowing to one of his trap markers. "From New York, matter of fact. Name was Marin. John Marin. Ever run into him?"

"Marin!" Robert said excitedly. "Odets has a Marin watercolor. I remember now, it was signed, 'Deer Isle, 1934'!"

"Nice fella, Marin," Eaton said, lifting the marker and the trap into the boat, then throwing the wiggling green lobsters into a barrel.

Katherine closed her eyes as she lifted her face to the sun.

How beautiful she is, Robert thought.

The two weeks were gone.

"I'm so glad we did this," Katherine said as they lay in the large bed the night before they were to leave. "We needed it. We needed to reestablish ourselves."

When they got back to the hot and airless apartment, which had evidently been closed up, there was a note on the kitchen table. "Went to the Cape with Alex. See you in two weeks. Love, Mike."

"Two more weeks alone." Katherine smiled broadly.

"Uh-huh." Robert smiled back, but felt a twinge of disappointment.

Mike came back tanned and energetic, with talk of the Cape, and Alex and Irwin Shaw, and "What a great time we had with the actors from the Cape Playhouse. You shoulda been there."

Robert had loved the month with Katherine but wished he'd also been with them. Katherine could see that nothing had changed.

"Do you really think it's a play?" Robert asked again as he drank coffee with Mike in the kitchen.

"The mysteries of marriage? Are you kidding? Of course it's a play."

"Why can't I make it work?" Robert shouted in frustration.

"Because you're not attacking the emotion," Mike shouted back. "Look at your own marriage."

"What do you mean?" Robert asked, stunned.

"Where would you have rather been, in Maine with Katherine or with me and Alex at the Cape?"

Robert was silent.

"You do admit a conflict, don't you?"

Robert nodded.

"But you don't face the conflicting emotion." Mike was sounding like Katherine. "How the fuck do you expect to write a play about it? And it's even harder with your parents, because you have the perspective of a child."

"Do you think there's something wrong with my marriage if I want to be with you and Alex?"

Mike looked steadily at Robert, his dark eyes intense, before answering. "No. I think it's the nature of marriage itself, the nature of life. There wouldn't be any theater without conflict. Katherine is terrific. I don't know a better woman. But as long as you both assert yourselves, your individuality, there are problems. Alex can't stay married. You can't dance at two weddings at the same time. And there's no doubt Katherine resents the time we spend together."

———————

Robert struggled with the play as Mike screwed his way through August and Hitler rampaged through Europe. By fall, Robert was entirely blocked.

"Put it aside," Mike advised. "You can always come back to it. Right now, you're just jerking off." Mike rose from the kitchen table. "Got to go. I have to meet Alex early today. We've got some problems. The Three Sisters are going to kill each other." Mike was Alex's assistant on the Chekhov play.

———————

The apartment was quiet. Robert walked into the living room, looked at the photos of himself and Mike at Jarama, the political posters, the Chagall, his books, his life. He took Scott Fitzgerald's *The Crackup* from the shelf and opened it. He was startled to see Jim Lardner's handwriting. It was a book they'd traded in Spain. Lardner had been the last American killed there. The memory fit his mood of despair.

But the next morning he started a new play. It had to do with the dream of being a big-league ballplayer, but had the same father and son. Katherine told Mike it was a metaphor for Robert's wanting to be a big-league playwright.

On the opening night of *The Three Sisters*, Alex went to the Café Royal alone. He knew it was going to fail, and he felt responsible. When it did, he went to Hollywood.

"I've got to make some money," he said in excuse. But

they knew Alex had to get away. His other protégé, Clifford Odets, was giving his new play to another director.

———————

Mike made it through the winter of 1940 by replacing an actor in a show that was running. The cold-water flat was freezing, but Robert managed to finish his play, and in the spring of 1941 he found a producer. As they celebrated in a French restaurant in Greenwich Village, Robert gave Mike most of the credit for having encouraged and guided him.

"Bullshit!" Mike said. "You did it yourself. All you needed was a kick in the ass."

Katherine was hurt by Robert's nonrecognition of her role, but said nothing.

———————

In May and June, the Russians complained of concentrations of German troops on their borders. On June 22, Hitler invaded the Soviet Union. A startled Stalin was totally unprepared. He'd believed Hitler when he said the German troops were only on maneuvers.

Alex was still in Hollywood, and Herman Finkelstein, baseball nut and well-known producer of comedies, chose "an old pro" to direct Robert's play, *The Strike Zone*.

"He's a hack," Mike said. "I guarantee you he doesn't have the least fucking idea what your play is about. I'd bet my life he thinks its about baseball. The last thing he did was *Getting Gertie's Garter!*"

Joe Harris was a smiling man, and they sat beneath his smiling portrait at his table in Sardi's. He regaled Robert with stories of former stars and productions, many of them hits of the twenties. Finkelstein assured Robert that Harris was right about revisions and casting, especially in the choice of a lightweight comedian who wanted to "stretch" and show that he had "range" in the pivotal role of the father.

Mike was right. They thought the play was about baseball. Robert's play was about dreams.

It didn't come through in Wilmington.

In Philadelphia, Mike played to empty houses in Odets's

new play. The audiences and critics found it pessimistic and depressing. They'd had enough of the Depression. They wanted to laugh.

They also wanted to laugh in Washington, where *The Strike Zone* was now playing. It was there that Finkelstein and Harris discovered that Robert had really written a comedy. Couldn't Robert write some one-liners to bring the act curtains down? He was aghast at their suggestions for rewrites, so they brought in a joke writer to "punch up" the script.

What should have been a high point in Robert's life was torture. He had no allies on the production except the assistant stage manager, who understood the play but was powerless. Alex was in Hollywood. Mike and Odets had their own problems.

Katherine took the train down on a Sunday, and they walked. At the National Gallery, Robert complained about the director; at the Smithsonian, he ridiculed the producer; at the Lincoln monument, he wished to be free of them all; and at the Washington Monument, he was suicidal. Katherine listened sympathetically, nodded, took his hand, and thought about the absurdity of "show business." She thought Robert was wasting himself.

The play that followed Robert's at the National Theater in Washington was a calculated comedy about the high jinks at the officers' club in Pearl Harbor. In New York, Robert and Mike closed in the same week. As the scenery was being carted to the dump in New Jersey that Sunday, December 7, Pearl Harbor was also burning and there were no laughs in Washington.

CHAPTER TEN

"The general will see you now."

Robert, Mike, Irv, and Milt Felsen, who'd been in Spain with them, from the Brunete campaign, rose and went through the door of the office in "Q" building on Constitution Avenue. General "Wild Bill" Donovan appraised them quickly and shook hands, smiling and holding them with his eyes. Athletic-looking in a well-fitting uniform, he'd been a World War I commander and Congressional Medal of Honor winner. He made it clear he had no time to waste.

"I'll come straight to the point with you guys," he said as they sat. "I need you. I'm setting up America's first clandestine service—work behind enemy lines, guerrilla stuff—and we're short of men with small unit or actual guerrilla experience." Donovan paused, looked at Irv. "That stuff in the Hemingway book true?" he asked.

"If the earth shook it wasn't because I had a girl in my sleeping bag," Irv said. "I didn't even have a sleeping bag."

Donovan laughed heartily. "I'll be frank with you," he said, sitting on the edge of his desk and folding his arms. "I've called you even though there are bureaucrats in this town who've warned me, despite what Hemingway has to say about you, that you're 'premature anti-Fascists'—read 'Commies'—because you fought in Spain. But this is my outfit and I'll run it my way. What concerns me is your combat experience against what are now our enemies, and you're the only guys in America with that experience. If you volunteer, I'm going to take advantage of it." Donovan looked at them for their reaction. They looked at him to continue. "Performance is my truth," he added.

"And truth comes out of the barrel of a gun," Irv said.

"I like that," Donovan said.

"Use it." Irv smiled. "But you might be labeled a subversive. It's Mao Tse-tung."

"*Touché*, Irv," Donovan said appreciatively. "I don't want to see your experience wasted when we need it so badly," he continued. "I want to train you in the latest methods of demolition, intelligence, weapons, murder and mayhem behind enemy lines." He scanned them again for their reaction. "I'll keep you together as a team. What do you say?"

The three men looked at each other.

"We volunteer," they said in unison.

"Why?" Donovan surprised them by asking.

"Because it's a continuation of Spain," Mike said. "Spain was only the rehearsal for this war."

Katherine shivered in the February cold as she walked with Robert and Mike to the subway at Sheridan Square. No one had slept. They had sat up all night talking, and in the morning, packed a few books. She kissed them both as the train rumbled in, watched their retreating backs as the doors closed, and walked back to the house alone. She drank another cup of coffee and left for school, not sure yet what she was feeling.

At the OSS training camp in the Maryland mountains—code name Shangri-la—a handsome blond man lectured them. It was rumored he'd been the chief of police of Shanghai, but his accent was both German and English.

"Deadly weapons can be very innocent. A pencil stuck in an eye, ear, or under the jawline can easily disable. A belt can be used to choke, a finger to gouge, a hand to tear a cheek or nostril. You must learn the soft parts of the body and go for them. Your enemy is not a sportsman. He will kill you if he has the opportunity, and your mission will fail. We are not training you to fail."

They had parachute missions at night with only a compass, survival hikes without food, hand-to-hand combat and disruption of communications. Irv could blow up anything. Mike loved the weapons training, Robert the radio transmitters. Milt became a great coordinator.

They became trained terrorists, although to many of the Ivy Leaguers in the unit it was all a gung-ho game, an Abercrombie & Fitch war.

———

Katherine discovered she liked living alone; studying and staying late at school. She missed Robert when she got into an empty bed, walked alone in the park, thought of things to tell him, but as she didn't share her medical life with him, she didn't feel his absence there. She crossed into his territory far more than he crossed into hers, and now she had to admit to herself she felt freer to focus on her own work. When she needed company there was Alex and Barkin's Sunday-afternoon "salons" of writers and artists, intellectuals and activists.

———

She traced her finger along Robert's body, noting its new hardness in the six months since she'd seen it.

Donovan did not want his new operatives thinking of home and kept the intensive training constant, kept them away from civilian life so that they wouldn't think about it.

"You've gotten strong," she said.

"And you? Have you changed?" he said quietly.

"Do I seem changed?"

Robert nodded.

"It's true. I've learned I like living alone. It's not that I don't miss you. . . ."

"Good."

"You mean that?" she asked, surprised.

"Yes. I want you to think about your future."

"Without you?" she asked, a little afraid.

"There's that chance," he said soberly.

"You have changed."

"I hope not." He sighed. "I've just become a more efficient killer, which gives me intimations of mortality."

Donovan had sped the team to his office by staff car, indicating his urgency. "I promised you guys a big one," he had said.

"Are you going to tell us?" Mike had asked.

"When you come back. I don't want you to have that information now. Take a week's leave."

The week had gone by quickly, and as Robert and Katherine talked, Mike said goodbye to his family. His mother's face was a smudged carbon of the hopeful one in the wedding photo. Mike's father's face could be his own. He looked at the rooms he'd grown up in, the scarred kitchen chairs, faded green bedrooms, the heavy dark furniture of the dark living room. Jesus still suffered above the old couch.

"Where you go, Mike?" his mother asked.

"It's a military secret, Momma," Mike's younger brother said proudly.

"And loose lips sink ships," Angela, his blossoming teen-aged sister, emphasized. "There's spies."

"Who am I gonna tell? Mrs. Scorcese downstairs? I'm more worried 'bout you than spies. You and that Ernie with the pompadour on the couch."

Angela and his mother argued about her boyfriend.

Mike found himself anxious to leave. He embraced them. His mother's knobby fingers patted his cheek. They're like worn flannel, Mike thought.

"Stay outa trouble, Mikey," his mother admonished him as they parted.

The sidewalks of Little Italy were crowded as he walked over to Third Avenue for a bus to Beekman Place. The doorman saluted Mike respectfully, opened the door to the large marble entry.

Maxine wore a cashmere dress that clung to her soft body. Mike enjoyed the subtle perfume as he kissed her, forgetting the cooking odors of his childhood. She took his hand and led him through the living room to the bedroom.

There was a fire and a bottle of champagne on ice next to the canopied Queen Anne bed. Caviar glistened in an ornate silver bowl. Maxine stopped in front of the fireplace. He held her as they listened to the Chopin in the background. They hadn't yet exchanged a word.

Mike tried not to hold her wealth against her. Maxine was an actress. As the daughter of a Pittsburgh steel magnate, she was hardly struggling. Mike's resentment against privilege almost melted as her dress dropped to the floor; she wore nothing beneath it. He stroked her fire-warm back.

"I love your skin," he murmured.

"So do I," she laughed as she took off his tie.

Maxine was the only one who could totally drain him, give him physical peace. "I won't die in battle," he said. "You're going to fuck me to death."

"Then we'll die together," she said, biting his nipple.

———————————

Robert and Katherine were also in bed. For all of Katherine's protests on the joys of living alone, she was suddenly overwhelmed with his leaving. She tried to hold back the tears.

"Let them come," Robert urged as he held her.

"I'm behaving like a little girl," she said, tears flowing. "I wanted you to believe I'm strong."

"You are strong."

"I don't want you to miss me," she said.

"You know I will."

Katherine and Maxine said goodbye to Robert and Mike at Grand Central.

Robert and Mike found Irv and Milt in the parlor car. They wondered where they were going.

CHAPTER ELEVEN

They reported to Donovan.

He leaned back, taking them in. "Torch is a combined American-British show." He paused for effect. "North Africa." He let it sink in. "Uncle Joe's been asking for a second front, and we've got to give it to him. Torch will have three landings on both the Atlantic and Mediterranean coasts. Your part in the show will be to aid the landings. You'll report to Colonel Sage at Shangri-la. He's your team leader. I think you'll like him. Ethel has *bon voyage* presents for you. Good luck."

Donovan smiled and shook their hands.

In the outer office, Donovan's secretary gave them each an expensively wrapped box from Abercrombie & Fitch containing a beautiful leather jacket.

Sage was a big man who'd been a fullback with the Redskins and the Bears. He had the hearty confidence of large, strong men, said exactly what he meant, and could make decisions fast, even in the middle of a play. He had no politics and was frank about his limitations.

"I'm depending on you guys to teach me the plays," the colonel said when they met. "I may be the captain of the team, but I been foolin' around in the locker room while you guys played the game."

They smiled at his candor. "We'll take care of you," Irv said.

The silence of the desert night was broken by a thousand-gun barrage that went on for five hours. The battle for El Alamein had started. On that same moonlit night of October 23, 1942, the submarine D-21 surfaced in Algiers harbor. The hatch opened and as the water ran from its conning tower five men emerged, inflated a rubber raft, and started rowing for the beach. D-21 slipped away silently, leaving only ripples.

As they neared the shore a light flashed, blinking twice, then darkness. It flashed again. They headed for the signal. As they pulled the raft out of the water and a man ran toward them, they drew their automatics.

"Good evening," the man said, slightly out of breath, swinging the flashlight, noting their drawn pistols. "I am from Saks Fifth Avenue."

Robert noted the pleasant French accent as the man waited for the countersign.

"We're interested in perfume," Sage said.

"I have the Chanel. Follow me." He turned and started up the beach. They holstered their weapons and pulled the raft with its supplies to an overturned sailboat.

"You can leave it here," the man said. They deflated it and stowed it under the hull of the wreck. Robert shouldered the powerful shortwave radio.

"I am Max," the man said, putting out his hand. He was of medium height and build and wore a fisherman's sweater and cap.

"We're Operation End Run," Sage said, shaking the hand. The others also took the hand that would either guide them or lead them to misfortune.

It was two in the morning when they slipped into the silent medina. A dog barked at their approach. In the apartment furnished with Moroccan leather hassocks, Max made mint tea and pleasant conversation until he asked for the date of the invasion.

"We're not sure," Sage said.

Max knew he was lying but didn't press. He'd be told when he had a need to know. After Robert sent a transmission to D-21 that they had rendezvoused with their contact, Max showed them detailed maps of the Algiers beaches.

"In the morning they were startled by the same Moorish melodies they'd heard in Spain, the same wail and beat. Robert and Mike went to the window, and moving a shade, looked into the street. Hot sunlight reflected off the white houses. Crowds of Arabs in multistriped jalabas shouted, haggled over prices in the market below, turned spits of roasting meat over braziers of hot coals watched by skinny dogs.

Mike smiled at Robert. Robert smiled back.

It was midnight, November 7, 1942, on the beach just east of Algiers, and the first Rangers were landing. With Max, the Operation End Run team guided them to the harbor installations, then to the city hall. By morning, they were in control of Algiers.

Donovan arrived and gave them battlefield commissions and commendations. Max took them to a restaurant in the French Quarter.

"Good as Maxim's in Paris," Donovan said. While they were eating, a well-dressed man approached. Donovan introduced him as Murphy.

"May I have a word with you, sir?" Murphy asked. Donovan went to the bar with him, had a whispered conversation, then returned as Murphy left.

Donovan's face was taut. "Hitler's gone into unoccupied France," he said. "Retaliation for North Africa."

On Valentine's Day 1943, Rommel counterattacked at the Kasserine Pass. His tough desert rats chewed up the inexperienced Americans, and he advanced at lightning speed, his new Tiger tanks leading. Donovan agreed to smuggle Max back to France, and the team was ordered to Souk-el-Arba, in Tunisia.

The C-47 landed at the primitive airstrip in the middle of a camel race. The desert encampment smelled of dung and gasoline. They made their way to the intelligence tent.

"Kidnap Rommel?" they all asked incredulously.

"Why not?" the colonel asked. "You guys have worked behind the lines."

"The British tried it with a whole commando unit and failed," Mike said heatedly.

"They failed because Rommel wasn't where he was supposed to be," the colonel said reasonably, stroking his large mustache. "They failed because of poor intelligence."

"Why is ours going to be any better?" Mike asked.

"Because you're going to do it," the colonel said simply. They looked at each other and shook their heads. "Look, I don't expect you guys to do the hot stuff. Just locate him, then I'll send in a Ranger group trained in low-level jumps for the squeeze play. We've got to do this now and we've got to do it fast, because he's kickin' the shit out of us. What do you say, Sage?"

Sage looked to his lieutenants. "Whattaya think, team?" They looked back doubtfully.

"I asked you, Sage," the G-2 colonel said. "You're their commander."

"I may be their commander, sir, but they do the work."

"It's insane," Mike said. There was a silence.

"His capture could appreciably shorten the war," the colonel argued back.

"For us, too," Mike said.

"I might have known," the colonel said cryptically.

"What?" Sage asked.

"That we'd blow it. We'll never get so close to him again."

"Send someone else," Sage said. "Get some volunteers."

"There isn't a better-trained team in North Africa."

The men looked at each other and against their better judgment agreed to the mission.

"Great!" The colonel beamed. "You know, they warned me that you guys were Commies, because of Spain. But I want you to know I'm proud to have you in my command."

He put them on a plane to Tebessa near Kasserine.

Kasserine was a mess.

Hundreds of burned-out vehicles lined the roads that twisted through the ravines. The wounded streamed back as reinforcements sought to stabilize the front and were dive-bombed by Stukas in the narrow passes.

"Jolly rugger, isn't it?" Captain Trimingham said as they followed their Arab guides past a burning Sherman tank. Trimingham was one of two British commando officers with them on what they called Operation Aida. It was Rommel's code word, and they hoped their radio transmissions behind enemy lines would be confused with his.

When Mike had seen the Arabs waiting for them at their rendezvous, their submachine guns slung like those of the Moors in Spain, it reminded him of having been captured and nearly executed in the churchyard. He still felt uneasy with them.

They started to climb the rugged terrain almost immediately. Some time after nightfall it grew quiet. In the dark they couldn't tell if they were on a narrow trail or following a small streambed.

Could the Arabs be leading them into a trap? Mike released the catch on his automatic pistol when the Arabs stopped. They'd motioned for silence. Now they could hear loose stones underfoot, and they moved rapidly up an incline.

A four-man patrol passed them, speaking German. They were behind the lines.

Robert set up his radio. He tested his signals to headquarters, then tried to pick up either *Donner*, Rommel's code for the Kasserine attack, or *Wustefuchs*, Desert Fox, his cable signature. Robert smiled when he picked up *Donner* coming in strongly, got a directional fix, and plotted it on their map.

The Arabs watched impassively.

Occasionally, they heard the rumble of trucks or the clank of tank treads moving to new positions, but for the most part the war had quieted for the night. They made their way through gullies and over ravines under an immense, starry sky. Robert thought of Antoine de Saint-Exupéry's poetic descriptions of flying through the Sahara at night with only the stars as guide and "a risk of death in a quest for a value greater than themselves." Funny how you remember certain lines, he thought. Is that what I'm about? He stopped when he nearly bumped into Mike on the narrow path.

It was two o'clock, and they'd stopped on a hill overlooking a camp. They could see the tents below them in the moonlight, but not much else.

"I think I'll have a look-see," Trimingham said.

"You'll stay right here," Irv told him.

"See here, lieutenant, I outrank you."

"You go down there, *captain*," Mike said, "and you'll get a bullet up your ass from me if the Germans don't get you."

"I'll have a word with the colonel about this," Trimingham said. He walked away a few paces and crouched down.

"He's trying to be a bit of a hero," Captain Stark, the other British officer, said. "His father's a general."

"He can be a hero on his own missions," Mike growled.

They zipped up their jackets against the desert cold and waited for first light.

In the morning, they discovered that the Arab guides were gone and that the camp was not an important headquarters. It was merely a communications center with ordinary soldiers having breakfast.

"Aida doesn't sing today" was the brief message Robert sent.

They found a shallow cave and tried to sleep. Robert and Mike sat back to back, their heads nodding. They could hear planes overhead and artillery in the distance.

"Don't go outside," Irv said to Trimingham, who stood against the light of the cave opening. "Too many spotter planes." Trimingham scowled over his large RAF mustache but sat down inside the cave.

"God, I'm hungry," Mike said, chewing on a fruit bar from their C rations. The radio came alive. It was Sage with new coordinates for a possible *Donner* HQ.

It took them five hours of steady hiking in the dark following the strong signals before they heard the cars and motorcycles coming and going from the front.

"Waiting for curtain to go up," Robert radioed.

They couldn't sleep in anticipation of what they'd see in the morning, but when they looked through their glasses wondering why it had grown silent, it was apparent the HQ had been moved. Robert's message "Fox escapes hounds" was answered by "Scratch Aida."

"Blast!" said Trimingham.

They hid as best they could in the scrub and at darkness set out for their own positions. After an all-night march they expected to be back behind their own lines, but Rommel's advance was so swift that in the morning they were still behind the enemy.

"We must be close," Irv said.

"Then let's keep going," Mike suggested. They all agreed, since they were out of food and water.

They followed a dry creekbed to the bottom of a ravine and had started to climb when Trimingham spotted a German sentry on a nearby ridge. Before anyone could stop him, Trimingham took a shot at him. The German dropped. Trimingham smiled like a child.

"Jol-ly!" he exclaimed.

"Are you crazy?" Mike asked furiously.

"He was an easy target."

"So are we!"

As if to confirm Mike's words, there was a rattle of small-arms fire. The bullets kicked up sand around them, and they started to run.

"I'm hit!" Milt cried out. Blood poured from the side of his head. Hiding behind scrub, Irv poured the contents of his sulfa packet over the wounded ear and quickly wound a white bandage around it.

"Can you run?" he asked.

"Yeah."

As they left their concealment, the bullets whizzed again. The gunners were following the white bandage.

Milt took another slug and went down. Robert stopped

and bent to him. The fire increased, and Robert clutched his thigh.

Mike dropped to his side. "The bad leg?"

"No."

"Can you move?"

"I don't think so."

They heard a tank's engines.

"Get going, Mike."

"I don't want to leave you."

"Then we'll both be captured."

Milt was having the same argument with Irv.

The tank was closer now, climbing a nearby hill.

"Go, before it's too late," Robert insisted. Mike shook his head regretfully, then crossed a streambed, followed by Irv. They watched from behind large rocks.

Robert and Milt tried to conceal themselves in some scrub, but Mike could see it wouldn't work. He and Irv cocked their automatics and aimed.

The huge gun on the Tiger tank appeared first, then the rest of it. It started to slide down the sandy slope toward Robert and Milt. Mike held his breath.

"Halt!" the gunner shouted to the tank commander. He'd seen the wounded men. The driver reversed his engines in a roar, and the tank stopped a few feet from them. Robert and Milt were sure they were going to be crushed. A machine gun was pointed at them, and two men came through the hatch and approached. They carried their machine pistols at the ready.

"*Amerikaner?*" one called.

"*Ja,*" Robert said. "*Verwundet.*"

The Germans cautiously examined their wounds and used their own first-aid kits to bandage them. The Germans took not only their weapons but their watches as well. Katherine had given Robert his for a birthday present.

Irv and Milt watched helplessly as the tankers tied Robert and Milt to the huge tank cannon like prize deer and then disappeared over the rise.

———————————

They were brought to a well-equipped surgery, where German doctors dressed and sewed their wounds. Milt's had bled a great deal from the bullet that had wounded his ear. The other bullets had torn away flesh but no bone.

"*Glücklich*," the doctor told them as an SS major entered.

They pretended to be deserters lost behind the lines, but Major Klein didn't believe them.

"Bad boys," he said, picking up their jackets. "I didn't know Uncle Sam issued Abercrombie & Fitch to his GIs."

"We bought them from officers," Milt said.

"Of course," the major said genially, letting them know by his tone he thought them liars.

They were saved further interrogation by the air-raid siren. As the bomber's engines were heard, the major rushed out. German casualties began to come in, and Robert and Milt were put aside. They managed to get rid of their cyanide capsules—giveaways that they were OSS men—in a container of bloody bandages. Robert almost laughed as he had when the capsules were first given to them. The label read, "Use with caution."

The all clear sounded, and the major returned to search them and question them again. Convinced finally that they were merely lousy deserters, he left in disgust, his low opinion of American soldiers confirmed.

"They should be shot, not healed," he muttered to the doctors.

A week later, as they flew over the Mediterranean with other prisoners, Robert could tell from the position of the sun that they were on their way to Italy.

———————

When Katherine got the telegram from the War Department, she was strangely relieved. Robert was out of the war. She looked at the wire again.

THE WAR DEPARTMENT REGRETS TO INFORM YOU THAT YOUR HUSBAND LT ROBERT THOMPSON 01168562 WAS WOUNDED IN ACTION AND CAP-

TURED BY THE ENEMY APPROX FEB 21 IN NORTH
AFRICA.

She went through Robert's papers looking for a phone
number.

"I'm sorry, General Donovan is not available," his secretary said. "He's out of the country and I don't have any
further information on your husband. I'm sorry."

She put down the phone and looked at Robert's typewriter. Would he ever use it again? She went into the living
room and looked at the photos of Robert and Mike, then
looked at the telegram again. Why was she carrying it
around with her? Was she holding on to some part of Robert? She put it on the coffee table, where it stared back at
her. "Damn Mike and Irv and their heroics!"

She felt as frustrated as when her brother had lain dying
in his room and they could do nothing for him.

She called Robert's parents, then Barkin.

Robert's mother heaved a long sigh, then started
weeping.

"Come right over," Barkin said. "You shouldn't be
alone."

Three weeks later a letter arrived from Mike telling her
that Robert's wound was not serious and he'd seen him
taken away alive. He didn't reveal any anxieties, and Katherine briefly wondered if he was withholding information. What Mike did reveal was his sense of loss, his feeling
that a part of him was missing.

Despite these sentiments, Katherine realized guiltily
that she was resentful that Mike was safe.

CHAPTER TWELVE

"*Raus! Raus!*" the guards called roughly, sounding like barking dogs.

The prisoners lined up along the tracks outside Naples, in single file, a guard every five yards, and then were loaded into freight cars. When no more could be wedged in, the doors were shut and locked and the number of prisoners was chalked on the wooden siding.

Some of the cars had barred windows through which sunlight filtered. Ventilation came from slits in the roof. They stood in the hot September sun for hours before starting to move north. They had to relieve themselves, and the cars began to stink.

The cars rattled and shook all night. Robert and Milt were hardly able to stand but because of the press of men could not fall. Robert's leg throbbed continually as he leaned against the wall in the dark limbo. He and Milt had been in a prison hospital in Italy since March, without proper medical attention.

———

Mike and Irv were sitting with their backs against the columns of the Greek temple at Paestum in the Gulf of Salerno on the second day of the invasion of Italy. They had been with Patton in the Sicilian campaign and had sailed from Palermo as part of VI Corps Intelligence. Now, on September 10, 1943, Mike smoked as they waited for Sage and listened to the artillery in the hills above them. He pinched out the glowing end of the cigarette with his fingers and field-stripped the butt.

Irv could read his mood.

"What's the matter?" he asked.

"I was just thinking about Robert."

Irv nodded.

It was night again as the train waited at the Brenner Pass and the border guards checked the prisoner manifests. They'd been fed only once that day—tepid water with some leafy flotsam.

"*Gemüsesuppe*," the guards had said, laughing. The "soup" had made them terribly thirsty. The men wondered if the Germans had intentionally used so much salt. Robert listened to the voices outside the cars to keep his mind off the pain in his leg. One of the guards was talking about his girl friend.

They slowly crossed into Austria. It was cooler, and their senses cleared, causing them to wonder where they were.

With daylight, they stopped, doors began to slide open, and there came the familiar command—"*Raus! Abfahlen!*" They fell out of the cars as a long line of guards watched them, guns pointing, dogs poised ready to attack.

It was a beautiful September morning on a rural road. They came to a crossing with various signs: MÜNCHEN 40 KM. DACHAU 6 KM. They turned left toward Dachau.

The village was small and quaint, out of a storybook. The German civilians looked at them as they passed, and they could hear children singing in a school. Outside the village, a sickly-sweet odor filled the air as the convoy passed rows of low buildings on both sides of the road. On their left, the buildings were of brick with smoking chimneys. The smell grew stronger. Beyond the barbed wire that lined the road they could see prisoners and guards. The prisoners wore striped uniforms.

"Must be a civil prison," Robert said to Milt. Milt looked at the prisoners and nodded.

"*Zie ruich!*" the guard on the truck commanded Robert. Robert looked at him and said nothing more.

The machine guns from the towers were aimed at them as they unloaded at the administration building. A captain strode before them, his high black boots brilliant in the sunshine.

"You are in Stalag 32. Obey regulations. Relax. You are out of the war." He turned smartly on his heels and left.

As they were marched to their barracks they noted the single strand of barbed wire surrounding the compound. They were already thinking of escape.

"It isn't electrified," Milt said quietly.

Robert nodded at a foot patrol with a dog, a huge Doberman. "But not insecure," he added.

They came to Barrack 97, a faded green building with broken windows. Inside they were delivered to Master Sergeant Biff Johnson. "Welcome to the summer camp," he laughed.

It was clean and spartan. Each wooden bed had a woolen blanket, and there was a wood-burning stove in the center of the cold room. It might have been a World War I facility. Robert noted the large cracks of light coming through the walls. I'd hate to be here in winter, he thought.

"You can take those two bunks over there," Johnson said, pointing to two neatly made beds near the door.

"What happened to the two guys who were in them?" Milt asked.

"Shot. Trying to escape," the former Air Force gunner said. "If you have such ideas, forget it, is my advice."

In the afternoon, Robert and Milt limped around the compound while the rest of the men threw a ball or passed the time trading cigarettes they never smoked. There was a road nearby and children of farm families walked home from school. The children laughed at them.

Dinner was a variation of lunch, with stale bread that tasted like pressed sawdust. At night, they listened to their nightly news broadcast on the BBC on a small radio secreted in the latrine. Air raids continued all over Germany, and the Allies were making progress in Italy.

On October 1 they heard that Naples was captured.

From the small Naples *palazzo* Mike and Irv had "requisitioned," the view from Posillipo was grand: ancient buildings, villas with gardens, monuments, and the harbor.

The *palazzo* owner, a Fascist official, had not liked leaving the marble entry, the enormous living room, the silk hangings and antique furniture, the kitchen that could serve a restaurant, and the cellar filled to overflowing with hanging cheeses, hams, salamis, cases of wine and champagne. His departure had been hurried. Mike and Irv had found warm bread in the brick oven. They feasted at the twelve-foot dining table on the black-market delicacies and drank two bottles of red wine.

"What we need is a servant," Mike said happily.

"The working class doesn't need servants."

"I'll cook, but I don't do dishes."

"Who needs to wash 'em? We'll just throw them out."

"Excellent idea, lieutenant," Mike said, cutting another giant piece of mortadella.

They drove their jeep down to see Sage, who'd installed himself in a luxurious hotel on the Esplanade of Santa Lucia overlooking the magnificent harbor. As they parked, they ran into Colonel Anderson, Sage's boss. Anderson had arrived when it was safe.

Mike and Irv had been among the first Americans into the city. They'd been supplying arms to the underground forces while the fighting was still going on. Colonel Anderson had tried to force them to work with Captain Trimingham again. "Trim" was now a major, working in Italy as an OSS liaison. Mike warned Anderson that the Englishman would end up on the casualty lists the first time his back was to them. Anderson didn't insist.

"Got anything lined up?" Sage asked as he sipped his bourbon and looked at the harbor traffic.

They smiled.

"Okay. What is it?"

"We're gonna turn the whole Italian railroad system into a huge information network," Irv said.

Sage's eyes widened.

"We want to get the dope on all German rail traffic

as soon as it comes through the Brenner Pass," Mike explained.

"How you gonna do that?" Sage asked incredulously.

"Does Macy's tell Gimbels?" Mike shrugged.

"You do that and Donovan'll kiss your ass in Macy's window!" Sage said, downing his drink.

They drove down the Spaccanapoli, past decaying monuments and baroque *palazzi* of the Spanish aristocracy, and turned down the Via Roma until the Vicoli, a spidery system of small streets and alleys of the Spanish Quarter. It was the working-class district, and from the decaying facade of a once splendid building, a red flag hung from Communist Party headquarters. There they met with the head of the Naples party, a veteran of the Garibaldi Battalion which had fought in Spain on the side of the Loyalists. Eugenio Reale was a heavyset, tough-looking man who'd been underground during the entire reign of Mussolini. After satisfying himself that Mike and Irv were indeed International Brigade veterans he took them to the headquarters of the railroad workers' union and suggested to Luigi Sabatini, head of the union, that he cooperate.

"For Comrade Reale, anything. For the Lincolns, my life," Sabatini said, embracing them.

Within a week every train that entered or left Italy was monitored, every station, railyard, and depot watched. Every rail worker became a spy. Unit designations, numbers of men and equipment, times of arrivals and departures—every German move by rail was reported to OSS headquarters in the former King's Palace in Caserta, north of Naples.

Allied Force Intelligence was doing handstands. Donovan flew in from his HQ in Algiers and promoted them.

Colonel Anderson looked at Mike and smiled. "And you told me only idiots get promoted," he jibed.

Then they started Operation Night Music. Mike named it after the Odets play he'd been in.

They recruited and trained twenty-two teams with radios for work behind the enemy lines. Mike developed cover stories. He worked with a costume designer from the Naples Opera House in gathering northern Italian clothing, mostly with Rome labels, to outfit the teams. Carla Romanelli was twenty-five, a southern Italian with olive skin, dark hair, sparkling eyes, and boundless energy. She was a female Mike, without his calculation. He loved being with her. Perhaps it was a reverse narcissism. In bed she was a match for him. To her, sex was fun. She was gay, playful, lighthearted, and intelligent. He had a better time with her than with any other woman he'd ever known.

At the reopening of the Naples opera, Mike hosted a party for the company at his *palazzo* with treasures from the basement. Champagne flowed and the eighteenth-century piano tinkled Mozart under the hands of the conductor. Mike sang aria after aria with the company. It was a magical evening in which he felt like a Medici.

"You were wonderful," Carla said at five in the morning as they ascended the marble stairs to Mike's bedroom.

"So were you," he said, reaching for her.

"Not on the steps." She laughed and ran to his bedroom.

———————————

It was getting cold in Bavaria, so the Germans took away their blankets. By the middle of November it was below zero outside at night and almost as cold in the barracks as the wind swept through the broken windows and the cracks in the walls. Some tried to sleep under their mattresses.

German Corporal Eberhard said they were lucky. "It's colder in Russia," he said.

Robert and Milt had volunteered to work on a neighboring farm, as their only chance for a little real food and the possibility of escape.

The wind cut through them as they rode on the open truck.

"*Vas ist das Geruch?*" Robert asked the guard as they passed the camp near Dachau.

The guard laughed. "*Brot. Das ist eine Bakerie.*"

"He says the smell is baking bread," Robert translated.

"*Welche gefangene bleiben in Lager?*" Robert asked.

"*Politische.*"

"He says the prisoners are politicals."

"Maybe." Milt shrugged.

They were dropped off at the farm without a guard. The farmer was expected to keep an eye on them—and to use his shotgun or rifle if necessary—though the military was not expecting escape attempts, since the chance of success was so small. So far, every attempt had failed and had been punished cruelly either by death or long-term isolation. The military prided itself on strict security.

The first week, the farmer was nervous and carried his shotgun all the time. But when he discovered his prisoner-laborers could milk a cow and had carpentry skills, he put them to work restoring his barn.

Willi Baumeister had been a jovial man, but the war was wearing him down. He was a veteran of the first "great conflict" and had been an early staunch supporter of Hitler's. But he had lost his first son at Stalingrad, and his second son, a smiling lieutenant whose picture was in the dining room, was also in Russia.

Willi's wife was a taciturn woman given to sudden bursts of tears as she embraced her ten-year-old boy, Frank. Frank suffered the embraces silently.

Soon, Robert and Milt were invited into the kitchen to share what meager food the family had, and Frank began to look at Robert as a replacement for his missing brothers. Robert taught him the rudiments of carpentry, and they did afternoon chores together when Frank returned from school.

By the first week of December it was bitterly cold. Robert and Milt had no outer clothing. The Germans had kept the Donovan jackets. They suffered in the freezing wind, and Willi felt sorry for them. He also worried that he might lose such good workers to illness.

"*Kommt mit uns,*" Willi said, leading them into the house and up to the older boy's carefully preserved bedroom. Willi gave them his son's woolen sweaters and trousers, as Frank smiled at them.

The large photo in the room of the two brothers, their arms around each other, moved Robert deeply, but the hanging uniform in the closet brought him up short. It promised escape.

But how could they use it? What kind of story could they

cook up for Milt, who didn't know German? Could he be a prisoner in Robert's custody? They worked on several stories, none of which was convincing.

"You've got a better chance alone," Milt said, and Robert reluctantly agreed. He decided that between Christmas and New Year would be the best time for an attempt. Guards would be on leave and the atmosphere more relaxed.

"But you know it's death if they catch you in that uniform," Milt said.

Robert nodded.

———————

Robert was whittling a walking stick for himself and a sailboat that was to be Frank's Christmas present. The afternoon light came through the window in the barn as Robert carved.

"Who is in the camp?" Robert asked in German.

Frank paused, looked about, and then answered *"Juden."*

"Juden?"

"Ja."

Milt stopped sawing at the mention of Jews.

"What is that smell?" Robert asked.

Frank looked away again, unsure if he should answer Robert's question. He looked back at Robert, who waited. *"Juden brennan,"* Frank finally said quietly.

Robert and Milt looked at each other.

"Ober sagen zie nicht meine Vater."

"Don't worry. I won't tell your father you told us," Robert said in German.

That evening, the men in the barracks refused to believe the smell was burning flesh.

Two days later, when Frank came home from school to greet Robert and Milt, a sour-looking Willi led his son into the house. When Frank came into the barn later to milk the cows, he was sullen. Robert asked what was wrong, putting his hand on the boy's shoulder.

Frank shrugged it angrily away. "I'll never tell you anything again!"

Milt had been right. There was an informer in the barracks, and Willi had been upbraided by the local Gestapo for his son's disclosure to the Americans. Robert took the child in his arms. Frank did not resist the gesture, though he looked away.

"You did the right thing," Robert said gently, "and I didn't tell your father. Someone else did."

Frank buried his head in Robert's shoulder. He wanted to believe him.

The week before the holidays, the guards began to leave the camp and only a skeleton crew was left. On Christmas Day they assigned only half a day's work. Robert and Milt stared at the concentration camp's inmates shivering in the wind. The chimneys smoked even today.

After morning chores they'd gone inside. Willi had built a fire in the sitting room where a small pine tree stood, decorated with strips of cloth. The sailboat sat under the tree. Frau Baumeister had made Robert and Milt woolen scarves. The fire crackled and there was a Brahms symphony on the radio. It began to snow. Then they heard the bell outside.

Willi went to the window, puzzled. "*Ist der Postmann,*" he said, frowning.

He went outside and returned with a blue envelope. Frau Baumeister trembled visibly as her husband tore open the fragile paper.

He put his hands to his face without a sound. Then he sobbed, "*Ist tot. Hermann ist tot.*"

Frau Baumeister went to her husband and embraced him, closing her eyes. Frank joined them slowly, putting his arms around their waists.

Robert wanted to embrace them himself. He could imagine a similar scene in Iowa. He looked at Milt, who was as moved as he was, but in that sobbing silence they felt like intruders. They left for the barn, eyes wet.

That night the radio played in the barracks. "I'll be home for Christmas," Bing Crosby sang on that Christmas Day, 1943.

———————

Katherine spent the day with the Barkins.

———————

In Naples, Mike cooked. He sang as he chopped, stirred, checked the Polish goose that was roasting, and puréed chestnuts. He had traded a provolone cheese for the goose, which had been found at Nazi headquarters. Mike laughed as he added sausage to the stuffing. It had been a long trip for that goose.

He was feeling good. The only thing missing was Robert. As he put another record on the phonograph, he thought of Katherine's letter, in which she'd told him she hadn't heard from Robert in months. Where could he be?

The Puccini was loud enough to drown out Carla's footsteps in the kitchen. She put her arms around his chest and nuzzled his neck.

"Taste," he said, giving her some stuffing.

"Hmmm . . . *bene* . . . *molto bene*. You are some cook. I marry you tomorrow."

"I'm busy tomorrow, but maybe next week."

"Next week, I am busy," she laughed. "What time are they coming?"

"Four. We start with champagne and *antipasti* . . . then *suppe di pesce* . . . the goose and my special ricotta cheese-cake. Tonight we are doing *The Barber of Seville*. I am playing Don Basilio, *maestro di musica*."

"I can't believe Giorgio gave the part up to you."

"I bribed him. With a salami."

CHAPTER THIRTEEN

Robert and Milt shared an onion.

Willi had gone to town with Frank, and there would never be a better time. Robert went upstairs to the bedroom while Frau Baumeister stood at her kitchen stove. His heart pounded as he mounted the stairs, trying to keep them from squeaking.

He worked quickly, stuffing the uniform in a military pack, going to the closet and taking boots and a small chest. He'd rehearsed all this before. He knew the chest contained family memorabilia, photos, baptismal certificates, military papers, and the Baumeisters' savings.

That gave him the greatest problem. He'd never stolen anything in his life. His hands trembled as he took half the money, not even counting it. It was necessary for his survival. "God, forgive me," he murmured.

He put the chest back, took a scarf from the dresser, and left, carrying boots and pack downstairs. He ran to the barn.

There he got dressed.

Milt looked at him appraisingly. "You could fool me," he said. "You've got about four hours." The truck always came promptly at five.

Robert stuffed the civilian clothes in the pack, checked the military ID in his pocket and turned to Milt. They embraced.

"Good luck," Milt breathed emotionally.

Robert ran to the woods in back of the barn and then

headed for the road to Dachau, some distance from the house. It wasn't long before a farmer's truck picked him up.

———

When Willi and Frank got back to the farm, Frank went to the barn to look for Robert and then ran to the house. He looked downstairs, and still not finding him, he went upstairs to his brother's room without knowing why. His heart sank when he discovered the uniform gone. He sat on the bed trying to understand why Robert would leave. He went downstairs, passing the kitchen, where his parents sat in silence. There were many long silences now that their second son had been killed. Frank said nothing about the missing uniform.

———

The farmer had dropped Robert off in town, and he sat at a bus stop. Were people looking at him, or was it his imagination? The young, pretty woman who sat next to him on the bench seemed to be glancing at him from the corner of her eye. A group of drunk and rowdy soldiers neared them, pointed at the young woman, and laughed as one of them made an obscene gesture.

The people on the bench grew uncomfortable. As the soldiers approached, the young woman slipped her arm through Robert's as if she were with him. The possibility of a fight threw him into near panic. It would bring police and discovery. But either her haughty look or the fact that Robert was a wounded soldier dissuaded them. Robert relaxed his grip on his walking stick as the soldiers continued down the street.

"*Danke*," she said, removing her hand.

"*Bitte schön*," he replied quietly. He was relieved to see the Munich bus coming toward them.

As they lined up to board, Robert heard a raucous alarm. It was an SS jeep followed by a truckload of soldiers. He hunched into his collar, heart beating.

———

Willi had looked everywhere for Robert. Both Milt and Frank maintained ignorance. Now Willi was in a panic as he explained to Frank and his wife that he'd be blamed, perhaps put in jail, or their rations cut. They'd have to lie. With a sinking heart, he rode his bicycle to a neighbor's farm where there was a phone. Within half an hour the road was filled with soldiers.

————

A police car screamed by as Robert got on the bus.

"*Vohinen?*" the driver asked, ready to punch a ticket.

"*Nach München,*" Robert replied, automatically offering to pay. The driver looked at him curiously and waved him inside. Robert caught the look of suspicion. Soldiers must ride for nothing, he thought. God, please don't let me be caught over something so stupid. He sat down next to a window and adjusted his arm in the sling he'd made from the dresser scarf as part of his "character." The young woman sat across from him.

After a tense journey in which the bus seemed to stop everywhere and to be filled with old men trying to make conversation with him about his Iron Cross and Stalingrad ribbons, Robert finally disembarked at Marienplatz, remembering his limp, using his walking stick, crossing to a broad, crowded avenue, and losing himself in the holiday crowds.

He went to a barbershop for a military haircut and shave. Would the barber slice his throat if he knew he was an escaped American? He was relieved when the chair was upright and the man smilingly patted his cheeks with 711 cologne.

Back in the street, he was waylaid by two drunken soldiers and steered by them into a noisy beerhall for a drink. The situation was surreal. He had fought Fascists since 1937, and now he was drinking with them in a Munich beerhall. The Bavarian music was loud. A tipsy soldier attempted a "shoe dance" and fell onto the sawdust-filled floor amid gales of laughter from other soldiers. One of his companions slapped him on the back and ordered more beer. He had to get out.

"Ich mus gehen," he said, escaping their camaraderie, the music, and the insanity of the situation. He headed for the train station.

PARIS   2200   32

Robert went to the ticket window and waited in line.

"Orden," the man at the window asked when his turn came and he'd asked for a ticket to Paris.

"Verloren."

The man looked at Robert sorrowfully, shaking his head, as Robert told him he'd lost his orders. Robert offered to pay. The ticket seller obviously had doubts but looked at the sling, the Iron Cross, the ribbons.

"Ein Moment, bitte," he said as he crossed to a uniformed superior at a desk. They conferred for a moment; then the superior picked up a phone as he glanced at Robert. Robert's heart stopped, but the man for some reason reconsidered, hanging up and nodding to the ticket seller.

Robert realized he'd been sweating.

The ticket seller gave him a form to sign. Robert signed Hermann Baumeister's name and unit designation.

"Kennkarte?"

Robert gave him the ID, making much of the wounded arm in the sling. He hoped the man wouldn't look at the photo too closely. The ticket seller was more interested in the signature. It didn't match.

"Meine Wunde," Robert said as if in explanation. The man looked at Robert's arm, scratched his nose and small Hitler mustache, and came to the conclusion that this soldier obviously didn't need any more trouble than he'd seen. He issued the tickets.

"Danke," Robert said, trying not to show his relief. *"Danke sehr."*

"Danken Gott," the man said quietly and nodded for the next person to come forward.

Robert looked at the station clock. It was almost seven. He bought a cheap watch in a station shop.

Exactly at nine, the air-raid sirens sounded. He followed a long line of civilians and soldiers to the tunnels of the station. Sitting in the narrow passageway, they were silent, listening to the sounds above. A sergeant shared some chocolate with Robert. He thought of Mike suddenly and wondered where he was. Mike loved chocolate.

At nine-fifteen the bombs started falling, and they could hear the answering antiaircraft. Robert looked at the stoic faces as they waited for the raid to end. Then he saw the woman from the bus stop staring at him. It was the stare that had drawn his attention and turned his head. She smiled. He smiled back. Was she following him? Her presence was a mystery. If she was trying to pick him up, she was going to extraordinary lengths to do so. She licked her lips as they looked at each other. Robert finally broke the connection by closing his eyes.

The all clear sounded, and the hundreds filed back into the station. If the train was on time, he'd leave in half an hour. He wondered about the woman as he watched the activity in the street. She'd disappeared. Back in the station he noticed two military police patrols. One of them, a poster version of idealized Hitler Youth, scanned him with cold blue eyes. Robert returned the gaze as he limped past. He was not stopped, but he was sure the throbbing of his temples must be visible as he nearly stumbled on the slight grade down to the track.

The Vienna–Paris express rolled in. Robert boarded through shrouds of steam, still gripped by the fear of discovery, closed his eyes, and rehearsed his story again as he sat in his compartment.

It did not fill up. A stout, well-dressed sausage of a man with a Nazi Party badge in his lapel sat opposite him, a thin, shrewish-looking woman in black sat on the inside corner, and an SS lieutenant sat at Robert's side. Only seven minutes late, the train left the station.

———————————

Just outside Augsburg, the woman from the bus stop entered the compartment and sat next to Robert. He was alarmed and intrigued. She began reading *Flowers of Evil*, tilting the French text toward him so that he could see it. Was it a code? he wondered, his imagination rampaging.

Did he resemble someone else she was supposed to meet? A misstep could mean disaster.

Burying himself in the *Berliner Zeitung* he'd bought, he thought of Katherine. Was she in the kitchen now, studying? The woman sitting next to him was close to her in age, but worlds apart in her well-coiffed, calculated, mysterious ways. Did Katherine have a life outside the hospital? Did she see anyone besides Alex and Barkin? The woman read and said nothing to him.

Near midnight, the woman left the compartment, to return with a picnic hamper. On the stroke of midnight, the SS lieutenant popped the cork of the Dom Pérignon and poured into elegant glasses. The woman smiled at Robert as she handed him one.

"Heil Hitler!" they toasted.

Robert choked. They looked at him in alarm. He pointed to his windpipe as if the bubbly liquid had made him gag.

They toasted Victory in the New Year!

Robert sipped. His hunger raged as she distributed caviar from Russia, ham from Poland, salami and cheese from Italy, *foie gras* from France on crackers from Holland.

The wine went to his head, and Robert escaped to an open window down the corridor.

"Where are you going?" she asked in German, joining him.

"Paris."

"Me too." She smiled. "Do you speak French?"

"Yes."

"I thought so." She beamed. "That's why I held the book so you could see it. I'm never wrong about people." She had a nice smile and a husky voice like Marlene Dietrich's.

"Amid the jackals, panthers, all hell's devices." He quoted from the French, knowing it would impress her.

"Merveilleux!" she exclaimed delightedly. "We are going to have a good time together. What's your name?"

"Hermann. Hermann Baumeister."

"Ilse Frank," she said, extending a strong hand. "Did you learn French in Paris?"

"No, school. What are you going to do in Paris?" Safer to shift the conversation to her.

"Getting married." She shrugged.

"Why are you following me, then?"

"You're very good-looking and you intrigue me."

Robert laughed. As they entered a tunnel the lights went out and she pressed against him suddenly. She sought his lips. He could feel their softness in the glancing kiss.

"I'm married," he said, taken by surprise.

"How quaint. But I've always felt faithfulness is for dogs."

Robert laughed.

They returned to the compartment together. The other passengers wondered if there was a relationship between them.

It was two-fifteen in the morning when they left Stuttgart. Robert looked out of the window and fell asleep again. He awoke to find himself growing hard. Ilse was stroking him. He put his hand on hers but didn't stop her as she worked open the buttons and massaged him with strong hands. He hadn't had an erection in months, and now was excited. She bent and took him in her mouth, her hand cupping his testicles.

With her head in his hands he stroked her hair gently, felt her smooth skin and working jaws, tried not to make any sounds. He couldn't tell if the others were asleep, and he bit his hand as he climaxed in order not to cry out. His orgasm was extraordinary, seemed to go on endlessly. He fell asleep again, exhausted, as she rebuttoned his pants. When he woke, he wasn't sure if it was a dream.

But the Gestapo officer checking papers with a Waffen SS was no dream. It was four-ten in the morning, and the train was at the French border. When the officer came to Ilse, he clicked his heels.

"Frau Frank," he said. *"Guten Morgen."* Was there anything he could do to make her more comfortable? And wasn't she supposed to be in first class?

"Ja." She smiled enigmatically.

"My compliments to the colonel," he said, saluting, and turned to Robert. "Papers, please," he asked, cold and official once more. Robert showed him his tickets. "Those won't do. I want your orders."

"I lost them," Robert said, trying to suppress his panic.

The Gestapo man narrowed his eyes, beginning to have the scent of the hunt.

"Identification." His voice was now cutting.

Robert fumbled for it. Tension began to grow in the car.

The officer looked at the picture, clearly unsatisfied. Noting Robert's walking stick and sling, he asked the others to leave the compartment. The Gestapo man drew down the shade of the doors. He ordered Robert to drop his trousers and examined the wounds on his legs. One was freshly healed, the others clearly older. The officer pointed to them.

Robert decided on boldness. "Spain," he said.

"Spain?" He'd never met anyone who'd fought in Spain.

"With the Condor Legion."

"And this wound?" He pointed to Robert's other leg.

"Plan Donnerschlag." Robert knew from his reading of the *Berliner Zeitung* that Plan Donnerschlag was the planned breakout of the Sixth Army from Stalingrad.

The Gestapo man stroked his chin and motioned for Robert to raise his trousers. Finding real wounds on his legs, he didn't ask to see Robert's arm. He opened the door, and the others took their seats once more, wondering at the outcome. The officer then made a great show of examining Robert's ID, obviously suspecting that Robert was a deserter, Iron Cross or no Iron Cross.

"Come with me," he ordered.

Robert's breathing stopped, and he began to tremble.

"One moment, please, lieutenant," Ilse said. "What's the problem?" Her voice rang with authority. He showed her Robert's ID. She shrugged. "He's with me."

Robert started breathing again.

The Gestapo man looked at her, clearly disappointed. He was losing an opportunity to show his superiors how alert he was, but his superior happened to be Colonel Volker, the man Ilse was engaged to. He now understood why she was in the wrong compartment. It was an assignation. If this sergeant was her lover and he revealed it, it could bring only trouble. Volker was the head of the Gestapo in Paris, and Ilse was the daughter of the party administrator for Holland. He gave the ID back to Robert, telling him sternly to get a new photo, saluted Frau Frank once more, and quickly closed the door behind him.

"*Danke*," Robert said as the others in the car looked at them.

"It's nothing." She shrugged. But her eyes searched his.

A half hour later, they crossed into France.

As they left Nancy, a porter announced the opening of the first-class dining car. It was filled with high-ranking officers and party officials. Robert was aware of the stares, and realized that Ilse liked to cause talk about herself.

"So . . . who are you?" she asked. Robert tried to look blank. "I know you're not Sergeant Baumeister."

"Who am I, then?"

"I don't know. But I was right to be intrigued. You are a man of mystery."

Robert laughed. "I'll try to remain so, to continue your interest," he said playfully.

It was her turn to laugh.

"What were you doing in Dachau?" he asked.

"Visiting a lover. He works in the camp."

Robert slowly removed his hand from hers. "What does he do there?"

"Administration. You have no idea how much work there is, the endless lists: gold from teeth, clothing, furs, spectacles, names and numbers, freight car schedules, increased production norms. Eichmann is very ambitious. My friend was so busy it hardly made the trip worthwhile. But I must say, there was something special about making love in the midst of all that death. Karl says he hardly notices the smell anymore."

Robert felt a revulsion he'd never known before.

"You think I'm perverted?"

"I think you're different," he answered carefully.

"Good." She smiled. "I don't want to be ordinary."

"Why are you getting married?"

"To please my father. He thinks Rudy Volker is a good

political match. Besides, Rudy will allow me to follow my own . . . pursuits."

He nodded. "Why did you intercede for me?"

Ilse smiled and took his hand again, not caring that others saw the gesture. "I'd rather have you in my hands than in the Gestapo's."

"What a little devil you are." He forced himself to gaiety, pressed her hand. The trip wasn't over.

"We'll both be in Paris. We can see each other," she said.

The food arrived. Despite his revulsion, he found himself attacking the croissants, the eggs, butter, and *confiture*. Hunger has its own morality, he thought.

Ilse didn't eat. She smoked and watched him.

Later that morning, they sped through the Château-Thierry country where his own father had fought. The sunlight came through the window and fell in broken slants on Ilse's blond hair. He couldn't rid himself of the image of her making love at Dachau.

His pulse quickened as they approached Paris. Ilse had gone back to her compartment in first class. The others stretched. He looked at the houses, the chimney pots smoking innocently in the winter air. The train rolled into the station.

He looked for Ilse on the platform, knowing he was safer with her. There were a lot of military police, and she could be his passport. He breathed deeply when he saw Ilse walking toward him with a Gestapo sergeant carrying her bags. She smiled at him and put her arm through his as they fell into step together. Then he saw it, old engine 77, the locomotive that had taken them from Paris to Perpignan. The old warhorse was still running.

A Mercedes staff car waited for her. As the sergeant loaded her luggage, he watched them out of the corner of his eye. Was that a note she'd slipped the *Panzergrenadier*? Who was he?

Robert took her hand and the piece of paper. "Thanks for everything," he said seriously.

"Call me."

He smiled and nodded.

The staff car pulled away. Robert looked at the bright Paris street and the clear blue sky and was overwhelmed. He was here! He'd made it! His eyes filled with tears.

"*Odéon, s'il vous plaît,*" he commanded a taxi.

It was twelve-thirty when he entered the Café Montparnasse.

CHAPTER FOURTEEN

The commandant of Stalag 32 was in trouble. So was Obersturmführer Wolff of the Gestapo. It was over a week since Robert's escape, and they hadn't found any trace of him. Headquarters for Allied War Prisoners in Berlin was in a fury. The escape would encourage others.

After a meeting in the commandant's office, Sergeant Schmidt was sent to the barracks with news that Robert had been shot. He'd been crossing a river and his body swept away.

"I don't buy it," Milt said.

"Why not?" Sergeant Johnson asked.

"Have you seen the ice outside? All the rivers are frozen."

"Maybe he's under the ice."

The others listened to the argument, divided in their opinions.

"They want us to keep thinking they're invincible and escape is impossible. I don't believe that crap about his body being lost."

Two days later, Milt was shipped to another camp, further convinced there was an informer in the barracks. Allied War Prisoners, Berlin, informed the International Red Cross in Geneva that Lieutenant Robert Thompson had been shot while attempting escape and described the events. Geneva informed Washington and wrote a letter of condolence to Katherine.

———————

Katherine had imagined this moment. When she opened the blue envelope with the red cross and the Geneva postmark, she felt the release of a tension, the bow unbent, the spring uncoiled. She sank to a kitchen chair and read the letter again, letting it slip from her hands. Her head fell to the table, and she covered it with her arms and began to sob, tears streaming uncontrollably. She lurched blindly to their bedroom and fell on the bed, body trembling, her lungs burning. It was hours before she rose unsteadily to wash her face. There was a dull pain in her chest as she picked up the phone to call Barkin.

"Hello," he said sleepily. Katherine was silent. "Hello," he asked again, a note of annoyance creeping into his voice.

"Who is it?" his wife asked from her side of the bed.

"I don't know."

"It's Katherine."

"Katherine! What's the matter? I didn't even recognize your voice."

"Robert's dead."

"I'll be right over."

Barkin stayed with Katherine until the following morning, when he had to leave for the hospital for surgery. They'd talked and wept all night. When he left, Katherine called Robert's parents.

It was winter dark when the phone rang, and Fred Thompson knew. The shrill ring in the cold bedroom shriveled his heart. When it rang again, husband and wife looked at each other with the fear of confirmation. Afterward, as he put down the receiver, he seemed to shrink visibly.

Robert's mother spent the entire day in her son's old room, rocking slowly, her arms around herself.

———————

It was cold as Katherine walked toward St. Luke's Hospital. The February wind came off the Hudson in swift gusts and swept down the Village streets. It had taken over six weeks for the letter to reach her through the bureaucracies of Berlin, Geneva, and Washington. Her cheeks and nose were red as she entered, and the receptionist smiled at her as she did every day.

Katherine could see Dr. Evans through the partition and knew Barkin was on the phone with him from the way Evans glanced at her. She'd have to suffer his condolences, and then word would spread.

"I'm sorry," he said. "Do you want to go home?"

"No, I don't want to go home. I want to work," she said firmly.

He nodded.

There were already glances of curiosity from the other residents who were gathering for morning rounds. They were on pediatric service, and as Katherine looked at the sick little faces she nearly broke into tears again as she realized she and Robert would never have a child.

At the end of the sixty-hour tour of duty she took Kenny Schwartz's rounds. He had a wedding to go to, and Katherine offered to take his tour. She did not want to go home yet. The other residents now knew, and they were subdued with her, which made her angry. She didn't want to be treated in any special way. Death was a fact of life. They should know that.

Alex came to the hospital. He was on his way to an opening, and in his long black coat and brilliant hat he looked like a dashing European impresario. He held her hand. "I'd like to do Robert's play again. As a kind of memorial. It was so botched the first time."

"If you really like it," she said.

"I do. When can I take you to dinner?"

"Soon, Alex. Soon. Let me get myself together. I don't want to bore you, playing the bereaved widow. I want to be good company."

"You are, no matter what role you play." He pressed her hand warmly. Was she misinterpreting the gesture, or was Alex interested in her? Katherine put it out of her mind and kissed him on the cheek.

Evans forbade her taking still another tour. She went home to face the apartment.

In the living room, she looked at the photos of Robert

and Mike. No tears came, just a dull longing. She sat on the couch to write Mike after putting Robert's favorite Mozart quintet on the phonograph.

She loved and hated the apartment, with its reminders of their relationship. She spent more time at the hospital, took the most difficult cases, sat all night at a child's bedside as she had at Robert's in Madrid. She lost weight. Food held no interest. Alex took her to see *Jacobowsky and the Colonel*, but she found no humor in the relationship between the small Jew and the Nazi colonel. The audience's laughter irritated her.

Finally, in the first week of May, she noticed the buds on the sycamore trees as she walked to the hospital. The air had changed, the wind from the Hudson now a fresh breeze. She looked around her. There were colors, sounds, faces, movements of life she had blocked out. She'd lived her own death, and now she must begin to heal.

Mike and Irv returned from Anzio to Naples. Donovan had commandeered a PT boat to see the action there. Katherine's letter was waiting. Mike sat on the huge bed in the silk-lined room holding a glass of red wine, which spilled as he read the first line: "Dear Mike, Robert is dead." As the red stain spread, he reread the letter, then stared at the wall feeling empty.

"Irv," he called with effort.

"Yeah?" Irv called back from his room.

"Robert's dead."

Irv rushed in, face drawn.

"Shot, trying to escape. Katherine wrote me."

Irv put his hand on Mike's shoulder. "I'm sorry," he said. He'd felt the same vacantness when Pete had been taken away.

"He was in a camp in Germany."

"Any word on Milt?"

"No."

Carla arrived later. It was dark, but Mike had not turned on any lights. "What's the matter?" she asked.

"My best friend's dead," he said without expression.

She put her arms around him. "I'm sorry, *caro*." She held him all night, held him as he shook, held him as he sobbed and trembled. In the morning, he drank black coffee and drove alone to the harbor. He sat on a bench staring at the harbor traffic, listening to the high-pitched squeal of gulls as they swooped in long arcs among the ships. He sat all day, and when it got dark he wandered the dock area.

His depression went on for weeks. Even food and sex had no interest for him. At headquarters they asked Irv what was wrong. They nodded in understanding, not really comprehending. They were office soldiers.

Then suddenly the color came back to Mike's face. It was as though an illness had taken its course.

"Let's have a party," he said to Irv and Carla.

But he didn't sing.

———————————

Barkin had Sunday-afternoon gatherings of musicians, painters, writers, actors, political activists. Katherine began going on her off Sundays. As she and Alex entered the large Riverside Drive apartment overlooking the Hudson, Barkin crossed to her, kissed her cheeks, appraised her professionally.

"Better." He nodded. "You're looking better." He led her into the crowded living room with its windows facing the sun-bright river. The intense light set off a couple standing near them in animated conversation. Katherine's heart lurched. Was it a trick of light that made the man look so like Robert?

"Katherine, do you know Larry Peters?" Barkin asked.

Slowly, she put out her hand.

"Nice to meet you," Larry said, taking it, holding it. There was a warmth to his smile and a softness in his brown eyes. He was wearing a worn tweed jacket and a work shirt like Robert's. Katherine felt a stab of pain as he continued to hold her hand.

Katherine noticed the paint pigment under his finger-nails and recovered. "You're a painter?" she asked.

He looked at his hands. "Sorry. I can never get them clean."

"You're not supposed to get them clean," Barkin said. "It's a badge of honor." Barkin got serious. "Larry's a ter-rific painter. He's the best new abstractionist I know."

"What do you do?" Larry asked softly.

"I'm a doctor. I'm a resident at St. Vincent's."

"I don't live far from there," Larry said. "I've got a loft on Hudson Street." Barkin watched Katherine's mixed feel-ings. "If you'd like to come over some time . . ." He let the invitation trail off as he weighed her reaction.

"Call me. I'm in the book," Katherine found herself say-ing. "On Perry Street." She excused herself and joined Alex, who'd been chatting with an attractive young harpist from the New York Philharmonic.

Barkin told Larry about Robert.

———————

"Well . . . finally reached you," Larry said over the phone. "I've been trying for two weeks."

"Sorry. I'm not home often."

"How've you been?" he asked.

"Busy." Katherine was flustered. She felt her holding on to Robert was in danger, and she wasn't ready to let go.

"You asked me to call," he said, sensing her distance. "Were you serious?"

She could tell he was ready to run from rebuff. "Uh . . . yes, I was. I mean, I'm glad you called."

"When can you come over?"

"Let me look at my schedule. Can I call you back?"

He didn't know if it was a stall but gave her the number.

Katherine was in the bedroom. She looked at Robert's typewriter, at his clothes hanging in the closet, and drew a deep breath before going into the living room to sort out her feelings. Robert would understand. Understand! He's dead, Katherine! she argued with herself. Then she called Larry.

When Katherine rang his bell, he came down to the warehouse entrance wearing a navy-blue wool turtleneck and baggy corduroys.

Katherine had dressed carefully, casual but neat, her hair pulled back in a bun.

"Hi," he said, taking her hand.

She liked the feel of it as they rose in the freight elevator to the top floor.

The space was huge and the light fantastic. It streamed in from the skylights and windows facing the river. In a corner was Larry's living area; the rest was work space. It smelled of paint, turpentine, and coffee.

Katherine looked about her. The walls were hung with large canvases. She crossed to an easel and looked at the painting on it. The brushstrokes were vigorous and the canvas vibrantly colorful.

"What do you think?" he asked.

"I don't know yet," she said.

"While you make up your mind, I'll get you something. Wine or coffee? I also baked some cookies."

Katherine burst into laughter. It was her first full, spontaneous laugh in months. How dear, she thought.

"I like your laugh," he said, and went to the kitchen area.

Katherine looked at the paintings on the walls, which had the same vigor as the canvas on the easel, the same assurance. The strokes knew where they were going, the palette was clear, warm, and sensuous.

"Cream?" he called out.

"No. Just black, please."

"Shall we have it over here?"

"Sure." She walked to the living area. The space seemed endless. She sat in a Victorian chair at a round oak table and sipped coffee, listening to the Bach he'd put on.

"Try my cookies."

Katherine took an oatmeal cookie and found herself relaxing. She closed her eyes. His chair creaked as he leaned toward her. She opened them. He took a cookie. She wasn't sure if she was disappointed. She looked around at the platform bed, bookcases, furniture.

"I made them," he said.

She looked at his hands. They were large and square, a worker's hands.

"I'm sorry about your husband," he said softly.

She nodded, thinking of Robert's hands.

The silences were long but not uncomfortable. Larry went along with them, not forcing entry into her mood. As they sat at the table, occasionally talking, the light changed and began to glow orange. Katherine crossed to the windows facing the river. The sun had begun to set, and she looked out at the river traffic.

How graceful boats are, she thought. She heard the floorboards creak behind her. As he put his large, gentle hands on her shoulders, she quivered despite herself. He brushed her neck with his lips.

"Please, don't," she said quietly.

He nodded, and they stood watching the river until it was dark and the lights of New Jersey came on, and she was overwhelmed by sadness and peace and calm.

What a magical place, she thought, and realized for the first time in months that she was lonely.

Though Mike's depression had lifted, Irv realized that he had again become the Mike of Spain, the tempter of death. Instead of merely conceiving guerrilla operations, he now insisted on carrying them out, dropping behind the German lines by parachute or sneaking through them with small partisan groups, often dressed as one.

"They'll shoot you on the spot if you're captured," Irv insisted angrily.

"So what?" Mike shrugged.

"Anzio Annie" was an enormous German cannon that played havoc with the beachhead. Its huge shells threatened ships and caused many casualties. All attempts to silence it, even by aerial bombardment, were fruitless, because it was on railroad tracks and after firing was withdrawn deep inside a mountain.

Angelo Bartoli, a handsome guerrilla leader educated at Oxford, offered to assault it from the ground, using the element of surprise. OSS was behind it, and Mike decided to drop in with the supplies.

Irv knew it was useless trying to talk him out of it. "Take care of yourself, shmuck," Irv said with warmth as he embraced Mike at the landing strip where the cargo plane was warming up.

"I won't do anything you wouldn't." Mike smiled and turned toward the C-47 as the cargomaster yelled to him to board.

The attack took place at night, and the Germans were indeed surprised. But it didn't take them long to recover. Half the guerrilla group were lost in the tunnel as they dynamited the gun. The rest scattered through the surrounding mountains. In the morning, German search parties and spotter planes were out. More partisans were captured and executed, but Mike and Bartoli managed to elude them. They showed up two weeks later at the beachhead. Bartoli told Irv that Mike was either the greatest soldier he'd ever seen or was just suicidal.

Irv knew he had to act. "Losing Robert's made him crazy," he told Donovan at headquarters.

"What do you want me to do?"

"Send him home on furlough."

"Good idea," Donovan agreed. "I don't want to lose him."

———————

Katherine was reading the Sunday *New York Times*. She was to meet Larry later that June afternoon at the Museum of Modern Art, then go for a walk down Fifth Avenue, perhaps take in a film. She wanted to see either *Les Enfants du Paradis* or Olivier in *Henry V*. It was a lovers' kind of day, although they were not yet lovers. Larry had not pressed her. As she thought about him, there was a knock at the door. She looked up. Another knock. Was it a neighbor needing a cup of sugar? Alex? Barkin? She opened the door.

"*Mike!*" she screamed, throwing her arms around him.

"Katherine . . . oh, Katherine," he said, embracing her strongly, kissing her, and then holding her at arm's length. "You look terrific." Mike looked at the carefully brushed hair, the dress. "You going out?" he asked with disappointment.

"I'll cancel," she said, then looked at him and smiled. "Don't just stand there."

Mike picked up his B-4 bag and closed the door. "I'm glad nothing's changed," he said as he entered the living room, looked at the pictures and furniture.

Katherine eyed him. "Everything's changed, Mike."

"Yeah," he sighed. "Make your call."

Katherine went to the bedroom. Mike looked after her and then walked into the kitchen.

"Larry . . ." she said.

"What?" He immediately picked up something in her voice.

"Mike Rossano just walked in."

"Strange," he breathed.

"What do you mean?"

"Just when things were going so well."

"Things will be all right," she assured him.

"No, they won't. He'll dig up Robert and you'll feel guilty."

"I'm not sure about that, but I can't see you today. I want to get the whole story."

"Of course." He hung up.

Katherine knew he felt threatened, hurt.

The living room was empty. Then she heard Mike in the kitchen. She smiled. Some things don't change. He entered with a pot of espresso and two cups.

"Who is he?" Mike asked, sitting, handing her a cup. "Anyone I know?"

"I doubt it. He's a painter."

"Abstract?" he asked, almost sarcastically.

"Very." She tried to smile against the tension in Mike's voice.

He merely nodded. "Serious?"

"I'm not thinking in those terms yet," she said. Mike looked at her over his cup. "He's dead, Mike," she said quietly. He nodded slightly. "Tell me about yourself. How come you're home?"

"Donovan thought I needed a rest. He thinks I'm cracking up, so he gave me a thirty-day furlough and arranged a flight."

"Are you . . . cracking up?"

He breathed deeply. "Let's just say I haven't been the same since Robert . . ." He didn't finish the sentence. He asked, "Have you gotten any other information?"

"Not really. I got a letter from Milt after Robert escaped. He was in a camp way up at the Baltic Sea near Poland, but every reference to Robert was censored. So there's nothing more than what I wrote you."

Mike drank the rest of the coffee in silence, then looked at the photo of himself with Robert at Jarama. He closed his eyes.

Katherine reached over and took his hand.

He looked at her, surprised at her touch.

"Tell me everything," she said softly.

Mike told her in great detail about North Africa, the fatal, stupid mission, the British officers, the wounding and capture of Robert and Milt, the invasion of Sicily, then his operations in Italy with Irv. He didn't mention Carla.

Katherine listened enthralled as the afternoon passed and the living room was filled with shadows as the sun went down.

They were sitting on the floor, their backs against the couch, in silence. Mike seemed to have finished, and there was nothing to be said. Suddenly, a sob escaped him, then another. Mike's face twisted in anguish.

Katherine took him in her arms.

He moved his head to her shoulder, then to her neck. At first she felt only his hot tears, then his lips as they brushed upward toward her cheek. A shiver passed through her as he sought her lips. He put his hand on her breast.

She felt a thrill of alarm, and moved it. "Please, Mike."

"Yes . . . yes . . ." he insisted, seeking her again.

"No, Mike." She took his hand.

"Why? He's dead." He breathed heavily.

"I don't want it. I can't handle it."

"It would be beautiful."

"I'm afraid."

"Of what?"

"Of you. I don't want to be used. I'd be another scalp."

"Never! You're Katherine."

She was startled. "What does that mean?"

"You know how much I've always admired you."

"I'm just a woman, Mike."

"You're more!" he insisted.

An insight struck her as he held her shoulders. "I'm Robert's wife," she breathed.

"Together we could hold on to him," he said urgently.

"I don't want to hold on to him, Mike."

Slowly, he dropped his hands from her shoulders.

Mike stayed in New York only two weeks of his month's furlough, then hopped a B-25 bomber being ferried to Italy.

At the end of June, Katherine got a letter of apology from Mike and read it before dressing for Larry's one-man show at the Contemporary American Galleries on Madison Avenue. He said it was grief that had led him to "the madness of that night."

She looked appraisingly at herself in the floor-length black gown as she put her grandmother's pearls around her neck. The mirror reflected an image of a woman she liked.

The opening was a huge success, and there was a party afterward at the gallery owner's Fifth Avenue penthouse. The view from the terrace across the park was breathtaking. Katherine stood with Larry in the spring night. He raised his glass to her.

"Thanks for being with me tonight," he said.

"Thanks for wanting me to be." They toasted each other.

The hostess took Larry into the living room to meet some prospective buyers.

Alex and Barkin came up on either side of her.

"We're glad," Alex said.

"Very glad," Barkin added.

The loft was dark with hints of green, red, and blue from the neon of the diner below. The colors pulsed as they crossed the creaking floor to the living area, where Larry lit candles. The walls were velvety in the glow. He took her in his arms and kissed her softly.

"Do you want some wine?" he asked.

"That would be nice. Red." He poured two glasses and held them to the candlelight.

"I could try all my life and never get that color."

"Some things are just not possible."

"When you're young, you think everything is."

"I know better," she said.

"Don't be sad tonight."

"I'm not. I'm very happy for you."

"I want you to be happy for yourself."

"I'll try," she said, removing her grandmother's pearls.

It frightened her how much his touch was like Robert's. The large hands caressed her gently and knowingly, his fingertips tracing patterns as if he were drawing. Her hand touched his leg, and she was surprised to find no scars. She shuddered with the shock of his fingers in her and reached up for him. Kissing him, she brought him down on her.

He was unhurried, forceful. Slowly, surely, they rose together, and she climaxed with him, gasped, and suddenly broke, her body convulsed by sobs. Her tears moistened them both as he held her.

"I'm sorry. . . ."

"It's okay . . . it's okay," he said gently, as he rocked her.

"I didn't want to cry." She continued sobbing.

"It's all right. I understand."

It was Katherine's last attack of grief. In the weeks that followed, she found herself falling in love.

"Let's go away," he said.

"I'd like that. Let me see if I can arrange it."

"I know a great place. Paul Marin used to paint there."

Katherine was startled. "Deer Isle?"

"You know it?"

"I've been there. It's beautiful."

Could she manage that? she wondered.

———————————

Deer Isle was unchanged, except that a bridge had been built from the mainland. Mr. Eaton remarked to Katherine that her husband had changed more than she had. She wasn't sure if it was poor eyesight or Eaton's dry humor. It was near the end of June, and the air was beginning to lose its raw spring edge.

To Katherine, there was an idyllic unreality about their relationship. Larry's interests were condensed into his work, not into movements or causes. He could understand Katherine's going to Spain with Robert and Mike, but it wasn't for him. He had not been drafted because of a punctured eardrum, but he sought no alternative ways to fight Fascism.

She felt the lack, but realized nothing could be perfect. During the day, she was content to watch Larry paint or draw; other times she would stare at the bay or read. At night, they listened to the news on the radio. The Allies had invaded France, Rome had been taken, the Germans were retreating in Russia.

"Turn off the radio," Larry said, lying in front of the fireplace, sketching. "Come here."

"No. I've been involved with myself for too long."

He frowned and continued drawing as Katherine listened to the end of the newscast. To Larry the war represented Robert, and the thought gave him a twinge of jealousy.

She turned off the radio and sat beside him on the hooked rug, looking at the drawing. "Is that me?"

"Uh-huh. You like it?"

"No." She laughed. "It's too idealized."

"You look like that."

"No, I don't. You just see me that way."

"How did you get so wise?"

"It's a reflection of pain."

"I don't believe that. Pain doesn't create either wisdom

or perspective. It destroys." He sighed. "I've seen it corrode a relationship." He stopped, then put the drawing aside and moved to her, his arms around her shoulders. They stared at the fire. He nuzzled her neck and stroked her breasts. She took a deep breath.

"Not in front of the fire," she said.

He dropped his hands. "It's hard for me, living with a ghost."

"I know. I'm sorry. Maybe we shouldn't have come here."

"Ghosts don't have territories. Robert would be with us wherever we went. I thought it would be a good test. And I love being here with you."

"So do I."

At the end of two weeks, as Larry put their bags on the train at Blue Hill, Eaton turned to Katherine.

"It's not the same feller, is it?" he asked.

"No," she said softly.

"Phew!" he said. "I thought my memory was goin'." He looked over at Larry. "He's a nice young feller too."

Katherine smiled and nodded. "Thank you."

As the train rattled through New Hampshire, Katherine looked at Larry's soft brown eyes. He caught her looking at him, raised his eyebrows questioningly.

"Do you want to talk about it?" she asked.

"Not yet. The wounds are still too raw."

Katherine nodded and pressed his hand.

Larry dropped her off at her apartment and went on to his loft.

Katherine's mailbox was stuffed, and she frowned at the bills. She opened her door and put down her suitcase, amazed at how quiet it was. She sat on the couch beneath the photos of Robert and Mike, looked at the Chagall on the wall and sorted the envelopes.

Her heart stopped. Her fingers trembled.

In her hands was the frail light blue paper of international mail with French postmarks and Robert's handwriting. She stared in disbelief, almost afraid to open it. The postmark was June. Robert had presumably died in January. Could it be a letter he wrote before that, long delayed? But he had died in Germany, not France. She was finally able to tear it open.

Her eyes filled with tears.

> Dear Katherine,
>   I'm in France!

He went on to describe his escape and attempts to contact her. With the Allied invasion, he had finally been able to get a letter out.

Katherine felt herself soaring, and then suddenly remembered Larry. She dialed his number.

"Hello?"

"He's alive! Robert's alive! I got a letter from France!"

Larry gently hung up.

Robert's mother was in his room at the farm when Katherine called. She'd never heard her husband yell like that.

"He's alive! Robert's alive!"

CHAPTER FIFTEEN

Inside the Café Montparnasse, Frenchmen drank coffee while Germans ate large sandwiches and drank beer. Robert crossed to the bar.

"*Eine bier?*" the owner asked, seemingly without interest. Robert immediately recognized the heavy man with the large nose.

"*Non. Un café au lait avec croissant.*"

The owner looked cautiously at Robert. There was something about him that pricked his memory. He spoke French without a German accent and had none of the boisterous swagger of the soldiers who came to his place. And what was he doing at the bar? Only Frenchmen sat at the bar. Where had he seen him before? he wondered as he brought Robert his order.

"*Merci.*" There was no one sitting on either side of him, and so Robert quietly asked the owner for Paul.

"Which Paul? I know many."

"Fresnay."

So . . . that's the game, the Frenchman thought. He's Gestapo and I've seen him in civilian clothes. "I don't know any Paul Fresnay," he said.

But Robert was still hopeful. He wrote on a napkin, "15th Brigade," folded it and pushed it forward. The man looked at it without expression. Robert tore it into shreds, and the owner swept them up with his hands as Robert drank his coffee.

Robert wrote on another napkin, "Lincoln." The man remembered him then, wearing a tweed jacket and work shirt with a woman next to him. Many Americans came through his café on the way to Spain, but almost no women, especially good-looking ones. What the hell was he doing in a German uniform?

"*Venez ici ce soir,*" he said, as he bent to refill Robert's cup. Robert nodded and ate the croissant, then went to the hotel off the Odéon where they'd stayed at the end of 1936. He fell into a long, dreamless sleep.

At eight o'clock he found a table from which he could see the door and ordered a sandwich and beer. Paul did not show. He ordered another sandwich and coffee, looked at his watch. Almost ten. Then suddenly he saw him. Even at a distance, he could feel the strength of the man as he crossed to the bar. The owner nodded toward Robert and slowly turned, but Paul gave no sign of recognition and left. Robert hastily put some money on the table and followed him outside.

He looked up and down the street, but Paul was gone. What now? he wondered.

Two men came from behind and stood on either side of him. Robert tensed. "*Promenade,*" one of them said, touching Robert's arm. They steered him into a small street and then an alley, where they suddenly threw him against a building and searched him. In the next street, he saw the glow of a cigarette in a doorway.

Fresnay embraced him. "What the hell are you doing in that uniform?"

"I escaped from a prison camp in Germany."

Fresnay raised his eyebrows. "Not so easy, huh?"

"My Iron Cross helped."

They laughed together.

After half an hour walking through a maze of back streets and dark alleys, they entered an old house and walked up five flights of worn steps without any lights. The apartment was small and dismal, with peeling paint and a smell of cooking gas. One of the men brought a bottle of wine from the kitchen. Fresnay introduced them as David and Jean.

"So . . . tell me from the beginning," Fresnay said as he relaxed into a chair with a glass of wine and a Gitane.

Robert spoke for over two hours detailing his experiences from his OSS training through his escape.

"You must be tired," Fresnay said as he stubbed out his last cigarette in the pile of others. He crumpled the package and stood, stretching, then led Robert to a room with a bed in it.

The lock clicked behind him.

"I don't like it," he could hear David saying in a hissed whisper.

"He fought with the Internationals. You are too young to know what that means. There is no record of even one turning around."

"There's always a first. His escape sounds phony to me. They don't give you a ticket to Paris from Munich because you have an Iron Cross and a wound. And that woman on the train who is supposed to be marrying Volker could be working with him."

"Your imagination is working."

"Healthy fear."

"What do you propose?"

"Have Falcon talk to him."

"All right," Fresnay agreed.

Robert saw the light under his door and knew he was being guarded. If "Falcon" didn't believe him, they might kill him. There was no hope of sleep.

He stared at the walls and ceiling.

In the morning, the door opened behind him. "Have some breakfast," Fresnay said pleasantly. The others were already dipping their baguettes into coffee. Robert watched David take his gun from the table and put it in his belt.

He joined them, trying to cover his nervousness. As he sipped his coffee, the apartment door opened. A man with a scarf hiding his face entered. Robert was sure this was the man to decide his fate. Silence fell as the man looked at him, then removed the scarf and revealed himself.

"Max!" Robert called out, standing.

"*C'est moi*," Max said, advancing. "How are you, Robert?" They embraced.

Fresnay breathed a sigh of relief. David and Jean looked at each other.

"We worked togther in Algiers," Max explained. He was now the head of French Resistance in Paris.

Max's hands had been in his pockets when he entered, and he put them back after the embrace. Robert saw why after David brought Max coffee. He had no fingernails. His teeth were also different. They were obviously false and not very good, giving his speech a strange clatter.

Robert repeated the story of his capture and escape.

Max smiled at Robert in his German uniform. "So . . . you've come all this way to work with us?" he asked cheerfully.

"Yes."

"Good. We need a radio operator."

David left the apartment.

"Now, describe this woman, Ilse, to me. You say she has come to marry Colonel Volker and gave you her telephone number?"

"Yes. She said she wanted to see me again." Robert described Ilse in great detail.

Max laughed, but there was a flicker in his eye, a tension of his mouth, that betrayed an interest.

The door opened again, and David returned with a young woman carrying a student's blue bookbag. Her hair was short, her eyes dark. Robert judged her to be fifteen or sixteen. Max introduced her as "Juliet." She smiled softly as she extended her hand. Then she took the radio out of the sack and put it on the table.

Robert bent to it. "And this is your Romeo?" he asked.

She nodded seriously. "Romeo" was underground slang for a clandestine radio.

"You know the type?" Max asked.

"Yes. It's one of the radios I was trained to use." Robert spun the dials as Juliet connected it. He put on the headphones and listened as he went from band to band. "Mostly German traffic."

Max nodded. "I'd like you to send a message," he said. "On 49.30." Robert turned to the frequency. "'Mother will tango tonight.' Send it just twice. They are waiting."

Robert expertly tapped out the message in Morse. He flipped to receive. The confirmation of reception came almost immediately.

Juliet, already disconnecting the set and putting it back in her sack, looked to Max for further instructions. He merely nodded for her to leave.

Robert watched her go. "Isn't that dangerous for her?"

"Everything is dangerous, Robert," Max said wearily.

"How old is she?"

"Seventeen. That's why the radio is safer with her. It looks as if she is carrying schoolbooks."

"What happened to your operator?"

"Arrested. He is being questioned at Gestapo headquarters, so we have to assume he will talk." Max rose and put out his hand. "Welcome to Paris and the Groupes Francs."

"The Groupes Francs?"

"Crocodile will brief you." As Max walked to the door, Robert noticed that he walked very lightly, almost tenderly, as if his shoes hurt. David went with him.

"The Gestapo tore out his fingernails, smashed his teeth, and then ran a rough file over them," Fresnay told Robert when the two men were gone. "Max said nothing. They poured boiling water over his head, then hung him from his elbows, which were tied behind his back, and burned his feet with a blowtorch. Max still didn't talk. They put electrodes to his nipples and balls. When he came to, they told him they'd tear out his eyes. He asked them to leave him alone for a few minutes to think. When they left, he smashed a glass and cut his own throat. He was afraid he'd crack. But he wasn't dead when they rushed him to the hospital. Fortunately, it was a civilian hospital where a few doctors and nurses were in the Resistance. We were able to rescue him."

Robert was silent, stunned.

"The Groupes Francs is our unit. It is for commando and assault work. The message you sent was to Lyon, which is a center for Resistance activities. You must think of a code name for yourself. I am Crocodile. Max is Falcon."

"I'll be the Wild Duck," Robert said, borrowing the title of his favorite Ibsen play.

———————————

Robert was given a room at the home of a wealthy Armenian Jew who posed as an oil-rich Arab, on the Avenue Foch, and the identity of a rare-book dealer. A new picture was taken for his soldier's ID, and other necessary papers like ration cards were manufactured in the basement of the Musée de l'Homme. In a cord suit and beret, Robert met Fresnay at various safe houses for briefing. But whenever his ability to pass lulled his sense of danger, he had only to look at the red, white, and black Nazi flag flying across the street from his window. It was Gestapo headquarters there at 84 Avenue Foch, and he could hear the screams at night from its basement.

The Avenue Foch was a beautiful, tree-lined street of millionaires' houses, and the SS guard waved to Juliet as she rode by on her bicycle and went across the street to 95.

Today she had not brought the radio. "They are searching everybody's bookbag," she said.

"That means that Magpie broke," Max said later at the café. "But at least he didn't name Juliet, or they would have come for her."

"He probably got away with saying he knew only her code name and that she carried the radio in her bookbag."

Max nodded. "We need a new system."

"I can monitor the Gestapo and SS traffic from my room and send from elsewhere. I'll keep the radio in my briefcase."

Max and Fresnay agreed. "Now, let me ask you something," Max continued. "Can you renew your acquaintance with Ilse?" Robert looked at him. "We have checked her out. She is the daughter of the Party administrator for Holland. Very powerful man. Ilse—"

"—is the way to Volker," Robert completed Max's thought.

———————————

She was delighted to hear from him.

"Hermann!" she shouted. "I'm so glad you called. You have no idea how bored I am. I have absolutely no one to talk to. You must come right over. If your *Kommandant* doesn't allow it, I'll have Volker talk to him. That's all he's good for anyway."

"I'm free," Robert said. "What time?"

"Come for lunch."

———————

The Hotel Crillon dining room was filled with highly placed Germans and Frenchmen doing business with them. The maître d' raised his eyebrows at the sergeant who asked for Ilse.

"You have a message to deliver? I can take it."

"No, I'm meeting her." The man's brows rose even higher, but he led him to her table. She smiled as she saw him. The Nazis and well-dressed Frenchmen looked at Robert in speculation.

Ilse put out her hand and a cheek to kiss.

"I'd given up on you," she said reproachfully.

"Busy getting settled," he said as he slid in next to her on the red banquette. "How have you been?" He surveyed the room full of black uniforms.

"Bored, bored, bored. No one to talk to. No one to sleep with."

"But, what about . . ."

"Volker isn't interested in me or any woman. I told you, it will be a marriage of politics."

"Then I don't think you should marry him," Robert said.

She took his hand. "At last, a friend who understands me. We'll spend the whole afternoon together. We'll go to bookstalls on the Left Bank, have a drink at the Café Fleur . . ."

Robert followed her eyes as she looked to the entrance. A tall, handsome blond man in a tight black uniform entered with another Gestapo officer, younger and more beautiful. They were heading for Ilse's table. Robert's heart bounced.

"Rudy," she said in surprised delight. "I didn't know you were lunching here today."

Robert was sure she knew perfectly well he'd be there. What kind of game was she playing?

"I needed a change from the Lancaster," the blond man said, looking speculatively at Robert.

"Hermann, this is my fiancé, Colonel Volker . . . and Captain Dietrich." There was a slight edge to her voice as she introduced the beautiful captain. "This is Sergeant Baumeister. We shared our trip from Munich together."

"Glad to meet you, Baumeister. I see you were at Stalingrad." Robert nodded. "Cold, hah?"

"No, very hot," Robert said, laughing.

"See how amusing he is, Rudy," Ilse said, laughing also.

"Yes," Volker mused. "What outfit are you in?"

"517th Communications."

"Safer than *Panzergrenadier*, hah?"

"I didn't ask for it, sir."

"Hermann speaks beautiful French."

"Oh," Volker said. Robert could see the mind working.

"So does Rudy," Ilse continued. "You two could be great friends, if you put rank aside."

Captain Dietrich looked coldly at her.

"Perhaps we'll have dinner together," Volker said.

The two Gestapo men left for their table.

"You see what I have in mind?" Ilse said.

"I don't want to be in the Gestapo."

"Don't be silly. It's a good job. And I'll be able to see you whenever I want." She slipped her right hand under the table and gripped Robert's penis, waving at Rudy with her left hand and smiling. He smiled back.

"What are you doing?" Robert gasped, removing her hand.

"Just being frisky."

"You just want to be outrageous."

"You know me so well," she said happily.

The orchestra played Strauss waltzes as they ate, and Robert watched the elegant lunch crowd at the Crillon. But the relaxed surface was disturbed by a Gestapo sergeant who hurried to Volker's table and whispered to him.

Volker and Dietrich, their faces grim, left immediately without so much as a glance at Ilse.

Robert did not find out what had happened until early evening after he left Ilse at the hotel. They had walked all day discussing literature and her "problem."

"Clisa's group bombed a busload of Luftwaffe pilots who were on leave sightseeing," Max explained. "They managed to get four grenades into the bus as the bastards were reboarding after a walk around the Arc de Triomphe." Clisa owned the house Robert was staying in. They were in the grubby restaurant of the Gare de Montparnasse eating sausage.

Robert drank coffee. "I had a good lunch today," he said, as he reported on his day.

"Sometimes things go too well," Fresnay said. "We'll never be able to get you a set of records or on the roster of the 517th."

"Yes, it's tricky," Max agreed. "How did you manage not to sleep with the beautiful Ilse? Or did you?"

"I told her I'd be crazy to since Rudy probably has her watched."

"Did she buy it?" Fresnay asked.

"For the moment."

Max leaned forward and spoke quietly as David watched for eavesdroppers. "Pepe has asked for our help in a rescue operation. One of his *cheminots*, Jean B., the man responsible for the Tréport-Abbeville bombing and the head-on wreck on the Paris-Lille line, has been arrested. On Thursday he is being transported to the Palais de Justice for a quick trial before execution. We cannot refuse. Crocodile will be in charge of our group liaison with Pepe."

Max looked at David, who nodded. They left together.

Fresnay explained that Pepe was a Spanish Civil War veteran and that Jean B.'s work had caused the death of hundreds of German soldiers, SS men, and officers, including a division general. He was too valuable to lose.

———————————

Robert was in the middle of a radio transmission when he got the phone call. "My car has broken down," the voice said. "I think it's a bearing."

Robert put the radio behind the false partition in the

closet and descended to the street. A black Citroën with police plates picked him up. They sped off to the Santé prison, passing the SS guards in front of Gestapo HQ.

Fresnay gave him a German machine pistol. Mike's favorite, he thought.

David sat in the back with them while a man from Pepe's group drove. They parked outside the prison behind a green van with "Produits Vert" lettered on its side. As they waited, two black Citroëns entered the street and parked behind them, dousing their lights. Robert could see a policeman standing at a second-floor window looking out toward the street as if getting some night air. He disappeared. Ten minutes later, he was back. As he took off his hat all the auto engines started and a police armored van emerged from the prison garage. One of the black Citroëns swung around to lead it, and the others fell in behind as if in convoy.

As they entered the poorly lit Rue Serpente traveling slowly toward the Palais de Justice, the leading Citroën stopped. The green van and the two other escort Citroëns stopped immediately behind the prisoner van so that it couldn't move. Two plainclothesmen walked toward the armored van, holding their automatics casually.

Fresnay went to the driver's side of the prisoner van while Robert went to the German guard's side. The driver looked questioningly at Fresnay, who showed him a package of cigarettes and motioned him to roll down the window. When he did, Fresnay told him the Citroën had stalled and offered him a cigarette.

The man took it, asking, "What do you want to do?"

"Take your keys," Fresnay answered, pointing his gun at his head. As the driver handed him the keys, the German reached for his pistol. Fresnay let go a burst across the driver into the German's chest.

They moved quickly. Opening the back of the van, they released Jean B., who was handcuffed to a stanchion, then replaced him with the driver, gagging him with a belt. The operation took less than three minutes.

———————

Colonel Rudolf Volker was in the elegant office suite of General von Choltitz at the Hotel Meurice being lectured. Von Choltitz, a former Panzer commander, was now responsible for Paris.

"You know what our Führer said to me when he heard about the twenty pilots killed on the bus?"

"No, my general."

"'Rudy must be getting soft. I'm talking to Himmler about it.' And now, this, last night! You can't even transfer a prisoner!" Von Choltitz's tone was cutting.

"He was not my prisoner. My prisoners don't escape."

"What about that Max? The one who cut his throat."

"He's the only one. And I'll get him back."

"How's that new Captain Dietrich working out?" Von Choltitz asked, switching tracks.

Did he know? Volker wondered. "Fine. He's a good staff officer."

"Give my regards to the beautiful Ilse," Von Choltitz said, ending the meeting. As Volker opened the door, Choltitz called to him. "I'll see if I can calm Himmler."

Volker closed the door, furious.

The following day, Robert had lunch with Ilse at the Crillon. "Rudy is in absolutely foul humor," she said.

"*C'est la guerre.*"

"It's not funny. And what were you doing on the Avenue Foch yesterday?"

Robert tried to look blank. "Me?"

"Yes. And in civilian clothes."

Robert's heart pumped.

"Probably meeting a lover."

"You think everyone has a lover," he said, trying to recover with a light tone.

"Everyone should." She leaned into him, speaking confidentially. "Have you been sent by Himmler to watch Rudy?"

"That's not even funny. It's absurd." He tried to laugh.

"There's something funny about you." Her eyes narrowed shrewdly. "My father has you following me," she said triumphantly. "That's it, is't it? That's why you won't sleep with me!"

This time his laugh was genuine.

"Don't laugh. I know you're some sort of secret agent. I called you at your 517th Communications yesterday. They never heard of you."

"I was there only briefly before I was transferred."

"Rudy is on to you," she said. "He had a meeting with Choltitz, who let drop that Himmler had someone here because of the recent 'incidents.'" She bent to him again and whispered conspiratorially. "Rudy's afraid of you. Isn't that delicious?"

———————————

A fearful Volker had decided to make a friend of his possible enemy. He had invited Robert to dinner and a musicale.

"How did you get your Iron Cross?" he asked across the glittering table in his mansion near the Bois de Boulogne. Volker sat at the head of the table, resplendent in a new uniform and all his ribbons, one of which was Hitler's special award to the Condor Legion. Dietrich was to his left, Robert to his right as the guest of honor, Ilse at the other end as his hostess. The other men were all Gestapo officers. The women were both German and French, in Parisian *haute couture*. Ilse wore a large diamond.

Robert shrugged modestly.

"Come now," Volker said. "Don't deny us. Soldiers love war stories." His accent was pure Berlin, and he listened for Robert's.

Robert made up a story of saving a tank commander's life at the risk of his own while killing a lot of uncivilized Russian peasants. The officers and ladies applauded.

Volker didn't believe a word of it. "Where do you come from?" he asked.

"Near Munich. A village named Dachau."

Munich, Volker calculated. High party connections. Hitler started there. Probably his father was an early party member.

"What does your father do?"

"He's a farmer."

A likely story, thought Volker. Well, it will be easy enough to check. He nodded and smiled at Robert.

As the Paris Symphony members played a late Beethoven quartet, Robert thought how insane it was to be there listening to chamber music with a group of Gestapo officers. He could see Volker looking at him speculatively, but Volker smiled pleasantly as Robert caught his eye.

Later, Volker poured Robert a brandy and took his arm, walking him into a corner to be alone. "How do you like Paris?" he asked.

"Better than Russia," Robert laughed.

"Would you like to work for me?"

"I like my present assignment."

"Your 'present assignment' is what?"

"Secret," Robert said, looking directly at Volker. "I'm under orders not to reveal it." Then he shifted ground. "I see you were in the Condor Legion."

Volker too was glad to speak of something else. "Yes. Glorious days. The beginning for us. What triumphs . . . Guernica, Barcelona . . ."

At that moment, Robert determined to kill Volker.

———————————

"It would be dangerous and gratifying," Max said. "The man is a beast." They were walking in the Bois with Fresnay. David was ten steps behind.

"What do you think is the best way to do it?" Robert asked.

"Let me think about it," Max said.

———————————

Volker got his call from Munich. Outside his window, the black swastika fluttered slightly in its red field. The caller confirmed that there was a Willi Baumeister near Dachau with three sons, one of whom was Hermann.

"Trace him for me, please."

———————————

Robert, Max, and Fresnay looked out the window of Robert's room and saw the same flag across the street.

"I think it's best to work on his fear," Max said. "Let yourself be seen in civilian clothes. In other words, blow your cover in a convincing way." He looked at Robert. "It's the most dangerous, however."

"Maybe not. The boldest play may be the safest," Fresnay argued.

"I agree," Robert said. "He'll be afraid to pick me up because of Himmler."

"One thing is sure," Fresnay said. "He's going to put a tail on you."

"*D'accord*," Max said. "And to reinforce his belief in the Himmler story, perhaps you should check into the Hotel Meurice."

"He is registered at the Hotel Meurice as a wine grower from Bordeaux," Dietrich reported to Volker, who was in deep thought.

"He and Choltitz are plotting," Volker said finally. "Choltitz doesn't like me and probably has his own choice for my job."

"What do you think we should do, Rudy?"

"Sit tight and stop these damned incidents," Volker said angrily, getting up. "I'll be in the basement if I'm needed, or you get a report from Munich. Call me immediately." Dietrich knew Volker always went to the basement interrogation rooms when he was tense.

"Ah-hah! I caught you!" Ilse said delightedly.

Robert turned to her in surprise. He was browsing in his favorite bookstore, the Rue Monsieur le Prince, down the street from the hotel he'd stayed in with Katherine and Mike. "Well . . . you caught me," he said, nonplussed.

"Who are you, 'sergeant'?"

"I'll tell you over a cassis."

As they walked down the street to the Café St. Michel, there were two men following them. One was David, the other a Gestapo plainclothesman. All four went to the same café.

"I'm in the evaluation section," Robert admitted, "and I report directly to Himmler. He's disturbed over the incidents here in Paris and wants a direct observation."

"So, Rudy was right."

"No one has ever accused Colonel Volker of stupidity." She looked at him carefully. "You're very handsome in that suit."

"Thank you. Now, I rely on you as a friend to keep our secret until I am ready to reveal it."

"I'll seal our bargain with a kiss." She leaned to him and put her lips on his.

The Gestapo agent wrote furiously.

———————————

"What the devil is going on?" Volker shouted at Ilse across his dinner table.

"Are you jealous?"

"Jealous!"

"Yes. I think you're attracted to our mysterious Baumeister yourself and are jealous of me."

Volker laughed. "You are a little bitch," he said, drinking his Chardonnay.

"Anyway," she said, shrugging, "he said he'd reveal himself to you when his report was ready."

"Why would he tell you that?" It bothered Volker that the man had revealed himself to Ilse. He must know she would tell me, he thought. So he wants me to know. What a clever game he plays. Perhaps he's looking for a bribe for a favorable report.

Volker smiled at his insight.

———————————

Robert made his move.

He invited Volker to lunch in a chic but out-of-the-way place.

Volker knew he was right as the Mercedes staff car pulled up to the Jockey Club at Longchamp, but still hadn't made up his mind what to do about it. Perhaps Ilse's father could advise him. The man was a master at political maneuver-ings.

The lunch crowd was mostly French. "They don't look like they're suffering too much," Volker said of the civilians as they took a window table overlooking the track. Then he tried to steer the conversation to Gestapo matters.

Robert countered with talk of literature, then Spain. He encouraged Volker to relate his experiences there, trying to stoke his emotions to the task before him. He'd killed, but never murdered.

Finished with coffee, Robert suggested a drive through the Bois.

Aha! Now it comes, thought Volker.

When Dietrich returned from lunch he found a message from Gestapo in Munich. Hermann Baumeister did have an Iron Cross, but had been killed at Stalingrad. Dietrich called Volker at Longchamp, but he'd already left.

They were on the Bagatelle leading to Longchamp Alee.

Robert tried to relax against the rich velour upholstery of the Mercedes, his shiny black briefcase with the small gold swastika on his lap. He focused on the death's-head insignia of Volker's cap.

"As you know, Herr Himmler has been concerned about 'events' in the Paris area," Robert said carefully, picking his way through the minefield of words. Volker nodded, wait-ing for the trap to spring as the driver made a right turn onto the main road. "I have here my report." Robert put his hand on his briefcase.

"Not too damaging, I hope," Volker said, smiling.

"Perhaps it can be fixed," Robert said, snapping open the latch of the briefcase. He checked the driver's rearview mirror for the black Citroën that followed.

So, he makes his move, Volker thought. "May I see it?"

"Of course," Robert said, putting his hand in the case and withdrawing the heavy Luger pistol. Volker swallowed hard, eyes widening.

Robert emptied the whole clip into Volker's body.

The driver slammed on the brakes at the sound of the

first shot, and the Citroën swerved to the side of the staff car, stopping. Fresnay leaped out, automatic in hand. He ordered the driver out, took the keys, and locked the German sergeant in the trunk as Robert continued to look at Volker.

"Come on!" Fresnay said urgently.

They left, Volker's dead face still staring in surprise.

CHAPTER SIXTEEN

The Gestapo was outraged.

The Germans conducted a sweep through Paris more thorough than their search for Jews. David was picked up. He'd refused to part with his gun, and it was found on him.

Captain Dietrich took charge of the investigation. The neighbors of 84 Avenue Foch couldn't sleep that night because of the screams. David finally told about Lyon. Dietrich then castrated him with a straight razor.

In the morning, Major Klaus Barbie, head of Gestapo in Lyon, got a call from Paris. Dietrich told him what he knew.

A meeting with the heads of the Lyon Resistance had been set up in the suburban hills surrounding the city. Robert, Max, and Fresnay, who'd left Paris until the atmosphere cooled, had agreed not to see each other before the meeting. Robert had lunch this quiet Sunday afternoon at a small bistro on the banks of the Saône. He tried to quiet his nerves as he looked out of the window at families and lovers strolling along the banks of the river in the late winter sun.

He left at one-thirty for the short walk to the funicular tramway, going over the signals. "Is Dr. Duclos at home? I have a sore throat and fever." Tram 23 came in and he got on it. When he reached the top, however, it wasn't Caluire. Puzzled, he looked at the rear of the already descending car. Dammit! How stupid! he thought. It was 33 I was supposed to take.

With the Sunday tram schedule he'd be more than an hour late. He cursed himself for his lack of professionalism.

The funicular ascended the long hill, and Robert sighed with relief when he saw the sign "Caluire." He walked quickly to the Place Castellane and nearly stopped. The house was surrounded by police cars and an armored troop carrier. Men with submachine guns were at its exits. Robert kept walking.

———————

"I have two of the three you described," Major Barbie said to Dietrich on the phone. "The one with the scar, and Crocodile. The third was not at the meeting."

"Damn!" Dietrich cursed. "Baumeister was the hit man."

"My informant is working on it. I'll find him."

"Take care of the other two. I don't want anything to happen to them. I'll be in Lyon tonight."

———————

Robert checked into a small hotel in Vienne and lay on the bed thinking of the pain Max and Fresnay would endure. Was Volker worth it? He thought about the Gestapo informer who'd tipped Barbie about the meeting. He had to be on the inside of the organization. How could a man live with himself afterward?

———————

Dietrich was sadistic even by Gestapo standards. He tortured them with a fury that went beyond professionalism. Nothing could make them talk about "Baumeister" or anyone else. He got no names.

Dietrich shot Max in the head.

Fresnay disappeared, Dietrich having another hell in mind for him.

———————

Robert went to Marseille, where he hid in the attic of a house near the waterfront. Nothing could lift his depression. Loss in action was expected, but this was betrayal of comrades. What price had been paid for it?

Only the promise of renewed action could lift his spirits. He decided to go north for the Allied invasion they knew was coming.

Mike got on the train from Rome to Naples, where the armada for the second invasion of France was forming. He saw Carla for the last time in her apartment near the Opera. They did not leave her bed for the entire weekend.

Robert worked with a group mapping German installations, gunsites, defenses, harbors, minefields. After the invasion he joined Patton's Army. He was in Normandy until the breakout from the beaches and then found that life at Patton's headquarters was too tame for him. He wondered if he was becoming an action freak like Mike and Irv. He left to go back to Paris to fight for its liberation and joined a Maquis group headed by Colonel Tanguy, a veteran of Spain.

No one in Paris was sleeping. Men, women, children, were at the barricades, and the first tanks of Le Clerq's columns rumbled through the Porte d'Orléans on the night of August 24. The following morning Mike entered with the main force at the Porte de Saint Cloud, met by tens of thousands of welcomers while shooting was still going on.

Von Choltitz's demolition teams waited for his order to blow up the main buildings of Paris, but he never gave it. He did not want to go down in history as the man who burned the world's most beautiful city. As Hitler waited for the news that Paris was razed, General von Choltitz, in full uniform with all his decorations, waited with his staff in the dining room of the Meurice. He thought de Gaulle himself might take his pistol and was not prepared for the confused young French lieutenant who wandered into the room and found himself capturing the highest-ranking German in Paris with his whole staff.

Outside the Ritz Hotel, a large group of Resistance fight

ers had gathered after taking the Chamber of Deputies from an SS group. They were ebullient as they passed bottles of champagne among themselves and recounted the battles of the day. There was less firing now, and singing could be heard.

Robert tipped the bottle back and drank too much, foam dripping from his chin. Colonel Tanguy, a large man, laughed as he took the bottle. Robert laughed with him before he saw the jeep approach, then brake to a halt. His heart stopped.

"Mike!" Robert shouted as he ran from the crowd.

Mike never remembered how he got out of the front seat or how many steps it took before he buried his face in Robert's shoulder.

Tears ran as they hugged each other's wet cheeks while the crowd of Resistance fighters watched and smiled.

"I thought you were dead," Mike said. "I thought you were dead," he sobbed.

———————

Fighting came to an end as darkness enshrouded Paris— the darkness of five years of defeat and occupation. As they stood outside the Place Vendôme, suddenly the arc lights of the Eiffel Tower blazed, then of Notre Dame, Les Invalides, Sacré Coeur . . . followed by voices. All of Paris was singing the "Marseillaise."

———————

It was three o'clock in the morning in New York. Katherine fumbled for the phone, wondering what emergency surgery had to be performed.

"Hullo," she said, struggling for consciousness. She heard the long-distance hiss and a woman speaking in French.

"*Oui . . . est Madame Thompson*," she answered, suddenly awake.

"Katherine?" the voice asked fuzzily.

"Yes . . . *yes!*"

"It's Robert!" he shouted.

"Robert!" she cried. "Oh, Robert, is it really you?"

"*C'est moi.*"

She couldn't speak.

"Are you all right?" he asked.

"Yes . . . yes . . . *yes*! Are you?" Her tears started.

"Yes. I'm here with Mike. In Paris."

"Thank God! Thank God!"

"I love you," he said.

"Me, too!" Mike shouted into the phone.

"Oh, Robert . . . Robert . . ."

Katherine's tears ran freely.

PART TWO

Character is destiny
—Heraclitus

CHAPTER SEVENTEEN

NEW YORK—1946

Katherine woke and looked at the illuminated dial of the clock; it was two-thirty. Robert slept soundly. She marveled at his look of childish innocence and its contrast to the vivid scars on his legs.

She thought of the Madrid operating room, then of Barkin's disappointment that she'd chosen psychiatry over surgery. Robert and Mike both had thought it was a good idea. "You've got the insight," Mike had said. She heard his footsteps in the hall on the way to the kitchen. He had not been sleeping well. Katherine wondered what demons were pursuing him.

Mike made a cup of coffee. As he stirred slowly, he thought of Carla. She had come to Paris while Robert and he were still stationed there. Carla had wanted to go back to the States with him, but he'd been with another woman. He wondered now if he'd made a mistake. He also wondered if he'd get the part he was reading for tomorrow. He picked up the script he'd left on the table and studied it.

"What's the matter?" Robert asked, having wakened to find Katherine staring into the darkness.

"Nothing," she said, stroking his face.

"Why are you awake?"

"I was thinking of one of my patients."

He reached for her and kissed her. At first, it was affectionate, but it grew in intensity.

She drew away. "Mike's awake."

"Oh," he said, understanding her reluctance. It also

started him thinking about Mike. Even with Alex's help, he'd been unable to get work, and it made him edgy. Robert got out of bed and put on his bathrobe.

"Where are you going?"

"To talk to Mike."

Katherine nodded, feeling a twinge.

Robert entered the kitchen. "What's the matter?" he asked, sitting.

"Nothing." Mike shrugged. "Just working on my reading." He looked directly at Robert. "You really think you had a rat in your barracks at the POW camp?"

"Milt was sure of it. I suspected that Air Force gunner, the guy in charge. When Milt voiced his suspicion that I wasn't dead and there was a stool in the barracks, they shipped him out to that camp near the Baltic."

"How would a guy like that behave?"

"Too well. You know, more security-minded, more German-hating than anyone else. But he'd have to have a crack someplace. Anyone ratting on his buddies has to show some sign of it."

Mike nodded. "What kind of sign?"

———

Mike was standing backstage at the 48th Street Theater in a line of other actors, working on being cold, hungry, and guilty. He also looked tired, as if he hadn't slept all night. The assistant stage manager called his name, breaking his concentration. He walked out on an empty stage illuminated by one large bare bulb that threw shadows against the back wall.

"Hiya, Mike," a voice called from the darkness of the theater.

Mike shielded his eyes. "Hi, Joe."

"You ready?" the director asked.

"Sure."

"Okay. Give it a go."

"Page one-four," the stage manager said.

Mike put down the script.

"Show-off," the director laughed.

Mike turned upstage briefly, closed his eyes, then

nodded to the stage manager, who began reading. As the scene progressed the director leaned forward. When they'd finished several scenes, the director conferred with the producer as Mike waited under the worklight. His breathing was deep.

"You sure you weren't a rat in a prison camp?" the director asked finally. Mike laughed in release. "You give me only one problem, Mike. You don't give me much chance to direct."

"There's a long way to go," Mike said seriously.

"Okay. We'll make the trip together."

———————

They celebrated that night at Sardi's with Alex.

"How's the play going?" Alex asked Robert.

"Slowly," Robert replied. He had returned to the play that had eluded him before the war. It continued to perplex him. The emotion of the play still resisted his efforts; the characters would not reveal their secrets to him. He looked around the room at the well-dressed diners, listened to the happy hum of conversation. It reminded him of the collaborators having lunch in the Hotel Crillon.

"Hi, remember me?" The question broke Robert's reverie, and he looked at the woman's face as she stood at their table addressing Mike.

"How could I forget you?" Mike lied.

"Ruth Gilbert."

"Of course. How are you?"

"I'm fine. How was the war?"

"We survived it," Mike said, pointing to Robert. He introduced them.

"What are you doing these days?" Mike asked. He now remembered picking her up in Sardi's, following her to the ladies' room. He also remembered liking her.

"I'm working at the Theater Guild. Casting . . . reading plays."

"I'll call you," Mike said.

She smiled at them and went back to her table.

"When do you go into rehearsal?" Alex asked.

"Two weeks."

Mike was a monk when he rehearsed. He had slept with Ruth Gilbert a few times before rehearsals started, staying over at her apartment because he knew Katherine was uncomfortable with his activities in the next bedroom. But once he started work, he saw no one.

He cooked once a week, usually on Sunday. An opera resounded throughout the apartment while the rich smells of garlic and tomato filled the rooms. Mike was singing again. He was working.

In Boston, *Stalag 15* got raves, and Mike was singled out for his performance.

In New York, Robert struggled with *American Dreams*, while Katherine, working to finish her psychiatric residency, woke early and went to bed late.

"Let's have a child," she said suddenly one night as they prepared for bed.

It had been an especially unproductive and frustrating day for Robert, and he stared at her in blank surprise. "What?"

"Let's have a child."

"That's what I thought you said."

"Why shouldn't we? We'll be able to afford it."

He was silent for a moment, then took her in his arms. "I like the idea."

Katherine nuzzled his chest.

Later, after their lovemaking, Robert observed, "You're awfully playful tonight."

"I feel good. I like the future."

"What about the present?" he kidded.

"I love the present."

On opening night in New York, Mike was electric on stage. Whenever he had a scene, Robert could sense the audience's tension. Robert looked at Katherine as she watched, the reflection of the stage lights caught in her reddish hair and pale skin, and felt the same pang of attraction he'd experienced in the Café Montparnasse. She sensed his glance and smiled at him, taking his hand. How lucky I am, he thought.

When the curtain came down there was wild applause. Mike got the biggest hand.

Katherine and Robert made their way through the back-stage crowds to Mike's small dressing room. The proud producer and beaming director were pumping his hand in congratulations.

"Does this mean I get a raise?" Mike joked.

"How about bigger billing?" the producer countered.

"These are my roommates, Katherine and Robert Thompson."

"I saw *The Strike Zone* in Washington," the director said. "Then I read it, because I suspected there was more on the page than appeared on the stage."

Robert was flattered.

"What are you working on?" the director asked.

"A family play."

"I'd like to see it when you finish," he said as he and the producer left for other dressing rooms.

Alex entered.

"Just in time," Mike said, reaching for the bottle of champagne in a cooler. "From Odets."

———————————

There was the crackle of success in the air at Sardi's, the electricity of a hit.

"You can always feel it," Alex said as they mingled at the party. "Everyone comes out of the woodwork to be part of it. When you've got a flop, it's like leprosy."

"Hi," Ruth Gilbert said, crossing to them. "To your performance." She raised her glass to Mike.

"I'll drink to that," he said, kissing her. "You here alone?"

"No. I'm with you."

"I thought I was with you," Maxine said, entering their circle. She was very appealing in an expensive gown.

"I thought you were in Pittsburgh," Mike said.

"I was, but I wouldn't miss your opening."

"Why didn't you call?"

"I love surprises."

"I think we are going to make an exit," Alex said, taking Robert's and Katherine's arms.

Ruth, who had been standing there in disappointment, went to the bar alone.

Mike frowned. "I heard you'd married Pittsburgh glass," he said.

"The merger didn't work."

"So you're richer than ever."

"The rich never talk about money. Are you free later?"

"Possibly."

She smiled. "Same old Mike."

At three in the morning Mike got out of Ruth's bed.

"Where are you going?" she asked.

"I can't sleep. I'm going for a walk."

"I'm sorry."

"It's not you. I'm just keyed up."

"Will you be back?"

"I don't know. Maybe." He kissed her and left.

The elevator man was new and proud of his job. Even at three-thirty in the morning he put on his white gloves and with a flourish moved the brass lever that controlled the ascent of the wood-paneled cubicle at 57 Beekman Place. He waited at Maxine's floor until she came to the door, answering Mike's ring, both as security and because he liked her breasts through the silk dressing gown.

So did Mike as he kissed her neck. "Hmmm . . . you smell good."

"So do you," she replied. "Who have you been with?"

"Alex."

"Alex wears Chanel?"

"He doesn't?" Mike asked innocently.

Maxine laughed slightly and led him toward the bedroom. The apartment looked even more luxurious than he remembered it.

The champagne was in a sterling bucket at the side of the bed.

"The ice is melted," she said reproachfully.

"I couldn't get away earlier."

"I fell asleep."

"I'll make it up to you."

"I was reading John Hersey's *Hiroshima*."

"No wonder you're in a bad mood."

"It's not the book. I'm not used to waiting for anyone until three o'clock in the morning."

"Then I'll leave."

"Why don't you just pour the champagne," she said, smiling briefly. Mike's manner still attracted her. No one else treated her that way.

He sat on the bed, took off his jacket, and poured the wine. "Here's to you," he said. The silk in the room reminded him of the bedroom in Naples. He drained his glass and leaned to her, kissing her breast. It was as if he'd never left, and there had been no war. Their lovemaking was as intense as it ever was, as synchronous as if there had been no interruption.

"I loved your performance," she said blissfully.

"Which one?" he asked, smiling down at her.

———————

"With those personal reviews, I'd say Mike is on his way," Robert said as he and Katherine undressed.

"I wonder what it's going to do to him."

"Why should it do anything?"

"Because nothing stays the same. Circumstance always makes for change."

"Come here," Robert said affectionately, holding out his arms. "I don't want to argue with you tonight."

Katherine moved into the circle of his arms and put hers around his neck. "Especially tonight," she said soberly.

"Why especially tonight?"

"Because I have good news. I'm pregnant."

"Why didn't you tell me earlier?"

"I was saving it for dessert."

Yet Robert knew she hadn't wanted her news to dim the brightness of Mike's success or compete with it. He fell happily asleep. But later, he had his usual dream.

He was in Dachau. The bodies were mostly naked and dead, emaciated, skulls accentuated, eyes staring, hands outstretched beseechingly. A man whispered to him hoarsely, the sound more gargle than speech. He turned from him, afraid of his own emotion. The man took his sleeve and held it, trying to speak again, as if his voice box were shattered. Was he saying "Fresnay"? Robert looked at him again. This skeleton couldn't be the man he'd known. Fresnay was dead. Tortured to death in Lyon. "Fresnay?" Robert repeated. The man nodded. Robert took him in his arms, the body weightless, and cried.

He woke up, remembering that day in Dachau.

Robert had felt he had to go back. And so, as Germany crumbled and the Allied forces smashed the last failing resistance, Robert had left the comforts of Paris he shared with Mike. He had talked OSS headquarters, Paris, into sending him to Dachau to confirm reports of the camp's activities.

Most of the cities he passed through were in ruins, blasted from the air and the ground. There was no food, little drinkable water, and a dazed population.

Robert was with a forward reconnaissance company of the Third Army when they took rubble-strewn Munich. He thought of his escape as he passed the wrecked train station.

The countryside was strangely peaceful. He made a left turn at the familiar crossroads and drove his jeep through town. It was untouched, a regiment of American infantry patrolling the streets. He passed the bus stop where he'd waited and thought of Ilse. When he came to the farm he turned into the dirt road. It was muddy from a recent rain and seemed deserted, the shutters closed. He shut off the motor and heard a sighing wind as he looked at the house and barn. They seemed smaller. He swung himself out of the jeep and walked to the barn, shouldering his carbine.

The door was closed. As he entered he could smell the lingering odor of the cows and their dung. On one of the beams he saw the boat he'd carved for Frank and wondered where he was, where Milt was. Katherine had written that she'd heard from Milt's wife, Roberta, that he'd been moved to another camp. He put the boat down and cradled his rifle when he thought he heard the sound of footsteps. He cautiously left the barn.

It was silent outside as he crossed to the house. The door was locked. He stepped back and looked up at the windows. He'd fantasized meeting them all again. Would they be glad to see him? The windows were shuttered, and he stepped to the door, slipping an envelope containing four hundred marks under it, then walked around the house once more looking for signs of life. He could not get over the eerie sensation of being watched.

"Willi," he called. Silence. "Frank!" Nothing. He frowned and went back to the jeep. As he turned to get into the driver's seat, he saw somebody disappear around the corner of the house. Alarmed, he held his rifle ready and crouched behind the hood of the jeep.

"Frank!" he called again. What an irony to be shot now at the end of the war by a fanatic.

"Robert?" came a small voice.

He turned to see Frank at the corner of the house. As Robert stood, the boy ran into his arms and hugged him. Robert lifted the child, returning the embrace, feeling like an older brother returned from the war.

Frank took him into the kitchen, which still smelled of soup. Robert looked at the undernourished child as he told of the increased hardships as the war was coming to an end. Willi had lost his spirit and hardly worked the farm now, as the cows had been taken from him for meat. Frank's brown eyes were sad, and Robert felt no child should have to endure what he had. He kissed the boy's cheek, knowing he'd always be connected to him.

———————————

Robert drove past the prison camp where he and Milt had been held. Germans were now behind the fence and

American GIs patrolled its perimeter. The wind brought the smell of the concentration camp as he neared it.

Nothing could have prepared him for what he saw. Nothing scratched the surface of this reality. To his right were low barracks, to the left the death factory. He had to stop the jeep as a bulldozer filled with bodies crossed in front of him to a large trench, where it deposited them. It backed up and returned to the large stacks of naked corpses collected for burial which had been left behind by the retreating Germans. The GI on the bulldozer was wearing a handkerchief against the gaslike odor that made it hard for Robert to breathe. Other GIs were also busy dragging, stacking, and burying.

He got out of the jeep and walked to a small brick building. The room he entered was cement, low-ceilinged, with shower heads. His nose twitched at the sharp smell. The door to the attached building was open. There was an iron stretcher on the floor. He stepped over it and into what looked like the furnace room of a large apartment house. Most of the furnace doors were open, and he recognized the sweet, sickish smell they'd known when passing the camp. More metal litters covered the floor and stuck out of the furnace doors. He walked to one and looked inside. There were ashes and incompletely burned bones.

Involuntarily he touched the still-warm body of the furnace and felt sick. "Baking bread," the German guard on their truck had laughingly said of the smell. Robert shook his head in dismay. Every day for years this had gone on in a routine manner, with "production schedules." He heard footsteps behind him, and a sergeant entered the crematorium.

"Can I help you, captain?"

Robert shook his head silently.

"I know what you mean. Difficult to take in, isn't it?"

"Can I go across the road?" Robert asked.

"Sure. There's a medical team there. Those poor people aren't any better off than the corpses."

Robert left his jeep and crossed to the barracks area. Outside, there was a mobile kitchen and ambulances. He entered one of the buildings. It was a men's barracks, and they were lying in tiers of bunks four and five high to the ceiling, with barely enough room for a thin body on the hay mattresses. The coarse striped cotton uniforms hung on bodies that were hardly more than skeletons, skin stretched so tight they were skulls with staring eyes. A few were able to move about; most lay helplessly staring at the medics and doctors as they examined and fed them.

Robert wandered through the rows numb with guilt at his own solidity. It was then, as he turned into another row, that he heard the croaking voice. He put it aside as imagination.

"Robert . . ." the voice rasped.

Robert was too stunned to answer. "Paul," the voice cracked again. "Paul Fresnay."

Robert took his friend in his arms. As he felt the weightlessness, the pitiful frailness of the once strong body, his tears began and he reached for Fresnay's hands.

The fingers were curled and misshapen. "Gestapo . . ." the broken voice told him.

———————————

A sob escaped Robert that woke Katherine. She took him in her arms, thinking of her own demons. They lay in each other's arms until they fell asleep again.

Katherine was gone when Mike came home the following morning. Robert was at the typewriter.

"Hiya," Mike said, entering the bedroom. "Got a minute?"

"Sure. By the way, there were some calls for you. Alex, your director . . . and Hollywood."

"Hollywood?" Mike laughed.

"A producer at 20th Century—Fox."

"What did he say?"

"To call him collect. It's all on the kitchen table. Where'd you end up last night, Ruth's or Maxine's?"

"Would you believe both?"

Robert laughed. "I'd believe anything. But don't tell Katherine."

"Believe me, I won't." Then Mike's eyes narrowed in the

look he reserved for serious questions. "Did you ever give anyone a hostile fuck?"

"I've practically never slept with anyone but Katherine. My first ineffectual rumble-seat efforts don't count."

"Ruth is sweet. I really like her. But Maxine is fantastic, and it's like I want to fuck her to death. It's angry, hostile fucking, and she loves it."

"Do you?"

"I don't know. That's why I'm asking."

"I haven't had the experience."

"Okay. . . . How's the work coming?"

"I'm slugging it out."

"I don't know if that's a good sign."

"I don't know either, but I can't let go of it."

Mike nodded and went to the kitchen. He made himself a pot of espresso and placed the call to California. Murray Silverman got on the phone immediately.

"Hi there, Mike."

"Hi," Mike said.

"Read your notices for *Stalag* this morning, and the studio report on the opening was terrific, just terrific. Can I ask you a question?"

"Sure."

"Were you in the war?"

"Uh-huh."

"See any combat?"

"Enough. I was in the Abraham Lincoln Battalion and the OSS."

"Great! Just great!" Silverman said enthusiastically. "I'm doing a war movie and I wanted to test you."

"I've already been tested."

"You've had a screen test?"

"That's not what I meant," Mike said dryly.

"I didn't think so. I'd like to fly you out."

"No thanks."

There was a silence. "Why not? This is a good part." The voice was a few degrees cooler.

"I'm not interested in testing. If you'd like me to, I'd be glad to read your script and get back to you."

"Do you know who you're talking to?"

"Not really, Mr. Silverman. I don't mean to be insulting. I just said I wasn't interested in testing. If you're interested in my work, come to New York."

Silverman hung up.

Alex laughed. "You handled it perfectly."

A week later, Silverman called the producer of *Stalag* for tickets.

———

"Why are you doing it if you don't care for the script?"

"I can do something with the part, and I've never been to Hollywood," Mike replied to Robert's question. They were having lunch in a small Village restaurant. "I've also found a new apartment," Mike continued.

"Oh," Robert said, feeling a twinge. "And when do you leave for the Coast?"

"Not till the middle of June. I'll be back in September. The apartment's just around the corner."

"That's great. But why are you moving?"

"I think it's time, Robert."

———

Although Mike moved, their schedules didn't change, and Robert continued to see more of Mike than he did of Katherine. He also continued his struggle with *American Dreams*.

In June 1946, Katherine finished her psychiatric residency, took a job in a clinic, and opened her own small office. Mike left for Hollywood to act in *Foxhole*, and Robert was about to give up on his play. Its theme always seemed to swamp the characters and become didactic.

At lunch, Alex suggested he think of another subject.

"Like what?" Robert asked.

"Spain," Alex answered.

CHAPTER EIGHTEEN

Mike enjoyed postwar Hollywood.

He was welcomed as a fine artist and as a war hero. The work was easy for him, and he translated strongly on screen.

"Who's that guy?" the studio head asked the producer as they watched dailies on *Foxhole*. Silverman had noted his boss moving forward with interest as Mike's scene came on.

"Mike Rossano," the producer said. "He's a New York stage actor I found."

"Make a term deal with him."

"I'll try. He's very independent."

"Independence has a price. Just make sure it's not too high."

The following afternoon Mike's agent came to the studio commissary to have lunch with him. He radiated success as he speared a shrimp and nodded to friends at other tables.

"You could do well here, Mike. The studio likes your work. They've offered me a term contract."

"No slave deals for me," Mike answered, biting into his corned-beef sandwich.

"We're all slaves to something," the agent countered smoothly. "Power, fame, sex . . ."

"Work."

"You want me to get you another picture?"

"I want to direct a play here, first."

"That's interesting," Ziggy mused. "At the Actors' Lab?"

"Yeah. There're a lot of New York stage people there,

and I'm interested in the theater. Movies are for quick money."

Mike chuckled as he drove through Beverly Hills on his way to Odets's house. The top of his convertible was down and the late sun warmed his face. He had disdained the offer but was secretly pleased. It was nice to be wanted, and he knew the studio would be back with a larger offer.

Mike tried to fathom what was going on behind Odets's blue eyes as he told him of the offer in the writer's beautifully furnished living room, surrounded by the magnificent art collection. It was as if Odets knew something Mike didn't, but wouldn't reveal it.

"When do the women arrive?" Mike asked Odets, who was making a party for him.

———————————

Shooting was completed on *Foxhole* in September. There was a "wrap party" on the set, which was a bombed-out village. They drank champagne and ate canapés in its ruined streets. Stavros Miarcos, the head of the studio, put his arm around Mike and steered him over to a bullet-pocked wall.

"You did a good job, Mike."

"Thank you."

"Why won't you take my offer?"

"I want to go back to the theater."

"Theater is nice, but who sees it? A few thousand people. Millions around the world see movies. Besides, there's no money in the theater."

"Who told you I was interested in money?"

"Everybody is interested in money. It's only the amount that's different. I'll double my offer."

"Thank you," Mike laughed good-naturedly. "But I don't believe in long-term commitments."

"You're not married?"

"I'm not married." Mike smiled.

"I'll get you yet." Stavros smiled back, wagging his finger in Mike's face. "I always get what I want."

"So do I," Mike answered.

Mike directed *Awake and Sing* at the Actors' Lab in Hollywood. Odets was ecstatic about the production, and Mike discovered something about himself: He preferred giving direction to taking it. He left for New York thinking of becoming a director.

He was also anxious to see Robert and read his play about Spain.

CHAPTER NINETEEN

Katherine walked through the late-fall streets of the Village toward her office. Her coat did not hide the size of her belly; she was due in a month. There was only light, early-morning traffic, trucks delivering bread and produce. It reminded her of dawn in Paris. Her fantasy was suddenly interrupted by a familiar voice calling her name. She looked up to see Larry Peters crossing the street toward her. She hadn't seen or spoken to him since the day she got the letter from Robert.

"Katherine!" he called again, catching up with her.

"Hello, Larry," she said quietly, unsure of what she was feeling.

He looked at her shyly, uncertainly. "How are you?" he asked.

"I'm fine. How are you?"

"Okay. The work's going well." He nodded at her belly. "I guess your husband got home all right."

"Yes." She blushed.

"Did you ever tell him?"

"No. I couldn't."

"Why not?"

Katherine's discomfort grew. She couldn't answer the question herself. "I probably didn't want him to know he could be replaced so quickly," she answered at last.

"I haven't been able to replace you."

"I'm sorry," was all she could manage.

He impulsively took her hand. "I still love you," he said.

"Larry . . . please." Katherine's cheeks colored.

"I've walked around the hospital and your apartment all hours of the day and night hoping I would see you. I've thought about you, dreamed about you. I can't get you out of my mind."

"Please, Larry," Katherine pleaded, withdrawing her hand. "I've thought about you, too. I'm not proud of the way I ended it."

"Can I see you again?"

"I've got to go," she said quickly. "I've got a patient." She turned abruptly and walked up the street.

Katherine's office was in a brownstone, and she fumbled for her keys, totally unnerved by the chance meeting.

Her patient came down the steps behind her. "You're late," she said crossly.

"I'm sorry," Katherine mumbled, realizing her hand was trembling as she fitted the key into the lock.

As the woman began her session, Katherine found her mind wandering. She was surprised at the residue of emotion still attached to the relationship. Suddenly, the woman began to cry and brought Katherine back to the room.

———————

Robert worked on his new play with a passion that had him forgetting to eat or shave for days at a time. The play flowed, character and plot growing together from his experience.

"How many casualties did we have at Belchite?" he asked Katherine as she was about to leave for her office.

"I don't remember, but I can look it up. Where are you?"

"Where Pete got wounded."

Katherine kissed him and left.

Five minutes later, Robert said, "Goodbye," and looked up when he heard no reply. Puzzled, he realized she'd left some time ago.

———————

Katherine walked from her office to St. Vincent's Hospital. She worked in the psychiatric clinic in the afternoons, until six, then did some grocery shopping and went home.

As she entered the apartment, she could hear the typewriter clacking.

"Hi," she called. Silence. "Hello?" she called again. The typewriter continued. Robert had taken over Mike's old room, and it was possible he didn't hear her. She put some water on to boil.

"Hi," he finally called out.

Katherine laughed. She entered the room and draped herself seductively across the doorway, her huge belly protruding.

Robert was still in his bathrobe. He looked blankly at her. "What are you trying to do?" he asked.

"Seduce you."

"In your condition?"

"Don't you find pregnant women attractive?"

"More than any other kind." He smiled.

She left the doorway and crossed to him, sitting on his lap. "Good day?" she asked.

"Hmmmm. . . . What about you?"

She was toying with the idea of telling Robert about Larry when she heard the sound at the front of the apartment.

"Is that the key in the door?" she asked.

"Sounds like it."

"Anybody home?" Mike called out.

Robert nearly dumped Katherine from his lap.

"Mike!" he shouted.

The two men met in the hallway and embraced.

"You growing a beard?" Mike asked. "And what are you doing in your bathrobe?"

"Working."

"Well . . . those are good signs." He saw Katherine in the doorway watching them. "Look at little mother!" he said excitedly and crossed to her, taking her in his arms. "You are about to pop. How do you feel?"

"Good, Mike."

Mike sensed the small holding-back in her greeting. "It's so great to see you," he rushed on excitedly. "What's for dinner?"

"Boiled water," Katherine laughed.

"It's good to know nothing's changed. I'll take you to Umberto's tonight."

———————————

Umberto's was one of the better restaurants in Little Italy, and the small, wizened man in the dark suit greeted Mike like a son, kissing him on both cheeks.

"How's you momma, Mikey?" he asked in a rough voice. "I ain' seen her awhile." Umberto had been a friend of Mike's father's, and his son, Sal, was a streetmate of Mike's.

"She's good, Mr. Pizzo. How's Sal?"

"Sal be here soon. He don' like come in early. I seen you sista wit' her kid. She look good. Where you been, Mikey?"

"Hollywood."

"Hollywood! Hey, big shot. Gonna be a movie star, hah?" Umberto led them to a good table next to Tommy the Priest and Carmine the Boss. Both men wore expensive suits and tinted glasses.

"Hey, Tommy," Umberto said as he seated them, "remember Mikey Rossano, Angelo's boy? He jus' come back from Hollywood."

"Hollywood! No kiddin'. You gonna be a star?"

"I'm tryin', Tommy."

"Well, we rootin' fer you, kid."

Mike was in a good mood as he described Hollywood, mostly in a deprecating manner, and told of his satisfaction in turning down Stavros.

Katherine tried to listen in a detached, professional way, tried to distance herself from her relationship to Mike to get at his real meanings. She looked about the restaurant at the people Mike had grown up with and tried to understand what it meant to be a first-generation American from a poverty-stricken background who could be thrust into stardom. Perhaps she knew Mike too well for objectivity.

Mike was aware of being judged, aware that Katherine was weighing his words. He was relieved when she leaned forward and became a friend again.

"Hey, Mikey!" Sal shouted, crossing to the table. He was tall and good-looking in a vain way. He and Mike kissed each other's cheeks as if they were old-time Sicilians.

"How you doin', shrimp?" Sal asked after being introduced. "Pop says you was in Hollywood. You shack up wit' any stars?" He looked apologetically at Katherine. "Excuse my mouth. . . . You have a convertible an' all that stuff?"

"Just like in the movies, Sal."

Sal turned to Robert and Katherine. "Anyone tells me when we was runnin' aroun' the streets that my frien' Mikey Rossano wit' the runny nose was gonna be a movie star, I'da called Bellevue for the straitjacket."

Katherine was the first to read *They Shall Not Pass!* She was in tears as she turned the last page. She called to Robert, who was waiting in the bedroom-study.

He came into the living room apprehensively. "Well . . . ?" he asked, even though he saw her wet eyes.

"It's so moving, Robert."

"What's wrong with it?" Robert had primed himself for failure.

"I don't see anything wrong with it," she said, surprised. "Perhaps I can't judge it objectively, but I think it's wonderful. When will Mike read it?"

"Tomorrow."

"It's devastating, Robert. Fucking devastating," Mike said, getting up and embracing Robert. "It grabs you by the throat and doesn't let go."

"Well . . . let's see if it devastates anyone else."

Robert gave the play to Alex.

Alex's office was on 57th Street near Carnegie Hall, in an old studio building with skylights. The room was decorated with props and posters and had a grand piano. Robert heard Alex playing a Chopin étude as he entered. Alex smiled and got up from the piano. He smelled as if he'd just come from the barber.

"Sit down, Robert. How's Katherine?"

"She's fine. Any day now."

"That's wonderful." Alex could see Robert's anxiety and didn't keep him in suspense with further small talk. He started by nodding enthusiastically.

"Terrific play, Robert. Just terrific. You've managed a large canvas and a complicated time scheme with compassion and emotion. The characters are interesting and develop well, the action is engrossing. It's expensive as hell and has to be done."

"What's wrong with it?"

"We'll see when we get it on its feet and it starts to walk."

"That means you want to direct it?"

"No."

Robert's face fell.

"I think Mike should direct it."

"Mike?"

"I don't know anyone else who would be better. Odets told me he did a wonderful job on the Coast with *Awake and Sing*."

"But that's a different kind of play," Robert objected. He had his heart set on Alex.

"True. But besides you, there's no one who knows the material better. Besides, Mike's got terrific instincts."

"Does he have the craft?"

"What he doesn't have in craft, he'll make up in talent." He looked at Robert frankly. "Why are you resisting it?"

"I hoped you would do it."

"Mike is better than I am for this."

"You really think so?"

"Yes."

"But will anyone produce it with Mike as director?"

"I will."

Robert's heart leaped. "You will?"

"Yes." Alex beamed. "Nothing would give me greater pleasure."

"That would be fantastic! Can you get the money?"

"Money comes to money. I've got a big hit on Broadway, so everyone is throwing it at me. When I have another flop, I'll be a bum again. Remember the lady who gave us the house that summer of 1939?"

"The one who wanted your body?" Robert said, laughing.

"The very one. Well, I'll just have to give it to her. Her husband is rich again."

———————————

It was two in the morning. Katherine had been in the delivery room for half an hour.

Mike paced and smoked. "Jeez, Mike, sit down. You're making me nervous."

"How can you be so calm?"

"I'm not calm. But at least I'm not falling apart."

Mike continued his smoking and pacing. A nurse walked briskly to Mike with a smile. "Congratulations, Mr. Thompson. It's a boy."

"A boy! Robert, a *boy*!"

"You can see your wife now," she said to Mike.

Katherine smiled as the nurse brought Robert, Jr., into the room. While Katherine cradled the child, Robert and Mike leaned over him.

"Thank God he looks like Katherine," Mike said.

"He is cute," Robert responded.

"I hope I'm not cute, Robert," Katherine said in mock pique.

The baby opened his eyes. "Look at that blue," Mike said. "Like the Mediterranean."

"I think you're getting carried away, Mike," Katherine laughed.

"Why shouldn't I be? How often do I get to be a godfather?" But Mike had hoped they'd name the child after him.

The nurse came back. "I think you should let Dr. Thompson rest now. You can come back tomorrow."

Katherine nodded in tired agreement.

The two men kissed her and left, walking through the late Village streets with their arms around each other.

"You want to come up for some coffee?" Mike asked.

"No, thanks. I want to get some sleep and then work on the opening scene."

"Okay. I have a casting meeting with Alex tomorrow. I'll

see you at the hospital at two." Mike looked smilingly at Robert. "Congratulations, buddy."

———————

"A boy!" Pete exclaimed. "That's great." Pete was behind the counter of his cousin's floral shop.

"Last night," Mike said. "Eight pounds, six ounces."

"A real heavyweight."

"I was more excited than Robert."

"Well, you know Robert. Captain Control."

"The nurse thought I was the father," Mike said, pleased.

———————

Katherine's room was filled. Pete brought baclava, Irv knishes, Milt champagne, Abe herring; Barkin's wife had baked a coffee cake. The sounds of the party could be heard all the way to the nurses' station, but no one complained.

———————

After four weeks, Katherine went back to a full work schedule. Robert had to share the study with Bobby. The clatter of Robert's typewriter didn't seem to wake the baby, and Mike took him to the nearby park at Washington Square, where he'd rock the baby and play chess with the park regulars. He didn't disabuse anyone of the idea that the child was his. Katherine met them at the apartment to breast-feed Bobby before going off to St. Vincent's for the afternoon. Then Robert and Mike worked on the play.

It was December and they were casting, set to go into rehearsal in the middle of January. Word had gotten out that the play was about Robert, Mike, and Katherine. The actors were nervous when reading.

Mike had been seeing more of Ruth than anyone else, seeking the kind of stability he envied in Robert and Katherine. Ruth's acceptance of his moodiness made the relationship possible.

———————

The actors had assembled for the first day's rehearsal on the bare stage of the Morosco Theater. Alex, as producer, made a short welcoming speech and turned the rehearsal over to Mike, who introduced Robert. Robert was nervous as the actors turned to him, but he spoke intently about commitment, his and theirs. When he was done, the actors applauded.

"Okay," Mike said. "Let's read the play."

The actors sat in a circle, Robert, Mike, and Alex at a table. There was a silence as the actors settled into the feeling of the Paris café.

"*Bonsoir* . . . my name is Paul Fresnay of the International Brigades. If you don't mind introducing yourselves, we can start with the chess players."

They had started! Robert was lost in the play as they read. Occasionally something didn't strike him right and he made a note, but for the most part, he was caught up in the emotion of the morning.

After the first reading, Mike looked at his watch. "Ten minutes, everybody." He turned to Robert. "Too long." Alex nodded in agreement.

"I thought it went very well," Robert said defensively.

"It did," Mike said. "But it still can use cutting for pace and emphasis."

"Robert," Alex said, smiling, "these are only the first steps on a long road." He took Robert's shoulder affectionately.

"It is a long road. It started ten years ago," Robert said.

———————————

On Valentine's Day, the Brigade had their annual reunion. Mike did not mention Florita. Ruth was pregnant.

The company went up to New Haven the following day.

Robert looked at his name on the marquee of the Shubert Theater and was thrilled. Mike was already in the theater. He'd stayed up all night with the crew while they set up the scenery.

The first run-through was rough. There were a lot of missed cues, and the play had no life as the actors tried to adjust to the complicated set and light cues. Robert was alarmed. Alex and Mike were calm. It was all perfectly normal.

Robert tossed all night after the first dress rehearsal. The following day was spent straightening out prop, costume, lighting, and set problems. No one bothered about the play, and Robert felt useless. He spent much of the day in and out of the theater, walking the Yale campus, and feeling anxious until it was time to pick up Katherine at the train station.

When she came out of the shower in his hotel room, Robert put his arms around her wet body and kissed her breasts hungrily.

"Are you all right?" she asked, surprised at his passion.

"Hmmmmm . . . I just feel as if I'm about to jump off a cliff."

"You are. But don't worry about it."

———————————

She sat alone. The three men stood in the back of the last row as the curtain went up on the Café Montparnasse at the end of 1936. The café set revolved and revealed the interior room in which they'd played their first chess game. As Fresnay made his entrance, Mike sat down next to the girl with a clipboard and flashlight who took notes for him. Alex paced.

Robert became uncritically involved. Mike watched the play. Alex watched the audience.

The first act ended to scattered applause, and the audience filed up the aisle.

"What'd you think?" Robert asked Mike as he walked up to him.

"Needs a lot of work," Mike said soberly. "When is Katherine going home?"

"Tomorrow morning."

"Good. I'll need your total concentration."

Katherine came up the aisle smiling. "It's alive," she said.

"Not yet, doctor," Mike countered. He was tense and subdued. Katherine noted his mood and went out to the lobby.

The audience warmed to the second act, and there was heavy applause at the final curtain. Robert beamed at Alex and Katherine.

"Don't let this fool you," Mike said. "New Haven isn't New York."

Later, in their room, after all the backslapping and congratulations at Kaysey's restaurant, Robert sat on the bed unaccountably depressed. "You know, Mike wasn't like this even in combat."

"He has more to lose now," Katherine observed.

They were in New Haven for a week. Except for performances, Robert was in his room rewriting.

"How do you feel?" Katherine asked on the phone.

"Great! I think all the changes have been for the better. Mike has been fantastic. Absolutely tireless and absolutely right. How's little Bobby?"

"I think he misses your typewriter, and he's always eating."

"Lucky guy."

At the end of the week, they went to Boston. The critics had been split in New Haven, but the Boston papers were unanimous in their raves, calling *They Shall Not Pass!* major theater. They had standing room only even for matinees.

But one night, as the audience sat in rapt attention, a man rose and shouted, "Commie propaganda! Go back to Russia!"

The audience tried to quiet him, but he continued his abuse.

"Sit down and shut up!" a man behind him finally shouted back.

"I fought in the Pacific for four years and I'm not gonna listen to this Commie—"

"I was with Patton from North Africa to Berlin, and I'm telling you—"

The fight that ensued between the two veterans made the newspapers and increased the demand for tickets.

"We should stay in Boston," Alex laughed.

But Mike remained concentrated on the work. "We've got to tighten the hospital scenes," he said in his suite at the Ritz. "I can feel the audience leaving us there. I don't want to let them off the hook for a minute."

He was relentless. "I think we ought to try something more radical for the opening," he said at a meeting of all departments. "We need more feeling of the period, more of the threat of Fascism, even before the curtain goes up. Like the Condor Legion song. Also, the lighting in the last battle scene is too general. It needs to be more specific, more dramatic, sharper." He turned to the stage manager. "And Jimmy, I want to see the music and lighting blended more smoothly in the scene changes." Mike was a perfectionist.

Robert hugged little Bobby and danced around the room with him. The baby shrieked with delight. Robert felt as though he'd come home from Spain and they were winning.

As Mike dressed for the opening he looked at himself in the mirror and saw his father emerging. I'm getting older, he thought.

Taxis and limos streamed through the dense traffic of 45th Street. The street was alive with the expectations of the evening. People hurried to box offices, to meet friends and lovers. There was that special excitement in front of the Morosco, the excitement of an opening.

The lobby was crowded with chattering couples in gowns and tuxedos. Katherine arrived with Paul Fresnay, who'd come from Paris. They sat with Ruth.

Backstage, Robert, Mike, and Alex stood in front of the assembled actors. "We've done all that is humanly possible," Mike said. "Robert has worked to the last minute. Alex has given us everything we needed. The rest is up to you onstage tonight. As the Loyalists said in Spain"—Mike dramatically raised his fist—"*Nos pasaremos!* We shall pass!"

Irv, Milt, Pete, Abe, and their women sat in the same

row with Katherine, Ruth, Fresnay, and the Barkins. Fresnay rubbed his fingers anxiously as the house lights dimmed and the Condor Legion sang. Katherine saw Robert, Mike, and Alex leave the stage door and walk up the side aisle to the rear of the theater. As the lights went out, the music segued to Edith Piaf singing of love, and the curtain went up on the Café Montparnasse.

Katherine took Fresnay's bent fingers in hers as his character entered.

At the back of the house, the three men also put their hands together.

There wasn't a cough all evening.

The audience sat forward, watching intensely, wrapped in the cloak of the story.

Onstage, the performances had ignited and blazed, ending with the fiery speech of La Pasionaria in the square of Barcelona.

"We shall never forget you!" her voice rang out. "When the olive tree of peace puts forth its leaves again, come back. Come back to us! Long live the heroes of the International Brigades!"

The curtain came down on a stunned silence. Then the applause exploded. The audience gave the cast a standing ovation. Then they started to chant, "*Author! Author! Author!*"

Robert loped to the stage and sprang onto it as the curtain stayed up on the last call. He motioned for quiet.

"Hemingway wrote, 'Our dead are a part of Spain now, and the earth of Spain can never die. Our dead will live in it forever.'"

Tears rolled down Pete's sightless eyes.

"The theater is a marriage of talents," Robert continued, "a collaboration. It may start as one man's vision, but it becomes that of many, none more important to me than Mike Rossano's, who has shared my life and my work." He motioned for Mike to join him. "And the man who is our stage father, Alex Tarasov." As Alex joined them on stage, they embraced the actors, and the audience went wild.

In the upstairs room at Sardi's the mood was exuberant. The plainly dressed vets mingled with the fashionable first-nighters. The backers had all their friends there, promising to let them invest in their next hit.

There was applause as Alex entered with a lovely young actress on his arm. He was in his opening-night Russian impresario uniform, radiating success. Robert and Mike, who'd been sitting with Katherine and Ruth, joined him.

"When will Ben get here with the notices?" Mike asked. Ben was the press agent.

"He's over at the *Times* now. He's got a deal with the typesetter for a copy of the proofs."

"It's probably the wrong time to ask," Katherine said to Ruth at the table, "but I've never been one for small talk . . ."

"I don't know what Mike wants to do."

"What do you want to do?" Katherine asked. Ruth was silent. "If you're going to terminate the pregnancy, you'll have to do it soon." Ruth nodded. "Do you want to marry Mike?"

"You know I do."

The party swirled about them. Katherine felt a pang of sympathy for Ruth, and a twitch of anger at Mike.

Everybody else was up. The vets regaled their listeners with stories of Spain as they all waited for the papers. Alex was high-spirited as he circulated. "What a night! Thrilling!" he exclaimed.

Ben suddenly rushed in, his cheeks flushed, his hand holding notices aloft like a banner.

"*Raves!* Raves, Alex!" he shouted.

Everyone crowded Alex as he read them aloud.

"'High drama at the Morosco' . . . 'mighty ensemble performances' . . . 'Robert Thompson is a strong new voice in the theater and he has in Mike Rossano a brilliant collaborator.' *New York Times.* 'Robert Thompson brought us a fine new drama last night, and Mike Rossano guided a gifted cast in a gripping evening.' *Herald Tribune.* Even the *Daily News.* 'Despite its content, there's strong drama at the Morosco brought about by two great talents, Robert Thompson and Mike Rossano.'"

"We did it!" Mike said emotionally. "We won!" Robert

nodded, unable to speak. Mike took Katherine's hand and drew her to them.

———————

The following evening, Fresnay cooked an onion soup while Robert and Mike bathed Bobby.

"You know," Mike said. "I think I'm gonna marry Ruth and have that baby."

Robert smiled and punched Mike on the shoulder.

After Fresnay's dinner they took a taxi uptown to the theater. There was a long line at the box office extending out to the street. There was also a line of pickets, carrying signs and chanting.

"Back to Russia! Back to Russia!" the signs said. "Jew money," "Commie propaganda," "America First!" and "We fought the wrong enemy." The pickets, predominantly male, looked like American Legionnaires.

Mike and Robert looked at the angry faces and thought of Nazi storm troopers.

Alex emerged from the lobby, crossing to them. "They didn't waste any time," he said.

"Well, they aren't stopping anyone from going to the box office," Mike observed.

"We'll see," Alex said. He started into the theater, Mike and Robert following him.

"Did you ever think *we'd* be crossing a picket line?" Mike asked.

The picketing continued but didn't seem to have any effect on the box office, though there had been several fights in front of the theater and two mounted policemen were stationed there every night.

———————

Katherine had found a duplex in a town house on Washington Square which gave her an office and Robert a study.

"Now I feel like a real writer," Robert said.

Mike and Ruth got married there in April, and Robert started outlining a new play. But *American Dreams* still nagged at him.

In April 1947, the House Un-American Activities Committee came to Hollywood to discover the extent of Communist subversion of the film industry by left-wing and pro-Soviet writers, producers, directors, and actors. They named *Mission to Moscow*, a wartime movie, as a prime example of a sympathetic film about Russia. It had been made by Warner Brothers. A worried Jack Warner called for "an all-out fight on the Commies." Odets sent Alex the item from the *Hollywood Reporter*.

"I don't like it," Alex said to Robert and Mike. "I smell a witch-hunt."

Katherine reminded them at dinner that Hollywood had been the biggest supporter of the Spanish Loyalists in the United States.

"My ambulance in the Ebro offensive was donated by Jimmy Cagney. It even had his name on the side."

"And remember how they called us 'premature anti-Fascists' during the war because we'd fought in Spain," Robert said.

The committee's secret hearings at the Biltmore Hotel turned into a fiasco. They got very few "friendly" witnesses to testify, although they named many screenwriters as "Commies" and the committee called for their firing. But Louis B. Mayer told them, "Nobody can tell me how to run my studio."

The producers balked at government control and the committee left town, tails between legs.

But the picket lines around the Morosco were now beginning to affect business.

"Who's behind it?" Robert asked Alex.

"An underground hate group called the Committee on National Security. They've even got the Boy Scouts and the Campfire Girls on their list as 'Communistic and dangerous.'"

Robert was in his study working one morning in June. A poster of the play was behind him, and photos of himself

with Mike were to his right. Other Spanish Civil War posters and watercolors were on the walls. He was looking at
the photo Irv had taken at Jarama when the phone rang.

It was Alex. "We've got to close," he said. "We've fallen
below our guarantees to the theater. I'm sorry."

"Have you told Mike?"

"Yes."

Robert found Mike in Washington Square Park near the
chess players. Bobby was in the sandbox.

"It always happens when things are going great," Mike
said. "I think it's God reminding you that life will not turn
out well."

"C'mon, Mike, look what we've survived."

"Yeah." Mike grinned. "And a whole lifetime to go." He
went to the sandbox and swept the baby into his arms.
"C'mon, *bambino*, let's get a cappuccino."

They sat in the nearly empty restaurant. There were only
a few elderly Italians and some young hoods drinking espresso from small glasses and playing cards. Bobby was on
Mike's lap making a gooey mess of a cannoli.

"How's the play going?" Mike asked.

"It's not. I think about the other play."

"Let me read what you've got on *American Dreams*."

"Okay. How's it going with Ruth?"

"She's very sweet." Mike sighed.

"But . . ."

"But I don't feel anything but emptiness afterward." He
shrugged. Then, suddenly, he burst out, "I *want* to feel
something, goddammit!" Bobby was surprised by the sudden vehemence. "I feel nothing. No, not nothing. Anxiety,
fear of nothingness. It sounds like fear of death. But you
know I'm not afraid of dying." He was silent for a moment.
"I've never told anyone this before." He paused. "I always
blamed my mother for my father's death. Because she
wouldn't let him quit."

"But Mike, there was no work."

"I know there was no work," Mike said emotionally, "and
she thought his fears were nonsense. She *had* to think his
fears were nonsense. I know that. But she didn't know how
much he loved to work. He didn't tell her. He told me.

Every night he'd tell me how many rows of bricks he'd laid that day, and what the guys said and the jokes they told and how they whistled at the women. He loved to work, but he knew he should leave that job. He knew how dangerous it was." Mike grew more emotional. "We could have gone to the opera for years. He would have been to the opening of our play. He loved the theater. Do you know what it would have meant to him to see my picture in front of the theater? He would have been at my wedding and shown us all how to dance! He would have taken his grandson to the park."

Mike was near tears, but his mood was broken when Umberto crossed to them.

"Hey, Mikey . . . *come va? Que se dice?*"

———————————

Mike slammed the script on Robert's desk.

"You're not Bertolt Brecht, for Christ's sake!" he said heatedly. "You're not seeking alienation of the audience. You want identification, but you're distanced from the relationships."

"I still can't hook into the emotion."

"I don't know why. There's nothing more explosive than family relationships. Look at Greek drama. Look at me! I'm a walking example of the pain."

Robert was silent for a moment as he looked about the room, then turned to Mike. "Maybe I should change the geography. Make it someplace else besides Iowa. Maybe the closeness is what's choking me."

Mike nodded. "Try it. You may be right. What I do know is that you're on to something potentially very powerful here. Now let's take Bobby for a walk."

"You take him for a walk," Robert said excitedly. "I want to think."

———————————

Robert began exploring the old family neighborhoods of Brooklyn and imagining the lives within their houses. It seemed to free him from the emotional irons he'd been bound in.

Katherine had been working hard establishing her own

practice while maintaining her work at the clinic, for she felt a strong social responsibility to those who couldn't afford private therapy. She presented a paper to the American Psychiatric Association's annual convention on the battered child and the battering parent cycle. It was widely reprinted, and she was now getting invitations to speak at other conventions.

———

In August, they went to Deer Isle with Bobby.

Mr. Eaton tried to be discreet in his inspection of Robert. He looked familiar but didn't look like the man who had been with Katherine the last time she'd been there.

"Must be the same fella," he told his wife. "She don't seem like the kind of lady who switches around."

"They're both tall and they do look alike, but I don't think they're the same," she insisted.

"You think it's their baby?" he asked.

"I think it's her baby, but I wouldn't swear about the father. You know how city folks behave."

"No, I don't," he sighed, putting his hand on her small breast.

"Now, don't get too familiar, Clyde," she laughed. "We only been married forty-five years."

The island was as beautiful as ever and still largely undiscovered. Eaton worked his lobster traps and knew every cranny of the coastline. Katherine and Robert went to Burnt Cove alone while the Eatons took care of Bobby. They looked out at the serene water, the lobstermen working, the gulls swooping for fish. They were lying down, surrounded by trees, the sun filtering shadows on their faces.

Robert reached for Katherine to make love to her. Katherine took his hand and held it firmly in hers. She couldn't do it. She had made love with Larry in this same place.

"What's the matter?" Robert asked.

"I just want to lie here."

He bent over and kissed her. She returned the kiss lightly.

"There's something," he said.

"No. I just don't feel like it."

Robert removed his hand and sat up, angry, puzzled.

Katherine wanted to remove the tension but couldn't bring herself to tell him the truth. Neither could she make love to him here. Why not tell him? she wondered. Did she not trust his reaction? She put her arms around his shoulders.

"I love you, Robert. I just want to lie here peacefully without passion."

Robert seemed to accept this, yet something told him there was more.

They lay in the small wood for an hour, looking at water and sky, then walked back to the Eatons' for lunch.

———————

Mike was edgy. Ruth continued her job at the Theater Guild as a play reader. Mike also read a great deal, and many of their evenings were spent in silence except for the turning of script pages. Mike had lunches with Alex. He hated unemployment, and nothing was going on during the summer except stock. Mike was beyond that.

"When do you think Robert will finish *American Dreams*?" Alex asked.

"I don't know. It's a tough one. It might not be this season. At least, not the first part."

"What about another play?"

"I haven't read anything that interests me, including the ones that go to the Guild. I guess the best scripts are still not coming to me. Are you going to do the Giraudoux play?"

"I think so," Alex answered. "Also, Inge is working on something interesting. You should call Harold Freedman when he gets back from Maine. He handles more good writers than any ten agents."

Mike nodded. Alex could see he was distracted. "What else is happening with you?" he asked.

"Well, I miss Robert . . . and I've been thinking about other women."

Mike was delighted when Robert returned in September and Ziggy, his California agent, called.

"I've got something for you, kid. Right up your alley."

"What is it?"

"I'm gonna make you a director."

"I am a director."

"A movie director. Terrific script. Real balls."

"That'll be a first for Hollywood."

"Don't be such a snob, Mike. This project has guts. Did you see *Crossfire*?"

"Yeah. It was pretty good."

"Damned good. And made money. So, Fox wants to do the Gentile side of anti-Semitism, and the head of the studio thinks it's a great idea for you to direct it."

"Stavros does?"

"Yeah. He knows talent when he sees it."

"Sounds interesting. Send me the script."

"It's called *Loyalties*, and it's in the Fox pouch on its way to you."

"You knew what bait to use, you son of a bitch," Mike laughed.

"Why do you think I'm the best fisherman in Hollywood?"

CHAPTER TWENTY

Instead of staying at the charmingly seedy Château Marmont, the hotel he'd used before, Mike rented a small house on Tigertail Road in Brentwood, with a pool and a view of Beverly Hills from its wonderful kitchen. Ruth stayed behind. She told herself that the Theater Guild had a busy season ahead, the baby was due in November, and Mike would be tied up with the picture, and so she'd be better off in New York. Mike totally agreed.

Katherine held a dim view of the arrangement.

Ziggy arranged a lunch between Shirley Day and Mike at Chasen's. Shirley, whose star was rising, was also a client of Ziggy's, and Fox was interested in having her in *Loyalties*. The fact that her husband was a big producer at Fox didn't hurt.

Shirley was a lean, tanned blonde with Eastern chic. She was intelligent, sure minded, aloof and porcelain cold. On screen, her presence radiated glamour and unattainability. She was perfect for the part.

Ziggy was all smiles as he led her toward the strategically placed corner table where Mike was already seated. Her eyes flicked over him, and an eyebrow arched slightly when he did not stand for her arrival. She put out her hand. The fingers were long and strong, the palm cool.

Her eyes did not turn away as Mike inspected her face. Arrogant bitch, he thought.

Ziggy could feel the tension already between them. "Shirley saw your play in New York," he jumped in.

"It was very good," she said, her voice surprisingly warm and husky.

"Thank you," he said modestly.

"It was obviously deeply felt. Ziggy told me you fought in Spain."

"Among other places." Mike felt himself holding back, as if letting her draw him out.

"My husband considered it as a film. He's a great admirer of yours. But he couldn't get it through the studio. They were afraid of the demonstrations." There was a slight silence, and they could hear the conversational hum of the expensive restaurant and feel the eyes on them.

"What did you think of the new script?" Mike asked her.

Shirley spoke easily, words flowing in articulate rhythms of her perceptions of character and nuance of story.

Mike had been prepared for an actress without too much upstairs and instead had found a mind to match his. She had worked in the theater and was enthusiastic about rehearsals, which were unusual in Hollywood, and could help Mike with the studio in gaining the extra time.

———————

It was a "honeymoon." Rehearsals were harmonious, and as a result of the extra preparation, photography went smoothly. On his first picture, Mike was on schedule and on budget, and the early reports from the front office were ecstatic.

"See if you can get Rossano for another picture," Stavros Miarcos told John Farrell, Shirley's husband.

Farrell invited Mike to dinner at their mansion in Bel Air.

Mike envied and hated Farrell's good looks, his money, his charmed influence. He also envied him his wife.

"What do you think you're going to do after this picture?" Farrell asked over coffee.

"I'll go back to New York."

"You could do very well out here," Farrell said with promise in his voice.

"I'm doing well in New York," Mike countered.

Shirley watched the skirmish over her cup.

Farrell nodded. He did not make any offers. John Farrell would not accept rejection and so decided to wait.

Mike worked with his usual concentration, taking only Sunday off to have Odets and other friends over for dinner. Occasionally he'd sleep with a minor actress. The rhythm of his life was broken only by the subpoenas his friends received to appear before the House Un-American Activities Committee in October of 1947.

By October, the American Legion had joined the committee's cause. A boycott of any film named by the committee would be instituted by the legion's ten thousand posts.

Hollywood was in a stir. There were meetings all over town. For the most part, those in the industry were outraged at the Congressional committee's attempts to control the contents of their movies. Few believed their films had any Communist intent. From Chasen's to commissaries, from front offices to studio sets, friends and co-workers argued. Were there any among them who were truly threats to the security of the United States?

"What do you want me to do?" Mike asked Odets, who was anxious about his friends.

"Can you go to Washington with the delegation?"

"I'll be shooting."

"How about money? Lawyers are expensive."

Mike donated a thousand dollars to the defense of the nineteen men to appear in Washington.

A short time ago a contribution of a thousand dollars would have seemed inconceivable to him. There were periods when his father didn't make that much in a year. Memories of "skin soup," boiled water with potato skins, never left him. They were with him as he stared at Bel Air ceilings or listened to Malibu surf. But the defense of these men who shared his views, who'd supported what he'd done in Spain, was essential. "It's me I'm defending," he told Odets when he gave him the money. Odets nodded in agreement.

"Any one of us could be called, Cliff. That's why we've got to fight this thing," Mike said.

Of the nineteen "unfriendly witnesses" he knew well

Ring Lardner, Jr.—an Academy Award winner whose younger brother, Jim, had been the last American lost in Spain—and Dalton Trumbo, Albert Maltz, Alvah Bessie—another Lincoln veteran—and John Howard Lawson. He knew less well Eddie Dmytryk and Adrian Scott, who respectively had directed and produced *Crossfire*, the first anti-anti-Semitic picture Hollywood made. He didn't know Bertolt Brecht, who lived in nearby Santa Monica.

Mike went to all the strategy meetings, which were held in Edward G. Robinson's house. It was decided that they would cite the First Amendment, ratifying free speech, rather than the Fifth, as their defense. Refusal to answer the committee because of the possibility of self-incrimination would seem suspicious, as if they had something to hide.

Shirley sat near the tennis court, wearing a large hat that shadowed her face from the sun, a light lavender-and-peach dress that made her look like an Impressionist painting.

Mike was distracted by the soft pastel presence. He was an aggressive and intense player and wanted to beat Farrell badly. After a particularly hard volley, in which Mike sent him from one corner of the court to the other, he smashed a drive that Farrell couldn't return.

"You sure you just learned this game?" Farrell asked breathlessly.

"Motivation." Mike's new tennis whites were dripping.

"That's what that say about you. Shirley loves working with you."

"I can speak for myself," she said, putting down her pink lemonade.

"Of course you can, dear. And I'm sure you've told Mike. I'm just reinforcing it. Stavros says the picture's sensational."

"I hope so," Mike said, hitting a fiercely burning curve.

Where Mike played strongly but choppily, Farrell played smoothly, as he did everything else. He didn't even seem to sweat in the Sunday-morning sun. The sets were close, but Mike won.

Shirley smiled under her hat as the two men shook hands over the net.

"Why don't you two go for a swim? I'll join you after I make a few calls," Farrell said.

They changed in the poolhouse. The rustle of Shirley's clothes in the next room excited him.

When they emerged, she smiled at him, then pushed Mike suddenly. "Last one in is a rotten egg," she shouted, running for the pool.

Mike ran after her. When they surfaced together, he had his arms around her waist.

"Got you."

As she slid from his grasp, swimming away, her breasts brushed his hands. He caught her again, and they kissed playfully.

Shirley looked toward the large house and splashed water in his face, laughing in high spirits. "Flirt," she said accusingly.

"I want you," he said seriously.

"You say that to all the girls."

Farrell came toward them from the house. He was tall and strong and smiling.

"Having fun?" he asked, diving perfectly.

God, I hate him, Mike thought.

The living room was Moroccan, with a tooled leather ceiling and arches painted in copper and gold leaf. There were hassocks and beautiful rugs, modern sculpture and paintings, but no books to be seen anywhere. Mike never saw books in Hollywood except in writers' houses.

"Arabians are fast, but they're temperamentally unsuited to polo," Farrell discoursed. "Morgans are strong, but thoroughbreds are faster, although they have weaker legs and have to be carefully wrapped." Mike was thinking only about the kiss. "I see I'm boring you with all this horse talk. What do you think about the committee and the subpoenas?"

"They've got to be stopped now," Mike responded. "Otherwise, they'll be dictating what kind of pictures you can make. It's like Spain. If we'd stopped the Fascists there, maybe World War Two wouldn't have happened."

"I agree," Farrell said. "They've got to be put in their place. Skouras agrees and is working out a strategy with Goldwyn. Jack Warner, of course, is impossible. Were you here when they had that strike at Warner's?"

"No."

"It was unbelievable." Farrell shook his head. "Like a steel mill at the turn of the century. They brought in strikebreakers with baseball bats and tire irons to beat up pickets, while the police tear-gassed them and the fire department hosed them. Your friend Lawson was on the picket line."

How does he know Lawson is my friend? Mike wondered.

"Warner put up a big sign outside the studio gates," Farrell continued. "'Good citizenship, good pictures.'"

Shirley was silent.

———

A Committee of Five Hundred was formed to defend the "unfriendly nineteen" and the First Amendment, among them four U.S. Senators. It was a Who's Who of Hollywood: Thomas Mann, Humphrey Bogart, Lauren Bacall, Gregory Peck, Charlie Chaplin, Katharine Hepburn, Eddie Cantor, Paulette Goddard, Danny Kaye, Walter Huston, Rita Hayworth, Kirk Douglas, Henry Fonda, Irwin Shaw. Thousands throughout the country sent contributions.

The night before the nineteen were to fly to Washington, seven thousand people attended a rally at the Shrine Auditorium, with Gene Kelly as chairman. Kelly brought the house down when he appeared in a leg cast and crutches.

"Honest! I broke my ankle rehearsing." Then he got serious. "I'm here because of the Constitution of these United States and the Bill of Rights, both of which I believe in and which I believe are being subverted by something called the House Committee on Un-American Activities. So do many others."

Shirley squeezed Mike's hand as they sat next to each other. Farrell had not gone, pleading work. Kelly introduced some of the nineteen, their lawyers, and many performers. The atmosphere was enthusiastic and electric; the committee didn't stand a chance before their power.

Mike and Shirley ran into Odets as they were leaving. He smiled at them, his blue eyes appraising. "Pretty fantastic, huh?" he said, as the crowds milled about them, passing on their way to their autos.

"Yes, it was very exciting," Shirley said.

"By the way, Mike, Bob Rossen asked me to invite you to a screening of *Body and Soul*, if Julie didn't get to you yet."

"Great. I've been wanting to see it."

Odets left them. Mike looked at Shirley. "It's early. How about a drink?" he asked.

"Sure."

"My place?"

She thought a moment. "Okay," she said, nodding slowly.

———

The October moonlight made her skin seem pale. It reflected through the glass doors of the bedroom from the garden and pool. A slight breeze brought the scent of flowers, which mingled with the perfume of her skin. It's like silk, he thought, as he slowly stroked her. Her body was almost boyish in its slimness. Her eyes watched him as he bent over her, lingering with his fingertips.

Her long fingers caressed his cheeks and moved down his chest, circling his nipples, descending his abdomen to his pelvis. She caressed him, then guided his throbbing organ. As he entered her, she opened, then closed about him.

Shirley's eyes were shut as her breathing finally settled. Mike stared at the moon reflections. He had never felt such stillness within himself.

———

"I'll see you tomorrow," he said, kissing her. They stood in the street next to her Cadillac convertible.

"Yes," she said quietly. "And thank you."

"For what?" he asked, surprised. He heard the telephone ringing in the house.

"For this evening." She also heard the ringing phone and

got into the car. She turned once, blew him a kiss, and sped off.

Mike stood in the silent street, looking after her. The ringing stopped.

He sat looking at the moonlight in the pool, trying to deal with his emotions. The phone rang again. It was Ruth.

He tried to focus on her voice, but he was annoyed with the intrusion.

"The doctor says the baby may be early," she said. "When do you think you'll be back?"

Mike struggled with this reality.

"I'm also a little ahead of schedule, although I've got a lot of cleanup."

"Please try to be here," she said.

———————————

Earlier that evening Robert and Katherine had gone to bed. Robert stroked her in the usual way.

"Robert, I'm exhausted. I'd just be a lump."

"Goodnight," he said, covering his anger.

He turned from her and thought of his play. It was going well, but slowly, like bending iron. Then he thought of the rally that night in Hollywood. He got out of bed and went to his study. It was one o'clock when he rang Mike, but there was no answer. He didn't feel like going back to bed, so he stalked his bookshelves. There was the book Jim Lardner had lent him in Spain, and now his older brother, Ring, was in trouble. At two-ten, he called again. Still no answer. Puzzled, he checked the number, read a few more pages, and dialed again. Busy.

"Mike?" Robert said, finally reaching him.

"Yeah. What are you doing up so late?"

"I couldn't sleep."

"Is it the play?"

"Partly."

"How's it coming?"

"Very well. I'm anxious for you to read it. I should have a first draft in a few weeks."

"That's great. How's Katherine?"

"Busy. Between her practice, trying to found a children's

psychiatric clinic, writing for journals, and lecturing, she's at top speed all the time. Until she falls into bed exhausted."

"With no time for you?"

"You always know the right questions, you son of a bitch. How was the meeting tonight?"

"Very exciting. Everybody's rallying to their defense. We think the committee's going to get whipped."

"I hope you're right."

"Hollywood is too powerful, Robert. They can't fuck with these moguls. They believe they're royalty and they don't like their domains invaded by shmucks like Richard Nixon. Besides, all this is bad for business."

"Well . . . I can't wait to see you and get to work."

"Same here, buddy."

The next morning, the nineteen flew to Washington.

———

On the set of *Loyalties*, Mike greeted Shirley warmly. She gave no sign of any change in their relationship.

Odets came by the studio for lunch.

"What the hell are you doing?" he asked Mike as they ate in the commissary.

"What do you mean?"

"C'mon, Mike. Don't play dumb. You're crazy if you get involved with her."

"How do you know I'm involved?"

"I wasn't born yesterday. Shirley is one of the original Rhine maidens luring ships to the rocks."

Mike ignored the comment and shifted the conversation. "When do the hearings start?"

Odets looked at him with his piercing blue eyes. "Okay, Mike. You're a big boy. The hearings start on the 20th."

———

They were held in the Caucus Room of the old House Office Building. The room was packed with newspaper and newsreel cameramen, banks of lights illuminating witnesses and the delegation from Hollywood who came in their support. The nation wanted to see Humphrey Bogart,

Danny Kaye, Lauren Bacall, John Huston, and others in new roles. Right now, Jack Warner was playing the starring part. He assured the committee there was no Communist content in his films and volunteered the names of a dozen writers he thought were Communists.

There was a stir among the producers. Warner was not playing their script. Eric Johnston, the president of the Motion Picture Association, had assured the lawyers for the nineteen that there would be no blacklist. "Any statement purporting to quote me as agreeing to a blacklist is a libel on me as a good American! We're not going to go total-itarian to please this committee."

But J. Parnell Thomas, chairman of the committee, had quoted the producers as agreeing to establish a blacklist throughout the industry. That would effectively block em-ployment of anyone named by the committee by every company making films. Johnston was outraged, as were other producers. And now Warner was saying he'd fired or barred from his studio Alvah Bessie, Gordon Kahn, Ring Lardner, Jr., Emmet Lavery, John Howard Lawson, Albert Maltz, Robert Rossen, Dalton Trumbo, John Wexley, Clif-ford Odets, and Irwin Shaw.

There was a parade of friendly witnesses who named thirty-five other Communists. Among the friendly witnes-ses were Gary Cooper and Ronald Reagan. Cooper said he'd read "quite a few" scripts "tinged with Communist ideas" but couldn't remember any of them "because I read them at night."

Congressman Richard Nixon asked Adolphe Menjou what tests indicated to him people were Communists.

"Well, I think attending any meetings at which Mr. Paul Robeson appeared and applauding or listening to his Com-munist songs."

Ginger Rogers's mother, Lela, attacked Odets through *None but the Lonely Heart*, a picture written and directed by him, starring Cary Grant, because the *Hollywood Re-porter* had said it was "pitched in a low key, is moody and somber throughout in the Russian manner." "We turned down *Sister Carrie*, by Theodore Dreiser, because it was open propaganda like *None but the Lonely Heart*," she testified.

John Lawson was the first of the "accused" to be called. He was refused permission to read a prepared statement as the "friendly" witnesses had been allowed to do. Thomas ordered the committee's attorney to begin questioning about the Communist conspiracy in Hollywood.

"Are you now or have you ever been a Communist?" became the litany of a decade. The interrogation became a yelling match between Thomas and Lawson, who shouted, "This committee is on trial before the American public. The question of Communism is in no way related to this inquiry, which is an attempt to control the screen and to invade the basic rights of Americans in all fields!" He called the friendly witnesses "a parade of stool pigeons, neurotics, publicity-seeking clowns, Gestapo agents, paid informers, and a few ignorant and frightened Hollywood artists."

The guards removed him forcibly from the hearing room, and he was cited for contempt of Congress. Some cheered his performance. Most thought he'd gone too far. Phillip Dunne, the screenwriter, saw it as "Jack's major tactical blunder."

In the afternoon, Johnston took the stand and chastised the committee for its unproven attacks on the industry. The producers intended to keep the screen free of subversion and government coercion. But he also invited them to investigate Hollywood. "I told you we welcomed it, that we sincerely do." It was the first indication that the producers were either playing a double game or were afraid.

The next morning, Dalton Trumbo was also refused permission to read a statement and was dragged from the stand as he attempted to do so.

The pattern was clear. Friendly witnesses could read lengthy statements, unfriendlies could read nothing.

The newspapers attacked the committee for its tactics. "The most un-American activity in the United States today is the conduct of the Congressional committee on Un-American activities," wrote the *Detroit Free Press*. The *New York Times* echoed its sentiment.

The committee changed tack.

Albert Maltz was then allowed to read a lengthy attack on them. They suffered in silence. They called Alvah Bessie, another screenwriter, with an Academy Award nomination, and he too read a statement.

"In calling me from my home, this body hopes to rake over the smoldering embers of the war that was fought in Spain from 1936 to 1939. This body, and all its previous manifestations, is on record as believing that support of the Spanish Republic was and is subversive, un-American, and Communist-inspired. That lie was originally spawned by Hitler and Franco, and the majority of the American people, in fact the majority of people all over the world, never believed it. And I want it on record at this point that I not only supported the Spanish Republic but it was my high privilege and the greatest honor I have ever enjoyed to have been a volunteer soldier in the ranks of its International Brigades." Bessie refused to answer any questions that incriminated himself or others.

Bertolt Brecht testified he was not a Communist and proved so brilliant a witness Thomas found himself thanking Brecht for his appearance. He was the eleventh witness. They called no more.

The initial reaction of the country was one of such hostility to the committee and its tactics that none of those who had testified was fired.

Under the title "Hollywood Fights Back!" there were two nationwide radio broadcasts featuring sixty top stars, directors, producers, and writers. Hollywood was swept by an almost unified solidarity against the committee, and its residents felt strong.

Mike was at a party with Shirley at Odets's house for some of what were to be called "the Hollywood Ten." As Mike crossed the room to refill Shirley's glass, Odets intercepted him. "Watch out for the rocks," he said.

Afterward, with reflections of the moon on her body, Shirley leaned over Mike. "It's never been so good with anyone as it is with you."

"I feel the same."

She kissed him gently. "I have to go," she said. "We're

leaving early in the morning for Santa Barbara. Polo matches."

"Can't you stay?"

She shook her head. "John expects me to go with him. Root for the home team and all that. Zanuck likes it."

Farrell called from Santa Barbara between matches. "How about some tennis tomorrow morning, Mike?" he urged.

Mike won some hard sets from Farrell. It occurred to him that the slick producer was playing a "customer's game" and letting him win, but his ego brushed the thought aside.

Shirley sat next to him on a hassock in the Moroccan Room. He could smell her hair and the fragrance of her skin.

"You going back East when you finish photography?" Farrell asked casually.

"About a week later."

"Why don't you stay longer?"

"My wife's going to have a baby, and Robert Thompson is finishing a new play."

"Families are nice. I wish I could convince Shirley of that."

"Hah!" was all Shirley said.

"You think there's a part for Shirley in Thompson's play?"

"I haven't read it yet."

"She'd like to work with you again."

"Why do you always talk as if I'm not here?" Shirley asked, draining her pink lemonade.

"Sorry. I know you're not very forward about your own desires. By the way, I've got a script that might work for you both." Farrell threw the line away.

"I'd like to read it."

"Just happen to have a copy in my study," Farrell said, smiling, and left the room.

Shirley put her slender hand on Mike's neck and kissed him. As he put his hand on her breast, she moved away.

Mike wiped the lipstick from his mouth and adjusted his tennis shorts, hoping his erection didn't show. He remained seated as Farrell gave him the script. He put it on his lap.

Cool customer, Farrell thought. Doesn't even bother to look at it.

———————

"He offered you a picture, didn't he?" Odets said to Mike later that afternoon.

"Yeah. What about it?"

"With Shirley as star . . ."

"Yeah," Mike said grudgingly.

"Shmuck. Don't you see what they're doing?"

Mike refused to see it. Shirley could not be bait. As tough as he was, he could not conceive of that kind of corruption. "You've been here too long, Cliff. The sun is rotting your brain."

"It's not the sun, my boy. Power corrupts, but money corrupts absolutely."

As Mike read the script, Odets's insinuations intruded on his concentration. The screenplay was mediocre. Not bad enough to toss aside, but not worth doing. He called Farrell two days later and told him so.

"What about rewrites?" Farrell asked. "I'll get any writer you want."

"The idea is too small to rewrite."

Farrell did not like being turned down and wasn't willing to give up.

———————

During the last week of shooting on *Loyalties*, the studio had a sneak of *Foxhole*. The only thing worthwhile in it was Mike's performance.

"My God, you're an actor," Shirley said.

As they lay together, Mike finally asked a question that had been bothering him. "How come your husband always leaves us alone?"

Shirley was silent.

"You taking the Fifth?" he asked.

She sighed painfully. "Why do you ask?"

"It dawned on me that it was peculiar."

"Does it matter?"

It was Mike's turn to be silent, then he answered, "Truthfully, yes."

"Because you think there's something beyond my feeling for you?" she asked.

Mike looked steadily at the beautiful face. "What does your 'feeling for me' have to do with John's leaving you alone with me all the time?"

"I guess it's never occurred to you that he could be with someone else."

"No," he said with obvious relief. "I couldn't imagine it." He smiled.

"And that we have an 'arrangement,'" she continued.

"Why stay married?"

"There are reasons I won't go into." Her face clouded, and she turned from him, ending the discussion.

———————

Mike finished shooting two days ahead of schedule. Stavros put his arm around Mike's shoulder affectionately at the "wrap" party.

"I understand you turned down Farrell on *Bedtime Story*."

Mike nodded.

"Why? It's a good script."

"It's a lousy script," Mike said scornfully, "and would make a mediocre movie at best."

Stavros laughed. "That's what I like about you, Rossano. No bullshit. What do you want to do next?"

"If Robert Thompson's play is good, and I think it will be, I'll do that."

"Maybe there's a movie in it. If not, just tell me what you want to do and we'll make it."

"Dalton Trumbo has an idea I like. There's also his book *Johnny Got His Gun*, which I think would make a hell of a picture."

Mike could see Stavros's eyes cloud.

"That book's too tough. We'll talk about the Trumbo idea some other time," he said, ending the conversation and crossing to a group of producers.

Shirley came up to Mike. "Hi. Having fun?"

"Not really. Our Lord just asked me what I wanted to do next, and when I told him Trumbo had an idea I liked, you'd think I'd farted." ·

Shirley laughed. "You are wonderful. He thinks a great deal of you. Everyone does."

"What about you?"

"You know how I feel," she said seriously.

"I know what you tell me. Would you leave your husband?"

"Is that a proposition?"

"I'll have to think about it." Mike smiled. He wasn't sure himself.

"Don't think too long. My offer is good for two minutes only."

"Would you go to New York with me?"

"No."

"Deal's off." He smiled again, masking his disappointment. "I couldn't live here full-time." ·

The softness had been getting to Mike. He needed some grit in his life. And the energy of New York.

He saw Shirley once more and was in conflict over leaving. He was convinced he could truly love this woman, wanted her as he'd never wanted anyone before, even though he'd not been able to fathom her depths fully. Was that what intrigued him?

"You'll be back," Odets said to him in parting.

CHAPTER TWENTY-ONE

Robert and Mike walked through Shubert Alley to Sardi's. Alex waved to them through the heavy lunchtime crowd. As they approached his table, friends and admirers slapped Mike on the back and shook his hand, welcoming his return.

"Good to see you, Mike," Vincent Sardi said as he led them to Alex's table. "Hope you're going to stay for a while."

"This is home," Mike replied.

Alex embraced Mike. "How was the flight?"

"I hardly noticed it, I was so glad to get back."

"Have you read it yet?" Alex asked.

"I just got in, Alex. I'll read it after lunch. What do you think of it?"

"I won't say. It's just the best play of the decade."

"I'm glad you didn't prepare me," Mike laughed.

Robert fidgeted in his study as Mike read in the living room. When he'd finished, Mike stood in the doorway. Robert looked up at him. Mike looked somber.

"Well?"

"You've really done it. You've combined emotion and idea in a brilliant concept. It's going to be tremendous. Needs some work, but it's all there." Mike smiled now.

Robert smiled in return, and they stood for a moment in

front of the picture of themselves taken ten years earlier. The phone rang. Robert picked it up and listened.

"It's Ruth." He handed Mike the phone.

"Uh-huh . . . uh-huh. . . . We'll be right over." He hung up. "Ruth is getting contractions every fifteen minutes." They left together.

———

Ruth had a girl, whom they named Antonia and planned to call Tony.

Robert saw that Mike was disappointed. "Be glad it's a girl. She and Bobby can get married."

"Yeah," Mike said. "That's right."

Ruth looked pale sitting against the pillows in the hospital bed.

Mike looked at her and felt sorry for her. Life with him wasn't going to be easy.

The usual gang of vets came to the hospital. The gaiety was there, but it had no depth. Katherine wondered why. Perhaps it was because Ruth had not shared the experience of Spain with them. No, it was not that, she decided. It had to do with Mike and Ruth. There was no joy between them.

———

The following day, November 21, 1947, the *New York Times* carried an item that Spyros Skouras, president of 20th Century–Fox, had made public a resolution of the Fox board of directors "to dispense with the services of any acknowledged Communist or any employee who refuses to answer a question with respect thereto by any committee of Congress of the United States and is cited for contempt thereof." That meant Ring Lardner, Jr., despite his Academy Award.

On November 24, the Motion Picture Association held a secret meeting at the Waldorf Astoria. That same day, J. Parnell Thomas won contempt citations against the Hollywood Ten. The next day, the MPAA issued a statement on behalf of the major studios that "we will forthwith discharge or suspend without compensation those in our em-ploy, and we will not reemploy any of the ten until such time as he is acquitted, or has purged himself of contempt, and declared under oath that he is not a Communist."

RKO fired Adrian Scott, producer, and Edward Dmytryk, director of *Crossfire*; Fox fired Lardner; MGM suspended without pay Lester Cole and Dalton Trumbo, who was the highest-paid screenwriter on the lot. The other five were not under contract.

"I thought you said Hollywood was too powerful," Robert reminded Mike.

Bosley Crowther, film critic of the *New York Times*, wrote, "It should be fully realized that this action was engineered by the major New York executives, the industry's overlords, and not by the 'Hollywood producers,' who form a different, subordinate group."

The Ten did not give up. They intended a fight up to the Supreme Court. The Screen Writers' Guild voted to resist a blacklist and to support a bill in Congress to abolish "the committee."

Mike and Robert contributed another thousand dollars.

In the mornings, they worked sharpening the play. After lunch, they walked their children in Washington Square Park, played a game of chess, and continued talking about the play.

Alex was so enthusiastic about the new work that he decided to forgo an out-of-town tryout and play previews in New York. "It may sound risky," he said, "but in this case, I don't think it is. And we'll save a lot of money that we can put into advertising."

Alex had volunteered to produce again. The three formed a partnership, and theater investors, untouched by the Hollywood hysteria, were beating down their door. Rehearsals started in January.

———————————

Mike carried on a charade of marriage, but Shirley was ever present for him. She shared their bed as Mike stared into the darkness at night.

Ruth knew it was useless to hope that he would love her, that the child would make a difference.

When rehearsal started, Mike concentrated only on the production, withdrawing any previous attention he'd given her. Ruth kept her unhappiness to herself, but Mike was aware of it, felt guilty, then resentful.

Katherine was busier than ever, and Bobby was left to the care of a nurse. The child missed his parents. They tried to be home before he went to bed, but it was seldom possible. They kept Sundays inviolate, yet as they walked up Fifth Avenue, each was preoccupied with work which couldn't always be shared. Often their attention to each other and the child was forced, but Katherine wasn't worried. After the play opens, we'll get back to normal, she thought. And there'll be the month of August together.

American Dreams depended on the pivotal role of the father for its power. They saw hundreds of actors. One, Len Soloway, stood out. He was a man who had never made it, just as was the character in the play. He brought a high tension to his readings that was partly personal, partly talent, partly understanding of the character.

"It's risky as hell," Mike said.

"That's what they said about you, Mike," Alex reminded him. "There's no one else who comes close to him."

"I'm not worried about his talent, Alex. I'm worried about a failure of will. He's scared to death of his opportunity. This could make him a star, but it's a high-wire act. He's so afraid of falling, he could cause it. And the play will fall with him."

Alex and Mike turned to Robert.

"It's your play," Mike said.

Robert looked at his closest friends for a moment, considering. "Let's do it," he said soberly. Then he smiled. "What the hell. We've never lived our lives safely before. Why should we start now?"

The cast came from the Actors' Studio, which had been recently formed as a continuation of The Group Theater. The mother was a veteran actress, the sons newcomers. The play was about dreams and values, about sons torn between an artistic mother and a father who represented commerce. A fantasy uncle represented the success of the American dream.

Rehearsal went well, and there were no problems until the previews. Len Soloway was a large man who felt small. He had struggled in the theater for years without particular distinction or success, although he usually got good notices. He looked and felt like a man on the subway, totally unnoticed, as he rocked his way back and forth between the unemployment lines and the dressing rooms of old theaters.

The first preview was a disaster. He threw everyone else's performance. Light cues were late and music came in too early. One of the risks of previews in New York was bad word of mouth. In Sardi's that night they talked about the disaster at the Morosco.

Those who witnessed the play the second night found it so powerful they walked through Shubert Alley stunned and shaken. On the third night, the first act was terrible, the second warmed up, and the third was brilliant.

The three men sighed and tore their hair at the back of the house, watching, waiting for the fall. If the opening was so erratic, they were lost.

Robert wanted to fire Soloway.

Mike insisted on keeping him. "I thought you didn't want to play it safe," he jibed.

"I don't. But I also don't have a death wish."

"I didn't think I'd see a failure of *your* will," Mike retorted.

Alex was silent. He was on the fence. He had no ideas for a replacement for Soloway.

"Let me have some more time with him," Mike said.

"Time! We open next week!" Robert exploded. But he relented, since there was no immediate alternative. We should have kept looking for someone else, he told himself.

Mike worked on Soloway's confidence. He knew the terror of the rising curtain, the feeling of being naked before strangers whose disbelief in you had to be overcome. But it was questionable how much he could rebuild the actor's ego in just one more week of previews.

That week was also up and down, with flashes of power

and missed opportunities. *American Dreams* was the most controversial play in New York. Arguments erupted between partisans who had seen good performances and detractors who had not. There had even been a fistfight at Sardi's bar. Those who had seen its power felt it was the most important play of the postwar period, perhaps of decades.

Robert and Mike had picked Valentine's Day for the opening night in remembrance of the holiday they had shared before going off to Jarama. Mike had not thought of Florita for a long time.

The atmosphere in the theater was unusually electric. There was the feeling of something monumental about to happen. "The three" were backstage, crowded into Soloway's dressing room. "You're going to be great," they assured him.

Soloway's eyes were doubtful despite his grateful smile.

Mike and Robert went to each of the dressing rooms with little presents and words of encouragement.

The backstage doorman stopped them. "I never seen such a play," he said. "I been around these theaters forty years, I never been moved like this one." As he spoke, a messenger entered the small space carrying a carton from a well-known liquor store.

The doorman signed. "These are for you," he said.

"Three bottles of champagne from Odets," Alex observed, looking at the cards.

"For American dreamers," he'd written, "my highest hopes for you tonight."

They went out front through the pass door and felt the excited buzz as they walked up the aisle. Katherine, in a pastel gown, waved and smiled. Robert nodded and returned the smile. His throat was beginning to constrict.

As the last critic was seated, Alex called backstage from the box-office phone. "Take it up," he told Jimmy, the stage manager.

The houselights dimmed, and the three men leaned on the low wall, concentrating on the stage.

Katherine pressed Ruth's hand.

As the curtain rose on a leafy scrim, music vaguely filtered through, setting the mood, then the lights came up slowly on stage, bleeding colors that revealed the impressionistic set: the back of the house that had been cut away, the houses next door, the city beyond, and playing areas downstage for scenes away from the neighborhood or in the fantasies of characters.

Backstage, Jimmy stopped Soloway before his entrance. "Break a leg and give 'em hell," he said.

Soloway nodded, with a faraway look on his face. He was already in character.

Mike was in his usual trance of concentration. It was as if he were willing Soloway's performance.

The opening lines were faltering, like those of a solo violinist unsure of his notes. Robert could hear the terror in the man's voice. He closed his eyes. He should have fought Mike and fired Soloway. Then the tension in the actor's voice relaxed and was transferred to energy. He began to hit the notes with precision and emotion.

Mike's hands unclenched. The performance had taken off on its own.

As the lights dimmed on the last scene, there was silence. The final solo had been played, and now there was darkness. Suddenly, the applause cracked out in thunderous bursts and became sustained. The critics ran up the aisles, putting on their coats as the curtain calls started.

There were seventeen.

The audience did not stop cheering. On their feet, they started calling for the author.

Robert leaped to the stage and embraced first Soloway, who had tears in his eyes, then the rest of the cast. He raised his hand for silence.

"Eleven years ago tonight," he said emotionally, "a group of Americans were in Spain on the eve of their first combat against Fascism. We were on our way to a place called Jarama, a valley we'd never heard of, a valley where many of us died. Mike Rossano and I were there together and have shared many battles since." Robert put out his arms for Mike to join him onstage. "My comrade in arms, and Alex Tarasov, our general." Alex also went to the stage, and they linked arms.

Admirers swarmed around them, wanting to shake their hands, touch them in some way, be part of the success. Irv, Milt, and their wives sat with Katherine and Ruth while "the three" circulated, received adulation and congratulations.

"Ben be back soon?" Mike asked Alex.

"Soon. But the suspense is not killing me," Alex quipped. "I'd just as soon let the dream go on."

"Raves! Raves!" Ben shouted like a newsboy, waving the papers. "All of them! Seven out of seven!"

"Listen to this from the *Times*," Alex shouted, brandishing the New York paper. "'A family play that challenges the American value system. Not since O'Neill has there been a voice as powerful as Robert Thompson's. Mike Rossano's probing and poignant direction has pointed up the values of the play. The performance by veteran actor Leonard Soloway is spellbinding in its harshness and lucidity. It is a play and a production that will stand as an American landmark."

There were shouts and cheers.

Alex continued to read the other notices, but Mike's attention was focused on Tracy Morgan. He'd never met the sex goddess while he was in Hollywood. They traveled in different circles, and he wondered what she was doing in New York. He'd wanted to meet her because he'd heard she was also talented.

When Alex had finished reading, Ruth watched Mike cross to the young star, who was stunning in a low-cut gown that revealed a spectacular cleavage.

"Hi," Mike said to her. "I'm Mike Rossano."

"I know." She almost blushed and put out her hand. "I'm so glad to meet you."

"What are you doing in town?"

"I'm going to study with Lee Strasberg at the Actors' Studio." Mike looked at her. "I've never studied," she explained. "I don't really know what I'm doing."

"Maybe I can help you." Mike smiled. The subtext of his

offer did not escape her. She'd been getting them since she was fourteen.

Robert crossed to them.

"How are you?" she asked.

"Somewhere in space," he replied.

Her voice was musical as Mike introduced them.

"I bet. What an evening. Your play is stunning. I was in tears."

"Thank you."

"Tracy is studying with Strasberg."

"You couldn't be in better hands."

"Except mine," Alex said enthusiastically, joining them.

"That's why I'm here. It's so stimulating in New York."

Robert shook her hand again and rejoined Katherine.

"She's beautiful," Katherine said quietly. Robert nodded in agreement, looking at Ruth's unhappy face.

"You here with anyone?" Mike asked Tracy.

She looked at him speculatively as Alex joined another group. "Unfortunately, I am. By the way, congratulations on your picture. I hear it's great and that Shirley's never been better." The way Tracy read her last line, Mike could tell she knew about Shirley and him. "Did you know it's opening next week?"

"What is?"

"*Loyalties.*"

"The studio never told me a damned thing," he said angrily.

"Well, that's Stavros for you. Shirley should be here next week for publicity." Tracy watched for his reaction.

———————————

Robert was distracted, and their lovemaking that night was brief and perfunctory.

"What's the matter?" Katherine asked.

"I'm excited. My mind is elsewhere. I can't get over it," he explained. "It's the kind of success I've always wanted."

"Your speech was interesting."

"How so?"

"In remembering Spain, you chose not to thank Mike."

"That's ridiculous," he said angrily. "I said we were comrades in arms."

"But not in the play."

"He didn't write the play."

"I know he didn't write the play, but you chose to ignore his contribution to it. You didn't thank him the way you did after *They Shall Not Pass!*"

"That was different."

"Yes, it was," she said, sensing his growing anger. "Forget it."

"No. I don't want to forget it. I want to know what you meant."

"All I meant was that I sense a subtle but important change. I don't know if you want to face the reality of Mike's part in the play's success."

Robert stormed out of the bedroom.

———————

In his own bedroom, Mike reflected on the evening. He too was aware of the difference in Robert's acknowledgment and was faintly resentful. He was also resentful that Stavros hadn't bothered to inform him about the New York opening. If he had had any thoughts about Tracy, they were now shifted to Shirley. Why hadn't she called him?

He left a message for her at the Plaza Hotel, where she was expected. When she didn't return the call, he left another message.

"Hello, Mike," her voice purred. "I'm sorry I didn't get back to you sooner."

"When can I see you?"

"Let me look at my schedule. They've got me on a roller coaster." She didn't sound too eager, and in the silence Mike was feeling bitter disappointment. "How about dinner tonight?" she finally said. "I've got the whole evening free." His heart lurched upward.

"See you at eight," he said coolly. Later, he told Ruth he had a publicity meeting.

———————

Tracy Morgan smiled at them from another table in the Oak Room. Mike recognized the man she was with, a studio executive. He was sure to tell John Farrell; they loved that kind of gossip.

Shirley seemed nervous.

"Maybe we should have gone somewhere else," Mike said.

"It doesn't matter."

Mike didn't believe her.

Later, in her suite, Shirley began to cry.

Mike took her slender, naked body in his arms. "What's the matter?" he asked tenderly.

"It's so good to be with you, Mike," she sobbed.

"Then why are you crying?"

"Because I feel so helpless, so manipulated. I hate my life. The only genuine moments I have are with you."

"What do you mean by 'manipulated'?" Odets's warning came back to him.

She caught the edge in his voice. "Being bought and sold like merchandise."

"Leave it. Come to New York," he said urgently.

"I don't seem able to."

Mike wondered who was manipulating whom. He realized with a pang that she could do it to him.

She left the next morning without calling.

Mike was stunned. He didn't even care about the notices that Robert read to him in his kitchen.

"'Mike Rossano makes a brilliant debut as a motion-picture director with *Loyalties*, a no-holds-barred look at anti-Semitism in America. Shirley Day has never been better and displays under Mr. Rossano's direction a hitherto unexplored depth, showing Rossano to be an incomparable director of actors. Coming from Broadway—'"

"Enough . . . enough," Mike said, pouring coffee.

"Enough is right," Robert laughed. "Two hits in one week. You're king of the mountain."

"And you know very well the mountain will crumble."

CHAPTER TWENTY-TWO

Ziggy called Mike almost every day with a new and more lucrative offer. Every studio in Hollywood wanted him, and the sums were astronomical. He could now earn more for one picture than his father had earned in a lifetime.

He was the man of the hour on both coasts. So why wasn't he happy? He enjoyed the attention and the offers, but some indefinable anxiety still gnawed at him. Perhaps he should talk to Katherine. In some ways she knew him better than Robert. But he knew he wouldn't.

Robert found himself relaxing for the first time in a decade. He did not feel compelled to work on a new play immediately, had no idea that pressed him to the typewriter. There were constant lines at the box office, offers of productions abroad, and more money than he'd imagined. So he read a great deal, reflected back on his experiences, made a trip back to Iowa to see his parents, played chess with Mike and spent time with Bobby. He was aware of how busy Katherine was, but her schedule didn't bother him. He was proud of her accomplishments.

In May, he went to Europe with Mike, who hadn't found a play or movie he wanted to do. There were productions of *American Dreams* in London, Paris, and Berlin. Robert had tapped into a universal stream of consciousness.

As they were having dinner at the Ivy Restaurant in London, Shirley and Farrell entered. Robert noted Mike's sudden tension.

Farrell headed for their table. "Well, Mike . . . nice to see you. Congratulations."

"Hello, Mike," Shirley said quietly.

Mike introduced Robert.

"Where are you staying? We must get together."

"We're at the Dorchester."

"Fine. I'll ring you. Loved your play, Thompson. Saw it in New York. We should talk about a picture." He swept Shirley off to their table.

Robert was surprised when Mike did not continue eating. "Is it over, Mike?" he asked.

"I'm not sure."

"Limbo is the worst place."

"Yeah," Mike sighed.

Farrell did invite them for drinks at his elegant townhouse in Eaton Square. He was pursuing Robert and perhaps could snare Mike in the same net. As he talked with Robert about his play, Shirley and Mike stood at the fireplace as if warming themselves.

"Why didn't you call me before you left New York?" Mike asked quietly, trying to appear casual to Farrell, whom he felt watching them.

"I couldn't," she said, smiling for the same reason. "John came and got me. That fellow we saw with Tracy Morgan must have called him. It's hopeless."

A butler freshened their drinks and stoked the fire.

———————————

"I'm here to do a steeplechase picture," Farrell told Robert. "And maybe I'll do something else here after that. I like England. It has class."

———————————

"Why don't you leave him?" Mike asked.

"I can't."

"You mean you won't."

"I mean I can't." Shirley put her arm through Mike's and crossed to her husband and Robert.

Mike wanted to leave London right after the opening.

In Paris, they took Paul Fresnay to the first performance. Fresnay took them to an Indochinese restaurant Ho Chi Minh had cooked in. "You are still involved in politics?" Fresnay asked them.

"Only with our art," Robert replied. They went to the Ritz and toasted their reunion on the liberation of Paris. From there, they went to the Café Montparnasse and ended the night at five in the morning having onion soup in Au Pied du Cochon at Les Halles.

Robert was happy with the German translation as they sat in the theater in Berlin. He had expected a larger-than-life representation of the play here, but found the acting surprisingly naturalistic and accurate. The audience responded strongly.

Although much of the city had not been rebuilt, the audience looked well fed and well dressed. He and Mike looked at the animated crowd during intermission.

"I still hate them," Mike said.

Robert nodded, remembering Dachau.

"Herr Baumeister! Herr Baumeister!" a woman's voice called over the crowd.

It took Robert a moment for the old name to register as the stunningly dressed woman made her way toward them.

"Ilse!" he recalled in shock.

"Do you remember me?" Ilse asked, beaming.

"Of course. Ilse Frank. How are you?"

She'd hardly changed. Her eyes were still bright and lively. The stubborn, sensuous mouth seemed a little harder, the cheeks less firm, but her figure in the black dress was slim, her breasts full, and they invited Mike's lingering inspection of her frank sexuality.

She threw her arms around Robert impulsively as Mike watched, puzzled and amused. A good-looking gray-haired man approached, his icy blue eyes missing nothing.

"This is my husband, Herr Glatz. Ferdy, this is Herrmann Baumeister and . . ." She gestured toward Mike.

"Mike Rossano," he said, intrigued. Robert had told him the story of his escape, but Ilse's name had not stayed in his memory.

Herr Glatz bowed stiffly in his well-tailored clothes.

"I knew Herr Baumeister during the war, Ferdy."

"Ah . . ." was all her husband said.

"But, of course, as I suspected then, your real name is not Baumeister."

"No, it's Thompson." He smiled playfully. "Robert Thompson."

"You are American!" she asked incredulously.

Robert nodded.

"You are the author of the play," Herr Glatz said.

"Yes."

"Ferdy, my friend is the author of this wonderful play! How intriguing. We must have a drink afterward and catch up. Where are you staying?"

"At the Kempinski."

"So are we. Ferdy is here on business. We are living in Düsseldorf."

After the performance, they rode past the cafés of the Kurfürstendamm in Herr Glatz's large black Mercedes. Ilse led them through the enormous lobbies of the Kempinski Hotel to the small, candlelit, wood-paneled restaurant. The waiters were obsequious to Herr Glatz as he ordered champagne and caviar. When it arrived, he looked at the vintage. It was a Cliquot, 1941.

"A good year," Glatz said, laughing. Ilse joined him. Robert and Mike did not.

"Let's go," Mike said quietly.

"Come . . . you must have a sense of humor about these things," Glatz said to Mike. "The war is over."

"The memories are not," Robert said.

Glatz sobered. "You are of course right. We also had our share of nightmares. I was on the Russian front."

"So was Herr Baumeister," Ilse said, "I saved Herr Thompson from the Gestapo." Glatz eyed her. Ilse told the story of the train trip to Paris. "We used to lunch together at the Crillon and you were an escaped prisoner! *C'est incroyable!*"

Herr Glatz proposed a toast. "In the next war, we shall be allies." He raised his glass.

Mike's jaw tensed, and Robert had to restrain him from throwing the drink in Glatz's face.

"To the defeat of Fascism," Robert said, raising his glass.

Glatz laughed. "As you wish. But you know we'll be allies against the Russians."

Robert ignored the remark. "What happened after Volker?" he asked Ilse.

"I stayed in Paris, for a while, married an idiot, and after the evacuation went to my father in Holland. Do you know he was executed?"

"No."

"Volker I didn't care about. He was an animal." Glatz's eyes began to glitter. "But my father was a gentle man. I know he could not have done what they accused him of. I know he did not round up Jews, including that Anne Frank. He was not a war criminal."

"What happened to Dietrich?" Robert asked. He caught Glatz's look at Ilse.

"He went to Brazil."

"Ilse . . ." Glatz said warningly.

"They called him the Beast of Warsaw," she continued, disregarding Glatz's warning. "He was a sadist even among sadists. The Vatican helped him to escape to Spain."

"Ilse is very tired and doesn't know what she's saying," Glatz said, rising and taking her arm.

She removed it from his grasp. "You may go, Ferdy. I am staying with my friend."

He sat down glaring.

"Order another bottle, darling," she said.

"You've had enough."

"Must I do it?"

Glatz frowned and called the waiter.

"That's how Bormann got out. Mengele too. Bormann stayed at our house in Bavaria. He was dressed as a priest." Robert saw Glatz's hand tighten on his glass to the point he thought it would shatter. "They were perverted, those men," she continued. "They were an aberration. My father was executed for their crimes. My father had nothing to do with concentration camps."

"But you knew about them. You made love at Dachau."

Even Glatz looked surprised.

"I was young and silly." She shrugged, then pointed at her husband. "Now, Ferdy was a good soldier, weren't you, darling?" He was silent. "Ferdy has an Iron Cross and a Hitler medal from Spain, where he knew Volker. Ferdy was a major in the Condor Legion and still has his uniform in the closet," she said mischievously.

He merely stared at them.

Mike stiffened when he heard "Condor Legion."

Robert looked at the man and could easily imagine him in his uniform. "And what are you doing now, Herr Glatz?"

"I am in business," he answered curtly.

"Very good business," Ilse laughed.

Robert waited for the laughter to die.

"Do you know who killed Volker?" he asked.

"No. It was never found out," she said.

"I did."

"You?" Glatz stared.

"Thank you," Ilse said unexpectedly.

"I had to do it," Robert said later in their suite. "I had to tell them. I wanted that satisfaction."

Mike nodded. "We'd better keep the door double-locked."

"That's paranoid."

"Maybe. You know, I wouldn't mind bumping off that Nazi bastard."

"We're too old for that kind of stuff, Mike," Robert laughed.

They took the S-Bahn into East Berlin. It was the least conspicuous and most interesting way to the Berliner Ensemble, where they had come to see Brecht's play *Mother Courage*, starring his wife, Helene Weigel.

Brecht met them in the lobby. "I saw *American Dreams*," he said, peering over his wire-rimmed glasses.

He was dressed in gray work clothes with a black tie and a gray wool peaked cap. "Very strong. And a good production, for a bourgeois theater. Of course, they have money, but money can be an enemy. I was impressed. Too bad I can't see Mike's production in New York, but I don't think I'd be welcome." Brecht had left the country the afternoon of his appearance before the House Un-American Activities Committee.

The audience was poorly dressed and the stage empty of scenery, but the image that soon filled it was somehow enormous. It was the small figure of a woman pulling a cart, her daughter walking beside it. The woman's voice was strident, her will rusted iron, her eyes fierce. Her small body dominated the stage.

They were riveted to her.

"I've never seen anything like it," Mike said at intermission. "Have you ever seen anyone fill a space like that?"

"Only La Pasionaria," Robert replied.

"You're right," Mike said.

After the performance, in a worker's café with Brecht, Robert told him of the comparison.

Brecht smiled. "Weigel will be pleased with that." He smiled again, then asked, "How are the Hollywood Ten?" Brecht had been the eleventh. "What is happening?"

"It's still in the courts," Mike answered.

"It will end badly," Brecht said.

CHAPTER TWENTY-THREE

"'And then the Little Red Hen asked, "Who will help me with the harvesting?" But, no one volunteered,'" Katherine read.

"No . . . no . . ." said little Bobby. He was in his Doctor Dentons, his face shiny, his eyes gleaming.

Robert and Katherine were in his bedroom in the house they had rented for the month of August on Deer Isle.

"And then what happened?" Katherine asked.

"They all wanted to share!" Bobby shouted.

"Yes," Katherine said.

"Again," Bobby insisted. He loved the story.

"Mommy is tired, but Daddy will sing you a song." She swept him up, hugging and kissing him. "Goodnight, my sweet Bobby," she said.

"Goodnight, Mommy." He turned to Robert. *"Ich bin der Doktor Eisen . . ."* The little boy closed his eyes and lay back on his pillow. Robert sat by his side and sang the same German song his father had sung to him.

The days were calm and beautiful. A small sailboat came with the house, and Katherine taught Robert about jibs and halyards as they spent afternoons on Penobscot Bay. Bobby would sit on Robert's lap at the tiller and play sea captain. Mr. Eaton would take Bobby out for the afternoon, allowing Robert and Katherine to walk for miles on the island's back roads and watch the sunsets over the bay.

On a Sunday in September, Robert, Mike, Katherine, and Ruth went up to Peekskill, New York, for a concert by

Paul Robeson. Mike had borrowed Alex's car, and they had taken a picnic lunch. When they arrived, they found the town in a state of tension. The American Legion was picketing with signs that read, "Go Back to Russia," "Burn the Commies," and "Jews, go back to New York."

The cold war had started. Berlin was blockaded by the Russians. Eleven top Communists were on trial in New York's Foley Square Courthouse for conspiracy to overthrow the government. There were rumors of Russian spies stealing atomic secrets. The Communists were winning in China. The people of Peekskill were angry and scared. The Russians would be at the borders of their town any day now. In the meantime, the Jew Commies from New York were invading to hear that nigger Commie sing.

Township and state police were waving their clubs and smacking their hands with them. Many baseball bats were in evidence, carried by both the townsmen and Robeson's bodyguards. The police tried to collect them. They were getting very nervous.

"Something's going to happen," Abe Osheroff said. He was a "marshal" and had been in Spain, having shared Mike's birthday in Belchite.

The large open field was filled with the many colors of fall as concertgoers sprawled on the grass.

Robeson received a standing ovation as he arrived and mounted the platform. As he sang songs of Bertolt Brecht, Negro spirituals, and the Chinese national anthem, the townspeople began to march on the crowd. An announcer interrupted Robeson to advise everyone that it was no longer safe to be there. Abe and other bodyguards got Robeson into his car, and they left.

The Thompsons and Rossanos got to theirs. "Do you believe this is America?" Mike asked.

Thousands of others went to their buses. As they did so, the Peekskill vigilantes attacked with their baseball bats. The police did nothing to stop them.

When the cars and buses pulled out, the state police directed them to a side road, because it was supposedly safer. But it was a trap, a gauntlet through which they had to pass. The local guardians of democracy had stockpiled rocks along the road and now smashed the bus and car windows. They also smashed windshields with their baseball bats. It was all Mike could do to contain himself as the passenger windows of Alex's car were splintered and the interior filled with shards of glass. They passed a stalled bus. Bloody faces looked out at them.

Finally they reached the main road to New York. Mike's hands trembled on the wheel.

"Do you want me to drive?" Alex asked.

"No. I'm okay. It's just that I realized if I had a gun I would have used it."

———————

In November, Mike found a film script he wanted to do. It was about a Mexican revolutionary. He left Ruth and the baby behind and headed back to Hollywood.

"I don't know why she puts up with it," Katherine said.

Robert shrugged and went back to his book after stoking the fire.

Katherine wasn't satisfied with the shrug. "How can he do it?" she asked insistently.

He put down the book. "Look, Katherine, he may be my best friend, but I can't answer for him. If Ruth stays in the marriage, that's her problem, not yours."

"He's a bastard."

"Okay, as far as Ruth is concerned, I'll admit that, and I don't know why she stays either, except out of fear that she won't find anyone else."

"She's an attractive woman."

"Then, she should have no problem." Robert went back to his book.

"Except one of confidence," Katherine said, wanting the last word.

"Right."

He didn't look up. He wanted to read. Reading kept him from facing his own major problem. What would follow his huge success with *American Dreams*? Most of the ideas he came up with now seemed trivial, especially as it was rumored he would receive the Pulitzer Prize for drama. He would have to reach that level again. And Mike was in Hollywood. Was Katherine right? Was he dependent on Mike?

He had thrashed about before, but now time was more pressing and more was expected of him. He thought back to a conversation he had had with Mike in Spain in which he expressed fear of winning. It was a responsibility. He discarded idea after idea, opening scene after opening scene.

Katherine still worked several nights a week, and even when she was home she worked. He felt lonely.

So did Bobby. "Where's Mommy?" the child asked as he said goodnight to him.

"Mommy's at a meeting. A board meeting of her clinic."

"Oh," he said thoughtfully. "Poor Mommy. She never has any fun. She's always at a meeting."

"That's Mommy's fun," Robert answered and kissed the child.

In the morning, as they were having breakfast, Bobby said to Katherine, "Mommy, can I go to a meeting with you?"

"Why, Bobby?"

"Because I want to have fun with you."

Katherine looked at Bobby and stroked his face, then raised her eyebrow at Robert. "Are you two ganging up on me?"

The more Robert floundered and the busier Katherine was, the longer the silences became. Only the sounds of pages turning and the crackle of the fire were heard.

Bobby came into the room in his pajamas.

"Why aren't you asleep?" Katherine asked. "It's nine o'clock."

"Give me a song, Daddy. 'Willi, Willi, vip, voom, voom.'"

"I sang it to you."

"Sing me another. 'The Lorelei.'"

"Not tonight. But tomorrow I'll give you two."

"Promise?"

"Promise."

The child went to Katherine. "Give me a song, Mommy."

"Tomorrow, sweetie. Mommy's busy."

Bobby frowned and went back to bed.

"Katherine . . ."

"What is it?" she asked without looking up.

"You might look at me when you talk to me."

"I'm sorry," she said testily, looking at him. "What is it?"

"Why are you so remote?"

"I'm not remote. I'm just busy."

"Maybe you've taken on too much."

"For you or for me?"

"For us."

"When you're totally involved in your work, I don't complain," she said reasonably.

"Okay, okay." He frowned and got up. "I'm going for a walk."

Katherine sighed and went back to her book.

The November air was crisp as Robert walked through the Village. The wind from the Hudson was fresh, without its winter edge, and he began to feel better. He hated these scenes with Katherine and wondered if they were inevitable in the course of a long marriage. She was right, of course. She did not claim his time when he was busy. Perhaps Katherine was basically stronger than he was.

As he tried to settle his resentments and angers, he reached the Cherry Lane Theater at its intermission. Robert liked theater crowds and headed toward them. He was listening to the comments on the sidewalk about the play when a voice called to him.

"Mr. Thompson . . . Mr. Thompson!"

He turned to see Tracy Morgan.

She came toward him with her hand extended. "Hi, remember me?"

"Of course," he said, taking her hand. "You were the naughty girl in *Kiss and Tell*."

"No . . . at the opening of your play." She saw then that Robert had been joking. "Gosh, I haven't heard the word 'naughty' since my father used it when I was a kid in Nebraska."

"I haven't heard anyone use 'gosh' since Iowa, and 'naughty' is a good word. It just seems outdated."

"Are you always so deep?"

Robert laughed. "You mean boring?"

"You're anything but boring. Intellectual, stimulating, powerful, profound . . ."

"I hope you're going to write the reviews for my next play."

"Oh, I'm a big fan of yours. *They Shall Not Pass!* knocked me out. I read it in one sitting. Was it really about you?" she rushed on ingenuously.

Robert nodded, somewhat embarrassed. "How's class?"

"Just terrific. I'm really stretching. Next week I'm doing Lady Macbeth. Lee and Alex and Gadge are wonderful teachers. I wish Mike were around the Studio. Have you seen Marlon and Jimmy in class? I'm doing a scene with Jimmy Dean. Maybe Chekhov," she rushed on.

Robert wondered if Mike had slept with her. "No, I haven't," he said, answering her question.

"You should come to class."

"Alex keeps inviting me."

The bell signaled the end of intermission. Tracy put out her hand. "I've got to go now, Mr. Thompson. Nice seeing you again."

Robert took her hand. "Robert," he said.

Her perfume hung on the sidewalk, then was blown away by a gust from the Hudson. He thought about her presence on his walk back to Washington Square. She was different without her war paint. Simpler, almost childlike. No, he edited, a knowing child.

———————

"I hate those scenes, Robert," Katherine said, leaning over him in bed. "I hate rough edges between us."

"So do I," he said, taking her in his arms. They gave themselves to their lovemaking wholeheartedly.

———————

If the theater was Mecca for actors, the Actors' Studio was its worshiping temple. Brando was there, James Dean,

Monroe, Julie Harris, Kim Stanley, Karl Malden. Marty Ritt, Bobby Lewis, Kazan, Lee Strasberg, and Alex were its high priests. Alex was the head of the directors' and playwrights' units.

In the absence of a concrete idea on which to work, Robert started going. He found the atmosphere stimulating and revitalizing. He loved watching actors work, and he loved their attention to him.

———————————

Christmas had come and gone. Robert and Katherine spent New Year's Eve with the Barkins, and Mike called that night to wish everyone the best. He also sent Hershey bars to everyone who'd crossed the Pyrenees that snowy night of 1937. Thirteen of them.

On Valentine's Day, Robert and Katherine joined their comrades at Pete's cousin's Greek restaurant. Many, in their forties, no longer looked hopeful about life.

The next day, Katherine flew to Atlanta to address the American Psychiatric Association. It was her sixth trip in as many weeks. Robert was restless. He had been going to Alex's classes twice a week now. It relieved the pressure of the blank page.

He was also tremendously attracted to Tracy.

He never thought of himself as compelled by sex, but he found himself fantasizing about her. Her figure filled his imagination, but he did nothing.

As he prepared to leave for the Studio, his agent called. "It's official, Robert," she said. "I just got the call from Columbia. You've been nominated for a Pulitzer!"

He was unsuccessful in reaching Katherine, and Mike had already left for the studio. Alex had heard it on the radio and delightedly announced it in class. Robert was pleased and embarrassed as Tracy clapped excitedly. Later, she did a scene from J. D. Salinger's "Uncle Wiggly in Connecticut." Robert noted a sweet, appealing quality, an innocence she normally didn't project. He looked at the eager faces about him in the rehearsal room and felt a part of the theater, a part of something larger than himself. It was an important and necessary feeling. The scene ended.

"Good work, people," Alex said. "Unfortunately, I see it's late for a critique. We'll do it on Friday."

The people in the room rose, stretched, and gathered in groups to talk about "the work."

Robert crossed to Tracy and congratulated her on the scene.

"Thanks. But congratulations to you. I'm sure you're going to win."

"Maybe."

"I see you two are getting to know each other," Alex said.

"Not as well as I'd like," Tracy said. "How about lunch?"

"Okay. . . . Alex, you free?" Robert asked.

"Unfortunately not. I've got a date with my barber, who's a Sicilian prima donna and hates to be stood up. See you Friday?"

"Yeah," Robert said. "Unless I start writing again."

Robert and Tracy walked through the theater district, although it was cold. They passed under the marquee of the Morosco Theater. The lobby was filled with a lunchtime box-office line.

Tracy looked at Robert's picture outside the theater. "You look very distinguished with that pipe," she said.

"Remind me to carry it, then," he laughed.

"I hear they're doing the play in London and Paris," she went on.

"And Berlin. I saw it there with Mike. We also saw *Mother Courage* at the Berliner Ensemble." He told her about the production as they approached Downey's Restaurant on seedy Eighth Avenue. The Studio people preferred it to the plusher Sardi's.

In one of the dark booths Robert found his nervousness replaced with humor. He could be very funny when he wanted to be. He enjoyed listening to Tracy's laughter, as her photo on the wall looked down on them.

They walked past the Plaza fountain, and Tracy put her arm through his. "I make a very good cup of coffee," she said. "How about it?"

"If it's not very large. I want to get some work done today."

Light from the bedroom window fell on Tracy's flushed face, her blond hair, her soft, creamy skin. She lay in post-coital contentment.

Robert seemed coiled within himself.

She leaned toward him. "What's the matter?" she asked softly. Robert didn't answer. "Was it me?"

"No. It's me. I've never done this before."

"Why did you?"

"Besides the fact that you're so desirable?"

"Yes."

Silence.

"I don't know."

"Are you being honest?"

"No."

"You're like a little boy," she said softly, "who needs attention . . . affection . . . and that's so thrilling. I love men. I need them. And when they need me too . . ."

Robert closed his eyes and turned his head from her.

"If you feel so bad, we don't have to do it again. Think of it as a dream. I do that, and the bad feeling goes away."

Robert turned to her. "When I was a kid, we lived out on a farm during the summers. They were hot, and after working in the field, or playing baseball, we'd run to our well. That well had the sweetest, coolest water I've ever tasted. We'd drink and pour it over ourselves. I've missed that well, and needed it, without knowing. With you, I tasted that water again."

"I'm glad." She smiled. "And your wife?"

"She's been that well."

"Some wells run dry."

"I don't know. Maybe I've spoiled it."

When Robert talked with Katherine that night in Atlanta about the Pulitzer nomination, he felt like a traitor, a betrayer of an ideal. She felt he was very subdued about such good news.

On Friday, Alex noticed that Robert and Tracy sat next to

each other and talked with the complicity of lovers. He thought Tracy was an interesting choice for Robert and made no judgments. He was surprised, though. She was more Mike's type.

Tracy was totally different from anyone Robert had ever known. Tending to be shy and serious, Robert had always sought out serious, intense people. Tracy was outgoing, fun, uninhibited, trying to be intellectual. Their relationship could be perfection, Robert playing mentor.

Sexually, she was wild and lovely, extremely competent in skills that Katherine had never been interested in mastering. Tracy evoked a passion and sexual energy Robert didn't know he had, and he became possessed.

But, polarized by the swings of sweet anarchy and puritan guilt, Robert was demonized, unable to write.

Alex brooded about it. He had not expected Robert to be so thrown. Tracy was a female Mike; they were both spontaneous and calculating. He was not certain that Tracy wasn't merely ambitious.

Every encounter in Tracy's bed was a revelation to Robert. He'd never imagined so many variations to an act he'd been performing for years. He soared and dived, swerved, skidded, and rose again on a sexual roller coaster. As spring arrived, they fell impulsively in love as Alex watched.

When Robert got the telegram that he'd won the Pulitzer for drama, he was in conflict as to whom to call first. He called Mike.

"That's fantastic!" Mike shouted over the phone. But after the congratulations, Mike grew sober. "Is it true about Tracy, Robert? Alex told me. I've been debating whether to call you."

"It's true," Robert said, after a long pause.

"This is very dangerous. You're not a son of a bitch like me who can handle it."

"You're probably right," Robert admitted.

Tracy idolized Robert, the Pulitzer Prize-winner and war

hero. Her hero. She hadn't imagined it would be so easy to get him, and having him made her a serious person rather than a fluffball Hollywood star. He legitimized her.

———————

Robert was a poor actor, and Katherine was aware of his turmoil, ascribing it to his lack of progress with his play. As they ate one night, she decided to open the subject.

"You're unusually silent tonight," she said.

"Pensive," he corrected.

"Is it the play?"

"I guess so."

"Nothing else?"

"No."

"You're not withholding anything?"

"No, I'm not."

She took his hand. "Look, Robert, I know I've been busy and not as available to you as you'd like, but don't be angry. Be happy for me as I am for you. Be happy that I've come into my own just as you have . . . that I can be effective with people who need me."

"What about me?" he burst out. "I need you too!"

Katherine was taken aback by the heat of his emotion. "Not in the same way."

"Do I have to be sick to get your attention?" he asked with further force.

Katherine was startled by the anger she felt from him.

The disquiet continued, but Katherine did nothing about the storm signals, although even little Bobby was aware of the tension. The songs and bedtime stories were half-hearted. Katherine wanted to believe the disturbed waters would calm once Robert got a play on course.

———————

Mike had done his own investigation of Tracy Morgan.

"Robert, you're out of your fucking mind," he told him forcefully. "Tracy Morgan is a carnivore. She'll eat you alive." He thought of Odets's warning to himself.

"Are we the pot and the kettle?" Robert asked.

"I understand your need for someone else, but couldn't you find a nice little understudy to have a fling with?"

"This is not a fling, Mike. I'm crazy about her."

"It's a fucking adolescent crush," Mike shouted. "Your need to be in love. Jesus, if you weren't so faithful to Katherine, this never would have happened. What are you gonna do?"

"I don't know. I wish I did. I'm torn apart."

"Be careful, kid," Mike advised. "This town eats gossip for breakfast."

Mike knew the currency of Robert's relationship with Tracy was being passed around when it came back to him at a Malibu beach house. As they listened to the waves crash, one of Mike's bedmates told him of the affair Tracy was having with his best friend.

"She's crazy about him," Rita said.

"How do you know?" he asked, alert.

"She told me. Tracy's *my* best friend."

"How many best friends does she have?"

"Very funny."

"Who did you tell besides me?"

"Nobody," she replied indignantly.

But Mike knew better. Rita would be dining out on her piece of news, spreading it around like honey, making her more important than she was.

Katherine decided that perhaps a vacation together would help them. She brought up the subject one night at dinner before settling into her office for the evening.

"I think I can take the month of August. Do you want to go to Maine or the Vineyard?"

"Analyst's heaven?" he said sarcastically.

She ignored the jibe at her profession. "How about Europe?"

"We might be casting in August."

"Will you have the play ready?"

"I hope so." Robert's mood was obviously negative and hostile.

"Robert, what is the matter?" she finally asked in exasperated concern.

"The play isn't working, that's all," he said with some heat.

Katherine resignedly went off to do her night's work. Besides her patients, she had the administrative side of her new clinic to deal with. It was successful and expanding. She had fund-raising and staffing problems. She had been going to Washington two days a week seeking federal money. She was also tired.

"Do you mind if we don't . . ." was often the answer to his attempts at contact.

Robert was increasingly resentful of his growing dependence on Tracy, which he blamed on Katherine. He also perversely blamed her for his guilt, and his inability to work. The play wasn't going badly, it wasn't going at all. "Dammit, Mike, why aren't you here?" he cursed.

But he wouldn't heed Mike's warnings about Tracy. Why should he? Even at thirty-four, he loved playing the Master Builder. Tracy, at twenty-four, was without much education but had great native shrewdness. She looked up to her mentor with awe, admiration, and love.

The underground stream of rumor surfaced. Mike, in his office, brandished the trades as if they were a weapon.

"It's in the fucking trades, that's what!" he shouted into the phone.

"Oh, no," Robert groaned. But a part of him was relieved. Pressure had to be released.

Mike read to him. "It's in 'The Talk of the Town.' 'Tracy Morgan's latest is none other than Pulitzer Prize-winner Robert Thompson, whose play *American Dreams* is wowing them at the Morosco Theater in New York. Seems the dazzling damsel met the scintillating intellect while studying at the famed Actors' Studio. Quite a marriage of mind and body.' Do you want to hear the others?"

"Spare me."

Robert faced Tracy in the large living room of her East Side town house.

Although Robert was in fragments, Tracy was calm. "I swear I didn't do it. I'm not a home-wrecker."

"How did they get it?"

"I told my former best friend," she replied quietly.

"Jesus!" he exploded.

Tracy looked at Robert steadily, coolly, and said with assurance, "If you want to stay with her, deny it. It won't be the last time you're in a gossip column." Robert was silent. "You don't want to deny it."

"I don't know what I want to do. I don't know how to handle this. I'm so damned inexperienced with women. I had one girl friend before Katherine!"

She took his arms. "Is there more than sex between us? There is for me," she said.

"I honestly don't know. I love being with you, touching you, talking. I think about you. I'm consumed by you. And I hate it. I hate the conflict between you and Katherine and the fact that it keeps me from working."

"I'm sorry. I didn't want it to end like this."

Robert was silent.

"Is this the end?" she asked.

Robert put his head in his hands. "I don't know. I only know it's the end of my life as I've known it."

"Then think of it as a new beginning," she said, taking his hands from his face and kissing him.

"God, I love you," Robert said.

———

The wire services picked up the *Hollywood Reporter* item, and it tore around the country. Katherine read it in an afternoon edition of the *Washington Post* on her way back to New York from a meeting with the Secretary of Health. Ordinarily she didn't have time for the late papers, but she was a captive of time on the train.

The item was near a continuation of a front-page story on Senator Joseph McCarthy, who was accusing the State Department of being "filled with Reds," and another story about the perjury trial of an important official named Alger Hiss who supposedly passed secrets found in a pumpkin.

When her eye fell on "Pulitzer Prize Playwright and Actress" it didn't occur to her it was Robert. She continued with the McCarthy and Hiss stories. It was only after reflecting on them that some random thought drew her to what she considered gossip. It startled and shook her. God, how blind and dumb I am! she chastised herself.

In their living room he denied it, shrugged off the story as rumor because they'd been seen together at the Actors' Studio. But Katherine knew the truth by the hands hidden in his pockets to avoid the detection of nervousness.

"Don't belittle us by lying!" she said furiously. "I've known something was wrong, but I believed you when you said it was your play. I guess I wanted to. My God, here I am an analyst, seeking reality for my patients, and I've avoided it myself. It was in bed with me every night, and I refused to see it. Why did you do it? After what we've been through together!"

"When I needed you, you weren't there for me. And she was," he replied angrily.

"What could she give you?"

"Attention! Affection! I was starving and didn't know it. You didn't see it. You were too wrapped up in yourself, your patients, your clinic. Everybody but me!"

"I admit I didn't see it. I thought you were stronger. That you had your career and I'd have mine. When you were busy or out of town and I needed you, I didn't say, 'Poor me,' and jump into bed with the first good-looking intern who came along." Her fury was building. "The only time I ever . . ." She stopped. The motion of her anger had carried her further than she'd wanted to go, or was it further than she intended? Did she now want to punish him with Larry? Or the even greater punishment of Mike's attempted seduction and replacement of himself for Robert? She stopped.

"Go on," he said.

Katherine stared back at him in silence.

"The only time what?" he pressed hard.

She knew the time had come. "The only time I had another relationship was when I thought you were dead."

He stared at her. "That's how you reacted to my death? You went out and fucked someone else! That's what my death meant to you!"

"No. Your death was worse than my brother's. I suffered more than at any time in my life. It was worse than the women's clinic in Madrid. I wished it was me. For months I was dead myself. How can I explain that I was trying to replace you? He was so much like you it scared me to death."

"Yes, I've heard about love and death," he said sarcastically, "but it didn't take you very long to replace me. I didn't know there was a statute of limitations on love."

"Perhaps you'd have preferred me to live only with your memory?" she cut at him, furious that he was trying to turn the tables on her. "You can't accuse me of infidelity." Was now the time to tell him about Mike?

"Yes, you were being faithful to my memory," he shot back.

No, she couldn't bring herself to do it. "I never betrayed an idea. An idea of *us*!"

Bobby came into the room rubbing his eyes.

"Mommy . . . Daddy . . . why are you yelling like that?"

Robert went swiftly to his son and picked him up, held him tightly.

"Katherine," he sobbed, crossing to her and grasping her with his other arm, holding them close, weeping. "Katherine, what have I done to us?"

Katherine broke. "How could you do it, Robert? How could you?" she sobbed.

"Forgive me . . . forgive me . . . I don't want to lose you both."

"Mommy . . . Daddy . . . what's the matter?" Bobby asked in alarm. "Why are you crying?"

Robert thought of the Baumeister family grouping when their second son was killed.

"You have lost us, Robert." Katherine withdrew from his grasp. "Please leave as soon as you can."

"Why?" he cried.

"Because the truth is not negotiable. Not between us."

"Jesus, I'm sorry," Mike said on the phone.

Robert slumped at his desk, exhausted. He'd been up all night. Katherine had taken Bobby to her parents' house in Princeton, feeling the break would be easier for him there.

"All because of that big mouth," Mike continued.

"It had to come to a climax, Mike. It couldn't have gone on."

"What are you going to do?"

"I'm waiting for a call from Alex on a sublet in his building."

"Damn! Do you want to come out here for a while? I've got plenty of room."

"Thanks, Mike, but I've got to get my bearings here and get back to work on my play."

Spain was only yesterday in his memory as he packed the books and pictures from his study. No pain he'd endured equaled this. "It wasn't worth it," he said to himself.

Katherine had found it impossible to live in the apartment while he was still there. His presence was too difficult, and she was afraid she might relent. Away from him, she could control her anger. She stayed with the Barkins until he was gone.

"I never thought I'd see this happen," Barkin said. "It was one of the strongest marriages—" He broke off, seeing Katherine's pained eyes, and took her in his arms. "Are you sure you're doing the right thing?"

"I can't do anything else and be myself," she said, burying her face in his shoulder.

Robert moved into the Osborne Apartments on 57th Street, across the street from Carnegie Hall and the Russian Tea Room. It was a classy old building where Alex and artists like Leonard Bernstein lived. He sublet it from a writer who'd been blacklisted, lost his TV employment, and moved to London.

Robert, immersed in his own troubles, had not kept up with life around him. It wasn't until the Hollywood Ten were sent to jail for their refusal to name names that he came out of himself.

He explained it all to Tracy.

"But that's un-American," she exclaimed as she signed a petition against the House Congressional committee in support of the Ten.

Then Alger Hiss was found guilty of perjury and sent to prison. Klaus Fuchs, a British scientist, was found guilty of betraying atomic secrets to the Russians, and his American confederate, Harry Gold, got thirty years. The Communist miasma was everywhere. Especially that summer when North Korea attacked the South.

Robert finally found an even keel and began to work again. The Studio sessions ended in June, and Tracy made a brief trip west. Robert saw a great deal of Alex and found a new life uptown. The Russian Tea Room became his haunt as much as Alex's. Robert now found himself out almost every night, and he loved walking in new neighborhoods. He saw Bobby at least three times a week and occasionally ran into Katherine at the end of an afternoon with his son. Katherine tried, despite her hectic schedule, to see more of the child. When Robert and Katherine did meet, the encounter was difficult. There was still a strong residue of feeling between them.

One night, while Tracy was gone, Robert was having dinner with Alex in their usual booth up front in the Russian Tea Room when Ruth came into the restaurant. She was ill at ease with the young man who held her arm as they were introduced to him. Robert recognized him from the Playwrights' Unit. He was good-looking and at least ten years younger than Ruth. He also had an almost worshipful attitude toward her that was balm to her hurt.

Robert looked at Alex as the couple went into the main room.

"Nature abhors a vacuum," Alex said.

"I hope he's good for her."

"From what I hear, he is. And talented to boot."

"Maybe Mike will direct his play," Robert quipped.

"Now, that is unworthy of you," Alex said, surprised.

"You're right." Robert was also surprised at himself for the corrosively cynical remark. What's happening to me? he wondered.

Robert loved the fullness and curve of Tracy's breasts, the hard flatness of her stomach, the inside of her smooth thighs, and her adroitness with her tongue. She laughed when he told her she was a "sexual miracle."

"I hope I'm more than that," she responded. She was ashamed of the fact that she'd risen from the ranks of extras through sex. For that reason, she doubted her talent, even though she was a gifted comedienne and one of the most highly paid stars in Hollywood.

"I have some news," she said on her return from the Coast. "First of all, Mike's picture is going very well. I saw the head of his studio and he's ecstatic over dailies. And . . . I have to go back to make a picture in September." She looked at Robert as he pondered this. "How about coming out with me? You'll love Malibu. My house is right on the beach."

"Well . . . there's nothing to keep me here except Bobby." He shrugged. "I can just as well write there."

"That's what I hoped you'd say." Tracy hugged him.

Katherine was at Martha's Vineyard for August. Deer Isle was too painful.

"Besides, it would be too cruel to Mr. Eaton to confuse him again," she laughingly told Barkin.

"It's good to hear you laugh," he said. ·

She did not laugh when Robert came to say goodbye. It was one of the strangest experiences either had ever had.

Robert sang Bobby all the old songs, and when the child had had enough, he reached for his father with tiny hands and kissed him.

"Goodnight, Daddy."

Robert swelled to the point of tears. "Goodnight, my big boy. Don't let the bedbugs bite," he said, his voice cracking.

In the living room he and Katherine sat on chintz-covered chairs across the room from each other. Robert's heart began to pound, and Katherine swallowed hard as they silently looked at each other. Then suddenly they rose and came together in the middle of the room, kissing passionately. Wordlessly they went to the bedroom and quickly undressed.

Their lovemaking had the sweetness of reconciliation.

"Katherine . . . oh, Katherine . . . I love you," he cried afterward.

They both stared into the darkness, listening to the waves and wondering what it meant.

"Please go now," she finally said.

"Are you sure?"

"No, I'm not. But go anyway."

When he'd dressed, they kissed more goodnight than goodbye.

Katherine curled up in her robe and wept. Bobby came into her room, crawled into bed with her, and put his small arms around her neck. She hugged the child to herself.

"Don't cry, Mommy. I'll be your daddy."

CHAPTER TWENTY-FOUR

Mike's embrace was exuberant and welcoming. Robert looked at his shining eyes and smiling mouth and hugged him in return. Without Mike a piece of his personality had been missing, the structure of his life incomplete.

At first he found the social life a novelty. He, Mike, and Tracy were eagerly sought after on the star party circuit, and he felt like a tourist in a foreign country observing native customs. A fresh start on all fronts was called for, and he made notes for a new play, shedding the old one like a worn coat. He rose early, went for a run on the beach, had breakfast with Tracy before she went off for costume fittings and makeup tests. Sometimes she ran with him along the water's edge, and he loved the stretch of her legs, the way she held her head to the sun, her fleetness, the sound of her laughter as they raced up the beach.

He worked in a small room over the water until lunch and then went for a walk to review what he'd done that morning. In the evenings, there were dinners and parties. He saw Odets, who told him that many friends were being forced to leave Hollywood. Lists were being compiled by various "experts," some without any known origin. Some came from police spies who had infiltrated various organizations, including the Communist Party. The recruiting secretary of the Hollywood branch of the Party turned out to be a policeman, and four former FBI agents published a bible of names in their monthly, *Red Channels*. But so far, the wheels of Hollywood still moved smoothly.

Robert missed the streets, the vertical beauty of New York, the eye contact of Manhattan, and his son. He called Bobby every Sunday. He also enjoyed Tracy and her big-finned Caddy convertible, her hair streaming in the breeze as she drove the Pacific Coast Highway at night or swam nude with him in the ocean after a party. He loved the slippery surfaces of her skin in the water. He grew tanned and shaggy-haired, and Hollywood paid homage to the Pulitzer Prize-winner.

But in time, he grew bored with trade talk, and real estate didn't excite him.

"Welcome to Hollywood," Mike said, laughing at his observations of local customs.

"Where are the real people?" Robert asked.

"You mean the poor people?"

"No. I mean the serious people."

"The serious people are in jail or abroad or hiding. The serious people aren't Tracy's friends."

Robert knew Mike was right.

"But there are other groups," Mike continued. "Thomas Mann and the German contingent who meet over at Salka Viertel's in Santa Monica Canyon." Robert's head rose in interest. "Then there's the English colony, the Malibu colony, and the untouchables."

"Except for the Germans, it sounds like I'm in the wrong place."

"Look, Robert, you've got a play running, and more money than you ever thought you'd make, so relax. Don't whip yourself. Enjoy Tracy while you're together."

Robert looked at him. "You don't think it's going to last?"

"Do you?"

Robert stared at him as if the possibility of Tracy being a short-term relationship had never occurred to him.

"I'd never have left Katherine if I thought it wouldn't last."

"Robert, we both know nothing is forever. If your work goes well, the rest will fall into place. In the long run, it's only our work that matters."

Tracy started shooting in October. She had to get up at five for her makeup call, but it didn't affect her life-style. Robert started begging off on invitations that didn't interest him; the late hours twisted his biological time clock, and he'd always been a morning worker. So Tracy went alone or with Mike. The two felt a strong but unexpressed sexual current. She also went with her leading man, Giorgio Vallone, an Italian who'd left his wife behind. Vallone was a handsome former truck driver with a radiant smile.

Robert found a few nonindustry friends one afternoon while exploring Santa Monica. One couple taught modern European history at UCLA. Tracy found them dull. Several Sundays he spent at Salka Viertel's salon. As Robert conversed with Thomas Mann and others, Tracy sulked in a corner.

On their way home, she exploded. "Why do they have to speak German?"

"It's their language," he explained reasonably.

"But they're in America!"

"They're more comfortable with it."

"Well, I'm not! I can't understand a single word," she said. She looked straight ahead, and they drove the rest of the way in silence. As she parked the car outside her house she turned to Robert. "And," she said, as if continuing the conversation, "those people can't do me a bit of good." She got out of the car and slammed its heavy door.

Tracy did not care for Odets. She felt he had no respect for her. "He thinks I'm a birdbrain," she complained.

Robert continued his visits without her.

Despite all this, his work began to flow again, and he felt the relationship with Tracy would regain its even footing when she stopped shooting.

He and Mike often went to meetings of writers and directors who were concerned with the unemployment of those on the "lists" and contributed to a fund for them.

"How's it going with Tracy?" Mike asked as they were leaving a meeting one night at Odets's house.

"It'll get better." Robert shrugged. "But the play's going well."

The following Saturday Robert suggested to Tracy that

they not go to the party they were invited to. "Let's just hang around with each other."

"There're some people I want to see," she countered.

"They don't interest me."

"Well, they interest me," she said, growing angry.

He tried to mollify her by taking her in his arms.

"Don't," she said. "You're a stuffy old man."

He was more surprised by "old man" than by "stuffy."

"Why do you have to be out all the time?" Robert said, growing angry.

"Because only failures stay home," she said heatedly. "And don't try to make me feel guilty for wanting to have a good time on Saturday night."

Robert almost laughed.

———————

After a party in Bel Air, to which Tracy had gone alone, she and Mike walked to their cars, star jasmine and jacaranda filling the air. As she reached hers, she turned to him. "Robert's probably asleep already." It was both observation and invitation. Each waited for the other to move, neither surprised by the tension between them.

Mike looked at her in the perfumed silence, their breathing audible. "Goodnight," he said finally.

Mike never mentioned the incident to Robert.

In November, Tracy started an affair with Vallone. He was a virile, bright, explosive man who spoke both French and Italian expressively, and was a Euro-Communist. He was a working-class intellectual Robert and Mike could relate to. Having found someone they found attractive, Tracy seemed to have all three. Mike knew intuitively what was going on, and then it was confirmed by Tracy's director. He debated telling Robert. What would it accomplish?

His mind was made up one Sunday afternoon as he and Robert walked along the beach, leaving Tracy and Vallone at the house after a lunch the actor had cooked. They talked about the Ebro and Katherine. Robert told Mike about their spontaneous lovemaking at the Vineyard and asked what he thought it meant.

It settled the question for Mike. "I think it means you should go back to her."

"Why do you say that?"

"Because you made a lousy trade."

Robert was silent as the waves swept at their feet. "You think so?"

"Yes. And so do you, if you want to be honest with yourself." Mike decided to tip the balance. "Tracy's having an affair with Vallone."

"What?"

"Billy told me."

"Are you sure?"

"It's dinner conversation."

Tracy looked up and smiled as they entered the patio. Robert was grim.

Mike took Vallone's arm.

"*Che cosa*, Mike?" the actor said in surprise.

"*Andiamo*, Giorgio. The scene's over." Mike led them to their cars, where he explained that Robert knew.

———————

"What the hell's going on?" Tracy demanded angrily.

"Why, Tracy? Why?"

She looked at him coolly. "I like him, that's why. He's fun and you're not."

"We're living together," he said, thrown by her arrogance. "What about trust?"

"What about 'trust'?" she flung back at him. "You were married when we started. You're still married, and not to me."

"I gave up my wife and child for you!"

"You knew what you were doing."

"I wish I had."

"If you recall," she said, "you wanted your wife and me too. Well, I want the same thing."

"Are you in love with him?" he asked.

Tracy laughed. "You really are old-fashioned. He makes me laugh and he's great in bed, which I can't say for you."

Robert was stunned by the leap to his jugular. He turned and left the patio, blood drumming in his ears.

Tracy went into the kitchen, poured herself a glass of milk, and chose a cookie.

Upstairs, Robert gathered his notes, put on his khakis, threw on his tweed jacket, grabbed his typewriter, and went out to the Pacific Coast Highway to hitch a ride to the airport. Some surfers on the way to catch the late-afternoon waves at Redondo Beach took him all the way.

He called Mike from the airport.

"I'm going back to New York."

"Good luck. Give Katherine my love."

Tracy threw the rest of Robert's clothes in the trash.

CHAPTER TWENTY-FIVE

As Robert carried his typewriter and briefcase into the lobby of the Osborne on 57th Street, Alex was going to dinner. He wasn't surprised to see Robert.

"It's over?" Alex said, more statement than question.

"It's over."

"You came to your senses."

"No. Tracy forced them on me." Robert tried to laugh.

"What are you going to do now?"

"Call Katherine."

———

"That was a short romance," Katherine said on the phone.

"Katherine . . . please . . ."

"You're right. I'm sorry. So, you're back."

"Yes. I'd like to see you."

Katherine sighed. She wasn't sure she wanted to see him. She was just beginning to get over the hurt. Why open the wound? She stared at the phone as if it might reveal the answer.

"Hello?" he said into the silence.

"I'm thinking, Robert."

"Please, Katherine. I'd like to come over now."

"Okay." She sighed again.

Was it a sigh of recognition, Robert wondered, a sigh of duty to their pasts?

Katherine found herself before the mirror examining her

face. She could not deny her excitement. That crazy last time together at the Vineyard had stayed with her. Was she still in love? Where had all those lines come from? Had they been there in the summer? Had she had so many gray hairs then? Katherine rarely looked at herself critically, as a man might look at her. Her heart pounded as she bathed and changed clothes. She chose a yellow silk blouse and gray skirt. No jewelry; she did not want to appear dressed-up. What *do* you want? she wondered.

Robert hurriedly showered and shaved, dressed in his old uniform of tweed jacket and gray flannels. His heart beat rapidly as he jumped into a cab on 57th Street and rocketed down Fifth Avenue in the December night. It was hard to realize he'd been in sunny Malibu that morning.

Katherine was surprised at how well he looked standing in the doorway, tanned and smiling. She'd expected a look of depression.

"Hello, Robert." Her voice had the slightest quiver.

"Hello, Katherine."

They stood appraising each other.

"Come in," she said softly. Katherine fought his attraction for her as she sat across the room from him. "You're looking well. Your hair is longer. It's becoming."

"Thank you. You look well too." He cleared the huskiness from his throat.

She looked frankly at him. "Robert, you didn't come here to talk about our looks."

"You're right. I'd like to start over."

"How do you know you'd like to do that? I'm not the same person you left."

"You can't have changed that much."

"How do you know I'm not vindictive?"

"You never have been."

"I told you, I've changed."

"I don't believe it. That night on the Vineyard told me you hadn't." Robert rose. "I would have stayed if you hadn't asked me to leave. I knew then I'd made a mistake."

"You didn't fight to stay."

"I didn't feel I deserved you. I've always felt I was less a person than you. Less idealistic, less giving, less strong, less deserving."

Katherine pondered this.

"Why did you leave, then? Why the affair with Tracy?"

"I was angry with you. I needed you and you weren't there."

"Did Tracy supply what you needed?"

"No. She supplied something else. Sex and vanity."

"Sex and vanity don't go a hell of a long way, do they?"

"No," he said quietly, looking at his hands.

"And now that she's found someone else, you're back."

"How do you know that?"

"It's not that I'm so smart, but it's unlikely your values would be hers. Your identity is in your values, and I don't think you'd trade them in for hers. If I thought so, you wouldn't be here now. Therefore, an inevitable problem."

"Why didn't I know that?" Robert asked.

Katherine looked at him and smiled. "Perhaps you don't know yourself as well as you should."

Robert nodded. "Oh, by the way, Mike sends his love."

Katherine cocked her head doubtfully.

"He was always against my relationship with Tracy. He'd said I'd made a lousy trade."

"He makes us sound like baseball players." Katherine's lips tightened. "Anyway, he should know. He's an expert."

Robert took a deep breath and leaped. "How do you feel about our trying?"

"I don't know. I haven't forgiven you. I'm not sure I can. And if I can't, I'm not sure we should be together."

"I'm willing to try on your terms."

Katherine looked at him. "I want to tell you about my affair."

"Why?" Robert was alarmed, not sure where it would go.

"Because it's about me and I want you to know."

He nodded uncertainly.

"It's not something I'm proud of, but not for the reasons you might think. It has nothing to do with being unfaithful, although I did feel unfaithful to what we'd shared. I'm not proud of having used another person to replace you. I did feel deeply about him. He's a good, talented person, and we had a wonderful time on Deer Isle."

Robert wasn't sure what was coming, and he wasn't sure he could take two rejections in one day. He tried visualizing Katherine in Maine with . . . What did he look like? he wondered.

"We'd made love at Burnt Cove, the same place you'd wanted to, remember?"

Robert nodded, remembering the incident, and kept his eyes fixed on her.

"I could have loved him, and I was shocked at myself, shocked that I could replace you so easily. When we came back from Maine, I found your letter. I never saw him again, except one day, by accident, when we met on the street and talked for a minute or so. It was painful. I could see how hurt he'd been." Katherine stopped, looked at Robert, and continued. "I was going to call him tonight. Just as you called. There's timing for you." She smiled.

Robert rubbed his face with his hands, then laughed. "Now I know why Eaton gave me those funny looks."

Katherine smiled again, remembering Eaton's relief when she told him they were two different men.

"I can't blame you," Robert said, taking her face in his hands. "I still love you."

"Robert, I don't know how I feel about you. I'm still very angry, although I can see my part in it. I don't think what you did was justified." Robert didn't argue. "I might still decide to call him. I just don't know what I feel."

Robert breathed deeply. "I'd like to see Bobby."

"Okay. But don't wake him. He'll never get back to sleep."

Robert looked at the sleeping child and turned to Katherine, putting his arms around her, his cheeks wet with tears.

———————

Robert did not pressure her while she tried to make up her mind.

Katherine debated seeing Larry but decided it would be the cruelest way to decide. It would be using him all over again. And how egotistical to think he's just sitting there, waiting for you to call, she told herself.

———————————

Robert moved back to Washington Square the day before Christmas. It was snowing as he pulled Bobby on a sled to Sheridan Square to buy a tree.

"Faster, Daddy!"

Robert started running, his lungs filled with the cold air and a joy he hadn't experienced in years.

On the way home they pulled the tree together, and later they all decorated it.

In bed, Katherine said, "Welcome home, Robert."

Mike arrived in February. "I need my sidewalk shot and some good conversation." At his apartment, he cooked one of his large dinners for his best friends and sang again.

Ruth was a silent shadow. She said little, the lines of her face expressing more, an unhappy woman unable to take part in her husband's success or to join his friends.

Mike had been enjoying his daughter. She was very bright and he loved taking her small hand in his as they walked, often to F. A. O. Schwarz, the toy store across the street from the Plaza Hotel, to buy her yet another stuffed animal. Then he'd take her to the Plaza's Palm Court for a hot chocolate. It's a long way from Little Italy, he thought.

"Just like in Naples," Irv said as he dug into Mike's pasta. "We had this villa belonged to a Fascist big shot we kicked out. Mike used to cook up a storm for the Naples Opera Company. And remember—" he nearly said "Carla," but stopped.

Robert and Katherine remembered when Mike cooked and was unemployed. Now he had one picture "in the can," was starting another, and had a hit running on Broadway.

"In the fall, we do your play, Robert," he said.

"You think you'll have the time?"

"I will always have the time."

"And I'll be standing in line," Alex said.

Bobby played in Tony's room. She had many more toys than he did. His parents always seemed to give him books or records as presents. But Tony didn't want toys. She wanted her father.

Katherine listened to the men's conversation. As often happened, it revolved around work or the wars they'd been in. They didn't consciously exclude women, but she looked at Ruth and knew she was thinking the same thing. She rose and left the table, knowing Ruth would follow.

In the bedroom Ruth began to cry.

"Why do you put up with it?" Katherine asked.

"I don't know. I still love him. It's stupid and hopeless."

"And self-destructive."

"I'm not strong like you, Katherine."

"It's not strength, Ruth, it's self-respect."

"I know. I don't have any. And Mike hates me for that."

———————————————

The following day, Robert and Mike took their kids on their sleds and had a snowball fight.

"God, it's cold as Teruel," Mike said.

"I don't remember feeling it as much as I do now."

"We're getting older, kid," Mike said jovially. "Let's go to Umberto's." They pulled the sleds to Little Italy, and drank cappuccinos while the kids made a gooey mess of their sweets, smearing the yellow custard on their faces.

"What are you going to do about Ruth?" Robert asked.

"I've offered her a divorce. She said it wasn't necessary."

Robert sighed, clearly troubled. Katherine had told him of the scene in the bedroom the night before.

"God, it's fourteen years, Mike. Can you believe it?"

"Nope," Mike said, smiling, and put his hand on his friend's shoulder. Then he impulsively kissed his little girl.

———————————————

On Valentine's Day, Katherine and Mike found themselves alone at their table at the battalion banquet. It was late and the songs had been sung, the stories retold, the tablecloths stained with wine and coffee.

"Thanks for telling Robert he'd made a lousy trade," Katherine opened.

Mike nodded acknowledgment. He could have left it alone, but made a move of his own. "Why are you always so critical of me?"

"Because in some ways you're a shit, Mike."

Mike was not prepared for the bluntness. "Why?" was all he could say.

Katherine looked at him as he recovered, wondering how far she was going to go. "I guess it's your treatment of women. I was shocked at seeing Ruth the other night."

"I've offered her a divorce. She doesn't want one."

"Why did you marry her?"

"I wanted to be like you and Robert."

"Such disarming honesty," she replied sarcastically.

"It may have been dumb or unrealistic, but it's true. I've always admired you. You know that. But you always looked down on me."

"I haven't, Mike. But you worry me. A man who uses women can't be trusted. He'll use other people or situations to his own advantage."

"What about women who use men?" Mike then leaned to her. "Besides, my relations with women are my business, and to the best of my knowledge, I've never abused one. Some I've used and some have used me, and that's life. Maybe you're concerned about my relations with women, but I think you've always been jealous of what Robert and I have together, that part of Robert you can't own or manipulate or even share."

As they stared at each other across the table, Robert, who stood in the door saying goodnight to Milt, could see the tension between them. He knew that a confrontation had been growing for years and hoped it wouldn't be bloody. An argument with Katherine would be risky now when the soil between them had so recently been dug up.

"I have never been jealous of your relationship with Robert," Katherine said heatedly. "I've always hated Robert's dependence on you."

"That's not why Robert left you," Mike jabbed. This time he waited for her to recover.

"Why did he leave me?" she asked, shaken.

"Because he's dependent on you, not me, and you

weren't there for him when he needed you. Robert had a good relationship with his mother and a cold relationship with his father. He's dependent on women, not men. You should know that."

"But I don't want him dependent on me."

"Because you want your freedom, just like me." He smiled. "You want your freedom to work. Without dependents."

Katherine knew he'd hit a fundamental truth.

"I may be a shit, as you say, but I recognize it," Mike said, concluding the argument.

"What were you and Mike talking about so intensely?" Robert asked on the way home.

"Who's a bigger shit, him or me," Katherine said.

"Who won?"

"It was a draw."

CHAPTER TWENTY - SIX

Mike went back to California in March. Odets told him that Dashiell Hammett had been sentenced to six months in prison for refusing to reveal to the House Un-American Activities Committee the names of contributors to the bail fund of the Civil Rights Congress.

Mike was on that list.

"It's the beginning," Odets said. "Thomas Mann said it's just like Germany in '34. I think he's right. You know there have been no protests over Dash except from Lillian. There were eight subpoenas this month and not a peep from the Committee of Five Hundred. Everyone's heading for the shelters. It's biblical. The plague is coming and everyone is afraid of an X on his door. It's the pink plague."

Mike looked blank.

"The subpoenas are pink," Odets explained.

"What are you going to do?" Mike asked. "You know you're going to be called."

"I know." Odets sighed heavily. "What do I do? What am I willing to sacrifice for principle? Who am I? How do I live with myself?"

"You're not thinking of 'talking,' are you?"

Odets looked at Mike carefully over his glasses and pushed back his hair. "The Jews believe informing is a crime punishable by death, and Judas is not exactly a hero, even to the Romans. But I have to admit my ambivalence, Mike. I don't want to inform. I don't want to name any names. I also don't want to be unemployed."

"You're a playwright, for God's sake."

"Sometimes I'm a playwright. Most of the time now, I'm a screenwriter. I'm a freelance for hire. That's how I make my living." He could see that Mike was disturbed. "Look, Mike, whom would I be sacrificing for? I never got a decent review from the left, even when I was in the party." Odets began to show the old wounds. "They said I wasn't positive enough, my working-class heroes weren't strong enough— why did I write about a dentist, a bourgeois, rather than a proletarian? I was too individualistic. You remember all that shit. That's why we quit."

"I didn't quit," Mike said. "Remember, I was thrown out."

"What's the difference? You wouldn't toe the line. You wouldn't crawl for them."

"Neither would you, and I can't see you crawling for the committee either. What the fuck is the difference who makes you crawl? Crawling is crawling! Remember La Pasionaria—'It's better to die on your feet than live on your knees!'"

"Yeah, I remember," Odets said. "Well, I'm not ready to die and I'm also not ready to live on my knees. I've got two kids who have a long way to grow up, but if I talk, how do I look them in the eyes? How do they look at their daddy? And if I don't, how do I support them? Remember Alex's line, 'survival without castration'? How do I do that?"

"Go back to the theater."

"Shit, I never made a living in the theater."

Mike looked at the expensive furnishings and brilliant art collection and knew what Odets meant by a "living." But he said nothing. He enjoyed that kind of living himself.

Odets looked at Mike keenly. "What are you going to do, Mike? You know you're going to be called."

"I hope I have the guts to die on my feet, Cliff."

———————

As Mike prepared his picture about a Central American revolutionary, April brought the plague. Death came in the form of that pink piece of paper, the subpoena to appear before a representative of the committee. It meant a dance of death either for oneself or for the people one had known, shared meals with, worked with, played with the children of, shared ideas with. The process server's knock at the door held as much terror as the midnight knock of the Gestapo.

There were few Joan of Arcs. Most did not accept burning. There were those who suffered in silence and those who fled to Mexico, England, France. A few committed suicide.

All over Los Angeles, people discussed the behavior of those who were called. Over dinner at the Brown Derby or Chasen's, at poolside barbecues, commissary lunches, on the set between takes, the conversation was about who "behaved well," who talked, who was likely to be called, and who ran.

An industry grew up around the pink plague. Every studio had a vice-president in charge of "security" with a fully staffed department entering and deleting names, advising production departments who was employable. Then there were the "smear and clear" people: Ronald Reagan at the Screen Actors Guild, Roy Brewer of the International Alliance of Theatrical and Stage Employees, the American Legion, *Red Channels*, and the lawyers who specialized in handling "loyalty" cases. There was even a psychiatrist tuned in to the special stress induced by "the problem." He always seemed to advise naming names and was later found not to be a psychiatrist at all but a photographer.

"It's spooky," Mike wrote to Robert. "People disappear. They're in the office next to you one day and gone the next. No trace is left. Names are gone from doors and parking spaces as if they never existed. If you call them, the operator says, 'Who?' When the subpoena comes, you're suddenly invisible. Everybody somehow knows and looks right through you. People who used to spill their soup on themselves trying to shake your hand look away."

Robert wrote that the same thing was happening in the TV industry in New York. Advertising agencies that sponsored programs were afraid to hire anyone listed for fear of boycott of their products. Although the theater was still relatively free of the plague, a few stage producers were afraid to hire blacklisted actors. One producer, Alexander H. Cohen, went out of his way to hire them.

"I thought we went to war to prevent the midnight knock," Robert said.

Lillian Hellman went to Washington at the committee's invitation and gave them hell as an industry watched. "I refuse to tailor my convictions to the fashions of the times," she told them. She did not go to jail and was not dependent on Hollywood.

"Lillian's got balls," Odets said at dinner. "We're going to need more than the courage of Spain, believe me."

Finally, Odets was called. "I'm scared, Mike," he said.

"I'll be over tonight."

Despite the fatigue of a day's shooting in the hot sun of the desert, Mike went to Odets's house without stopping to eat. He found Paul Robeson there. Robeson's passport had been lifted by the State Department, so he could not concertize abroad. They talked about Spain, Peekskill, and the mood of the country.

"This too shall pass," Robeson assured them. He radiated enormous strength, which he tried to impart to Odets. "The Spanish Inquisition also didn't last," he said.

"But they threw the Jews out," Odets said. "This is my country. I don't want to leave it."

Mike told the story of the men who'd deserted in Spain and the vote about whether to court-martial them.

"I voted for death," Mike said.

"Why?" Odets asked.

"Robert asked the same question. I told him, 'Shame is worse than death.'"

Odets looked at him. "How Sicilian," he said.

They talked all night. In the morning Odets took the plane to Washington. Mike still did not know what Odets would do. He doubted whether Odets knew. He went back to his revolutionaries in the desert.

There was a big battle scene on the schedule that day involving a train, many horsemen, and explosives. The scene went well: stunt men fell beautifully from their horses, wagons, railroad cars. Explosions took place on cue, wranglers brought horses to their knees and turned them over, hooves pawing the sky, and men screamed in pain. After the take, everyone cheered.

Stavros applauded as he watched from beneath an umbrella held by his chauffeur. He crossed to Mike as they moved toward the train for close-ups.

"I love this," Stavros said, waving his hand at the scene. "I love movies."

Mike wondered why he was there. Stavros hadn't come out all the way to Palmdale to tell him he loved movies or to see something he could witness in the comfort of his screening room.

It didn't take long for his hidden agenda to surface.

"By the way, how is Odets?"

"How should he be?" Mike fenced.

"I hope he's going to be sensible in Washington."

Mike shrugged. "He'll do what he has to do. Every man has to live with himself."

"That doesn't sound too good."

"Depends which side you're on."

"There's only one side, Mike. I hope you talked to him last night."

Mike stiffened. "How do you know I saw him last night?"

"I just assumed it," Stavros said blandly. "You're good friends, he has a crisis, it's natural."

He wants me to know he knows, Mike thought. And somebody else sent him here or he wouldn't come out to the fuckin' desert.

Stavros waited.

"Mike! Where do you want the camera?" the cinematographer shouted.

The two men looked at each other in the shade of the umbrella.

"Go back to work," Stavros said quietly, putting out his hand. Mike took it and was surprised by how rough it was.

"Thanks for the visit," Mike said, his tone letting Stavros know what he thought of it.

Stavros waved airily.

When am I gonna get shot down? Mike wondered. When is my luck going to run out?

Odets testified in secret session and gave the committee a hard time. He harangued them, he lectured them, he was caustic and belligerent. He gave them a history lesson, telling them what democracy meant. He insulted them. And he gave them six names.

"I can't believe it!" Robert exclaimed over the phone. "Odets! Why?"

"Why?" Mike echoed the long-distance question. "Who knows why? Who knows what a man will do at the moment of truth or what fear will break his courage?"

"You sound like you're apologizing for him," Robert said, almost angrily.

"I'm not. He can do that for himself if he feels he needs to. I'm trying to understand him." Mike felt tired.

"What's there to understand?" Robert barked. "By every rule of morality he failed."

"Maybe he's getting back at the God that failed."

"Mike, that's bullshit and you know it. He did it to save his standard of living," Robert said angrily. "God, what a disappointment."

Mike exhaled heavily. He knew it was at least partially true. "But Cliff says he didn't hurt anybody. He only named names the committee already had."

"C'mon, Mike . . . he could have talked about himself and no one else. It doesn't matter that he lectured them. What matters is that in the end he gave them what they wanted."

"True," Mike said.

"How are *you*?" Robert asked, coming down from his anger.

"Knocked out. It was a blow. Cliff knows how unhappy I am and it hurts him, but I just can't hide it." Mike wanted to change the subject. "How's the play coming?"

"Very well. It's really flowing. Alex has read some scenes, and he's excited. Are you still on schedule?"

"Two days ahead. And I've gotten permission from Stavros to bring the footage back East and edit it in New

York. If the play is ready, we can get it on in late fall or winter."

"That's great, Mike," Robert said in excitement.

John Garfield was called. He was afraid of losing his brilliant acting career but he felt he couldn't name anyone and still face himself. Yet if he remained silent it would be considered an indictment of his longtime friend Odets.

"What are you going to do?" he asked Mike one night at dinner in the Brown Derby.

"What I do may not be right for you, Julie."

"You didn't answer my question," Garfield persisted.

"When I was a kid I could have answered it easily. Right and wrong were a lot clearer to me. I shot one of our own men in Spain. It was during an attack and he tried to surrender. I killed him and didn't even think about it."

As Garfield pondered this, Stavros approached them on his way into dinner. "Well, two of my favorites," he said jovially. "Plotting a revolution?"

"No, just a palace coup," Mike shot back, smiling.

"Make sure you're well armed," Stavros said.

"We don't need arms," Mike said. "We've already got our guys inside. You know, boring from within . . . the great conspiracy."

"You're a funny guy, Mike, but I'd leave the comedy to Chaplin," Stavros said.

"I can take a hint," Mike said.

Chaplin had already been subpoenaed.

Garfield testified. He named no names.

"I didn't hurt anyone!" Odets finally blurted out one Sunday afternoon at his house.

Mike and Garfield turned away.

Odets took Garfield's arm. "Listen, Julie, you want to be unemployed, that's your own decision. I guess you're stronger than me. I couldn't take it."

"But Jesus, how could you name Joe Bromberg?" They had known Bromberg since *Awake and Sing*.

"Joe had been named ten times. I couldn't hurt him any more than he already was."

"You mean the last guy to stick a knife in the body doesn't count!" Garfield said.

Odets looked away. Mike was silent as the two old friends fought, thinking, This is what the bastards do to you.

CHAPTER TWENTY - SEVEN

Mike waited for two things. An invitation for tennis from John Farrell, who'd returned from Europe with Shirley, and the dreaded pink invitation to account for his past and ruin his future.

It was late, perhaps ten o'clock, when the knock came. He went to the door and opened it. It was a neighbor telling him his lawn sprinkler was still on.

"Thanks." He turned off the sprinkler and returned to his desk. He realized he was trembling. He looked at his script and tried to concentrate on the next day's work.

When the second knock came he knew it wasn't about a sprinkler. He got up heavily, feeling the nervous electricity up his spine.

"Mr. Rossano?" the man asked politely.

Mike noted that even in August he wore a tie. "Yes."

"Please accept this," he said, extending his hand with the folded pink paper.

What would he do if I refused it? Mike wondered. Would he sleep on my doorstep, come back night after night in his wilted shirt and crumpled suit?

"Thank you," Mike found himself saying as he took the summons.

The man, relieved, turned to his black Ford.

Mike stared at the pink paper in the moonlight. The Congressional summons was for the following week in room 1025 of the old Federal Building. Next week, he thought. I'm not ready.

Mike had finished his location work and was shooting interiors at the studio. It was a Friday, and he called Stavros. Stavros did not call back.

But Farrell did. "How are you, Mike?" he said heartily. "We've missed you. Especially Shirley. Talked about you all the time. Come over on Sunday. I've been practicing my backhand in England, and I'm going to whip your ass."

"You probably will. My game's rusty."

"I hear the picture's great. I've never seen such excitement around here. Zanuck's in the clouds, and Stavros is sure it's Oscar time. He's positively drooling."

So why isn't he returning my call? Mike wondered.

"Glad they're so excited," Mike said modestly. "I'll see you on Sunday."

"Shirley's looking forward to it."

———————

Mike called Robert that night to tell him.

"What are you gonna do?" Robert asked.

"Try to get a postponement."

"Then what?"

"Need you ask?" Mike felt a surge of anger.

"I know you're not going to name anyone," Robert explained, catching Mike's tone. "Are you gonna take the First or the Fifth?"

"The Fifth stinks."

When Robert hung up, he left his study and went to Katherine's office, where she was working. "That was Mike. He's been called."

Katherine looked up at him from her desk and bit her thumbnail. "What's he going to do?"

"If he can't get a postponement, he'll take the First."

"I wish I could be sure of that," she said.

"What do you mean?"

"You never can tell what Mike will do."

Robert felt a flash of hostility. He wanted to argue with Katherine about the remark, but felt he couldn't. He left the room and went back to his own study.

———————

Mike was disappointed when he got to the Farrells'. Shirley wasn't there. He was distracted and didn't play well.

"Your mind's sure not on your game," Farrell said.

Later, in the Moroccan Room over drinks, Farrell put on his most sympathetic look. "You okay, Mike?"

"What do you mean?"

"Just that you have your problems."

"Which problems are you talking about?"

"Look, Mike," Farrell said earnestly, "we're friends, so let's not volley back and forth. Everyone knows the committee is something to worry about. I'd like to help you if I can."

Mike's alarm system went off.

"Now, what are you going to do?"

So, that's the game, Mike thought. Farrell's the scout for Stavros. He won't call back until he gets a report.

"What am I going to do?" Mike echoed the question. "I'm not a rat. I don't squeal."

Farrell nodded as if in agreement, but said softly, "You're too talented for that position, Mike."

"It's got nothing to do with talent."

"Of course it does. You could be the best director in the world if you keep going. So don't fuck it up. You owe it to your talent, to the industry, and to the public. You would be selfish not to go along with the program."

Mike felt like laughing, Stavros's ploy was so obvious. Soften him up with some Farrell artillery and then make the main attack on Monday. As he speculated, Shirley passed the door. Mike hadn't heard a car drive up. Had she been in the house the whole time? Was she checking now to see if they were through with their meeting? Her perfume wafted into the room.

"And who are you going to protect in your misguided idealism?" Farrell continued. "People who are trying to destroy our freedoms? If those people were in power there wouldn't be any First or Fifth Amendments."

Now that the game was clear, Mike didn't pay any attention, thinking instead of Shirley in her white dress.

Farrell saw Mike turn inward and finished, "Think about it before you do anything rash."

That's the tack I'll take with Stavros, Mike thought.

Just then, Shirley entered. "Hi, Mike," she said, her voice low. She was smiling, but Mike felt the tentativeness as she crossed to him with her hand outstretched.

Farrell frowned.

"I thought you were finished," she said lamely, the smile diminishing.

"We have," Mike assured her, taking her hand. He'd forgotten the pleasure of her strong hands. "You're looking well."

"Thank you. You are too." Mike could see that she was glad to see him. "I hear *Blood and Earth* is just great."

"We'll see," Mike said. "What have you been up to?"

"I did T. S. Eliot's *The Cocktail Party* in London."

"And she was great," Farrell said.

"I loved the experience. I wish I could get John to move to New York. I really prefer the theater."

Is that her way of telling me she prefers me to John? Mike wondered. "I'm going to do Robert Thompson's new play in the fall. Maybe there'll be something in it for you."

"Oh, I hope so. I'd do a walk-on in one of his plays."

"Shirley has great enthusiasm and very little sense," Farrell said.

"I don't think that's true," Mike said.

"Neither do I," Shirley said, taking Mike's arm playfully, as if choosing sides.

"Okay. I know when I'm beaten," Farrell laughed.

As Mike walked to his car, Farrell took his arm conspiratorially.

"Stavros told me. Watch out for him."

The good-cop–bad-cop routine, Mike thought. "Thanks for the warning," he said.

"Let's have dinner next week."

Mike nodded.

But it was Stavros who invited him to dinner at his home in Bel Air. Mike had never been there. Not many people had. As Mike drove up to the huge iron gates of the mansion, they opened for him. The sixteen-foot iron grillwork in the forms of flowers, angels, sunbursts, and spikes reminded him of Italy. Only Italians worked iron like that.

The house was pink marble with blue columns delicately veined in white. A butler opened a golden door that had a bas-relief of Greek athletes throwing javelins and discuses, their penises covered with gold grapes. The furniture was French Empire, gold-encrusted.

It reminded him of the villa he and Irv had requisitioned in Naples. This guy must be a Fascist too, Mike thought.

Stavros came from another room, advancing through the Greek statues and vases that lined the enormous entryway. He padded along the marble floor in black velvet evening slippers with his initials woven in gold. Dressed for a quiet evening at home, he wore a yellow silk shirt and beige cashmere suit.

"Michael . . ." Stavros called, arms outstretched. Mike had never been called Michael in his life. "Welcome to Casa Stavros. It's good to see you. Did you have a hard day? The rushes were fantastic. What would you like to drink? How about a little retsina?"

"Retsina is fine."

As if he were a genie, a servant appeared with a silver tray.

"The stuffed grape leaves are wonderful," Stavros said, taking one. "My wife is so talented."

"Where is she?"

"Paris, shopping. You know, the new collections." He waved his hand airily. "Would you believe she travels with two empty Vuitton trunks wherever we go?"

Mike smiled, unsure of what his response should be. He looked at the giant goldfish in a marble lily pond.

"Beautiful, aren't they?" Stavros asked, following Mike's gaze. "I love nature."

Mike wondered when Stavros would get to his agenda. During dinner over some incredible Bordeaux that would make his head swim? Or would he wait for brandy and cigars in the intimacy of his study?

Stavros walked arm in arm with Mike toward the dining room, past erotically painted vases. "What are you thinking?"

"That I'm a camera on a long dolly shot."

Stavros exploded in laughter. "Wonderful! Wonderful! That's why I love artists. Always thinking of their craft. And you are a great artist, Michael."

Here it comes, Mike thought.

It didn't. "It's no accident that you were named after Michelangelo."

"My father's name was Angelo," Mike said.

"Of course. What did he do? What was he?"

"He was a bricklayer."

Stavros stopped. "So was I as a youth. And my father. In Athens. He still builds walls and terraces behind the house I bought him. He says if he stops working, he'll die."

"I can understand that." Mike looked at Stavros's stubby, powerful hands with a new and grudging respect.

Stavros caught the look and opened his hands to Mike. "You see, I'm just a simple working man."

The wines were superb prewar vintages, the food prepared to the standards of an international gourmet.

Stavros told him about his poverty-stricken childhood in the slums of Athens and then, as if struck by an idea, asked Mike what he was doing in November.

"I'll be in New York finishing *Blood and Earth* and working on Robert Thompson's new play."

Stavros put his hand on Mike's arm and spoke as if he were imparting a deep secret. "If you can manage it, you must come to France with me. In Burgundy, at the end of November, they have a gastronomic marathon known as Les Glorieuses at Beaune. On the third Saturday night, the Confrérie des Chevaliers du Tastevin has a banquet in the cellars of the sixteenth-century Clos de Vougeot, founded by Cistercian monks." He drew a deep breath. "You sit down at eight and rise again at one in the morning." Stavros swished the '36 Mouton Rothschild in his large glass and beamed. "One meal I had started with *saladier de jambon persillé dijonnaise rélevé de bonne moutarde forte de Dijon*, followed by a turbot with Meursault-Charmes that was round in the mouth, perfect for fish . . ."

Mike realized that Stavros was almost hypnotizing himself in his gastronomic reverie, bizarre in the light of the dinner's agenda.

"Then came a duck cooked to perfection, with a Savigny-les-Beaunes that restored the palate followed by . . ." Stavros continued the aria, describing desserts and cheeses, as their own soufflé was brought to the table with tiny strawberries.

"Taste these," he commanded, taking some. "They're wild. I have them flown in from France. They were picked yesterday by a peasant I know."

The soufflé melted on his tongue, and the strawberries played a counterpoint of slight tartness to the sweet chocolate. "And that was only the first meal," Stavros laughed. "You know what I'm going to do?" he continued. "I'm going to get a bunch of good guys together—you, Zanuck, Farrell, maybe Gable and Ty Power—and we'll go to Burgundy for an eating safari. We'll call it the Gourmets' Expedition."

Mike laughed, then pointed to the large dining room with its twenty-foot table at which they sat alone, and asked Stavros how he'd managed to get all of it.

"Luck . . . pure luck," he replied with his killer's smile.

And how many bodies have you buried? Mike longed to ask.

"Let's go into the study," Stavros finally said, "for brandy and cigars."

Mike was sorry he'd eaten so much. This was not a conversation for a full stomach. He accepted the fifty-year-old Napoleon brandy and vintage Cuban cigar.

"It's real," Stavros said of the Velázquez Mike was staring at. "I paid over a hundred thousand for it. Outbid the Metropolitan Museum." He laughed.

As they faced each other in large leather wing chairs, Stavros inhaled the fumes of brandy. "I'm glad you came over tonight," he finally started. "I want to know you better. We're all so busy, we have no time for friendships. I want you to consider me a friend. We have a lot in common."

"Thank you."

"We're going to have a great future together if you give me what I need. Then I'll be able to give you anything you want, your choice of property, star, writer—"

"Except those on the blacklist."

"You might as well ask for Leonardo da Vinci as your art director. They're just as dead."

"But they're not dead."

Stavros's voice took on an edge of annoyance. "Then let's just say they're 'not available.'"

Mike leaned forward. "Look, if you or any other studio head openly hires one of those people, you can break the blacklist."

"Assuming that I'd want to, and I'm not saying I do, except that it's a damned nuisance and I don't like anyone telling me who to hire and fire. But I've got a board of directors, stockholders, and the other studios to account to. We all signed the Waldorf statement."

"But—"

"That's it, Mike." Stavros's voice grew hard. "Don't push. And you never heard me admit there is a blacklist." He looked sharply at Mike, then sat back, puffed on his cigar, and continued, his voice now warmer, "Now, how can I help you with your 'problem'?"

"What do you mean?"

"I'm not without influence."

"Can you get the subpoena squashed?"

"That much muscle I don't have." He laughed. "What are you going to do?"

Finally. "Tell the truth," Mike said.

"Good. That's always best. Who are you going to name?"

"No one but myself."

"You know that won't satisfy them," he said, still reasonably.

"That's too bad. I've survived two wars and I'll—"

Stavros cut him off and leaned forward. "You'll be annihilated. And for what? Today's principle is tomorrow's garbage. You got the best future of anyone in this town. You want to dump it?"

Mike was silent.

"Now I'll speak selfishly. I've got twenty or thirty million tied up in you."

"My pictures don't cost that much."

"I didn't say they did. But that's the profit I see in them if I don't have seventeen thousand American Legion posts demonstrating in front of theaters where your pictures will play. And over the course of your career with us, there's maybe a hundred million profit." Stavros stood up. "You see how honest I am with you? I'm not going to lose our investment and I'm not going to lose our potential profits." Stavros stood so close to Mike he could not get up if he chose to.

"Do you know what *Earth* is about?" Mike said as strongly as possible. "It's about a revolutionary fighting for his people against oppression from those above. The black-list is the same kind of oppression. That film represents me!"

Stavros looked bleakly at Mike, and his voice was cold and penetrating. "You think I'm a fool? You think I don't know what you and your pictures are about?" His voice softened. "I know and I'll help you. But if you cross me, I personally promise you you will never make another picture. Anywhere. I'll kill you in this town. You know I have that power. Or . . . or . . ." He smiled. "I'll give you a chance to make your pictures. I'll give you a multiple-picture deal, scripts and cast of your choice as long as we can get them."

"The stick and the carrot, huh?"

"Works every time. Unless you're suicidal, and somehow I don't think you are. I think you're more like me than you'd care to admit. It's one of the reasons I like you." He sipped his brandy and let it sink in. "Now . . . I've already made a deal for you with the committee."

"You *what*?" Mike stood, causing Stavros to step backward. "You had no right to do that."

"All they want is one big name that hasn't been named and you're home free," he said.

"How about Tracy Morgan?" Mike joked. But he knew from Stavros's reaction he'd hit a nerve.

The tycoon's eyes clouded and his mouth tightened. It had not yet been announced, but Stavros had signed Tracy to a multimillion-dollar contract last week.

"What do you know?" Stavros asked.

Mike smiled enigmatically.

"That stupid petition for the Hollywood Ten she signed?" Mike looked blank not to reveal his hand.

"She wouldn't know a petition from Chasen's menu," Stavros laughed. "Anyway, she told me the signature's a forgery."

"I saw her sign it," Mike said, marveling at his luck. "If you look at it closely, you'll see my name above hers and Robert Thompson's below it." Stavros took a deep breath. "She also had an affair with Vallone, who's a known Communist. Guilt by association."

"Are you threatening me?"

"No. I'm showing you the absurdity of this fucking 'conspiracy.'"

"Good." Stavros nodded. "For your information I didn't see the petition because it doesn't exist."

Mike looked at him.

"It was somehow destroyed. Anyway, love clouds the mind. She never discussed politics with Vallone, because she's too stupid, and your friend Thompson is a jilted lover. Now, what are you going to do?"

"I'm going to think about your offer."

"Good. I'm glad I'm not dealing with a closed mind. But you don't have much time."

"Get me time. Get me a postponement. I don't want to have to think about anything but the picture, which is to your benefit. I need time for that decision."

Stavros appraised him, then nodded slowly.

———————————

Mike had his dream again.

The building was collapsing in slow motion. The bricks, cement, timbers, were flying about as the men fell through the air to the street. *"Poppa!"* Mike yelled. His father lay in the rubble, eyes beseeching, holding on to life. *"Poppa!"* Mike yelled, sobbing. The ringing phone released him.

"Hello . . ." he said, trying to surface.

"Mike . . . it's Cliff."

"What time is it?" Mike asked, drenched.

"It's about two. I couldn't sleep," Odets said.

"Are you okay?" Mike asked. Odets had been very depressed.

"Yeah. Look, Mike, don't do it. It's not worth it. Whatever you lose, it's not worth it. I don't know what I can ever do to make up for it. Be strong."

"Stavros is getting me a postponement."

"Okay." Odets sighed. "But don't give in."

"Try to get some sleep, Cliff."

"Okay, Mike. I'm depending on you. I don't want Julie looking at you the way he looks at me."

"Julie doesn't hate you, Cliff."

"I hate myself." There was a click.

Mike fell against the pillow in exhaustion.

———————————

The following afternoon as he was setting up a shot, he was handed an envelope with the seal of the United States Congress. The letter postponed his appearance before the committee indefinitely. He went to his dressing-room office.

"Thanks," he told Stavros.

"Indefinitely does not mean permanently, Mike. It means time to think things over. I can't keep the dogs off forever."

That night, over the phone, Robert said, "It only postpones the inevitable. When do you think you'll be in New York?"

"Less than a month," Mike said.

"That's great."

"How are things with Katherine?"

"They'll never be the same," Robert admitted. "You can mend a tear, but the fabric is never as strong again."

"It's like naming names. Even if you can understand it, things can't be the same."

Somehow, Mike wasn't surprised when Tracy called that night. She wanted to come over and "talk."

"I'm not in the mood," he told her.

"Maybe some other time," she said with promise in her voice.

"Maybe," he said, knowing he wouldn't.

He had a date with the Farrells the following night for dinner, but John called in the afternoon to cancel. "Stavros wants to have dinner with me, but why don't you go ahead with Shirley and maybe I'll be able to join you later."

Shirley was already seated at a softly lit corner table of Chasen's looking cool and elegant in lavender silk.

Mike bent to her. "I want you," he whispered in her ear. She laughed as if he'd said something funny.

Mike was conscious of the many eyes on them. Would they appear in some gossip column in the morning? "Seen at Chasen's last night, hot director Mike Rossano, recently subpoenaed by the Un-American Activities Committee, with cool, lovely leading lady Shirley Day, wife of Fox producer and Zanuck polo pal charming John Farrell. Shouldn't you be worried, John?"

John never showed up, and Shirley stayed away from anything personal. She knew that if they were drawn into conversation about themselves it would be sensed around the room by all those whose radar instantly read body language connected to changes in relationships. But she agreed to meet him at his house in Brentwood.

———————

His need of her was almost violent, and she lost herself in totally unmasked passion. Mike stripped her of the cool veneers she assumed for the outside world and drew out a tenderness she'd never known she possessed.

When they climaxed together, Mike cried.

"It's all right, Mike . . . it's all right." She took him in her arms.

"I don't know why that happened," he said, wiping his eyes.

"It's all right." She soothed. "It's all right."

"Why do you stay with John?"

"I don't know. I love him in a way. We're more alike than you'd care to believe. We're both ambitious, vain . . ." She changed the subject. "Why were you crying like that?"

"Because it's so good with you. Because of my father, because of Odets and Garfield and all the guys I've left dead on battlefields. Because I haven't let myself cry since I was a kid. Come to New York with me."

"I don't know if I can. I mean, I don't know if I'm ready."

Mike went back to New York in the middle of September after a huge party on the Mexican set of *Blood and Earth*. Stavros had imported a troupe of flamenco dancers whose heels and skirts swirled down the main street as piñatas exploded in the air. There were shouts and songs from the crew, who mingled with the executives. They all felt they had a hit as they ate, drank, joked, and danced.

Mike danced with Shirley, who was light on her feet and smiling. Yet her smile was dimmed for him as he thought of Florita. The trumpet player's cheeks puffed with the effort of playing the intricate high notes, but he did not play as well as Florita's father had. Shirley's colorful skirt swished at her ankles, and she held Mike's hands tightly.

But she was not going to New York with him. She was staying with Farrell.

"I'm just unlucky in love," he told her as the dance ended.

"Perhaps you should count your blessings," she said. "Maybe you're lucky and don't know it."

"What does that mean?"

"I was just being flippant. I can't go, Mike," she said, flushed from the dancing. "I just can't."

Stavros approached. "Shirley, you don't mind my borrowing Mike for a few minutes, do you?" he asked politely.

"Of course not. As long as you don't dance with him."

"Good sense of humor," Stavros said as he took Mike's arm for a stroll down the rural street. Stavros was wearing a costume designer's version of a Mexican cowboy's outfit, lots of silver and tinkling spurs. "I hope you know we usually don't allow a director to edit his picture away from the studio. It's a mark of our esteem for you that we're letting you take the footage to New York."

"I appreciate it."

"Let's talk about release dates. I think *Invisible Man* is a good back-to-school picture. It feels like a good October release, so we're starting the campaign next week." Stavros nodded to friends and flunkies as they strolled. "We'll release *Earth* in the spring. It's an exciting picture, and people are always excited by the change of seasons, especially spring. The sap is rising. We're going to do a big campaign." They got to the end of the street, and Stavros turned back. "Spend a lot of money on it. I hope you're not going to do anything to fuck up our plans."

"What do you mean?"

"I could only get you a delay, Mike. The problem of your past hasn't gone away. I assume that when you're called you won't shame me or violate my trust."

"I didn't make any promises," Mike said, trying to withdraw his arm from Stavros's grasp, but Stavros held it firmly.

"True," he said, "but it will reflect on me, Mike." He stopped and faced Mike. "I love your talent and I like you as a person, but if you don't respect our mutual benefit, I'll destroy you."

"It's very clever of him to release the first picture before you testify," Alex said as they had dinner at Robert and Katherine's. They all nodded. "That way, he'll get a few months' grace without any problems. That's probably the deal he made with the committee."

"He probably can't hold them off until *Blood and Earth* opens," Katherine said.

"Good back-to-school picture!" Robert said, laughing. "God, he's clever."

"And a killer," Mike said.

Bobby came padding into the dining room and seeing Mike, ran to him, shouting, "Uncle Mike!"

Mike spread his arms, and Bobby jumped into his lap,

kissing him. "Will you take me to the park tomorrow, Uncle Mike? I can play chess."

"I sure will. When did you learn?"

"Daddy taught me."

Ruth looked at Mike with the child on his lap, knowing she had never had that tenderness from him.

Later, they stared into the darkness of their bedroom.

"I don't love you," Mike said.

"It doesn't matter."

"Why? You can find someone else, someone who'll be better for you."

"It's too late."

"What do you mean? You're very attractive."

"Mike, please . . ." Her voice cracked.

Mike persisted. "Why are you cutting yourself off from possibility?"

"Because there isn't any."

"Why are you so hopeless?" he asked angrily.

"Because life for me is, Mike." Her anger also rose. She sat up. "I'll tell you why it's hopeless. Because I have cancer. I have to have a breast removed. Who wants a disfigured woman?" Her anger and tears burst out of her.

Mike was stunned. He put his arms around her as she sobbed.

Mike set up his cutting rooms at 1600 Broadway and a production office for *84 Avenue Foch* almost across the street at 1645. Robert's play was about his underground experiences in France and the betrayal of Max and Fresnay by an informant in Lyon. It was also about the betrayal of ideals for profit. Mike shuttled between the two buildings as they cast the play.

"It's in good shape, Robert," Mike said over lunch at Dinty Moore's. Alex agreed. "Whatever shaping and tightening we want to do, we can do in rehearsal and on the road. You agree, Alex?"

Alex nodded as he looked at the *New York Times*. "Pretty big ad for *Invisible Man*," he said.

"Yeah," Mike replied. "I can't figure out if Stavros is nervous about it so he's spending a lot on advertising." Mike switched the subject. "How many people are we seeing this afternoon?"

"About sixty," Alex replied, putting down the paper. "This morning I booked the Shubert in New Haven for the last week of November."

"Here we go again." Robert smiled.

CHAPTER TWENTY - EIGHT

"I'll bury you and dance on your grave!"

Stavros's long-distance threat still echoed in Mike's mind as he stared at the gingerbread ceiling of his Ritz Hotel bedroom in Boston. He looked at his watch. It was half past two. Heavily, he walked to the bathroom and splashed his face. His legs felt like lead. Yet only this morning he had left the committee room and marched down the halls of Congress arm in arm with Robert and Katherine as they'd marched in Barcelona. Proudly and with a light step.

He could still see Katherine's puzzled look as he left the witness stand this morning. She'd expected his collapse, and he'd surprised her. Katherine hated to be wrong. And Robert's smile. It had been worth anything to have Robert smile like that when he'd come through.

What was he going to do? He believed Stavros's threat to line up every other studio head and destroy him. The phone rang. He ignored it. It rang again.

Must be Robert or Alex, he thought and bent for the black instrument on the night table, nearly knocking the lamp over.

"Overseas call, Mr. Rossano," the operator said in her flat Boston accent. Mike felt a tremor in his hand as the hisses started again.

Stavros launched right in. "Michael, I think I was a little rough with you before. Forgive me, but you can understand how I felt getting that call from Washington. You embarrassed me, damaged my credibility." Although the words were damning, Stavros said them smoothly, without apparent heat. "I don't want to punish you, so don't make me. Give me a break, kid," he said, smiling into the small gilded mirror above the flowers on the table in the restaurant's elegant little phone room. "You won't be the first uncooperative witness to think it over. Dmytryk did it from jail, and he's certainly no coward. Now, I want you to call Martin Gang, the lawyer, you know who he is, and have him set up another meeting. Ask him to make it in secret, executive session, so there's no one else there," Stavros said pleasantly as if he were suggesting a lunch date. "They're expecting it. They're also expecting a big name from you, no rehash of old ones. You know who I mean."

"Who?" Mike asked, his throat dry.

"Mike, don't play games with me. A Pulitzer Prize-winner will do nicely."

"Robert was never a Communist."

"He was a sympathizer. He was in the Joint Anti-Fascist Committee."

"That doesn't make him a camp follower. He was also in the OSS and the French underground."

"Mike, don't split hairs. Your friend Irv was a Communist and in the OSS. Now, I'm telling you what you have to do." Stavros's voice was rising in anger. "Do it, or you're dead!" The phone clicked off and the connection was broken.

Mike took a deep breath and called Ziggy in Hollywood in response to Ziggy's call.

"I don't know what you did in Washington, Mike," his agent said, "but I had a rich offer from every studio in town. I was playing one off against the other and the prices were going into the stratosphere. Within one hour, every offer was withdrawn."

Mike called his film editor in New York, who'd also called while he was in Washington.

"They've ordered me to pack up, Mike. Stavros is taking the picture away from you. I was told to have everything back at the Fox lot by next week unless I heard from Stavros personally."

Mike bit his lip. They might as well take his child away. He slumped against the pillow. The phone rang.

"Let's take a walk to Durgin Park," Robert said cheerfully.

———————————

Mike forced himself to concentrate at rehearsals. Robert and Alex thought it was a kind of post-combat depression.

Mike's old nightmare of his father's death by burial returned. Burial was the image Stavros had used, and the dream changed. Mike was now buried under building debris as the child Mike clawed to save him. Then he had a new dream. He was on a snowy mountain trying to reach the top where the sun was. He slipped and slid as the high winds buffeted him, pushing him backward. It was freezing, and he woke in the large Ritz bedroom shivering, holding blankets about himself.

He didn't tell Robert and Alex about the pressures being applied, but he looked terrible. Finally, Robert asked him if there was anything beyond the contempt charge that was demonizing him.

"It's Ruth," Mike said. "She's afraid of having the mastectomy and she's threatening suicide. She says she has nothing to live for. I'm gonna have to go to New York this weekend."

Robert patted his arm sympathetically. "Let me know if there's anything I can do."

———————————

The curtain came down on Saturday night's performance of *84 Avenue Foch* to heavy applause.

Robert and Alex smiled in satisfaction as Ben Korn, the press agent, joined them in the back of the house. "They love it," he said. "I think we've got a big one."

Mike appeared through the backstage pass door into the theater and walked up the aisle toward them. "Good show tonight. Second act's much tighter, and the interrogation scene went like a buzz saw."

"You coming to Steuben's for a drink?" Robert asked him.

"No," Mike demurred. "I've got an eight-thirty plane tomorrow."

"Okay," Robert said and gave Mike a hug. "Say hello to Ruth for me."

Robert wondered at the slight shudder of Mike's back as he embraced him.

———————

Mike's early plane did not go to New York. It landed in Washington, and Mike took a taxi to the Madison Hotel, where the committee waited for him.

When the door opened to his knock, the scene was totally innocent, a group of men standing around drinking coffee and eating pastries. It looked like the hospitality suite for a large company. The men smiled and greeted Mike as if he were a potential customer.

"Some coffee?" they asked.

"No, thanks. Do you mind if we start? I've got to get back to New York to see my wife."

"Surely," they agreed pleasantly.

The members of the House Committee on Un-American Activities arranged themselves on the hotel furniture as the stenotypist readied her machine.

"Mr. Rossano," the chairman said, "thank you for coming down here on a Sunday."

"Thank you for seeing me."

"Well, Mr. Gang phoned and said you had something important to say to us . . . that you had had a change of mind about your position." Mike nodded. "We're grateful for that, for your cooperation. We don't like these contempt citations any more than the recipients do. We're just trying to do our job."

Mike nodded impatiently.

The chairman noted Mike's annoyance and signaled to his counsel to begin questioning.

Counsel rose and crossed the pink carpet toward Mike, who was sitting near the fireplace.

"Mr. Rossano, to recapitulate, you've already testified that you were in the Communist Party of the United States . . . in a cell in the Group Theater."

Mike nodded slightly.

"Would you answer please for the benefit of the stenographer."

"Yes," Mike said, having to clear his throat.

"And who was in that cell?"

Mike took a deep breath. "Clifford Odets, Phillip Loeb, J. Edward Bromberg, Art Smith."

"Anyone else?"

"Not that I can remember."

"Morris Carnovsky?"

"I don't think so."

"But he was in the Actors' Lab, in Hollywood?"

"Yes."

"A hotbed of Communist activity—"

Mike cut him off. "I wouldn't characterize it that way."

"How would you characterize it?"

"As an artistic organization of the highest principles, just as the Group Theater was," Mike answered strongly.

"With Communists in it?"

"I suppose so. But Communists don't have a monopoly on artistic scruples."

"We know they don't have any scruples."

"I'm not here to debate that," Mike said curtly.

"Quite so," the chairman interjected. "Now, I understand you've arranged this session because you have something new to tell us." He stressed the word "new." They looked at each other.

The chair nodded for his counsel to continue.

"So far, Mr. Rossano, you've given us only the names of people already named by others."

Mike's breathing became shallower as the counsel neared his target.

"Previously, you refused to name anyone on the Joint Anti-Fascist Committee with you. Are you prepared to do so now?"

Mike's heart stopped. He seemed hardly conscious, hardly in the room at all, immobilized by what he was about to do.

"Mr. Rossano?" the counsel said, as if calling him back.

A flash of anger started Mike's breathing again, and he turned to the committee members. But he was still silent.

"Mr. Rossano," the chair said ominously, "I hope you aren't going to disappoint us, that you didn't bring us downtown on a Sunday morning to rehash old names."

"Robert Thompson and his wife, Katherine," Mike said quickly as if the names had escaped him.

The committee members looked at each other and smiled.

"From 1938 to 1941 in New York City," Mike continued as if in response to the next question.

"Thank you, Mr. Rossano," the chair said. "That took a great deal of courage, and I'd like to commend you for your . . ."

A bilious gorge rose to Mike's throat. He ran to the bathroom and retched so violently he thought his insides would follow the bile.

———

Ruth was pale, her hair damp as she leaned back against the pillows. Mike took her warm hand, but she didn't seem to notice; she was floating under sedation, turned inward, away from him, escaping him. The heavy scents of the room reminded him of the funeral chapel his father had lain in. But the death was his own.

His despair matched hers as they shared the flower-scented silence. And tonight, there would be Robert and Alex.

———

He met them for dinner at Loch-Ober's, a splendid restaurant of deep walnut and silver, but he merely picked at his food, said little in response to their own confident spirits. There was nothing they could say or do that would change Ruth's condition or his own. What a Sunday! Mike thought. Was Odets right? Would he soon be calling people in the middle of the night trying to explain what he'd done, or would he rationalize it? After all, he'd only told the truth about their membership in the Joint Anti-Fascist Committee. Should he take a full-page ad in the *New York Times* and explain his position?

Robert and Alex could not understand Mike's withdrawal, his avoidance of eye contact, Mike who always sought engagement. Could he be feeling guilty over his treatment of Ruth?

"He's taking Ruth's illness very hard," Robert said to Alex later in the street.

Alex merely nodded.

———————————

There was always excitement at the Morosco Theater when Robert Thompson and Mike Rossano did a play there. It was their favorite theater, their good-luck theater.

Katherine entered with the Barkins and Paul Fresnay. Her turquoise gown and reddish hair set off her almost lavender eyes and pale skin.

Alex greeted them, dressed in his usual impresario outfit, to which he'd added a silver-topped walking stick and gray doeskin gloves. There was a lovely young actress on his arm whom he introduced to Katherine as Christine.

"You're well turned out tonight," Katherine kidded.

"And you are radiant as ever, still fixed in the orbit of my desire."

"Getting a little flowery, aren't you?"

"It's age. Would you believe I'm fifty?"

"I'd believe it if you told me you were twenty-five," she laughed. "Where are the boys?"

"Backstage, of course."

There were shouts across the lobby. "Katherine! Hey, Barkin! Alex!" They turned to see the group of men making their way toward them, subway riders among the carriage trade in their plain suits. Katherine smiled, and there were embraces and kisses. They were all strong-looking men.

Christine wondered who they were as their names passed in introduction, Irv, Milt, Pete, Abe. There was an energy and warmth about them.

"Well . . . shall we make an entrance?" Alex asked. As they crossed to the ticket taker, Christine leaned to Alex and asked in a whisper, "Who are they?"

"Friends of Robert's, Mike's and Katherine's. They were all in Spain together."

"Spain? What were they all doing there?"

"I'll tell you some long, rainy night."

The houselights went down, and the curtain rose on Gestapo headquarters at 84 Avenue Foch, in Paris. When Fresnay saw the black swastika in its blood-red field he shuddered involuntarily. Katherine, sitting next to him, felt it, and took his large hand, pressing the misshapen knuckles.

The play was more melodramatic than the audience expected, and they tried to adjust during the first act. The applause was warm, respectful, but not enthusiastic.

Robert and Mike walked across the street and to the corner to avoid contact with the intermission audience.

"Not exactly overwhelmed, are they?" Robert observed.

"They'll warm up," Mike responded.

The audience did warm up, but there was no cheering for the author at the end of the play.

Still, the conversation at the party at Sardi's was animated. Perhaps the notices would be better than the audience's reception. They often were.

Mike was at the bar with Alex. Robert sat at a large round table with Katherine, the Barkins, and other veterans of Spain, waiting for the notices.

"It's like waiting for the artillery to start," Abe Osheroff laughed. He was a tall ox of a man who looked as if he could knock down telephone poles.

Irv's broad face broke into a grin. "And you don't have any to answer," he said.

"Geez, remember that bombing on the way to Brunete where George Carver got killed?" Pete said, adjusting his dark glasses.

"Yeah, I broke the world record for the hundred-yard dash while still carrying my machine gun," Milt said.

Roberta, Milt's wife, looked at Katherine as if to ask, "How is it men always get back to war stories?" Fresnay listened without comment.

"I'll be right back," Robert said, going to the bar. As he talked with Mike and Alex there was a stir.

Katherine's head turned with the others to see the famous face and form of Tracy Morgan as she made her way toward Robert.

She took his arm. "How are you?" she asked huskily.

Robert didn't answer for a moment, assessing his feelings.

"Okay. And you?"

"Fine. I just finished a picture and came back to New York for a while," she said.

"Good," Robert said, then excused himself and returned to Katherine.

Tracy watched his retreating back, then turned to Mike and Alex. "How did it go tonight?" she asked. "I had to be someplace else."

"Okay. Coming back to class?" Mike asked coolly.

"If Alex will have me." She smiled at him as if to make up for Mike's lack of warmth.

"I'll have you any time," Alex laughed.

"Are you uncomfortable?" Robert asked Katherine.

"Only slightly. Are you?"

"I felt nothing," he said.

When Ben entered with the notices it was not with the charge of success. "They're so-so." He shrugged. He distributed the morning papers, and people quickly turned to the theater page.

"More melodrama than drama" . . . "characters more types than individuals" . . . "well crafted but dispassionate . . ." But one partisan wrote, "Exciting and important theater, a must-see for the intelligentsia."

"Well, it's not a complete flop," Mike sighed as he sat with Robert, Katherine, and the others.

"You can't get a knockout every fight," Pete said, putting down his white cane and rubbing his sightless eyes behind the dark glasses.

Robert watched Tracy work the room. He also noticed something else. People were looking over at them and then away, as if embarrassed. He began to feel a strange atmosphere. It was palpable, charged. He caught Alex's eye at the bar. What was he trying to say—"Better luck next time"? He wondered if it all was his imagination and went back to the morning paper.

Irv went to the bar for more drinks. As he waited for the bartender, he glanced over the shoulder of the man next to him who was reading the front page of the *Times*. His mouth fell open. As the man turned the page, Irv startled him by grabbing the paper and returning it to page one.

It was almost at the same time that Robert also read the news item:

ROSSANO NAMES THOMPSON AND WIFE

Mike Rossano, noted stage and film director, in secret session with the House Un-American Activities Committee, last week named Pulitzer Prize playwright Robert Thompson and his wife, Dr. Katherine Thompson, a psychiatrist, as members of . . .

Robert didn't finish. He put the paper down and stared at Mike. He felt faint, nauseous, and intensely angry.

Mike felt the look and wondered at its puzzled hostility. Then he felt other eyes on him. Katherine caught the headline in Robert's hands, and Mike followed her eyes to it. He shuddered at the chill that enveloped him. Their eyes locked in the stunned silence of the room, and a current passed between them.

Heavily, Mike rose. He walked toward the door as though it were the last mile and everyone in the room his executioners.

Robert sat empty and bereft. He felt as he had when he'd fallen in the battle of Fuentes.

How could he do it? Robert asked himself. We loved each other.

Why was I right? Katherine wondered.

Alex shook his head in pain.

Fresnay thought back to his first impression of Mike in Paris that December of 1936. "Here is the survivor."

———————————

"Goddammit!" Mike yelled into the phone of his study. "They weren't supposed to release that until next month!"

"It's a fuckup, Mike. What can I tell you?" Stavros said soothingly into the gold telephone. The silk of his pajamas rustled as he shifted his heavy weight in the large canopied bed. The script he'd been reading fell to the floor. "I'm sorry."

"Christ, what timing! What kind of ghoulish asshole would release that on the same day as the opening?"

"Mike, it's a mistake. Nobody on that committee has the brains to do it on purpose."

"God fucking dammit! I was sitting right next to them!" he screamed into the phone. Ruth came into the room. Mike waved her away. She blinked and left.

"Mike, it would have been rough whenever it came out," Stavros placated. "I admit it's a bit much—"

"Thanks for the admission."

"You're upset, and I can understand that, but it's late and there's nothing to be done. We'll talk tomorrow. When are you coming out?"

"Sooner than I expected." Mike slammed down the phone.

Stavros put his down gently and smiled. Then he dialed John Farrell's number.

"It worked," he told Farrell. "He'll be out here, 'sooner than he expected.'"

Mike stared at the photo of himself and Robert at Jarama in 1937.

———————

Robert, Katherine, and Fresnay walked most of the way back to the Village in silence. Fresnay had come from Paris just to see the play in which he was a character and was staying with them.

Robert burst out, "How could he do it? How could I have been so wrong?" There was a silence which they didn't try to fill. "Why did he name you too? And how did you know he would crack?"

Katherine's prediction had lain like a bomb between them. She carefully considered her answer.

"You'll think it strange," she said at last, "if I connect it to his relationships with women."

"I don't get it." Robert stopped.

"It's complicated and I'm not sure I understand it totally myself." She sighed. "Neither did Mike the night we had that fight at the vets' banquet. You know I never trusted his sense of self-preservation, the ruthless part of him." Fresnay nodded. "It's that part, the part he keeps to himself, that prevents him from giving himself. A man who uses women will also use men. Am I making any sense?" Robert nodded slightly. "I think he named me because he knows I've never trusted him completely, because I expected him to crack the first time you were called. He's always resented me. Not only because he felt I saw his fatal flaw but because he felt I came between you." Robert felt as if he were hardly breathing. "At one time, he would have sacrificed himself for you, even given his life, but his life wasn't worth much to him then. He had little to lose. In that way he's changed."

Robert took her arm, and they started walking again. "What part do you think his being thrown out of the party plays in all this?" he asked.

"A large part," Katherine answered. "I think there's enormous anger at being forsaken. He might have transferred his love for his father to the party and then had his love rejected, his individuality rejected. What could be worse for an artist? I have to wonder if he was so heroic in Spain because he needed to prove his worthiness."

"Maybe you're right," Robert said. "Remember the six guys who were caught trying to desert in the ambulance?" Katherine nodded. "Mike and Irv voted for the death penalty for them, but most of us voted to return them to their company. Within a few days, three of them were killed while trying to atone with heroics."

A light snow had begun, and Robert's step was slower. "The snow reminds me of Paris that first night. It seems a lifetime ago."

Katherine looked at Robert's crestfallen face, feeling with him Mike's betrayal, the loss of their idealism and youth.

———————

Mike was up all night. In the morning he made two calls.

"I can't talk to you, Mike."

"Let me explain."

"There isn't any possible explanation." Robert hung up.

"I couldn't talk to him, Katherine," he said, turning to her with tears in his eyes. "I couldn't talk to him!"

The second call was to Stavros.

"If Thompson goes to jail for contempt, I'll blow the whole deal. I'll take an ad in the *New York Times* with all the details."

"Don't worry, kid," Stavros purred. "He'll get off with a slap on the wrist, and nothing'll happen to his wife. Nobody's interested in a doctor. Just get your ass out here."

———————

Robert's slap on the wrist for contempt of Congress was a fine of a thousand dollars and the loss of his passport for an indefinite period, which meant he couldn't go to Paris for the French production of *84 Avenue Foch*.

Katherine was never called before any committees, and there was no fallout from Mike's having named her.

———————

Mike finished the editing of *Blood and Earth* in Hollywood. Although he'd offered to take Ruth with him, she refused.

"I don't want to be a part of your infidelities," she said pointedly, referring to more than his relationships with other women.

That New Year's Eve there was no word from Mike. The veterans of the Abraham Lincoln Battalion did not mention his name on Valentine's Day.

Joe Bromberg died of a heart attack. Odets spoke the eulogy for his longtime friend, who'd been virtually unemployed since having been named. He died in London. Not many in the Hotel Diplomat in New York for the observance knew the full irony of the afternoon. Odets had named Bromberg when he'd testified.

Alex asked Robert if he wanted to go backstage with him to see Odets.

"I couldn't," Robert said.

Mike wrote to Robert, but the letters were returned unopened and marked "Refused." He saved them in a drawer with his underwear.

Shirley was in Spain with Farrell, and Mike filled his tormented nights with compulsive, unsatisfying sex and *mea culpa* phone calls.

Blood and Earth opened the Cannes Film Festival and was an instant international hit. When it played in New York, Mike refused to go there for the premiere. Stavros said he understood.

Alex talked Robert and Katherine into going to see it with him. They left the theater filled with admiration and loss. It had been a fine piece of work; the battle scenes had an authenticity not seen in Hollywood films, and it was compared to the great movie classics.

JOHN GARFIELD DIES

Robert put down the paper. He'd felt a lurch in his belly as he read of the actor's death by heart attack. How many casualties will there be? he wondered.

"It's our fault," Mike said angrily as he threw himself about Odets's living room. "If we had backed him up . . ."

"If . . . if . . . how many guys do you know who would be alive today *if* they had chosen to go right instead of left? How many dead heroes are there all over the world?"

"Julie wasn't trying to be a hero. He did what he had to do!"

"Just like us, huh? You afraid you too will die in bed with a woman, Mike?"

Mike shook his head in surprise, as if Odets had hit him. "I don't think there's too much chance of that, Cliff. I've become impotent."

"You!"

"Her name was Julie, and I thought that had something to do with it."

"That's a bit Freudian."

"That's what I thought, so I went to bed with an Althea. Same result."

"Maybe you should go to an analyst."

"Not a bad idea. I've never fucked an analyst."

But Mike was worried.

———————————

Stavros kept his word, and Mike chose his next film without fear of refusal by the studio. *Taking a Fall* was about corruption in the world of boxing, with an informer as hero. It was written by a man who'd also named names and created a context in which informing was the heroic and honorable thing to do.

Robert worked on a new play. *The Inquisition* was a period piece about the Salem witch trials with a resister as hero.

The same preoccupation still bound them together.

August on Deer Isle with Bobby was wonderful. They walked, talked, sailed, made love, and Robert finished his play. He also sensed that Katherine kept a part of herself in reserve from him. He was afraid to question it.

"Did Uncle Mike do something bad?" Bobby asked one day.

"Why?" Katherine looked at him.

"I don't see him anymore," he said.

"Yes," Katherine responded.

"What did he do?"

She tried unsuccessfully to explain. Robert was silent.

———————————

The Inquisition was done in the fall, but it never caught fire. Audiences were not moved by the hero's convictions and sufferings; they seemed to feel confession was preferable to death. Perhaps they reacted poorly to the archaic dialogue, or perhaps the period prevented them from identification.

"Listen, even Joan of Arc wouldn't get much sympathy today," one theatergoer said.

Alex blamed himself. He thought he'd approached the play too intellectually.

Taking a Fall, Mike's movie, was contemporary and filled with action. His hero was young, there was a sympathetic love story, the script was compelling and intimate, the language was of the streets, and the rhythms were fast. It also had an extraordinary actor in the leading part.

Mike's picture won an Academy Award. Robert's play closed. Katherine wondered how Mike felt about that.

It was painful for Robert not to be able to go to Paris, where *The Inquisition* was a hit. It was the second time Paris had applauded a play of his that Broadway had rejected.

Robert was not finished with the subject of informing. Katherine wondered if he was trying to hold on to Mike through the subject.

The time of his new play, *The Dock Brief*, was contemporary, the plot classical. It even had a character who commented on the action like a Greek chorus. But the emotion was personal, involving love, jealousy, and betrayal. *The Dock Brief* had its partisans, but it was not a wild success.

Soon afterward, a blacklisted actor and friend from the Group committed suicide by throwing himself in front of a subway train. The man had been named by Mike.

Mike shuddered when he heard of Leopold's death. He'd worked with him in *Awake and Sing*.

On the surface, he was as cocky and confident as ever, but inwardly, he felt corroded, and his impotence continued. Then he had his first film disaster.

Stavros had had a brilliant notion. Put his star director together with his star comedienne, Tracy Morgan. Mike had been attracted to the idea of doing a comedy. Perhaps a change of pace would alter his mood.

It had all gone well until Tracy invited Mike to her Malibu beach house for the weekend. In terror of not being able to perform, Mike turned her down. Tracy had been furious at the rejection, and her warmth turned to frost on the set.

"What the hell's going on down there?" Stavros demanded in the screening room. "This is supposed to be a comedy. I haven't laughed in three reels!"

"Mike says it's supposed to be a social comedy," Silverman said.

"Yeah, well, tell him if he wants to send messages, use Western Union. Tell him I want laughs."

Mike did not know how to get them, and Tracy, a skillful comedienne, wouldn't help him.

The picture slipped quickly to the bottom half of double bills in second-run houses and drive-ins.

At night, Mike often stared at the black waters off the Malibu pier. It was five years now since his appearance before the committee.

In 1956, the writer who won the Academy Award for best original screenplay did not appear at the ceremonies. He didn't show because he didn't exist. The name was a "front" for blacklisted Ned Young.

When it was discovered, the absurdity of the situation caused the ice to crack, though the thaw came too late for many who had been destroyed. Many others who had been forced into exile in foreign countries started to return.

Odets was now writing movies for Elvis Presley.

Mike made several trips to New York. He saw Alex, who urged him to stay. He saw Ruth and his daughter, Tony. They did not urge him to stay. He was a famous stranger.

On February 14, Mike walked up 41st Street toward the familiar Greek cafeteria, his collar turned up against the cold, his hands jammed deep within the pockets of his overcoat. He looked through the steamy plate-glass window and saw the men and women. Taking a deep breath, he entered.

The room was filled with music, talk, and the smells of

food. Pete Seeger sang "The Four Insurgent Generals."
How many times had he sung those words himself? Mike
wondered as he stood there, unnoticed, afraid to move
farther.

Robert and Katherine were seated across the room, Irv
and Pete were at the bar, Milt was talking to his wife, Abe
was doing a cossack dance to the music.

When Seeger's song ended, Mike was slowly discovered,
and a stillness settled on the room. As Robert's and Mike's
eyes locked, Katherine held her breath. Finally, Robert
turned away. Mike's heart sank.

Irv began to sing.

> "There are rats, rats
> In bowler hats and spats
> In the store, in the store . . ."

The song became a drumming chorus.

> "There are rats, rats
> In bowler hats and spats
> In the quartermaster store."

When the last verse finally faded, they stood watching
Mike, wondering what he was going to do. He stood there,
rooted, before he finally turned and left.

Robert lay next to Katherine staring at the patterns of
light through the shutters of their bedroom.

"Are you all right?" Katherine asked.

"He's gotten gray."

"What?"

"His hair is gray. And did you see his face?"

"Yes."

"Sad, wasn't it?"

She nodded.

"He always said, 'Shame is worse than death.' Do you
think he'll ever stop hating himself?"

"I don't know," she whispered.

"It must have taken a lot of courage for him to show up tonight."

"Or need. The need for forgiveness, absolution."

Robert sighed, and tried to sleep.

———————

There were no patterns of light on Mike's ceiling. Ruth had put heavy drapes over the windows, creating an early tomb. She too was awake as Mike lay next to her. His body felt heavy, thick and lifeless, his energy drained away.

"I tried," he said.

"What?" Ruth asked.

"Tonight. I tried."

"Oh." She had no idea what he was talking about, nor did she really care.

———————

In 1958, Robert's passport was returned. He and Katherine traveled now that Bobby was away at boarding school. Katherine went to psychiatric conventions, Robert to see productions of his plays abroad.

Mike did another picture which was neither good nor bad. The Bel Air circuit buzzed as Mike had another failure—was he out of touch?

Stavros settled his contract. After his performance in Washington, Mike had gotten half a million dollars per picture. Now it took a day for anyone to return his phone calls. Hollywood was merciless.

He rented his Brentwood house to a hot young director and left for New York.

CHAPTER TWENTY - NINE

Robert outlined and discarded several plays.

Mike was not happy with any of the screenplays he'd been developing, and none of the stage plays he'd read appealed to him.

In 1962, he went to visit his daughter, who was away at boarding school in Bucks County, Pennsylvania. George School was lovely. The fieldstone buildings with their white columns were nestled among trees. There was a bright eagerness about the students, so unlike the Malibu teenagers. Mike was glad his daughter was there.

Tony had mixed feelings about the visit. She was proud and apprehensive. Apprehensive because she wasn't sure what she'd talk about with her famous father and worried about what he'd think of the school's production of *American Dreams*, which she'd directed.

Mike looked at her across the table in the colonial restaurant, the oil lamp glowing on her dark skin, pointing up her eyes, Mike's eyes. Fifteen! How could she be fifteen so fast? He filled with feeling.

"You know in the second scene of the first act where Harry is playing football with the boys," she said eagerly, "I decided to sneak in a little music. You know, like on a football field, just subliminally, as if Tommy was remembering it."

"Music is always tricky," he said seriously. "I'm anxious to see how you've used it."

He marveled at her intensity and resolved to be a better

father. He regaled her with anecdotes of the original production. Although he was smiling, Tony could see the hidden pain when he talked about Robert. But he also made her laugh with his stories of Hollywood, and he enjoyed her interest. He realized he wanted her approval. She gave it, but Mike could sense the wariness, the inner reservations. She wasn't going to be hurt again.

"Have you seen Bobby Thompson?" she asked as they were leaving their early dinner.

"No," Mike said in surprise. "Why?"

"Bobby goes to George. You'll probably see him tonight."

Would his father be there too?

The theater lobby was crowded with chattering students and their parents. Mike immediately recognized Bobby as he entered. He had Robert's long body and Katherine's complexion and hair. When Bobby saw him, he shouted, "Uncle Mike!" and ran to him, embracing his favorite figure of childhood. Then Mike could feel him tense as Bobby censored his feelings.

"I didn't know you were at George School," Mike said.

"Didn't Tony ever tell you?"

"We haven't talked much. I've been away." There was a pause. "Actually, I've been an absent father, but I'm trying to remedy that."

Bobby nodded gravely in the same way his father did when considering an emotional question.

"Are your parents coming up?" Mike finally asked.

"Tomorrow."

Mike was both relieved and disappointed.

He was pleased with the production. Even though the father was played by a seventeen-year-old, he had surprising range. And Tony had done a good job. She understood and was able to project the subtler currents of the play. Mike was free with his enthusiasm and praise as he went from group to group backstage, exciting them with his presence. Tony smiled, holding her father's arm as if she didn't want to let him go.

Mike had breakfast with Tony at the inn the following morning and left feeling optimistic about their relationship.

Robert was also pleased with the production, but his eyebrows went up as Bobby told him Mike had been there.

Bobby couldn't read his father's reaction. "I can't help it, Dad. I know I'm not supposed to, but I still love him."

Robert nodded gravely, but said nothing.

Does Robert still love him? Katherine wondered.

Robert started a new play about the nature of love, loyalty, friendship, and betrayal. It was a play in which he sought to understand rather than to judge actions like Mike's, understand rather than to justify Tracy's part in his life. While he was working on it, Clifford Odets died. He was just fifty-seven.

Robert, Mike, and Alex took separate planes to the Coast. Alex could not choose one over the other. How sad, he thought, that we can't be together at a time like this.

Odets had had a lingering death, physically and artistically. His last job had been as a story editor on a TV series. Even as he lay dying in the hospital, he told a parade of visiting celebrities that he would make a comeback, that he had no less than six plays outlined, that he would once again regain his place in American arts and letters. His blue eyes never lost their intensity. Perhaps he even believed what he said.

In the memorial chapel Robert and Mike sat on opposite sides of the room. They had seen each other but hadn't spoken. Alex sat alone up front and grieved as much for that lost friendship as for his protégé Odets.

The service was simple, the room crowded with stars from Broadway and Hollywood. People on both sides of the blacklist came to mourn a genuine talent who'd become a casualty. Robert, Mike, and Alex each spoke of what Odets had meant to them.

After Robert spoke, Mike followed him back to his seat with his eyes. Then he saw her. Shirley smiled, pale, but still beautiful.

Mike crossed to her after the service as people milled about, seeing and being seen. "How are you?" he asked nervously. "When did you get back from Europe?"

"Last month. I finally left John."

"Well . . ." Mike said, inhaling deeply. "Can I see you?"

"I'd like that."

Mike saw Robert looking at them from across the room. "Tonight?" he asked.

"It can't be soon enough." She smiled.

Robert was so fixed on Mike he didn't see Tracy at his elbow until she took it.

"Hi," she said.

Robert turned to her reluctantly.

"How are you?" she asked softly.

"Okay. You?"

"I never apologized to you," she said. He nodded in a small way, not indicating acceptance. "How long are you going to be in town?"

"I'm leaving tonight."

"Oh . . . that's too bad. I thought maybe—"

"I'm leaving tonight," he said, cutting her off.

"How was it?" Katherine asked on his return home.

"Not exactly a celebration."

"Did you talk to Mike?"

"I couldn't."

———————————

When Robert finished *Things Past*, he gave it to Katherine.

"What an exorcism!" she said.

"But is it any good?"

"It's incredible, Robert."

Every producer in town wanted to do it, but Robert gave it to Alex, who was now artistic director of the new Lincoln Center Repertory Company. Alex wanted it as the opening play.

"Are you going to direct it?" Robert asked.

Alex took a long time to answer. "No," he said finally. "Mike is better. Especially for this play."

"I can't do it," Robert said, shaking his head.

"Think about it."

"Some wounds never heal," Katherine said as Robert described the meeting with Alex. "But you and I are still married. I'm not sure that in the deepest part of me I've completely forgiven you." Robert was silent. "Can you work with him?"

"I don't know."

"Robert, you have to think about whether there's a statute of limitations on punishment, and who else is being punished."

"Are you trying to convince me Alex is right?"

"No. You have to convince yourself."

"He's changed, Robert," Alex argued. "For what you've gone through together, you owe it to him to at least talk."

Robert sighed heavily and nodded. "Okay. I'll talk to him."

They met backstage at the Morosco. The theater was dark, and as they crossed to each other under the bare worklight, they were aware of the ghosts of characters they'd created together on its stage. Their eyes held until they were so close they could feel each other's breath, hear it in the silence.

"Let me off the hook, Robert," Mike finally said.

"Can you let yourself off?"

"No."

Robert looked away into the dark house, to the farthest reaches of the balcony, as his heart beat rapidly. He fought for composure as he turned back to Mike, but his anger began to slip from him.

"How could you have done it, Mike? We loved each other!"

"I didn't want to lose everything."

"You did."

"I thought I'd never work again. I was afraid of being crushed like my father."

"Your father never hurt anybody! You were a Judas, Mike. You sold me!"

"Not for money."

"You could have survived very well in the theater. You survived at my expense."

"Do you know what it cost me to do that?" Mike said painfully. "To name you and Katherine? Do you know how many times I wanted to drown myself?"

"In self-pity," Robert said coldly. "We loved each other and you sold me out and you didn't drown yourself. You sold yourself out and everything we ever believed in and you went on working, while I lost my passport so I couldn't even get away from the insanity or see my work performed where it was appreciated."

"I wrote you. You returned my letters unopened."

"I didn't want to read your apologies."

"Because you wanted to keep your anger."

"What should I have felt for your betrayal? Pity? Understanding? Poor Mike, he only did it for his career."

"Like a lot of others, including Odets."

"And look what it did to him! I would have died for you before selling you out, because we were special, Mike. Not only to the times but to each other."

"That was war, Robert. It was easier. I wouldn't have survived these years without work. I would have ended up on a subway track too. Work is the only thing that matters to me. My work *is* me. I have no other identity. I even became impotent!" Robert looked at him in surprise. "Yes, me, impotent. Can you believe it? Why can't you accept the fact that I could love you and still betray you? You should be able to understand. You loved Katherine but you betrayed her."

"That was low."

"No. I'm trying to make you understand. You were swept along by something you had no control over. When we walked down that hall in Congress together, I felt strong. I felt the way I did when we marched together. My strength lasted through the hearing. When we got back to Boston and Stavros threatened me and Ziggy told me all the offers had been withdrawn, my will to resist collapsed."

"Mike, you wanted the death penalty for those six guys who deserted. They were also scared. You shot that Spanish sergeant when he'd tried to surrender. He was afraid too."

"You're right. I've thought about that guy and what he might have become if I hadn't killed him. But at the time nobody blamed me. Everyone thought I was right."

"I didn't. But I couldn't criticize you for it because you were my hero."

Mike looked away into the empty, dark theater. "Some hero," he said, and turned back. "Do you think character is fate?"

Robert considered. "Sometimes." They stood in silence for a moment. "I guess sometimes character is overwhelmed by circumstance."

Mike held his breath as he looked up at Robert, waiting for him to continue.

"Let's try," Robert said finally.

———————

They began rehearsals of *Things Past* with the cautiousness of former lovers trying to reconcile. Robert, though unsure, went along with Mike's desire to cast Shirley as "Katherine." She turned out to be a good choice, having the same liquid coolness and intelligence. "Tracy" was a young actress from the Actors' Studio who seemed destined for stardom herself. Onstage she radiated sexuality, yet offstage she was simple and unpretentious. Perhaps she felt intimidated by Robert's and Mike's reputations. The two actors playing them were certainly inhibited at first and tiptoed around the characters' sensitive areas. And Mike did not probe too searchingly where he was vulnerable. The atmosphere was tense.

It became especially so when they were doing improvisations to get at underlying truths. Often the play became confused with reality, a Pirandello-like situation: Art was imitating life and couldn't be distinguished from it.

The actor playing Robert, who was the protagonist, was a volatile and exciting man with firm convictions of his own about the part and the play. In the middle of the reconciliation scene, he suddenly broke from it and faced Mike, as if Mike were the real character in the play.

"Why'd you do it?" he shouted. "I want an answer!"

Mike stood there stunned as the rest of the company watched in silence.

"We were more to each other than any husband and wife have ever been! We owed our lives to each other!" His eyes blazed in fury and hurt, and he suddenly started punching Mike. When they were pulled apart, the actor left the theater. He could not be found for a week, during which he'd gone on a monumental drunk.

Alex was worried that the dynamics of the play and rehearsals were like a bomb that would go off and blow the production apart.

In the middle of it all, Ruth died.

The service was small. A few people from the Theater Guild, a few actor friends, the young writer who'd been her lover, Mike, Tony, Robert, Katherine, and Alex. Bobby had come down from the George School with Tony. The small group went to the cemetery. It was a beautiful day, cloudless and windy.

Mike threw flowers on the coffin as it was lowered. "Forgive me, Ruth," he said in a dry and husky voice. "I was a lousy husband. I hurt you and you never forgave me and you were right. I never helped you accomplish anything but the death you wanted for yourself." As he looked at his daughter and at Robert, he began to break. "I wasn't any kind of father, but I'll try to make up for it, Tony. I betrayed my best friends, and I'll never forgive myself for that."

The group turned and walked to the limousines that would take them back to the city. Tony had her arm through her father's. Bobby walked with his parents.

"Oh, the sweetness of confession," Katherine said, but not without sympathy.

———————

Mike bought a brownstone in the west sixties, and Shirley moved in with him. Their sex life was as fervent as ever.

Rehearsals continued to be explosive, mixing reality with theater. Robert tried to remain objective and often inserted into the play lines or ideas that came from the actors, making rehearsals exciting and often thrilling.

For Robert and Mike it became an emotional roller coaster.

———————

Katherine had never seen Robert so nervous. His fingers fumbled with the studs of his tuxedo shirt.

"Let me help you," she said, crossing to him, but her own fingers trembled as she tried to fit the small black buttons through the small white holes. They both laughed as Robert took her hands. He kissed her. "I love you," he said.

"This too shall pass. And wonderfully."

Shirley was already at the theater. Mike felt as he had before going into battle, his stomach muscles a hard knot.

The opening-night audience was high, and their fever rose as Robert, Mike, and Katherine took their seats. The evening was special. Not only was it the opening of a new theater, it was the return of two heavy hitters with material that was clearly about themselves, the reunion of two major talents who had been estranged.

Alex checked that all the critics were seated, and the houselights went down.

Mike closed his eyes and listened.

Robert was drawn into the play, unsure whether his own emotion was shared by the audience.

Alex knew that it was.

At the first intermission, the theater buzzed with excitement and enthusiasm. The three stayed in their seats, not wanting to be pointed at in the lobby. But they were silent.

When the lights went down for the last time, the applause was thunderous. On the first curtain call the audience was on its feet. After the leading actors had been called back several times the audience started chanting, "*Author!*"

Mike looked at Robert and extended his hand to him, his eyes beseeching. Robert looked at the hand, then at Mike. The audience watched the two men. Shirley, standing on-stage, held her breath.

Robert was paralyzed.

Katherine took Robert's hand closest to her in her own. The warmth of it moved Robert. Slowly, he lifted his own and took Mike's. Mike's hand was dry and hard, but his eyes were soft. Softer than Robert had ever seen them. In the midst of the audience they were totally alone, captured by their past and their present.

The shouts broke through Robert's thoughts, and he slowly removed his hand from Mike's. He stood up and walked to the stage, then motioned for silence. The audience was still, waiting for his words. None came. With one hand he pointed to the assembled actors, with the other to Mike. Tears streamed down his cheeks.

The house went wild.

———————————

Shirley held Pete's arm as his cane lightly tapped the sidewalk in front of the Morosco Theater on their way to Sardi's. The theater was half in ruins, a demolition ball hanging next to the bulldozer in the backstage alley.

Robert and Mike looked briefly at the ruin and, flanking Katherine, crossed the street toward Shubert Alley.

They were deep friends.

They were scarred survivors.